Rebecca Harding Davis

John Andross

A novel

Rebecca Harding Davis

John Andross
A novel

ISBN/EAN: 9783337048662

Printed in Europe, USA, Canada, Australia, Japan

Cover: Foto ©Andreas Hilbeck / pixelio.de

More available books at **www.hansebooks.com**

JOHN ANDROSS.

BY

REBECCA HARDING DAVIS,

AUTHOR OF "LIFE IN THE IRON MILLS," "DALLAS GALBRAITH," "WAITING FOR THE VERDICT," ETC., ETC.

ILLUSTRATED.

NEW YORK:

ORANGE JUDD COMPANY,

245 BROADWAY.

JOHN ANDROSS.

ILLUSTRATIONS.

JOHN ANDROSS.

CHAPTER I.

THE Niagara Express, just before sunset at the close of a sultry July day, was puffing slowly into Lock Haven, a small lumber-town which is the key of access to the wild mountainous district of Pennsylvania, from the rich coal and oil valleys below. As the smoking engine came in sight, a runner from one of the inns hastily pasted up a written placard on the wooden wall of the station, where it would face the car windows, reading it aloud to half a dozen lounging men and boys:

"'*Mysterious Disappearance—Supposed Murder.*' A hope it a'n't no murder, a'm sure. But——," gloomily wiping the paste off his fingers inside of his trousers pockets, "Joe Vanderpoelen came down from the mountains last night, and he says there's them there as hints of suicide, but a says, 'For what reason?' a says. 'A man don't kill and bury hisself out of sight for no reason at all, Joe,' a says. A always did like to get at the common sense of a matter."

"Them Vanderpoelens has always got some cock-and-bull story going," observed the station-master scoffingly, squirting tobacco more vigorously as the train approached.

7

"This a'n't no Vanderpoelen story," patting down the wet edges of the bill. "Old Judge Maddox is down himself about it. Hasn't been out of the mountains for two years. Sending telegrams right and left. He come to meet Doctor Braddock when he gets in. He's looked for on this train."

"Rough news for Braddock."

"So a says," eagerly. "A thought of him first one. A just sent Jimmy up for the 'bus, so's a'd be here to break it to him myself in case the judge's not about. Never do for him to hear it first from strangers, or by the placards. Hi! here she is!" as the train came up alongside of the station.

Dr. Braddock and a stranger, a large showily dressed man, came out of the cars and halted, as people do in the country, to watch the train steam leisurely off, leaving a wavering line of bituminous smoke across the hot blue sky. The bill-poster stood irresolute. There was always something in the gloss and primness of the doctor's tall, lank figure which daunted one of the great unwashed, but to come off of a long and dusty journey immaculately gloved, and with such snowy shirt cuffs and a high beaver hat instead of a slouchy felt, was to mark the gulf between them offensively.

Dr. Braddock touched his hat. "My team here, Joseph?"

"No, sir. A'll drive you up to the Fallon House? A'd better now?" Joe needed to bolster his courage before he offered himself as a sympathizing friend to a man who touched his hat to him. The doctor's companion had turned his bold laughing eyes on the men on the platform, called one of them a lout for dropping his valise, and so was hail-fellow-well-met with them already. Dr. Braddock had never been hail-fellow-well-met with anybody in his life.

"No, we'll wait," he said. "Andross," turning to his

friend with a polite mannerism that tried to be cordial, "Andross promised to drive down from the mountains to meet us. I depend on him to make your two weeks' holiday what it ought to be. He said the first thing to look to was the larder, and he was right there. The air up yonder makes a stranger ravenous. It's too late for venison, but he promised to have trout and partridges for supper if he scoured the Nittany range for them. Here he is!" as a wagon, swung low for mountain roads, and drawn by a black horse dashed down the dusty street. "Why, that is not John!" crossing the platform; "that's the judge."

Joe, afraid that his ill news would be taken from him, hurried after him. Braddock, zealous Presbyterian as he was, was known to be so irritable a man and so easily rasped by trifles that Joe had a curiosity to see how he would deport himself when met by a great disaster.

"You don't observe the placard, Doctor?" carefully standing in front of it. "'Mysterious disappearance. Murder in the Nittany Range.' Why there ha'n't been such eggsitement in Lock Haven since the war—no, sir. Mr. Andross being such a popular man too——"

"Who is murdered?" pushing him aside. "What is this fellow chattering about Andross's popularity for?" sharply to Judge Maddox. But Joe, whose blear eyes were as keen as a ferret's, noticed that the doctor was not startled by the ill news. "If a'd av told him Andross hed killed hisself, he'd not have been surprised. He was lookin' for ill news of him, take my word for that. Lookin' for it;" he told up in the bar-room afterwards.

Judge Maddox, who in his blue cloth coat looked not unlike one of the round-bellied, blue-painted oil-barrels on the platform, gently patted Joe on the back with his pudgy hand. Murder or not, there was no need of offending a possible customer. "Ah! Joseph, is it you? And how's that mare you bought do? Balky, eh? Tut,

tut! Just a word with Dr. Braddock. Come in this office, Clay," rolling into a square closet where a man stood writing. "Mr. Stiles? Just give the doctor and me a moment here. Got rid of that dyspepsia yet? Tried podophyllin? Don't dabble in medicines, hey? Right, right!" shutting Stiles out of his office. "It's Andross, Clay. He's gone."

The judge's face was at blood heat, but he did not wipe it. It was noticeable that Dr. Braddock made no exclamation, and before he spoke at all shut the window.

"What do you mean by gone? Is he dead?"

"God knows! How can I tell? Busy at his accounts at nine o'clock Saturday evening, and walks out; walks out without a coat—in his waistcoat—leaves the blotter on the open book, desk unlocked, lamp burning, and never comes back. Just as if the earth had opened and swallowed him. Place all alight from the furnace, yet not one of the hands saw him. I've not eaten a full meal since. Nor slept. Counted the clock strike every hour last night. I said to Anna, if Braddock were here some of the horrible responsibility would be off my shoulders. You and Andross being just like brothers. Very rare to find such friendships between Americans. Germans, now, are more addicted to that sort of thing. Why I've seen two six-foot red-whiskered fellows kiss like school-girls; but that's not Andross, poor fellow! It's wretched, wretched! Got such a turn after the soup yesterday thinking of him, I couldn't eat another mouthful. Such a light-hearted, jovial fellow you know! 'Poor old baldhead Elisha,' my little Joe called him," chuckling. "I checked that in Joe promptly. Don't like forward children. Well, what do you think, Braddock? I telegraphed for the police. None of your country bunglers—a sharp city practitioner. D'ye think it was suicide? Or how about those old shafts on the ridge? The men tell me there's some man-traps near the ore banks sixty feet deep. Well, what d'ye think, Braddock ?"

"You sent for the police ? I am sorry for that."

"Hey ? You don't say so ! Why, I told Anna first words Braddock will speak will be, 'Have you sent for the police ?' And you really think we'd better not have them ? Well I am astonished ! I'll go and telegraph at once for them not to come. Better trust to our own wits. They're a pompous lot ! Low, uncultured fellows generally, dressed in the little brief authority of billies and white gloves, you see ! Too much for them. Well, what do you think, Braddock ? Was it murder ?" his bulgy gray eyes quailing a little.

"Murder ? What possible motive could anybody have in killing Andross ?"

"Just what I said. Best-hearted fellow ! Wouldn't hurt a worm ! The old shafts now. He might have wandered out, and accidentally—there would not be a chance for him there."

"John knows the Nittany Ridge thoroughly, and it was not likely he would purposely wander beyond it."

Dr. Braddock paused before each reply as if to choose his words. His whole bearing, since he heard the news, had been noticeably cautious and repressed. Even the judge, whose perception was of the dullest, observed this unwonted reticence in the usually quick, outspoken young man. He was, like Joe, disappointed that his news had produced so little sensation.

"I thought, Braddock," irritably, "you would have some plausible theory at least about it ?"

"Yes, yes, certainly. Give me time."

"You're in a measure responsible for Andross. You stood sponsor for him at the Works. It was on your recommendation I put him in the office ; you know that."

"Well, you've had no reason to regret it, Judge."

"No, not till now. But whatever it is to you this has

been a terrible shock to me.　If the fellow had died in his bed, like other people, it would have been another thing. But at my age a man is shy of sensations.　After fifty all trouble is apt to go to the liver or bowels.　Jake at the mill says it was suicide ; but that's absurd."

Braddock was silent.

"That's sheer nonsense.　What trouble had that fellow to make him go cut his throat ?　If he had, more likely his brain was affected, and he's wandered off into the mountains and will turn up again all right."

"In that case he would not have left the desk open."

"Stuff !　Do you suppose if a man is so mad as not to care for his life he'll care for my cash-box ?"

"Yes," promptly.　"There's nothing sticks in even the maddest brain like the idea of duty—duty that has been promised and paid for."

"Oh ! all men are not machines.　Nor Braddocks," chuckling.　"You might go hang yourself at twelve o'clock, but you'd wind the mill clock at eleven.　Jack was a different breed—a different breed, sir.　As jovial, jolly a dog as ever I knew, especially after a glass or two of dry sherry—he always took his wine too dry—but as to a nice sense of honour, I don't know.　No.　I don't know about that, Clay."

The doctor crossed the room and tried the door.

"Not so loud," he said, irritably.　His mouth was parched, and he had the uncertain haste of movement of a horse that has been under the curb too long.　"You forget, Judge, that Andross was my friend, and that in all likelihood he is dead."

"Why, nobody heard me.　Who is that strange fellow that came with you, anyhow ?"

"His name is Ware.　A poor devil of a newspaper man out for a holiday."

"And what's he here for, eh ?　Wants to write up the

Works, I suppose ? I want nothing written about the Works. I want to run the business clear of print."

This last idea had apparently banished Andross and his mysterious fate from that fat substance inside his pulpy head which the judge frequently mentioned as "the best brain in the state, sir." Two ideas never subsisted there together. Yet it was a serviceable brain in its way ; had served to amass a fortune for its owner, and prompted him to show kindness to every unlucky dog, whether man or beast, that crossed his more fortunate path.

"You know well enough, Braddock," he muttered, "that I mean to keep the Works out of sight of the public until I'm sole owner, and now you bring this interviewing pump——"

"He never heard of you or the Works," said Braddock, uncivil and blunt as usual. "He wants," with a shrug, "to interview Nature. He has had a great deal to say on the way up about the Great Mother."

"I wish him joy of her acquaintance. There's no need for him to meddle in this mess about Andross."

"No. There is my horse and wagon at last. I'll drive Ware out," opening the door.

"All right. I'll keep along-side. This ghastly business has knocked me up so that——How this town is looking up, hey ? There's a new row of shops now, very neat —very neat. Pay eleven per cent, I judge. But oh ! you're off, eh ? " turning to find himself alone, and puffing slowly out.

Dr. Braddock's sallow face relaxed as soon as the judge's "chud, chud" of talk died out behind him. He halted a minute on the vacant side of the platform out of sight of Ware and the men. He was a man accustomed to fling all his emotion into words at once. Ill-conditioned and bigoted, both words and emotions often were, perhaps, but always quite open and bare for God and his fellow-man to judge. "It is either a fool or a knave who must have secrets," he always said.

Yet a secret had just been forced on him, and a necessity for controul of tongue and even eye, at the very instant when he fairly staggered under the chance that death had taken out of the world one of the two or three people who were his friends in it. For Braddock was as narrow and bigoted in his affections as his creed.

Mr. Ware, however, soon cut short his pause for breath.

"Where the deuce have you been, Doctor? Sick? You look pinched about the nose and jaws. Nothing wrong, I hope? I should dislike confoundedly to be confined in this dusty town over night. I catch a whiff of the mountain air already!" his wide, red nostrils expanding. "Come, come! Let's go. Why, I looked to see you all fire at the first breath of your native hills. You have no touch of the Swiss homesickness which should belong to all mountaineers."

"There's no necessity for homesickness. I've only been gone two weeks."

"Shall we go?" Mr. Ware drew long breaths as though his chest was oppressed, stretched out his arms, the red rising and fading in his large thin-skinned features. His chest was so broad, the grasp of his arms so wide, his exaltation of feeling so assertant that even Joe repressed his first inclination to snigger, and looked on respectfully. "Pardon my impatience," he said, wiping his forehead with a delicately fine handkerchief, "the near approach to Nature is like music or a fine picture, it affects my nerves like an electric battery and—a—. Some stamina is lacking in my bodily organization which you more phlegmatic, bony people have——"

There he broke off abruptly, turning away as if conscious that his audience would not understand him. It was Mr. Ware's habit to make his small talk into an oration, and thus break off abruptly, his fine brown eyes gazing rapt before him, "finishing his remarks," as some coarse joker had said, "to infinity." ·

Braddock meanwhile was sponging his horse's nostrils as carefully as if he had been handling a baby. His trouble might pinch his face and load the blood in his veins, but assuredly his nag would not suffer for it. Had he not been rebuked in church session for squandering time and money at horse-fairs, and it was even hinted at horse-races? "He ought to have been fed two hours ago. You know I never drive him on a full stomach!" he said to Joe so fiercely that the judge called from his wagon:

"There, there! Come, Doctor, I want you to be up on the ground early. We must take measures to-night;" and added aside, "What are you hectoring that man for, Clay? he might be of use to you yet; and for a brute beast, too! It's unbecoming a professor of religion," and then bowled off.

Dr. Braddock sat stiffly upright. His companion, big and buoyant, had an air of laying claim to ownership of the sun and all about him. With his rolling dark eyes and large gesticulating hands he gave you the impression that he would have settled himself just as easily on Charlemagne's stone throne or a shoemaker's bench as the buggy-seat. Braddock had no impression about him except to wish heartily that he was back in New York. He had hoped this crisis would never come. Now that it had come, it needed all his skill and well-known friendship for Andross to cover it from ordinary observers. But what could he do with this fellow's absorbing eyes and ready note-book in pocket beside him?

He never had learned to alter one of his words or to conceal a look.

He found out presently that Ware was talking to him. Ware's was a portly orotund voice for a young man, but musical withal.

"Yes, it was an old master's mate gave me that dressing-case—thorough type of the old Jack-tar, as you find him in Cooper. Bit of gratitude, that was. I heard a man was down with Asiatic cholera; went and offered myself as nurse. Town was in an uproar, but I brought the man through. So, after his next voyage he brought me this. Chinese, you see, complete. Look at the carving of that ivory and these inlaid flagons. But you don't care for such things, Braddock? Now I do. I want the commonplaces of every day to be æsthetically shaped and colored before they touch me. I've been a blacksmith in my day, and lived in the ashes and dust; yet it pleases me to think that when my dead bones are in the coffin, white satin padding will come between them and the boards."

"Very sensible people do have such whims sometimes," said Clay apologetically, wishing to be civil.

"Now you are not quite callous to outside impressions," in an encouraging tone; "not quite, or you would not be here. Laird told me how you studied medicine and tried journalism, and finally left New York to be clerk in these out-of-the-way iron works, because here was your home. The mountains had their hold on you."

"I wanted to make money, and I came here as the most likely place to make it."

"Laird told me you had saved some money and were anxious to double it soon," with a quick side glance.

Braddock had no secrets. "A trifle—but my savings for three years: about seven thousand dollars."

"You ought to have put it into Laird's hands. It would have grown like weeds in a barn yard. He is head of a ring in New York and Philadelphia. It's omnipotent, sir. It holds one city at least, lawmakers and law-givers, so—" closing his large fingers on a dandelion seed on his palm. "Yes. If Laird was a friend of yours your money would have yielded a thousand-fold."

"He was well enough disposed to me. But I may

have had a prejudice against planting my money in such dirty ground."

"Oh-h ?" with the same quick, furtive glance. "Well, I have had just such a fancy in my time. Porter, the pork dealer in New Haven, asked me once to go in with him. A sure thing it was, but I declined. 'I may have stood over the forge,' said I, 'but I can't see the name of Julius Ware going all over the country cut into greasy hams.' Foolish. But I have these idiosyncrasies. Can't cure myself of them any more than of my cleft chin."

Braddock was silent. They had run into another blind alley of conversation, the only way out of which was that by which they had entered—Ware.

That never-wearied subject sat tranquil, combing his magnificent red beard with his white fingers, and glancing alternately admiringly down on it and questioningly over the rolling hills, as though inquiring whether Nature knew who was coming.

"Oh, by the way !" he said presently, "this friend of yours who was to have provided the trout—Andross—has had some adventure, they say ? Missing, eh ?"

"Yes."

"Too bad if there has been murder or that sort of thing. But not likely. We newspaper men know how such reports grow. He'll turn up all right. Without the trout, probably. More's the pity."

"Come up, Tom," said Braddock, with a queer tightening of his lips.

Tom was carrying them lightly from the farm lands into the higher levels ; they had left Judge Maddox far behind ; the sun was bright ; a cool damp wind met them from the forests full of astringent piny smells. Ware heaved a sigh of luxury, threw his cap down at his feet, and stretching back, clasped his hands behind his head. He never could be still a moment. He had been the best smith on the forge so far as thundering blows went ; now

that he had neither hammer nor anvil, and was cased·in
by broadcloth clothes and an education, some restless force
in his blood worked itself off in incessant motion of brain
or body.   Just now, his brain having nothing before it but
Andross, he employed his body in what he would have
called "feeling of" himself—the mass of hair (significant
live hair he knew it to be) ; the thick, white prize-fight-
er's throat ;   the   white,   stubby-fingered   hands.   He
glanced critically and approvingly down at his brawny,
well-shaped legs and then at Braddock's, all of whose
members unfortunately had a lean and hungry look.

"But," appearing to remember lazily after awhile the
subject of conversation, "don't you think now, Braddock, it was a little Quixotic in you to bring this Andross
into the office with you ; to adopt—christen him, eh ? A
middle-aged poor devil with neither kith nor kin, I hear."

"No ; neither kith nor kin."

"No friends but yourself.   And you pick him up, charcoal burning and half starved, and get him work—shoulder him ?   Now, I'm one of the most impulsive of men, but
I never go into partnership with incompetency.   Never."

"You don't know Andross or you would not use the
word."

"I know," with a triumphant laugh, "that he was a
man of education burning charcoal at middle-age when
you saddled yourself with him.   Depend on it, if a man
reaches thirty-five without making his mark there's some
part of the machine lacking.   I wonder what scrape the
fellow has tumbled into now ? A woman, eh ? I heard
a hint of that at Lock Haven."

"Your information seems to have been minute, Ware."

"Oh no !   Just a few words of gossip with the men
on the platform while you swabbed Tom's mouth.   I
don't confine myself to the Brahmin caste for my friends,
I find companions among soldiers, priests, and Pariahs.
Besides, the press"—touching himself lightly on his im-

maculately glossy white shirt—"absorbs information above ground as the long-armed polypi draw in their dinners under water. And it is about as hopeless an undertaking to fight one as to fight the other, eh ?"

"I suppose so."

Doctor Braddock sat more stiffly erect, while his companion lolled back again, feeling that he had, by a lucky image, put the relative position of press and public forcibly. His imagery, hair, beard, legs : here was unfailing matter for contemplation with which he never wearied himself, and, oddly enough, seldom tired his companions. There was something so genial and responsive and full-blooded in the intent look of the brown eyes and grasp of the hand of this big, warm-colored, confidential fellow, that most women and all men turned to him with a sense of relief from the ordinary mass of bilious, abstracted American citizens, and listened with interest to the lively disquisitions of Ware on Ware. Just now, however, he represented to the man beside him the world at large. Braddock certainly had shouldered Andross; and he would have liked, according to his custom, to fight his battle for him with a few furious, telling blows. It was terribly hard, he thought, that he was forced to do nothing but sit passive and speak inanely in monosyllables. As for Ware and the press or the world, the simile held good ; they were like flabby, long-armed polypi, trying to draw his secret from him.

Stopping to water his horse at a wayside spring, Braddock heard Judge Maddox signalling him behind. Night was beginning to fall, and they had just turned into the gloomy mountain passes ; the judge was tired of being without a listener.

"My wagon is stouter than yours, Clay," he said, "I'll take Mr. Ware, if you choose."

He began to reflect that he was horribly cut up just now, and Braddock would be a dull companion for a few days until this miserable business was settled, and Andross, the only good company on the mountain, was gone. Besides, it might be as well to have a friend in a newspaper man, in case he threw the Works into the market.

" I'll take charge of Mr. Ware to-night," he said, after the exchange was made, "while you go to work at the mystery ; and for God's sake, Clay, get to the bottom of it to-morrow."

Braddock nodded curtly, and they drove off ; he turned the horse up a sharp defile which would bring him half an hour sooner to the Works.

" It's rough on you, I know, old fellow," he said, apologetically to Tom, just as if he had been a man.

Passing a gap he could see the lights twinkling in his mother's window. It was there they were to have had supper, and he thought of Jack, as he had seen him a dozen times, in his shirt sleeves, anxiously broiling the venison, " which nobody but the hunter ought to touch," while his mother stood gravely by, dish in hand. He remembered now another trouble, which this news had driven out of his mind ; the difficulty he would have in satisfying his mother that he had done wisely in refusing his money to Laird. She had known Houston Laird when he was a boy in the Jersey village where she was born, and before Clay started had been sounding his praises.

" As pretty a boy as you would see, and good-natured to silliness. No ; he played his marbles and mumble-the-peg as fair as need be ; and if he were the scoundrel you say, it would have showed itself then. Just as the twig —you know. Sent me a photograph of his wife when he married—quite the family man. You're too suspicious, Clay. Silly, Houston Laird may be, but he has nothing to do with packed election boxes and Rings, take my word for it."

His mother was Scotch-Irish, and consequently was her own pope, from rules of faith to the colour of a cap rib-

bon ; religiously loved her friends and hated her enemies.
She had the Scotch-Irish thrift too, undiluted by American swagger or generosity. She knew to a dollar the
amount of Clay's hoardings, and what the especial chance
in life was that he hoped to command by them.

"She'll think I ought to have given it to Laird to turn
over for me, and asked no questions," moving uneasily on
his seat. "But it's *clean* now anyhow."

He put his hand in his pocket. Braddock had his mother's blood. At any other time he would have enjoyed
the rustle of the crisp bank-notes and even the smell of
them, and the plodding back over the last five years to
think how they had been earned. But he forgot them
now, even while he held them. Going by one of those
gorges of the Muncey range, in which the mountain
has been torn asunder ages ago by volcanic action, he looked into the chasm between the shattered walls of gray
rock rising to the sky, down which a low watery moon
threw uncertain shadows, and suddenly saw, as in a vision, Andross lying there, his face turned upward to the
sky. Who knew but that he lay in that very chasm,
"with the old bulgy check suit on at which we laughed,"
his thoughts ran on, "and the torn felt hat? Such a
slouching fellow as he was!" The slouching, yet handsome figure lay stiff, with a bullet through the heart, it
might be, or a cut in the throat, which to Braddock
meant worse than murder, for he could guess out of what
part of Andross's hidden past the stab might have come.
He urged Tom up the rocky path. Horses generally filled
too large a share of the world to this narrow-minded,
few-ideaed young fellow ; but just now there seemed to
be nothing in it but the slovenly, happy-go-lucky man who
lay dead somewhere in these gorges. He had shouldered
Andross soul and body, and he set out on the search for
him with much of the same feeling a woman has for the
child to whom she has given birth.

CHAPTER II.

THE Works, as the Gray Eagle Furnace was called, lay under the shadow of a spur of the mountain. The roofs and walls of the old wooden building, gray with age and charred by falling sparks, were one in color with the limestone rocks about them. Dull reflections from the smouldering furnace threw bars of red light through the rising fogs down as far as Bear Valley. The men came from the inside and stood in the doorway, leaning on their ash-rakes, as the doctor drove up, with the curiosity with which they would look at the chief mourner at a funeral, though every man there knew that he understood Andross better than that fellow Braddock. As for the story that had been whispered about, that Braddock had brought him originally from some coalings in Clinton county, that they could swear was all bosh. Who ever heard of setting charcoal burners to keeping books? You didn't make silk purses out of such sow's ears as that, and Andross *was* a silk purse; the very finest gentleman they had known ; a different make of a man from that supercilious, pious prig, Braddock.

The mystery or murder had warmed all Gray Eagle Gap into a genial, excited fellowship. One or two quarrels had been made up, and double drinks had to be taken at the usual times for bittering, such was the heat of public feeling. The men detailed themselves in off hours in voluntary searching parties ; popular prejudice ran high against Maddox for not closing the Works, if for nothing else than a mark of respect ; a dozen times a day somebody suggested how zealously Andross himself would have gone into the thing and scoured the mountains day and night. It was a thousand pities, as Spellin said, he couldn't have joined in the row his death caused; everybody felt that. Braddock would engineer the matter as though he were on horseback and everybody else on foot. Even Spellin the superintendent, when he came out to meet him, spoke in a critical, defiant way. His broad jaws were a shade less purple than usual, he having lopped off his whiskey a glass or two daily since the occurrence took place. He nodded gruffly.

" I suppose you'll take this business in hand now. It's not been suffered to drag so far. The two cricks has bin dragged up to the gate, and the old ore banks searched; but there's hundreds of worn-out shafts there."

" Yes. Very good. Yes."

Braddock was trying to pass, but Spellin filled up the doorway.

" In my opinion the place to operate in now is Bear Valley. 'N there's no time to lose," sharply. " If he's fell inadvertently, we kin yet save the body."

" Certainly. You're quite right, Mr. Spellin."

" You'll go up to Bear Valley right away then ? In fact I sent the men there to wait your orders."

" At twelve o'clock," deliberately drawing out his watch. " It is now ten. I have business in-doors in the meantime. Don't let me be interrupted. Good evening, Mr. Spellin."

Spellin turned into the Works, not deigning to glance after Braddock as he crossed before the furnace to reach his office. " He takes it as I thought he would, cursedly cool," he thought; " just like his Scotch-Irish blood ! " But when one of the men hinted the same thing, he sent him with an oath to the right about pretty quickly. " Bosses " might be disagreeable to each other, but they must preserve the prerogatives of their order.

Braddock shut the door and locked it. The room in

which he stood was his own office ; inside was Andross's den, as he called it. He struck a light ; he had driven with furious haste to come here ; had felt as though he could scarcely keep from knocking Spellin down as he barred his way ; yet now, being here, he trimmed and retrimmed the lamp, threw some waste-paper in the empty stove, and stood with his back to it, his hands behind him, as if there were a fire, his neatly trimmed whiskers oddly black against his pale face.

He was so sure of what he should find ! He looked about his square office as though it were new and unfamiliar to him. There was a queer, suggestive contrast between its trig carpeted comfort and that den beyond. Braddock made a home according to his notions of a home, out of even that twelve by fourteen closet. The stove was polished ; the waste-basket held every clipping of paper ; desk, inkstand, pens, were in faultless order; the varnished book-shelves were lettered above each department. History, poetry, belles lettres, etc., etc. To be sure, there were not often more than a dozen books in each. Braddock meant to have a complete library, and after the text-books of his humanities, had begun with English standard authors—Hume, Addison, Scott, Chaucer, etc., all bound alike in durable calf—adding to them steadily as he could. That a book suited his whim or mood never yet had tempted him to buy it. Time to gratify caprices when the proper solid foundation of knowledge was laid. He went to the book-shelves now and took from a locked drawer beneath, the sole volume that was not new and shining. It was a first edition of Dryden, tobacco-colored with age, the edges of the leaves clinging in dead bits to his fingers.

When Braddock brought Andross to the Works, that poor creature had only the decent suit which his discoverer had bought at Bellefonte for him ; at the end of the first three months, therefore, Braddock handed him his salary, advising him to run down to Philadelphia and get clothing for the winter. Two days after Jack dashed into the office exultant, and unrolled this book from sheets of tissue paper.

"Look at that, Braddock! Heard of the auction of old Pepitt's library in New York just in time to catch the owl train and go over. I knew nothing would delight you more! Just look there!" his eyes sparkling and his fingers unsteady as he turned the mouldy leaves. "A first copy of Dryden, 'Glorious John'! There's no doubt it's genuine, sir, genuine! I know this very book. I was with Louis Pepitt when he bought it. I'd back that old fellow's eye for a genuine first edition against any man's in America! and Lord! what a palate he had for wines. His decision was infallible. There, Braddock. I am so glad to be able to give you a little pleasure," looking full in his face as he handed him the book, with his blue eyes wet and bright.

Braddock would very much have preferred a new copy, in uniform binding with his other books, but he did not say so, knowing that the poor fellow meant well. The rest of his money he had laid out on a vase of rare Venetian glass, big enough to hold a single flower, which he carried up to give to Clay's mother. He was a happy man that morning. His miserable or terrible past, whatever it may have been, weighed no heavier on his light heart than did the shabby coat or trousers patched at the knees. He put a fern leaf or two in the vase and set it on Mrs. Braddock's mantel-shelf between the two enormous potichomania urns of wax fruit which she had made herself.

"I know just where to pick up such things, or of course I could not have afforded it," he said, touching it with a sigh of pleasure. "Who knows now but this may belong to the days before the Marano work? There is not a hint of color in it."

"Oh, Venice, indeed!" said the old lady vaguely. "I remember reading a good deal about those doges and their underhanded ways. When Clay was a baby I had more time for secular reading than I've ever had since. It was kind of you to think of me, Mr. Andross."

She turned the vase about, looking at it admiringly, though secretly she thought it but a poor thing, smoked and cloudy, beside her real cut glass decanters, which Mr. Braddock had given her just before he died, and which were locked up in the spare chamber cupboard with her red and gilt china. The old lady prided herself upon her taste, and when Clay brought her anything which did not suit it ("and Clay had no more eye for colour than a turkey-cock"), she laughed at it and him; but she would no more have so hurt this Andross, whom she had known but a month or two, than she would long ago have thrust pins into her baby, when she had a baby of her own.

Braddock could not help thinking of all this now, nor of how Andross was always ready to go with his mother to the little wooden church to listen to old Macintosh during the long, hot mornings. How her clear, delicate voice (Braddock had always been proud of his mother's voice) was lifted up and strengthened by Jack's wonderful baritone! When the two sang together, all the rest of the congregation halted in their race to get through the tune, and Braddock, who had no ear for music, felt the tears come to his eyes and his throat choke unaccountably. He believed as gospel in the election and fore-ordained damnation which Macintosh preached, but he had often an excuse for staying at home; while Andross, whom he suspected of being an infidel, walked regularly beside the old lady to hear the curses of the law, cheerful and light-hearted as a child.

He was a child in too many of his ways, Braddock thought, going into his den and carefully turning his back upon the desk. When he had money to buy clothes, had he not expended it all upon linen fine enough for a prince of the blood ? The fellow dropped money as water from a sieve, for any whim of his own or for whoever chose to fleece him. No use for Braddock to advise or beg him to put his salary in a savings bank, to insure his life, or buy western lands, or to tell him, as an example, of the seven thousand dollars which he himself had been able to save. Look at these heaps of books, now ! Some in paper covers, others in costly English editions and bindings, thrown pell-mell in the corner as one would orange rinds after the juice had been sucked. German, French, Greek, all together.

One month Andross would take up Descartes' old doctrine of naturalism, and argue that the complete man must first go back to the savage condition and imbibe all human experiences as he rose slowly to civilization. "Saint Simon had the idea, but was a coward. Could not carry it out," he said. The next day he would be *en rapport* with nothing but the product of generations of culture ; there was a fine flavor of repose, he declared, of certainty in knowledge and assured place in the universe which belonged to the castes of the Brahmin, the Faubourg Saint Germain, the slaveholder in a nation ; of course, tyranny, slavery, all such things went to make it up, but wasn't it worth the whole of them ? A costly thing, but all good things were costly, etc., etc. In an hour he might break out a fiery Radical and outrant any red bonnet of the Commune ; for Andross, who would nurse a hurt dog for weeks, was the blood-thirstiest of men in his talk. But whatever the caprice of theory or hobby of study, the books were not spared to humour it, and once having served their purpose were thrown aside.

Braddock, usually as hasty of motion as of tongue, stood hesitating and halting through the office, trying to recall all these faults of the man—how weak he was, vivid, erratic : of different flesh and blood, indeed, from the smart, common-sensed young men who had been Braddock's class-mates in college, "any one of whom would have snapped at the place which he had obtained for Andross." It was such steady-going hacks that were fit for work, he thought, irritably, and not John ; John was like those winged creatures you read of in the old mythologies—you never knew one minute whether in the next they would be soaring in the clouds or grovelling in the mud. His vices were vices of the blood, perhaps ; and if so, hopeless. The clock pointed to the half hour. He had tried in that wasted time to summon all of Andross's petty faults before him, very much as the judge looks in the face of the convict to find proofs of his evil nature before he pronounces sentence of death on him.

But he could defer his work no longer. He had already heard Spellin tap at the door once or twice and go away swearing at his delay. He lowered the window-shades, tried the lock of the door, turned up the lamp. Then he put his key in the desk and opened it.

When Braddock was in haste to catch a train or finish a job, he fumed and trembled with anxiety and impatience ; but once he had gone out to save a drowning man at Cape May, and he had when making ready, they said, been the coolest, quietest man on the beach. He was cool and quiet now. His hand was as steady as that day when it held the drowning wretch with a grip like iron, now as he drew the account books out and opened them.

Nobody had access to these books but himself and Andross. The key to the desk he had in his pocket, the duplicate had been left in the lock the night Andross disappeared.

He turned over the leaves rapidly : when a man knows what footmark he is looking for the trail is easily found. Here in May, on the debit side, the company was charged three thousand for timber : the last cipher was of paler ink than the first ; again in November another added cipher. Both marked paid. The alterations had been made within a week ; a little more time and they would have been as black as the original writing. Braddock closed the books, took up the lamp, and shifted it to the other side of the desk, set the blotter and pen-holder in order, glanced furtively from side to side, and then took from its inner hiding-place the bank-book. One would have thought from his stealthy, colourless face that he was a thief making his final successful haul, so strongly were guilt and terror marked on it.

He opened at the last cut pages : "July 18th," the day before Andross's disappearance, a check drawn for six thousand dollars. There was no proof there. The company, of course, banked in Lock Haven, and either Braddock or Andross brought up the money for the monthly payment of the hands, or the debts due on lumber, whenever it was convenient to go down and return in daylight, not deeming it safe to carry large sums of money through the wild, mountainous passes. July the 18th was not the time for paying the hands, but there was no matter for suspicion in the fact that Andross had drawn it then. The fact that the cash-box was empty proved nothing ; for only the two men knew of the secret lining in an old unlocked chest of drawers in Andross's room where it was their wont to put the money until pay-day. There was still a chance ; what if, after all, he should put his hand into the old hiding-place and pull out the roll of notes ? If it was empty Andross was dead. He would never live after he had been dragged so low as to steal. Braddock lay down the check-book, got up from the desk-stool, and crossed the room. Heaven knows what spasmodic whim made him try to hum a tune as he went, but it was an effort ghastly enough. He pulled out the rattling drawer (in which, for precaution sake, Andross had stowed some ragged winter clothes, laughing at his skill in blinding the always expected burglar), lifted a thin board at the back and thrust in his hand.

It was empty when he took it out.

Five minutes afterward an authoritative bang came to the door, very different from Spellin's rap.

"Braddock ! Doctor, I say ! It's not possible the man's asleep ! Here, it's I."

"Coming, Judge, coming," unlocking the door. Maddox's round figure pushed it open.

"Just got your friend off to bed. Lord, what a tongue that man has ! Always was considered a good listener, but he wore me out ! Mixes a nice salad, though ; deucedly nice. You might as well have come down to supper as stayed drowsing here. Spellin came to say somebody had better be sent to Bear Valley, but I told him you knew what you were about, and then I just walked over to see what it was you were about."

Braddock not answering, the judge dragged a bench out and sat down on it with a thump.

"Hu ! What a pull up hill this is ! Here, let me trim that lamp; your hands shake like a drunkard's that hasn't got his bitters. Well, well. No wonder it knocked you up. Andross was as good a fellow——" heaving a sigh and smoothing his fat little legs with melancholy strokes. "Aha ! you've been looking over accounts, eh ? Well, you are the devil of a fellow for business. Newcome, down at Lock Haven this evening, was running me pretty hard about leaving my affairs to you and Andross. 'Anybody could cheat you out of your eyes, Maddox,' he said. 'Always could.' 'Just the reason,' says I, ' that I get these fellows about me whose eyes nobody will throw sand in.' Eh ? But I keep a sharp look out myself," wagging his head. "I mean to go over the books with you and see if Andross had them straight. By the way, there's the check-book. Meant to go into the bank down

"WHY, ANDROSS DREW SIX THOUSAND DOLLARS THE DAY BEFORE HE WAS MISSING!"

in town to-day if I'd thought of it.   Hand it over here, Clay."

Braddock handed it over.   He walked quickly to the window, and stood there with his hands thrust deep into his pockets.   The judge spoke to him once or twice, but he did not answer.

In his right breast-pocket there was a roll of greenbacks which he had taken to town to give to Laird.   He could feel them pressing against his chest.   It seemed to him as if all the days and years of work which he had paid for them came back in that moment.

When he had drawn these savings of his from bank, a short time ago, his mother had touched the money with her finger, laughing significantly.   "There is your chance to marry, Clay," she said.   She knew very well that Clay, like most quiet, long-headed men, had looked forward to marriage since he was a boy, but she did not know that lately he had done it with a definite, settled purpose.   So definite, that these notes seemed to carry not only all his past life but all his future with them.

Andross was dead, of that he felt convinced.   To protect his name from shame was he to give up ——

"Why, God bless my soul, Braddock, here's —— Why, Andross drew six thousand dollars the day before he was missing !   By George, this puts a different face on the affair !"

"In what way ?"   Braddock came up to him slowly.

"He did not leave one dollar in the cash box.   Not one single red cent !   I searched it myself."   The judge was standing now, the blood heating his flabby face, his voice thick.

Braddock took the check-book from him, the leaves of which he was flapping excitedly, and shut it quietly.   "Andross never kept large sums of money in the office, sir.   We had a place in his chamber where we hid it."

He stopped, took up the lamp and set it down again.

"Well ? Well ?"

" I'll go and look there."

" Yes. Of course, go and look there. I tell you, if that fellow was a thief, after all —— "

He was out of the room but a minute, and came back with a small brown roll in his hand.

" There is your money, Judge. Six thousand. Count it and see if it is correct."

The judge did count it, wetting his thumb and filliping the notes down on his knee with shaking hands.

" Six thousand—yes. All right. Well, thank God for that ! It wasn't the vally of the money, Clay. But I'd not for ten times the sum have thought Andross a thief. One has such a regard for that fellow, you see."

Braddock stood buttoning up his waistcoat, which was open. The dull light made his face ghastly. " Yes, one has a regard for him," he said quietly.

CHAPTER III.

WHEN the two men were outside of the office and Braddock had locked it, the judge folded the money and put it in his pocket. "I'll take charge of this until you come back from Bear Valley, Clay. By the way, you're to stop at the house, and take a cup of coffee or something."

"I haven't time for that."

"Anna wants to speak with you about Andross."

Braddock went without reply, as a matter of course. Anna Maddox when she was a baby in arms had been able to do what she pleased with her father; he had had half a dozen other children, but none of them he thought had a hand so soft or eyes so innocent and affectionate. Every man or boy who came near her since had followed his example. They might love other women better, but it was she whom they obeyed; her whims that they delighted to humour; they wished their own wives or sweethearts had such soft clinging hands, or knew the affectionate trick of her blue eyes.

Braddock, with the stunning fresh weight of his sacrifice upon him, with the thoughts of Andross's dead body so real that he felt as if he could stretch out his hand and touch it, would have given much for one cheery word from the woman whom he meant to make his wife, but would not allow himself or her that comfort; yet he gave half an hour to Anna. Any other man would have done the same. Braddock remembered too as he came up to the door that his trousers were muddy, and his face unwashed. Whereas, if it had been Isabel's door, and he had been covered with Andross's blood, he would not have once thought of any annoyance or feeling she might have had about it.

The garden through which he passed was a real rest and pleasure for any hard-worked eyes and brain. Andross had planted and kept it in order. Andross always said Anna was only an educated Maud Muller, and ought to be framed by all the gracefullest simplicity and freshness of Nature ; no tree but the elm or waving willow should hedge the house in which she lived ; no flower without perfume should bloom in her garden. The very lights, Braddock thought, as he knocked at the hall door, burned more softly here than elsewhere ; the lamp-shades were of Andross's choosing ; the bow-window for flowers back of the hall he had planned, and, in fact, for lack of carpenters and glaziers, almost built. It made a background of massed colour now for Anna, as she walked up and down the matted floor waiting for Braddock. The scent of the flowers was faint, her dress was delicate and cool ; that was all he saw. No man ever went away from Anna and remembered her muslins or merinos ; they only felt as never before that they had been in the presence of a woman, and were apt to talk a good deal thereafter of how the tenderer sex was vine-like and helpless and loveable, and to think of themselves in the relation of an oak.

Braddock, when he was with his betrothed, had always been so busy confiding his plans and consulting her that he seldom remembered whether she was a good-looking woman or not, but he noticed the face of the judge's little girl every day. Sometimes she would put roses or starry white flowers in her curly, light hair, and so plumed and vaunted herself that the dullest man would be enchanted with her vanity, as apparent as that of a baby just beginning to be conscious of its body.

To-night, however, her hair was straight, her nose

pinched, and her eyes had dark purple rings about them. She hurried up to Braddock, the moment he opened the door, in a timid, fluttering way that reminded him, modest man as he was, of a little boat scudding under shelter of a man-of-war.

"You've heard it?" she cried in her little falsetto of a voice. "Oh, Dr. Braddock, it's so dreadful—so dreadful! You men can bear to talk about him as dead, but it is quite a different thing to me."

The voice was such a weak and plaintive pipe, she looked up at him, patting her hands over her hair, so helplessly, there was such a bloom of youth and innocent passion over her whole delicate body, that Braddock, with all his Scotch common sense and coolness, was bewildered with a new rush of emotion. He felt as if he had not half mourned for Andross, now that this little creature unconsciously gave him a glimpse into her heart.

"I did not know," he said bluntly, "that Andross and you were lovers, Miss Maddox. This makes the matter worse, and God knows it was bad enough."

"Oh, no, no," she protested, "it was not love at all. It was only friendship. But if he is dead, what shall I do? Oh dear, what shall I do?" She shook with her sobs from head to foot, the tears rolled over her small, pale-tinted face as she stood looking up to him.

"Tut, *tut!*" said Braddock, and took her hand.

He was seriously pained for the silly, indiscreet little thing; but what the deuce had the judge been about to allow a man like Andross to obtain such a control over her? Was he blind? Of course, in the office or with men, John, though taken from a coaling-hearth, was fit for any place. But with this lovely woman, frail and pure as a white rose-bud——.

"Mr. Andross was a friend to us all, Miss Maddox. I am going now to Bear Valley to see what can be done. In the meantime——"

"Not _was_. Don't say was! He is only a friend to you, but he is all I have. *All!*"

"In my opinion," sharply, "that's not right. Where is your father, child? Do all his care and love for you go for nothing against this bow-window and flower-pots' and jimcracks which a stranger has made for you in a year?"

She drew back from him with a certain childlike dignity which had its force.

"What are his gifts to me?" with an indignant gesture. "He was congenial with me. He understood me. No one else does. I am quite alone now. You do not understand what I have lost."

Dr. Braddock looked down at her in a dumb dismay and then he looked—at his watch.

"If there is any chance that Andross is not dead, every moment we lose may be worth his life. I must go at once. Tell me what can I do for you?" stooping over her with that caressing tone which all men used to Anna.

"Take me with you. It was for that I sent for you."

"With me? To Bear Valley? Impossible."

"It does not matter to me about the possibility," smiling. "I intend to go."

"You forget the danger of the road, and the time of night and ——" stammered Braddock. He could not, with those clear blue eyes looking into his, hint at any other objection which worldlier women would have foreseen. "There comes your father. He will tell you it is impracticable."

"Dr. Braddock," laying her hand on his, "my father is no judge of this matter. Neither are you. If Andross is dead or in danger, it is my right to go to him. If," looking him full in the eye, "he has done wrong, I can bring him back. I am nearer to him than you."

Braddock was silenced as by a blow. After all, there was a higher law of love and helpfulness before which danger and conventionality were trifles. If she loved this poor criminal, a word from her might do more to save him than all his efforts or Macintosh's exhortations. But how did she come to suspect there had been wrong-doing? Women had eyes like ferrets, no matter what their youth and innocence.

Judge Maddox came in while he was searching for a word.

"What, Braddock, not off yet? Anna, you ought to consider poor Andross and not detain the doctor. Andross has been kind to you, I'm sure. The handiest fellow about a house, you see, Braddock."

"So kind that he is quite necessary to me, papa, and I propose to go with Doctor Braddock to find him," tying on a pink opera cloak and drawing its bewitching hood over her head.

"Absurd, Anna! Are you mad?" But Braddock noted that the judge's face wore a look of alarm which hinted that he thought the matter settled when Anna planned it. "Why, the road to Bear Valley is up the steepest side of Gray Mountain, dangerous for the surest-footed horse in daylight. It was there that Roskyns killed a panther last January; and as for rattlesnakes ———. Besides, what would people say if you went scouring the country at the dead of night with one young man in search of another?"

Anna's fair skin crimsoned a little.

"Yes, I knew there were snakes, and Roskyns told me himself about the panther," she said so regretfully that Braddock doubted for the moment if the hope of an adventure had not tempted her, and looked at her in perplexed wonder.

It is women like Anna that are sphinxes to men, and are therefore treated with a sort of awe-struck homage.

"Then you'll not go, my dear?" blustered the judge, but doubtfully.

"Certainly not, papa, if you disapprove of it," with a bright, affectionate smile which caused Braddock as never before to reflect how exquisite a thing was filial obedience. The judge began a dribble of directions, warnings, and advice to him, in the midst of which Anna disappeared.

"Here's your horse," as they went out of the door. "Joe has brought him up. Now be off, and good luck, and God bless you."

Braddock lost no time. The heels of his horse struck sparks from the flinty road. In half an hour he had left the Works and all trace of human habitation behind and reached the gorge between the mountains. His only path up the heights was the bed made by the current from a mountain spring, dry in summer, but in which the mossy boulders lay green and slimy. The solitude was absolute ; the unbroken forest, filled with the inexplicable noises which belong to the woods at night, stretched like a vast wall on either side of him to the horizon. There was an opening at last, where an old Indian trail crossed the bed of the brook, and in the dim moonlight which the thinner foliage admitted, he saw a dark moving figure waiting apparently for him. Coming closer, he found it to be a horse and a woman on it—a woman with a small-featured, baby face, looking beseechingly at him out of a pink hood.

CHAPTER IV.

"I TOLD you I was coming," said Anna gently. "What the deuce," Braddock began inwardly, but he only answered, "Yes, Miss Maddox," and quietly dismounted to lead her horse by the rein. If it had been Isabel or anybody amenable to reason, he would have continued hot in his wrath ; but who could crush such a white dove as this by displeasure ? Before he had gone a dozen yards he forgot, in the feeling of how sublime an act of devotion this was in the child, the discomfort of stumbling up a mountain pass, leading two horses, one or the other of which perpetually tramped upon his shins. She had forgotten danger, propriety, even the obedience to her father which he had thought so admirable, to follow the call from the one human being she loved. Braddock, narrow, clean-minded man, looked at her from time to time with a wordless awe and tenderness. She had dropped the reins instantly at his bidding and sat quite helpless but for his guidance, her hands folded outside of the cloak over her breast, her pure face turned heavenward. As a chance ray of light touched it she seemed a saint to him. If she had persisted in holding the reins and managing for herself, very probably he would have turned back and marched her straight to her father as a self-willed little minx.

Braddock was a commonplace fellow who liked life to go on in an orderly jog-trot way : breakfast, office, dinner, bed, like so many due bills to duty paid and receipted. But to-night with his hand on this girl's rein, passing through these dreadful solitudes, he felt as if he had suddenly opened up the depth of the realities of human life in all its vague mystery—God overhead, the fires of hell waiting, and death at hand. Andross, the stout bright-faced fellow who counted pig-iron with him every day, was in fact a lost soul, that for years had been struggling out of vice and the darkness and underside of life into higher levels—with what fierce agony of effort Braddock now could see. He had failed; if he were dead yonder in the mountains, had failed for all eternity. This little girl at whose silly vain chatter Braddock had laughed indulgently every day, suddenly rose into a height far above him, as one of God's messengers, going through night and danger and risk of shame unappalled upon her errand.

He wondered, with the awe with which one would look at a drama whereof heaven and hell were the background, whether if Andross was alive she could save him; whether he were one of the elect or one of that countless multitude condemned before Time was. These were terrible realities, to which Braddock had hitherto approached only through vague Sunday reflections or Doctor Macintosh's prayers. He had an uncomfortable sense of sacrilege in applying them to this every-day business and these every-day people.

If any human agency could be sent as a Saviour to the lost wandering soul, surely this pure woman was fit for the errand. He thought of Jephthah's daughter going out upon the mountains ere she offered herself a sacrifice; of Una unharmed on her pilgrimage by beasts of prey; whatever images his narrow imagination and scanty reading supplied him with, of fair, of saintly, he bestowed upon her as he walked humbly at her side.

Anna bent down to look curiously at the wet rocks. "Now, I suppose if there are any rattlesnakes anywhere they would be here?"

"Nothing would harm you on your errand," cried Braddock, almost in a state of religious exaltation.

"No, I don't really suppose a snake could reach me up here," she piped in her sweet, pleading little voice, drawing her legs up higher on the horse. "Besides, it would attack you first. Of course you're armed in case we should meet a bear?"

"No. There's no danger from bears in this time of the year. Don't be frightened. Keep your thoughts clear, for your great errand. Though if we find him alive, it will be given to you what to speak."

"Oh! I'm never at a loss for words. Papa calls me a perfect chatter-box. I shall scold Mr. Andross roundly for giving us all such a fright; he'll have no petting from me, you may rest assured of that. Well, now, I was sure we would meet a panther or something," in a most pathetic cadence. "My cousin, Mrs. Large, was in a party once which was attacked by wolves in the Pyrenees, and such a talk as all her family have kept up about it! It has been their *cheval de bataille* of conversation ever since, and here have I lived all my life right beside wild beasts, plenty of them, and never had an adventure! I was quite sure of one to-night."

There was something dampening to Braddock's enthusiasm, it is true, in these little dribbles, but the fountain was so pure! He looked up at the clear, delicately cut face, and felt the small hand laid confidingly on his shoulder, and was with Una and all the heroic, saintly company again. The child was but a child, but because of her simplicity the fitter for God's messenger. After she had kept silence five minutes it seemed to him that the chance rays of light made a halo for her head.

Anna was thinking what a pretty pose hers was on a horse. Braddock was like a knight—a much better figure for a knight than Andross, who was undeniably stout and wore no beard either; and this cloak she had on, how lucky it was soft cashmere instead of any stiffer stuff—it draped so well.   Only, white would have looked better than pink.

They came out now from the thick forest into an open space—a range of ridges from which the underbrush and trees had been partially cleared.   Here and there upon the cleared space lay portentous dark shadows.

"You must dismount here," said Braddock.   They had reached the district of the abandoned ore-banks full, as he knew, of old shafts from sixty to two hundred feet deep and left open, save for the brambles aud berry bushes which covered their tops.   "You could not take ten steps here on horseback without peril of your life, and I really don't see," in perplexity, "how it is possible for you to advance even on foot."

"Oh, I am sure *you* will take care of me," murmured Anna.

Yesterday, indeed up to nine o'clock this evening, Anna had cared for nothing in the world so much as Andross.   When she suspected him of guilt, her devotion (very genuine of its kind) rose to fever heat.   She remembered one of her songs about the "one who ne'er would flee from the tiger slain, but soothe its dying pain," etc., etc., and had been singing it through her tears all day.

But Andross was so provokingly long in being found, and Braddock was like Greatheart or Sir Galahad. Really, she never had observed how finely cut a nose and chin he had, nor how well his pale, lean face was thrown into relief by the black whiskers.   She had always thought him a bigoted and sour sort of man, and a good deal of a prig; but now——

"You will take care of me," she said again, in a musical whisper which would have reminded a sharp woman of Rosalind's murmured, "Woo me, woo me," which thrilled the listening forest of Ardenne.

It thrilled Braddock uncomfortably.

" Perhaps I had better get you to shelter," he said, with awkward haste. "I had a superstitious fancy that you would be guided somehow to Andross, but I can find him as well by myself, probably."

"What are you going to do with me, then?" holding his arm with fluttering, feeble hands.

"I'll take you to Colonel Latimer's. There is a light from his windows—that red speck yonder."

"Oh, dear! Isabel Latimer is such a dreadfully sensible, unfeeling creature! But one would not like to be dragged out of an old shaft like a rat in a hole, to be sure. Well, Dr. Braddock, you can take me wherever you choose."

They reached the colonel's house in a few minutes. It lay in the mouth of the gorge, surrounded by the brawling waters of the creek, but Braddock knew the way too well to be in danger of pitfalls. He knew, too, that the light was in Isabel's window; she had waited, perhaps, for some message, on his return, which he had forgotten to send. No matter; she would forget her disappointment now, in sympathy with this child and her errand. He lifted Anna from her horse as reverently as though it had been Godiva herself, and opened the door, which was unlocked, according to the habit of the mountains.

Miss Latimer came down the stairs the next moment with a light in her hand. Her eyes sparkled at sight of Braddock. The doctor was in such haste to show his heroine to her that he forgot he had not seen her for a week. People were more apt to think of Isabel's sympathy than of Isabel herself.

He left the little pink-draped figure by the door.

"It is Anna, Miss Maddox, Bell; come and help the poor child! She—I was going in search of Andross and she would come with me. I thought it would be better to leave her here. You could take care of her."

The sparkle was quite gone out now from Isabel's eyes.

"Miss Maddox would not be very efficient in a searching party, I imagine," eyeing her across the hall with an amused laugh in her face.

Braddock remembered angrily that women were always hard on women, yet even the hardest, he would have supposed, might soften to that lovely little enthusiast.

"At least you will be kind to her, and give her what comfort you can?"

"I should suppose that, just now, would be water and towels.   Why, Nannie!" advancing cheerfully, "what a woe-begone, drabbled object you are!   Go up to the front chamber, you know the way, and go to bed directly.   I must speak to Dr. Braddock alone a moment."

"Sending me off like a baby that she may take possession of the doctor!" thought Anna; and then the vine-like creature, after the habit of vines, being thus summarily robbed of one support, put out its tendrils in search of another.

"To bed, Isabel?" she said coldly.   "How can any of us sleep when Mr. Andross is lying dead in the mountains?"

Braddock's face was filled with the tenderest pity, but Isabel listened calmly.

"You at least will be much more apt to sleep if you are in bed," she said good-humouredly, and watched her without speaking until she had gone up the stairs.   Then she turned to Braddock:

"You need look no further," she said, "Andross is here."

CHAPTER V.

"ALIVE? Alive?" He could not say anything more. The blood in his veins stood still; something choked his throat. Braddock was surprised at himself; he had not known he cared so much for anybody, much less this idle fellow.

Isabel turned to him suddenly. "You love like a woman, Clay." She had only touched him on the arm, but her eyes grew wet and her cheek burned so that it seemed as if she had kissed him.

"Why didn't you tell that poor little creature and send her to bed comforted?"

"Time enough for her to know to-morrow. Mr. Andross is in the front room. He thought you would be here early in the evening, and has been waiting for you."

"I'll go to him. Good-night, Bell." After he had taken the lamp from her and hurried across the hall, he remembered that they had been separated longer than ever before. He ought to have been more tender in his greeting—have kissed her, he thought, reddening. But then Bell was not a woman to care for caresses or any trivial expressions of affection. Andross was nearly right when he talked of her Roman head; both features, he thought, and character were of the old Roman mould—graver, more liberal than American types. Yet she need not have put that poor little Maddox girl so utterly out of the question to-night in her large, good-humoured way, as though it were a gnat she was brushing aside.

He stopped a minute at the door, behind which was

Andross, not to steady his nerves, for Braddock would go about all the business of life in a matter-of-fact way, would die most probably, as he had made love, in a politely respectable fashion. He would have been very glad if Andross could have come right into the office to-morrow morning, and they could have gone on with work, smoking cigars and talking over the morning's Herald and Tribune together as usual, without any pother of welcome or confession or reconciliation. Braddock, the Presbyterian, might hate sin, but Braddock, the man, hated a scene more, and besides he had that terrible embarrassment of shame upon him with which an innocent man faces a guilty one dear to him.

When he opened the door and Andross came to meet him, it was Braddock who looked the criminal.

The men shook hands.

"Ah, Braddock! You came up this evening?" said Andross, gulping through commonplaces as men do, though death be tugging at their throats.

"Yes."

"Have a good run up?"

"No, behind time. The train was delayed at Williamsport as usual. The company takes no oversight of these branch roads. Why, Andross!" as they came up to the light. "You've been ill. Sit down, man, sit down!"

Braddock had never in his life perhaps expressed sympathy with mental trouble, but the gaunt face and sunken eyes of the man whom he had left a fortnight ago plump and hearty were things he could talk of fluently. "What is it, Andross? You look as if you were struck with death!"

"No. I'm too toughly built. A man of my constitution don't die of grief or shame; more's the pity. Twice out in the mountains I tried to put an end to myself this week, but it ended like Göthe's going to bed with a dagger and poison. It seemed to me there must be a chance for me yet, if only in the fact that you could be as patient with such a man of straw as you have been with me." The face he turned on Braddock was full of a fine sensitiveness, and eager and appealing as a woman's. But the doctor turned from it impatiently. A man of straw, indeed ! He had not will enough to put the knife to his throat after he had made a thief of himself. Braddock walked up and down once or twice before he could reply.

"Your nervous system is run down, I suspect," he said drily. "Go to bed now, and in the morning I'll see what will be best to give you. Quinine, probably, or bromide of potassium."

Andross laughed. "You're more practical than I thought. You dragged me out of hell once, and you know it; and now, when I have gone back again, you give me bromide of potassium."

"You forget, Andross, that I know nothing of your past life. I never knew what curse had brought you as low as you were when I found you—whether it was drink or cards or women. Nor do I know how it took hold of you again. What does that matter for me? My words of advice would prevail nothing if there is a sentence against you——" He stopped short there. He could not believe Andross was one of the multitude foredoomed for destruction. He was standing in front of Braddock in his shirt sleeves. The light fell on his bared neck and uplifted head. In spite of the gauntness and haggardness of the man there was still that certain air of youth and springiness and wholesome energy about him which Braddock always had told himself could only belong to one whose life had been temperate and cleanly.

"He has been neither profligate nor debauchee," he thought, trying as usual to find a reason for the blind faith he had put in him.

"No. It was none of those ordinary vices that dragged

me down. There never seemed to me to be any great
temptation in them." He paused a minute. "I don't
know why I should say anything more to you. I have
no wish to come whining to you about any exceptional
hardness in my lot."

"I have no wish to know your secret, Andross,"
coldly. At that there was a weak, uncertain quiver in
the face of the guilty man, peculiar to him. The moment, like a woman, that he had thrust sympathy away,
he craved it more greedily.

"It *has* been harder than other men's. I've been
tangled in a net, by no fault of my own, since I was a
boy, and it has held me down. You know whether I
have struggled faithfully against it or not. It's not
worth while to struggle now any longer."

"Bah! That is sheer folly," vehemently. "If you
tell me that all your struggles may be unavailing to
insure your salvation for the next world, I can understand you. But there's no power which can prevent a
man from leading a decent and honest life in this, if he
chooses."

Andross had turned from him and stood leaning on the
mantel-shelf, still looking down into the open, fireless
hearth. He did not move, although the tall, black-a-
vised man beside him, in his eagerness, had caught him
almost roughly by the arm. Outside, a sickly gray light
began to struggle through the night at the east. The
wind had died out. There was silence that might be
felt in the mountains and in the sky. Even to Braddock's unimaginative soul it seemed as though there was
a listening pause in Nature while this man's soul that
had come so close at times to God, stood for the last time
at the crossing of the ways, to choose between life and
death.

And only he, Braddock, held him by the hand. It
was he who had been appointed his brother's keeper. It

would have been so natural and comfortable to go back to every-day ways and gossip about politics or the next week's yield of pig-iron, and to shut their eyes to this awful undercurrent of sin and remorse and death below. It was the first time in his life Braddock had dared to speak in such wise to a man. The shame and the novelty of it made his voice hoarse and his commonplace salesman's face set and rigid, while Andross, usually all nerve and fire, was heavy and motionless as a log.

"I am not fit to talk to you. I never can talk of religious matters, Jack. If it was Dr. Macintosh now——. But for God's sake, be a man. It seems to me as if you stood on the edge of the pit. There's no force that need compel you to go down it. There are no devils to enter into a man now as in old times."

He stopped, confused. His creed, taught him in the village church, told him that there were devils; that there was no hope for Andross if he had not been born with his name written beforehand in an invisible, unalterable list yonder; but the every-day experience he had gained knocking around from the Works to New York forced him to believe that no man was a thief or liar but by his own free will. A theologian might reconcile the two; but Clay was no theologian.

Andross answered as from far-off reasonings of his own. "You're mistaken. There are forces outside of a man nowadays—here, all about him—just as strong to compel him to ill-doing as ever there were in the wilderness or in hell. Talk of your devils—Satan and Apollyon!" with a sudden discordant laugh. "*I* don't know them! I'd sooner run the risk of facing the whole batch of them than one little red-headed man I know. They'd do my soul less harm. None of their flames are as terrible as a policeman's tap on the shoulder—that is," catching his breath, "if I were a poor wretch who knew he was in danger of a jail cell while he was trying to be an honest man and a gentleman." He pushed up the window as though choking for air, but none came: a sullen torpor, dark and breathless, held the night.

"I don't follow you clearly," said the doctor drily. He sat down by the table, pushed some books back to make room for his elbow, looked at his pink, well-shaped nails with a face of grave rebuke. "I know that sort of infidel heterodoxy is fashionable, but I confess I never understood it. To compare the Author of all evil to a policeman is a belittling view of the truths of Holy Writ, to my mind."

"I'll tell you frankly, Braddock, where I stand," as though he had not heard him. "For years I have been in the hold—not of a man, nor a devil, but of a corporation. That sounds commonplace enough, don't it? You could easily get out of that halter? Wait one minute, Braddock. The purpose of this club or organization is unmixed evil. As for its power—it has money. Unlimited money. It buys and sells at will the government and interests of the city where it belongs: it controls the press, the pulpit, the courts. The best men are muzzled by it, are forced against their will to serve it. What was I to fight against it? It needed me, and it has an absolute hold on me—I can't tell you now how it gained it." Just then he caught the doctor's keen black eyes under their suspicious brows fixed on him.

"No, I'm not making melodrama out of this matter. I've been the slave of this Thing. I've been forced to work for it with both body and brain; though, you would say, God gave me both to make an honest Christian man out of me. I suppose He did——"

"I think I should have been able to master any such force as that," dogmatically. "If a thing is wrong, there's the law. There's public opinion to back you in putting it down."

"You might fight against a man. But a powerful

corporation meets you with the brain power of a multitude of men, but with no conscience, nothing to which you can appeal. It buys the law. It buys public opinion."

Braddock had been reading Andross's face with its protruding forehead and weak chin.

"Now I understand you pretty thoroughly, John," he said frankly. "You'll not mind if I'm candid, eh? I'm a pretty sharp reader of human nature, you know, and it strikes me that the difficulty has been in yourself. Your imagination is always at white heat, you know: you've exaggerated some ordinary political club into a monster that devours men's souls and bodies. You do that sort of thing a good deal, Andross. And then you—well, I don't say that you're not strong in a certain way, but——"

"I understand, a man of straw."

"Now don't be hasty. If you'd said a man of wax—. I mean that you are influenced by people whom you like, unwarrantably. Now *I* should have said to these people calmly, 'I can not do as you require. *It is wrong.* To the law and the testimony.' What possible hold could they have on you which would resist that?"

There was a pause.

"No matter. They did have it. They have it yet. I can not explain that to you, Braddock," hastily. "I went to the coaling hearths to escape them. When I came here I thought I was still out of their reach. It was the first time I had ever seen the way clear for me to be like other men, even in the matter of earning money honestly and being paid for it. You and Maddox had confidence in me. I thought I could make a position for myself here, and some day marry, and have a home and wife and children as other men can do."

"Yes, I understand, Andross," gently, thinking of the child up stairs. "Well——?"

"That was only a week ago. Then they found me out. I am in their power, Braddock, as if they had a

halter about my neck.   I had the choice to go with them
or buy them off."

Both men were silent for awhile.

"Go on," said Braddock.

"I—*bought them off.*"

He watched the doctor furtively.   Braddock stood
with his back to him.   A damp, chilly wind blew through
the room, heavy with fog.   There was a break in the
solid rampart of gray behind the Muncey range, an opening as into a new firmament full of shifting, uncertain
colour.   Andross long afterward remembered that red
watery depth together with the breathless pause of
waiting.

Braddock, he saw, was not surprised at his last words;
he knew him already then to be a thief?

While he stood like a miserable convict, his weak
mouth open, staring at the doctor's back, Braddock was
running over the whole situation in his own mind.

He could not bear that this poor creature should go on
and confess his crime; he would as lief have had him
commit hari-kari beside him.   Let him confess it to God.
If they did talk of the money, then he must explain that
he had replaced it, and that would be a miserably mean
bit of bragging.   It would crush Andross to the earth;
for he knew how the money had been saved and for what.
"He'd never look me in the face, going about the Works,
knowing he owed me such a sacrifice as that," he thought.
And he was going to bring back Andross to the Works.
He believed he would be honest in future, not because of
this rubbish he had told him about a Ring, but because,
because——Well, he always had believed in Andross.

For Braddock could give no better reasons for any of
his opinions than for having an aquiline nose on his face.

While he was thus sharply debating the matter, and
deciding that when Andross was in the office he could
keep a supervision over him, that the judge should suffer

no loss, that poor wretch came up behind him, and laying his hands on his shoulders, turned him around. His face was ghastly.

"Look here, I'm in your hands, Braddock; you're the only friend I've got in the world. Do what you please with me."

For a moment the doctor could not collect his wits to reply.

"There now! there now!" loosening Andross's hold. "I don't like scenes, John. Go to bed, and report yourself at the Works early in the morning. That's all I can say to you."

"Do you mean——" Could it be that the loss of the money was not yet discovered? There was a chance then that he might replace it? He had meant to replace it until the consciousness of being a thief had driven him mad.

"I mean that you are to come back to the office and go to work. If your old enemies trouble you let me know. I'll attend to them," with an inflexible crook of the eyebrows and cocking of the chin, which in anybody else, Andross would have quizzed as intolerable conceit and priggishness. But the humbled fellow looked up to the young doctor as one of the saints of the earth.

"I'll go down then, Clay. If you say so. It's a chance for me to be a man again."

"Very well. I'm going back to-night. Explain to Miss Latimer in the morning that I've gone."

"Yes. She——it was Miss Latimer found me in the mountain to-day. If it had not been for her I should not have been alive now. I think God made her different from other women."

"Oh, it was she that found you, eh? Well, good night." He took Andross's cold hand and dropped it quickly, going out hurriedly without meeting the dreadful pleading look which he knew was fastened upon him.

"He does not know!" said Andross with a long breath. He felt for the minute as though he were an innocent man.

"He would have been alive whether Bell found him or not," ran the doctor's thoughts. "He has not strength of mind enough to kill himself. And as for Bell, how is she different from all other women? That little thing of the judge's, now—her devotion and exaltation of nature were something really remarkable. Bell is the dearest girl in the world, but as for being different from other women—nonsense '

CHAPTER VI.

A S long as the night lasted, Jack Andross knew that
in spite of his reprieve he never should hold up his
head among men again. He felt his hands, muttering to
himself that this was the flesh of a thief; he recalled the
faces of all the men he had seen in rogues' galleries and
the dock, and told himself again and again that he was
no better than they: just as he had been talking to himself for days up in the hills, taking out his pistol now
and then and cocking it. Why in God's name had he
not used it, and put an end to all this intolerable misery?
Presently, however, the day began to break, and, being
feverish, he went to the window to catch the cold air,
and then waited to see the red light on the creek beside
the house. The water went brawling over the stones; it
was like voices talking; another minute and one could
tell what they said; the colonel's big dog came rushing
through the currant-bushes up to the house knocking the
dew off them like rain. Andross whistled to him: "Hah,
you scoundrel! After sheep, eh?" he said. Then he
leaned farther out to see the chickens come clucking up
from the barn, and finding some crackers in his pocket,
whistled to them and threw out the crumbs. He must
remember to bring the colonel some Poland hens next
time he drove over to Millhall. Just then the old black
man who was Bell's cook and maid of all work opened
the kitchen door, and looking up touched his hat to
Andross.

"Pretty fa'h mohnin, sah. Gwine take a bath 's
usual?" For Andross often came up to spend the night

with the colonel. He nodded and went down to Otho
for towels. "'Rival in de night, sah! Doctor from de
Wohks and young Miss Maddox."

Andross threw the towels over his arm, and crossed the
yard stopping at the gate. "Is Miss Maddox here now,
Oth?" he said, without looking back.

"Yes, sah. Doctor's gone back."

As he passed along the creek bank he was conscious
only of an agony of shame, not remorse. He could face
God or the world, but not this woman.

But the water in the creek was deliciously cold, and as
he came back from his bath the wind blew in his face, a
flock of king-birds flew about him chirping, his feet sank
up to the ankle in mosses: through the brown needles of
the pine the Indian pipe thrust its fairy pillars of carved
ivory. He stooped to dig out a clump for Bell, remembering that she preferred them to flowers, and then
climbed the rocks to gather the laurel whose waxen clus-
ters tinged the whole mountain pink. The laurel and
the cold and the dawn, even the chirping birds, in spite
of himself, filled him with a strange delight with which
Rings and stolen greenbacks had nothing to do. He
would not give up his chance! The world was a good
and kindly world! If he told the whole story to all his
friends in the mountains they would understand and forgive him. He would go and make his confession to Anna
—now!

He went scrambling down the cliffs, loaded with his
laurel, when he caught sight of the colonel near the barn.
After all, what was the use of confessing to everybody?
These people were not in God's place to forgive sin. He
would tell Braddock, of course. He wished he had done
it last night. But he would replace the money—he
always meant to replace it—before he told Anna. He
could not drive her from him now, until he had won her.
In the meantime there was Colonel Latimer, a man of

honour like no other, why not consult him? He would go at once and tell him the whole story. So he scrambled on dropping his laurel with his face in quite a glow of satisfaction at his rational decision. The colonel was a man of the world as well as honour. He would know what a Ring was, and why he had been as one might say, compelled to—borrow this money, and would set it in the proper light to Braddock.

The colonel had dragged on his trousers and run down barefooted to stop Towers, the miller, whom he saw going by with a string of eels. "The very thing!" he whispered excitedly to Bell, nearly upsetting her in the hall. "I've lain awake half the night contriving a decent breakfast!" He had just paid Towers double price as Andross came up, and was soothing Oth's wrath about it.

"God bless my soul, man, suppose it was swindling. When you look closely into the matter Towers has eleven children and an aguish wife. Eels are eels in a case like that. Halloo! Mr. Andross," with the eels still in one hand and holding out the other. "I was chagrined beyond measure to be in bed last night when you came. It's this confounded leg of mine. Neuralgic. Not a symptom of gout in it. I'm a little careless, too, for a man of my age. Just ran down barefoot—pressing business with—well, Otho. Look at that, sir. You can understand a sunrise like that better than any man I know."

Rain which was in the air thickened the sky without darkening it, so that it absorbed the dawn into retreating depths of nebulous gray, within which shone a golden lustre. Below, the unbroken hills of green forest rolled wave after wave to the horizon's edge, except where the precipitous heights of the Nittany Range heaped their gray rocks in inextricable confusion.

The colonel's house, standing in the gorge, was shut in on every side by these threatening recesses, which even at noon were gloomy, and fit haunts apparently for any beast of prey; but the damp soft light gave to them now a strange tenderness and cheerfulness: the gigantic cedars on the upper peaks showed but a black fringe against the sky; the mountain springs, discoloured by the pine roots, ran in glittering brown threads over the rocks to the pasture lands. The morning framed it all into one glad homelike picture; the very windows of the dilapidated old house in the gorge behind them shone yellow in the glow, but the whiff of smoke from the chimney was red; the blood-coloured beet-tops and the tomato vines were thick set with dew, every chicken and duck or pigeon scrambling for corn about Oth's heels at the kitchen door had its cheery cackle or coo. The colonel stood in the gateway swinging his eels to and fro in his enthusiasm, waving them to the finest points of view. His suspenders dangled about his legs; his thin, high-nosed face cut the wind like the prow of a boat; his bald pate rose into heights above it as if to assert its baldness; never before, Andross thought, in all his length and leanness, had he been so absurdly long and lean as now. But there had always been something about the colonel from the days when he was a dashing young fellow on the town, which attracted all women: it attracted Andross in precisely the same way now. Braddock was a little ashamed of his father-in-law's vagaries, but Jack watched him with a good deal more tender respect than he would have showed to the colonel's noble daughter.

The colonel turned away with a half sigh when the glow began to fade. "Here, Otho, take your eels. No, Mr. Andross, town can't give us that, eh? I've no doubt that you are homesick as I am sometimes for it; opera, theatre, libraries, and the people, sir, and the stir—the being close to the heart of things, eh? But the sight of the sun coming up over old Nittany sets me all right again. I don't wonder the young fellows born here come back, after trying the West, and fall to ploughing over the boulders. 'Pon my soul! I'm glad to see you!" energetically as they went into the house. "Do you know it's two months since anybody has broken bread with us?"

Andross glanced down at his muddy and ragged trousers; he was beginning to come back to the world and the ways of it. Colonel Latimer whispered more energetically than before: "I see! Hunting rig is not the thing to appear in before the ladies. Now don't say a word, my dear fellow. I'll bring up a pair in five minutes—a little too long, but we'll turn them up. Nothing like soldiering for making a man a tailor. Go right up to your room."

Andross went up dazed and silenced. How could he break in on the old man's single-hearted delight in his guest, or in the pure beauty of the morning with his vile nightmare story of Rings and robbery? Presently, after breakfast, as soon as they were alone. How in the deuce was he to get into the colonel's trousers? He laughed, and with the laugh the story of the stolen money was a dimmer nightmare than ever.

"Here you are!" The colonel tapped at the door. "They're very loose for me—there is a difference in our size probably. Now come down as soon as possible. Bell has a delightful surprise for you: a companion for you over to the Works, if you persist in going."

He knew, of course, that the colonel meant Miss Maddox. She had often last winter driven up with Andross to the gorge and spent the night with them.

Everything then was to go in the old way. Just as though he were not a thief!

He was standing before the glass ready to shave, and saw his face red with pleasure, and his eyes kindled at the thought of Anna. He looked at the razor. Better he should draw it across his bare throat now than deceive her and be as he had been to her!

Here's linen, Mr. Andross; and put this pink bud in your button-hole, and no woman will see the fit of your trousers." He heard the door close behind the colonel, and his steps as he went into his own room, and afterwards, being dressed, down-stairs; but he still stood irresolute, not yet determined how he should go to meet Anna.

In the meantime the poor little woman had seen her lover, whom she supposed to be dead, standing in the gate with the colonel, and had sobbed and cried her joy out behind the window-curtain. The tears were little drops, and the sobs little sobs, perhaps, but they were real. She would like to have gone down and hung on his broad breast, and combed his shaggy hair with her tiny pink fingers and smoothed the pain or trouble out of his heart with her touch. He was all the dearer because of his breadth and shagginess and mysterious grief. A different man from that lank, neat Braddock, that *résumé* of all the moral virtues! She was glowing through all her delicate flesh while he was in sight, and chilly and shivering from head to foot as soon as he was gone; she was the woman Shakspeare loved to draw; her bounty as boundless as Juliet's, looking and longing from a window long ago, her love (while it lasted) quite as deep.

Usually she did not favour Isabel with her society when in the house, but she crept into her room now, and asked leave to dress there, and hung about Bell, taking down her mass of fine brown hair, and dressing it again with her more skillful, swift fingers. "How white and stately your neck is!" she said, kissing it, and then curling her arm about it and resting her head on Isabel's bosom just as a baby would. Usually Bell was irritable when indifferent people kissed or touched her, but she patted the pale little face kindly enough as she lifted it off.

"Your head aches, Pussy?"

Anna sighed but said nothing. "She thinks nobody

can have feelings but herself, the—the intellectual Glumdalclitch," she thought spitefully. She had a nice little talent for giving well-fitting nicknames, and was rather pleased with this. "I did not care for *her*," she thought, still looking at Bell with wide, tearful eyes. There was an aching weight of love under her doll-like waist to give to somebody, and the soft, red lips were hungry to be kissed. "I'll go down to your father until breakfast is ready." The colonel was always overflowing with tenderness for the pretty little girl, and she felt that she sadly needed a comforter.

"Very well, Nannie."

"I see that Mr. Andross is back," stopping to chirp to the birds pecking at the window-sill. "So nice to see him back all safe again. We're all so fond of Mr. Andross. Tweet! tweet! How can you make these wild birds know you? I have canaries always: Lily, I call my little darling now."

"Don't like to cage things," gruffly.

"Oh, I must have something to pet and love!" turning her pleading eyes to Bell. "I've had such a disappointment in Fidele! I gave her gin regularly every day to keep her the proper size, and in spite of all my care she's grown into a great coarse beast! I had to send her away. I'll run down now. By-by birdies!" and she went down singing in a bird-like voice that made the old house alive with music.

Bell looked after her perplexed. "Well, she's an affectionate little thing! But I really thought she cared for Jack!" She never could have guessed Anna's habit of suddenly folding up her secrets and hiding them just as she did her lace collars and little puffs of scent-bags. The little lady's thoughts did not run into the Land o' the Leal of which she was singing. "Jack called her the 'ox-eyed.' She's like an ox!" nodding her head viciously back. "Just as slow and stupid and obstinate when her feet are down. I threw her off the trail about Andross, at any rate. Poor fellow!" and the soft eyes slowly filled.

"Oh, Colonel! I thought I should find you here!" running up with both hands out. The colonel, his coarse, gray clothes in martinet order, his scant gray hair brushed up in a top-knot to cover the bald pate, took them in his and bowed in a tender, soldierly fashion over them. But Anna could not wait to hear his old-fashioned compliments. "Come out to the garden; we've plenty of time before breakfast, and—I—I have something to say to you. Don't be frightened!" with a piteous sob, when they were scated behind the grape-trellis—"Oh, you dear Colonel, you look more frightened than I am! Oh, if I had such a father as you!"

"Why, the judge spoils you, my child! You're nothing but a petted little baby! Tut! tut!" as her warm tears rained on his wrinkled hand, wondering if Maddox could possibly be stern with such a creature. "Really, my dear! I'll call Bell. Bell is the kindest soul if there's trouble——"

"No, no!" drying her hot cheeks. "I'm quiet now. But I could not control myself any longer. I've been so unhappy! It's about Mr. Andross, sir."

"Mr. Andross?" gravely. "Yes. Well, my dear?"

The colonel suspected no acting in Anna, and indeed there was none. The whole of her force of body and soul spoke truthfully in every look and word.

"He has had some great mysterious trouble, and I must help him. I want to be of some use in the world, and I'm so little!" twisting the soft, snowy hands together. "He's—he's a good friend of mine, sir."

"Yes. I understand, my child."

Her lovely, imploring face was upturned to his. "Now I think," chirping like a bird, "that he has committed some dreadful crime."

"God bless my soul! Andross!"

"Yes, indeed, sir. I suppose that is why he went away the other day. So I thought I'd ask you what it was. Was it drinking? or gambling? or what?"

"Tut! tut! These women! I thought you'd discovered a murder at least. Why no, Miss Maddox. Mr. Andross always appeared to me to be a perfectly temperate man, and so far as I know, can't tell one card from another. I suppose he was out gunning or fishing. It's hardly fair to ask a man to expose every hour of his life, when you look at the thing closely."

"You don't think he is very fond of women, sir? Suppose he had a wife concealed somewhere?"

The colonel reddened like a girl; he turned away from the innocent face watching his. "I never have seen any more dangerous affections in him than for old china or rare editions." He looked at her with a meaning smile. "It's not for me to hint that he cares for her," he thought. "Now, my dear," rising, "we must go into breakfast. My advice to you is to talk to Mr. Andross himself, and offer your aid to reform him. You have some unwholesome megrims in your head, and I think Jack can cure them."

He led her gallantly along the unweeded path, joking about every subject but her lover. "For he must be her lover," he thought. "And Maddox approves, or he would not throw them together. God bless them both. I've helped them together with that advice, or I'm mistaken."

For the colonel was a born match-maker. Every young man in his eyes was a noble fellow, and every maiden exceptionally pure and beautiful, and all that was needed to regenerate the world was to drill them in couples, as Noah did the animals into the ark.

CHAPTER VII.

ANNA, with the conviction full upon her that she was the heroine of a tragic drama, thought fit to greet Andross, who was waiting at the hall-door, with a shy blushing dignity, very sweet and lovable.

"You look so well this morning!" said Isabel, holding out her hand to him heartily.

"Come, children! To breakfast! to breakfast!" cried the colonel, as Oth, having slipped on a white apron and turned from cook into waiter, opened the door with a flourish.

The table was bright, the scent of roses and coffee mingled deliciously. They all hurried in together. How could he stop then and there, and begin the dreadful story of his life? He had come down prepared to make confession, and here he was instead, opening his napkin and telling the colonel the price of beef in Lock Haven.

"Try a piece of this sirloin, now. They killed their young heifer at Judge Maddox's yesterday, and Sam brought over this steak a few minutes ago."

"Yes, sah, just in time. Very lucky, sah!" ejaculated Oth.

"It's our turn to kill a sheep to-morrow; don't forget, Bell. The beans are ripe enough to send round with it to the neighbors."

It was just the commonplace homely talk to bring Jack back to his old self. If Braddock had had the weight of crime on his conscience he could neither have eaten nor drunken; but Andross was made of different metal. He had been half starved on the mountains, and the beef was deliciously cooked, the butter fragrant with vernal grass; they all laughed and talked gossip and of the news in last week's papers; they lingered lazily over the meal, after the colonel and Bell's careless, happy fashion; the window was open, and beyond rose old Nittany, his robe of sombre cedar white with chestnut-blooms; the running water outside whispered and talked aloud at times; it was impossible to Jack not to fancy that they were real footsteps and voices growing cheerfuller every minute. The sun struck a warm beam across Anna's tender little face, but he would not look at that; he turned to watch it light the bunch of laurel on the table into rosy splendour. He was going to drive Anna back to Gray Eagle mountain presently, and then go to his work in the office. As for crime or danger it began to be as far off and long ago to him as the old stories of the war which the colonel was telling. He, too, had his old stories to tell, and he knew how Anna hung on every syllable, as Desdemona on the Moor's.

"It was my short-sight that always bothered me," the colonel said. "It never played me such a trick though as in the battle at Antietam—you know, Bell? I've told you the story a dozen times. I suddenly saw an opening where I thought my regiment could be used with effect, Mr. Andross, and brought them up at a gallop, cheering as we came, when I met Joe Thompson—Thompson of Chicago—you may have heard of him; a grain man formerly, colonel like myself; shot before Richmond, poor fellow, plumb through the heart. 'Where the deuce are you going, Tom?' he shouts. 'To the front!' I cry. 'Stop, stop!' he hallooes after me, like John Gilpin's wife when the mare ran away with him. But on we went up the hill, my men cheering louder than ever, and, I fancied, laughing. Well, sir, it wasn't until we had gone up the hill and come back again, bringing the enemy's cannon with us, that I discovered it was Joe's regiment I had taken and left my own in the van. One-third of his poor fellows were left on the ground. But we took the guns!"

"Short sight," laughed Andross, "would have been a serious obstacle in my way; for, when I was appointed to my captaincy, I did not precisely take Hardee's tactics on the parade-ground, but I copied the orders I had to give in shorthand on the palm of my glove, and read them off."

"You were in the army, then?" asked the colonel.

"Yes," with some embarrassment, "for two years. I was forced to give up my commission then and go back to business."

Colonel Latimer caressed his scanty imperial triumphantly and looked at Anna. "Here's a vicious criminal for you! This brave soldier!" his eyes said.

Andross saw the glance, and was driven by it into resolution. The colonel was his ally; he should know all as soon as breakfast was over.

Just as they rose from the table the splash of a horse's feet coming through the ford was heard, and the next minute Braddock came in with an odd air of repressed excitement in his stiff figure and lean face. Anna was first to coo out a welcome, especially cordial because of the admiration she felt for his neat new office suit and dazzlingly white linen.

Andross, dear fellow, always had a towzled look, like a brigand in the chorus of an opera. It was picturesque, but not gentlemanly.

"I came to drive you over home, Miss Maddox," the doctor said. "But I started so early that I shall be glad of a cup of coffee if Miss Latimer will give me one." He sat down by Isabel with that change in his voice as he named her which always brought the blood to her cheeks.

"Why, Andross could have taken charge of our little

girl," said Colonel Latimer, bluntly. "Maddox has trusted her to his driving a hundred times."

"I feel responsible for her safe return this time," replied the doctor drily. "A drop more cream, please."

Anna leaned back in her chair looking at him through her half-shut eyes. She knew as plainly as though he had told her, that for some reason he would not trust her to Andross for an hour. Was it because Jack was less his friend than he had been, or that she—was more? She got up and sauntered thoughtfully out into the garden. Andross, after one angry stare at Braddock, rose with a sudden cowed look.

"Can I speak to you one moment, colonel, before I go?" he said.

Braddock nodded to him kindly as he passed. "I told Sam to bring over the mare for you, Jack."

"Thank you. I don't know yet whether I shall— whether I shall go back to the Works at all or not."

After they had gone out, the doctor said abruptly: "If that man does not come back to the Works, Isabel, it would hurt me as though some one had died. Yet he's very faulty—very faulty, indeed."

"Why would you not leave Anna with him, Clay?"

Now Isabel was too blunt and large-natured to be susceptible to small jealousy; but she was startled at a certain expression in his face, and the effort he made to hide it from her. She had been leaning over to put a laurel-bud in his button-hole; she waited, her gray eyes fixed on his. "You came for that reason? You have had no sleep at all, and certainly did not come directly back to take a cup of coffee with *me?*"

"No, not you, dear. But Anna—really she's nothing but an innocent baby; and the judge gives her her way too much. She is one of those women whose love is for life and death, Bell. And if she were disappointed in a man it would kill her. She has not your resources of strong common-sense, you see.   I think somebody ought to protect her."

"You are very kind, Clay; and right," she added, after a pause.   But she began to crumble bread for her sparrows, and the bit of laurel fell to the floor.

"There he is with her now!" starting up.   "I must go at once, Isabel," hurrying out to his buggy.

Miss Latimer stood silent and grave in the door for a minute or two, and then went down to the gate, bidding the doctor and his companion good-by, ready to laugh with them both as usual.   "One never knows whether Miss Latimer is in earnest or not when she jests with one," complained Anna as they drove off.

The doctor did not answer.   Bell's easy good-nature jarred on him.   He wished indeed her sensibilities were deeper, more earnest—like this dear little creature's, for instance.

The little creature was dumb and cold to him all the way home however.   Andross had spoken but a few words to her, and they were of no import.   But his face had appalled her.   "What bar did he see between us?" she wrote in her diary that evening.   "Was he taking leave of me forever?   He is in imminent need and peril. *I* will be true to him.   As for C. B. ——?   I shall not deny that there *have been times* when his soul has called to me and mine *has answered.*   But I am tired of hearing Aristides called the just!   I wash my hands of him.   I shall leave him to his proper tailor, and proper church, and—proper wife!   Let them dwell in decencies forever. While I—alas!   What fate betides Andross?   There—just Heaven, lies *my* doom!!"

CHAPTER VIII.

"YOU wished to consult me about something, eh? Take a cigar," said the colonel when they were alone. "He wants to know how best to ask the judge for his daughter," he thought. "The poor fellow has but a clerk's salary, and Maddox has laid by a pretty sum; there's the hitch, no doubt." And the old man knitted his brows, studying over for Jack the old problem which he had not solved for himself, of an empty pocket and the ills which it is heir to.

"I wish," said Andross in a sharp, hurried tone, "to make a plain statement of a business affair to you, and to ask your opinion as a man of honour and of the world. I—I hardly can tell what is right and what is wrong"— leaning against the fence, his hand to his mouth. The colonel, however, unlike Braddock, did not speculate on its weakness.

"Business? Very well, go on," nodding. "I know nothing more of honour than yourself, Mr. Andross; but as for the world, I'd be very sorry," straightening his hat on his gray hair solemnly, "very sorry that such a lad as you had detected the insincerity, the iniquity of it as I have done! Necessarily, sir, necessarily! Age brings us that wisdom." He stopped and waited with the air of a' blasé Solomon and Areopagite judge rolled into one. Andross was tempted to laugh, but went on:

"About 1857 a man of much repute in Philadelphia died. He was the father of—of a friend of mine. He belonged to an old Irish-Kentucky family—headlong, generous, fond of good living. A scholarly man, too, but with no more knowledge of money——"

"Than to count the debts he couldn't pay," laughed the colonel. "Bless you, I know dozens of that old stock. Never paid butcher or baker until they came as beggars, and then flung them all that was in his pockets, eh?"

"Something very like that. But no character stood higher than this man's in the city for integrity and benevolence. It does so still. The boy was left at his father's death at college, his bills unpaid, without a penny. A friend of his father's took notice of him—studied his capabilities pretty closely, I suspect, and finally charged himself with his support and education. When he was ready to go to work, through this friend's influence, a situation as superintendent of certain manufactories in an inland town in Pennsylvania was found for him, with a high salary."

" A very unusual post for a college boy."

"Yes; he was totally ignorant of the business, and is so to this day."

" How's that? The friend dropped him into what in Bowery talk was a good thing, eh? Pay and no work?"

" He worked well for his wages," bitterly. "This friend was the president of a great corporation; it does not matter what, but one that needed bills passed at Harrisburgh sometimes, and was able to pay for the passage. To do this they must have tools in the Legislature, and to help elect these tools was the business of this young fellow. He was popular with the workmen ; he soon found that his duty was to manipulate them; any man who voted against his employers was discharged. The man was a careless dog, but not unjust; there was much in this sort of work which disgusted him, but what could he do? His benefactor had indulged him like a petted boy, humoured his every whim, nursed expensive and fantastic tastes in him. He loved the man. It was not only for his salary he bent his head until they put the yoke about his neck."

"I'm sure of that!" energetically. "I'm sure he was a noble fellow! Blood tells, sir. He came of a good strain."

"After awhile other work was exacted of him. He was sent to Harrisburgh to 'lobby!' You know what that is. He soon found that the little of good which he had, the lazy good-humour, the friendly manner, was the stock in trade upon which these men were working. They presumed on it—they took him into their secrets, and then, when he rebelled and would have left them and made an honest man of himself, they dared not lose him. He knew too much."

Colonel Latimer nodded gravely, but said nothing. He began to watch Andross closely as he talked, finding apparently some new meaning in his carefully-worded sentences.

"Matters went on in this way for a year. They made him the cat's-paw by which much of the trickery and bribery or dirty work of any kind needed by an unscrupulous, powerful body of men was done. When he——"

"Pardon me! One moment. Your friend's story does not hang together well. A young fellow with abilities as fair as his could have made enough in any legitimate business in six months, to pay off the trifling sum in which he was indebted to his patron. Men are not held as serfs by an I. O. U., Mr. Andross. Or perhaps," noting his change of countenance, "you have not told me all the hold they had upon him."

"No, I have not." After a moment's pause he went on, with a still more guarded and cold manner: "When he began to make arrangements to go into some other business, his patron, as you call him, came to him one day. There was no hint of threat, you understand, of dishonesty in the work they had set him, or of dread that he would betray them. It was all civil, friendly business talk. 'You're talking of leaving us,' he said. 'I'm sorry for that. You've got into the ways of the office and the routine in which the company like things to be done. It will be hard to find another man to fill your place. By the way,' and he drew out his pocket-book and began to unstrap it, 'here is an old document I have had in my possession some ten or twelve years. As long as you were one of the firm, as I might say, it was properly kept in the firm. But when you leave us, of course we shall not feel entitled to retain it. The matter there is of public interest, as you see.'"

"What was in the paper?" eagerly. "A bribe to keep quiet, eh?"

"Such a bribe as no money could have equalled. This —this poor tool's father, it seems, had committed a forgery. It was known only to the leaders of the Ring. They reaped the benefit of it, and afterwards held him by the neck throttled, and drove him as they chose, just as they had driven his son. 'When you leave us,' said this kind guardian, 'to make an honest livelihood, as you say, your love of justice, no doubt, will be gratified by seeing this document in print. It will cause a little stir in Philadelphia, I suppose, for the old man was a favorite there, and it seems a pity, too; now, don't it? for his reputation stands fair to this day.'"

"What did the boy do?"

"He could not sacrifice his father," said Anaross, whose excitement had died out and who stood dully, his hands in his pockets and head sunk on his breast. "Very likely it was all a lie. What did these blood-suckers care for an old man's good name who was dead long ago? But he had no way of proving the lie; and he stayed in the works."

"That was the end of it then?" with a long breath. "He was wrong, sir. He should have held by his integrity. And yet if I thought my child would give up my honourable name from the grave——Well, well! The boy had rough lines."

"So rough and so vile that he escaped; ran away absolutely like a thief in the night, and found a shelter where they could not follow him. As long as they did not know where he was, he was safe from their plan of vengeance. He found at last honourable work and friends; one day an agent, one of the underlings, the spies of this company, stumbled upon him by accident, and threatened to tell of his whereabouts. He was a man to be bought off by a comparatively small sum, and this poor, weak wretch bought him off with money—that he had stolen."

"Good God! What insensate folly!"

"Perhaps so. You would not have done it. Braddook would not have done it. He was a weak man, as I said. Now, Colonel Latimer, what can be done with such a man? Say that I am his friend; am I to stand by him? is there any hope for him, that after knowing his story, you, for example, would take him by the hand—that he could work his way in the business community, in society, love, and marry as other men do?"

Now the colonel, knowing the astuteness of his own judgment and Jack's youthful ignorance of the ways of the world, had been forming during the whole narration his own sagacious interpretation of it. It never occurred to him that Andross was the hero of his own story; but he knew it was some sharper who had trumped it up to impose upon him. The colonel had been, since he was a boy, the victim of every impostor who chose to practice on his credulity; to-morrow, as to-day, he would empty his pockets to the most palpable cheat and swear he was a true man; but in the meantime he inveighed vehemently against the world in general as iniquitous, and per-

petually guarded his friends against imaginary swindlers.
He was fairly mounted on his hobby, now.

"My dear boy," he said energetically, "depend upon
it, you've been scandalously imposed upon! I know the
world. Be guided by me. This friend of yours wants,
no doubt, to borrow money of you."

"No," with a queer smile.

"Well, he wants you to indorse him socially, back him
up somehow; take my word for it." A vivid and bright
idea flashed on the colonel. It was this unknown scoundrel lurking in the neighborhood, no doubt, who had
tempted Jack into the mountains; he wanted to drag him
down into his own slough; it was this disreputable intimacy which stood between Andross and Anna, which she
suspected to be secret crime; and Braddock, having discovered it, began to look upon Andross himself with suspicion, as he had seen that morning.

"Now, sir," with vivacity. "Let me judge this man
impartially for you."

"It is just that which I ask you to do," said Jack with
a pallor about his clean-shaven jaws. All morning he
had despised himself, as he talked, for his confidences.
Braddock, any other man, in the toils of these men,
would have fought out of them, not have gone whining
his story to one or another. Andross, like a woman,
must have sympathy at every step. But he was satisfied
now that it was a wise thing to do. The colonel was a
more merciful judge than any other he would meet; if he
condemned him it was useless to struggle back for honesty or honourable position again. If he said there was a
chance——. "I want your judgment," he repeated.
"Much depends on it for me."

"Yes, I see. I see. Well, it is my opinion that this
fellow, according to his own story, is a dead-beat, as the
police would call him, of the worst kind. Why, look at
it; he's the son of a man careless about money, and a

forger. Blood tells, sir. No sooner does he leave college than he goes into the business of bribery and corruption up to the elbows; according to his own showing, mind you! Then he runs off from his employers, and when traced by them, steals another man's money to buy them off! It all looks badly, Mr. Andross. Even if the extenuating facts be true, I shall be very much inclined to question whether his birth and the influence of his business had not demoralized his moral sense, so that stealing came confoundedly easy to him. An honest man would never have thought of bribing the agent, certainly not have robbed another man to do it. My advice to you is to let him alone, to dree his own wierd. Don't saddle yourself with a weak, wicked fellow at your age. You have a good prospect before you now, and such a man as that would drag you back irretrievably, injure you in every way, in business, or—or your plans nearer home. You follow me?"

"Yes. You are easily understood, Colonel."

Jack began to button his coat mechanically, turned his face, which was as unlike to the real Jack and as vague and hard as a mask taken after death, down the road, as a man does whose business is finally over, and who is in haste to go.

"One minute, Mr. Andross." The colonel, vain of his shrewd judicial decision, wanted to give the whole of it. "I am the more convinced of the falsity of the whole story, because I happen to know that the statement respecting the power and corruption of the Rings is grossly overstated. That sort of abuse of great corporations is all political jobbery. Why, to credit the newspapers, you'd suppose these men scruple at nothing —not even murder! All clap-trap! Oh! I know the world. These stories are set afloat just before election. Very naturally these great corporations have their favorite candidates, and these vile rumours are started by men envious of their better luck, or by some discharged work-men. Your friend, if not one of those who have origi-nated the scandals, has been weak and wicked enough to believe them."

"Weak and wicked? Yes, I believe you are right."

Was he right?

Andross's brilliant dark eyes stared at the colonel as though he saw a ghost in the daylight; but it was the spectre of himself, as this man showed him. Was all the honesty of which he had boasted a sham? Had his father been a forger and given his tainted blood to him? He had slipped easily into the work of bribery at first: had taken the money with but little hesitation to bribe the spy last Saturday. Braddock would never have been so tempted. To be sure he had been in a hell of remorse ever since, but what did that matter?

"Yes, trust me," the colonel broke in; "the man, even if his story be true, is thoroughly demoralized. Better leave him to his fate."

"Yes, he had better be left to his fate."

"That's all right, then. The fact is, Mr. Andross, I don't want to see you ruin yourself. I take an interest in you—everybody does to a curious degree. You've got that sort of magnetism, that strong personality about you, which makes people your foes or friends on sight." He unlatched the gate, for they had turned to the house, and gossiped on, not noticing that Jack neither heard nor answered. "It's a power, sir. It's not exactly virtue, nor good looks either. Henry Clay had it. By George! there are some tones of that dead man's voice which have more power over me even yet than any living man's logic; and that little doctor, the Boston laureate, he's full of it as a connecting wire with electricity. I dined with all those fellows once, and Emerson appeared to me to be a bit of sheer intellect, looking at men and women as a profitable drama; every one of us gave him our best. Why, even I, a dull experimenter in furnaces, believed I had something for him. Hawthorne was like one of his own beautiful uncanny ghosts; but Holmes was a man of men. Well, you have that same human attraction in you," looking down at him kindly. "Odd, isn't it? Men that have it impress one as women do; that's why I talk in this unpractical fashion to you, I suppose," breaking off with a laugh. "Well, now that this business is settled, what shall we do? stay with us to-day, Mr. Andross, or must you go down to the Works?"

Jack roused himself; he had heard only the last sentence. "I'll go down to the Works. I must see Miss Maddox again before—before I go."

Must he go? Even as he spoke that desperate courage which belongs to men who lack backbone, nerved him. Why not stay, work his way, keep his secret—marry Anna? Why not catch some good from life as it passed?

"I wish you could stay. Or come back this evening. There is a friend of mine coming up to-day from Philadelphia, whom I should like you to meet, to convince you how unjust these stories about Rings are. My friend controls one of the most powerful in Philadelphia and New York, and a more estimable man I defy you to find, in every relation of life. Tender husband and father, head of Christian associations, aged workmen's homes, hospitals—I don't know what charities——"

"What is his name?" Andross stopped short in the wet path. He looked for an instant, white man as he was, like a slave when the bloodhounds catch sight of him hidden in the swamp. But the colonel was busy lifting his tomato-vines on to the posts, and did not answer at once.

"What did you say was your friend's name?"

"Oh? I beg your pardon. These vines are so beaten down by the rain. He's really more a business acquaintance than a friend—Laird is his name. Houston Laird. Are you not going to the house?" as Andross turned and walked hastily but uncertainly away. He followed and fell in step again with him. There was silence which the colonel found awkward.

"How long does Laird stay with you?"

"Only a day or two," looking suddenly at Andross, struck by a change in his tone. "I'll bring him over to the Works to-morrow. In fact, he mentioned having business there with some one, in his letter; probably Maddox. But I want," heartily, pressing closer, "I really am anxious, Mr. Andross, for you to meet Laird. It would tend to disabuse you of your prejudices; and besides he might be able to serve you in business relations. He is really a financial power in the country, as you know; and the most genial, friendliest fellow! He delights in gathering young men about him in his office— religious clubs and so forth—and shaping their future course."

"Yes, I have heard of Mr. Laird and the influence he has over young men."

"Ah?" with another perplexed scrutiny of Andross's face. "I wished to mention you to him especially. It can do no harm?"

"No. It can do no harm. The truth is, Colonel Latimer," abruptly, "I am probably the person Mr. Laird wishes to see in the Works. We have met before in a business relation."

"In a business relation—I did not know that!" stammered the colonel, and a moment after began to talk of his turnips. It was not like Andross to be so reticent, and, considering his anxious efforts to serve him, scarcely civil.

CHAPTER IX.

TOWERS, the miller, who was down in Lock Haven that day, drove Mr. Laird up in his buck wagon. He charged him a dollar and a half: "putting on the fifty cents extra, Colonel," he explained a week afterward, "because he druv the mare as no hurs shud be druv. She's lame ever since. 'He's a millionaire, he can stan' it,' I said to myself. But he lays me down seventy-five cents. It was cursedly shabby."

"Tut, tut, Towers, Mr. Laird had not any change; here's your money," tossing down a note, one of the very thin roll in his watch fob. "The next time, don't talk in that way of a gentleman."

"So he left this fur me, did he, eh?" with a suspicious glance from the note to the colonel.

"That fellow, who brought me up, Latimer," Laird had said ten minutes after arriving, "wanted to overcharge me. Talk of rural simplicity! I find Hodge has just as itching a palm at the plough as his cousin in town. But I let him see I was not to be imposed on."

"Well, well. The poor devil has eleven children and an aguish wife," hesitated the colonel.

"No doubt," promptly. "And I'm ready to give liberally to the wife and children," thrusting his hands into his pockets, his blue eyes lighting his face agreeably as he touched the money. "But how could I give alms if I did not watch these rascally workmen? I venture to say, Latimer, that I pay my employés, from the head clerk to the porter, ten per cent. less than any other man in my business. By prudence like that I am able to give to the poor—pay my tithes to the Lord."

Mr. Laird withdrew to dress for dinner, which he did always as carefully for the colonel's picnicky board as for his own. He stopped on the stairs, however, as Colonel Latimer escorted him up. "You did not answer my letter, Colonel? You have a couple of thousand left of your capital, you say. Let me take charge of it for you. Put it into this new National Transit stock, and I insure it to pay a hundred per cent."

"Tut, Laird. I can't be hampered with thinking of money. Besides, next month I expect to succeed wholly with my experiment. Maddox has consented to give me the furnace for a few days for a final trial, and I shall need all the money I can raise to reimburse him and pay my expenses." They had reached the upper landing by this time. Laird stopped and bridged his hawk-like nose with his glasses. "'Pon my soul! I've known many a mad inventor, but you're the worst of the lot. Think of the fortune you've sunk in this thing already, Thomas. You have no right to sacrifice your daughter to your whim: leave her at least enough to keep her from beggary."

The colonel laughed. "What do you want for her? She has plenty to eat and to wear, and that fiddle-faddle work of designing brings her in abundance of pin-money. Bell's like myself. She likes to vagabondize leisurely through life, looking out for the green, warm places, and carrying no impediment in the shape of unnecessary baggage. No, sir. Isabel would rather I should use that money and succeed in making one bar of pig-iron, with wood instead of charcoal, than that you should pay me a thousand per cent."

Laird laughed, looking back with the door-knob of his chamber in his hand. "If the discovery would pay you anything when you make it, there would be some sense in your having made ducks and drakes of all that your father left you."

"Pay *me?*" his thin face heating. "Why, you certainly understand, Laird, my object is to make this business less a monopoly, to put money into the pockets of the poor man, not to take it out with a royalty. Smelting can be done at one-third the cost by using lumber instead of charcoal, the price of the pig-iron reduced proportionately—and—I'll go for my papers and show you the whole thing in a nutshell. Just wait one minute."

"To-night—after dinner. I'm quite sure I understand all about it now," nodding and laughing as he went in and shut the door. He laughed again to himself now and then while he was dressing, muttering "of all the cursed idiots!" but in the same tone with which he would have spoken to his own children when their childish folly pleased him.

Laird, especially now in his trousers and shirt-sleeves, was a gross-looking fellow: short, squat, his heavy-jawed, high-featured face set off by red whiskers, and mustache. One could guess at a glance that the power indicated in this face was that of a bold, unscrupulous speculator, and that the strongest taste and enjoyment of the man lay in his wine and dinner, the "feeds" with which he and two or three of his clique usually finished the day; but there was a trait, a sixth sense, which lay under his relish for high percentage, or terrapins, that insensibly raised him a level above his compatriot feeders: it hindered him from ever saying a coarse word before his children or such a man as Latimer. When all the betting world was down at Jerome Park, Laird went off for a lazy day's fishing in the hills; when his friends filled their boxes at the Academy of Music, chuckling over the broad shoulders and broader jokes of the Opera Bouffe, or delighted at Edwin Booth's pretty pictures, Laird jeered at them; yet he

went night after night to watch old Rip's parting with
his daughter, and was not ashamed to be seen wiping the
tears off as he came away. The colonel's unconscious
self-sacrifice touched him now with a certain pathos, just
as did the white hairs of the old man coming back to his
own to find himself forgotten. It was a thing which he
felt Houston Laird might have done in another and a
better world. "'Can't be hampered with thinking of
money?'" he repeated, drawing on his boot and looking
reflectively at the toe. "That was finely said in Latimer!
Confoundedly finely said! And he means it! That old
fool don't care for money any more than I do for the dust
on my shoes. Neither does old Farroll, starving himself
and his family to found his Inebriate Asylum—drunken
bloats!" Laird felt himself a better man for Latimer
and Farroll's whims just as he did after listening to Joe
Jefferson's wonderful rendition of nature, or one of
Thomas's noble symphonies; but it did not follow that
he had the least intention of imitating those heroic old
idiots, any more than he had of going about the country
acting or fiddling.

When his boots were on, he dressed himself with scru-
pulous care and quiet, hanging as sole ornament to his
plain black watch-guard a dull, cracked antique, of which
he had lately become the blest possessor. He never risked
wearing it in town.

"She will appreciate it," he thought. In the hurry of
pushing the National Transit stock during the spring he
had really forgotten that when he met the Latimers in
town at Christmas he had asked Isabel to marry him.
Of course it all came freshly back now, and as he trimmed his well-shaped nails he half made up his mind to
do it again. "I can afford to marry whom I choose," he
thought. It was in obedience to this sixth sense of his
that the ideas of a wife and money were kept strictly apart.
When he went down the stairs he found Isabel, drawing,

as usual, sitting in the window. It was a hot day. Laird's eyes, used to the fulness and rainbow colouring of city drawing-rooms, Persian carpets, brocatelle, buhl pictures, and old china, opened with a sudden sense of coolness and rest on the bareness and still, pale lights of this room; the floor of yellow pine, the sweeping curtains of thin gray lawn, the big round table covered by books, papers, pipes, and sewing, in most comfortable disorder. The light was sifted in through a honeysuckle, its crimson tubes flaming in the sun, and touched Isabel's white neck and reddish-brown hair as she bent over her pencil and blocks of wood. Outside, a purple butterfly sat on the moth-eaten window-sill, and flapped its gold-dusted wings drowsily in the still heat; the mountain alone looked threatening and gloomy, its gray boulders shouldering aside the grass, and coming offensively to view in the bright light; the water of the creek babbled sleepily over the stones all about the house. Miss Latimer turned with a ready smile to meet Laird, and then went on with her work; he put his eye-glass over his nose to regard her. Women just then wore large hoops and stiff stuffs ruffled and fluted and buttoned at every inch. Isabel's lavender-coloured gown was soft and heavy, clung closely, and moved with every motion of her body. It was the fashion, too, to heap the head with false curls and pomatum and jute, height on height, while Bell's own soft hair waved loosely up to a knot above her high, narrow crown. Her truthful appearance, her simple, direct manner, was the charm that had conquered Laird. He began to run over in his mind the lovely girls with their trained manners and artistic dress, whom he was used to see, against the background of those brilliant city rooms. This was like a strain of one of Beethoven's symphonies—they were the Opera Bouffe.

He drew a hickory-woven chair up, and, lying back in it, looked at her at his leisure. Bell dotted and rubbed on composedly. Isabel and her charms were, as usual, so far from her own thoughts that a man's gaze upon her produced no more blushes or shrinking than if he had betaken himself to staring at the mantel-shelf. Men never show fantastic homage to such women, and Laird did not.

"Up in town," he said abruptly, "what with the hurly-burly and the trading, it is hard to imagine the mountain wrapped in his solemn gown, like a monk yonder, and you here, cool and quiet. I wish I could take a picture of you both with me. I've a picture of a winter landscape that I often like to look at in summer; very nicely done, indeed. It's by Richards."

She adjusted her tools.

"I wish old Nittany could have his likeness taken," glancing up the height with kindling eyes.

"And for yourself——. Ah, Miss Latimer," smiling, "it is not your pictured presentment I wish to take with me—it is the real woman. You know that."

"You think so when you see me with old Nittany for a background; but in town you would find me as out of place as one of those boulders stripped of its grass and moss."

There was a short pause.

"You have not reconsidered the subject of which I spoke to you last winter, then?" lowering his voice and leaning forward, his arms resting on his knees. "You have never thought of giving me a different answer?"

Bell looked at him.

"Never. I supposed you had forgotten that matter long ago, Mr. Laird."

Laird could not tell her that he had not thought of her for six months; he heaved a profound sigh and shook his head sadly, sinking back in his chair. She might at least show some little sign of interest in it; a downcast eye, a blush. Her whole mind was given, instead, to trailing

the partridge-berry vine properly over the moss which she
was copying. When Houston Laird talked of marriage,
Bell saw no more cause for blushes than if he had consulted her on the colour of his coat or any other business.

"I wish," he resumed presently, in a low voice which
over most women would not have lacked power, "I wish
I could make you understand how you represent something which I have not in my life, but should like to
have. It is your great simplicity. You are so downright,
do you see? I like the very sweep of your garments—
straight and full. Yes, I like that in you very much,"
eyeing her from head to foot. "I wish you would marry
me, Isabel. It would be—well, wholesome for me. I
could get back to a simpler way of life. I prefer simplicity, a classical severity in dress and music, even in religious rites. Now you did not think that of me, eh? You
never would have thought of me as living or dying in the
high Roman fashion, I'm certain?"

"No," she laughed. "Cato's was not the rôle I should
have chosen for you. To tell you the truth, I always
think of you as the modern Aladdin, building palaces of
jewels by rubbing on miraculous nothings called stocks,
as unreal as old lamps."

He shot a keen glance of suspicion at her; but Isabel
never was guilty of a sarcasm in her life. She worked on
tranquilly.

"Why not let Aladdin build for you, then, or your
father? Put the idea of marriage aside for the present,
and let me be your friend. Miss Latimer, I do understand the old lamp, Speculation; with a touch or two on
it, Colonel Latimer shall be as rich a man as he was
before the war."

Bell was rubbing out a false stroke. She finished before
she answered.

"He was no happier man then than now. He slept on
the same iron bedstead, wore as coarse clothes, ate a baked

potato for his dinner.　If he had one dollar or a million, it would go alike into lumber and ore."

"And come out—slag?"

"I'm afraid so," choking down a sigh.

He watched her with a perplexed frown for awhile. "Perhaps," suddenly, "it is this very wealth and luxury you would dread as my wife?　The responsibility of the children?　They should not be in your way.　John is at Annapolis, and the little girl has her governess, and as for the rest it should be in your hands.　I'd be glad if you'd remodel the house, unfurnish and ungild as you choose.　Now, there's the carriages," thoughtfully; "that gold-mounted harness: I never liked it.　It drives everybody to talking of Laird's patent stirrup.　I began as a saddler, you know, Miss Latimer.　That harness was to please—the children's mother.　But we would drive in an undertaker's wagon, if you wished it!"

"I do not wish it.　I will never take the place of your children's mother in any way."　Isabel's tones were more gentle than before, but Laird knew that he was answered.

"I'm very sorry, Isabel," he said gravely.　"You are mistaken, I think."

The pencil paused irresolute in her hand an instant over the block.　The natural and decisive way of ending the matter would be to tell him of her engagement; but at the mere remembrance of Braddock, hot blood crept up into Isabel's honest face which had not warmed under the smothered passion of Laird's glances.　Even to her father she had never spoken of her lover.　She thought of his love secretly even to herself with a shyness akin to pain.

Laird saw the blush and mistook its cause.　"I'll have her, soul and body, before the year's out," he thought; her coldness had roused a balked sense of indolent passion within him.　But he determined to let the matter rest for the present.

CHAPTER X.

AFTER Mr. Laird's rejection he leaned back so quietly in his chair and looked so persistently at his *intaglio* in the sun that Miss Latimer began to feel alarmed. He was suffering more deeply than he showed, no doubt, poor man! No matter how little nonsense a woman has in her, she always has a sentimental regard for a rejected lover, and bewails secretly the irreparable wound which she feels he must bear to the grave.

"Aha!" he cried presently. "Who's here? Coming with your father?"

Isabel sighed with relief, but answered rather shortly that "she did not know the man."

"Surely I know that roll and the patriarchal length of beard, and the hat set cock-a-hoop on one side! It certainly is Ware! Prepare yourself for black-mail, Miss Latimer."

"Who is he?"

"Reporter for the Daily Critic. If there's a shameful story to be told of you, he'll write it and charge you so much a line to keep it out of print; if there's a chance for gross flattery of you, he'll print it first, and send you the bill for it as an advertisement next day. But what brings him here?" anxiously. "Ware goes nowhere without the chance of grist to his mill. He follows a crime as a buzzard the carrion. What can he want here?" He rose uncertainly, but sat down again and was idly turning his seal in the sun, and smiling when colonel and Ware entered. The colonel presented his guest with a good deal of *empressement* to his daughter. He had a measureless respect and awe for the press, and the least worker on it. He only read the papers which defended the opinions he had formed beforehand, and therefore found in them nothing but pure truth.

"Mr. Ware represents the New York Critic, Bell," with an effort to speak coolly. "They have heard of my experiments in New York, it appears. The public want information on the subject, and Mr. Ware is going to furnish it to them."

Miss Latimer's face was in a glow at the words. She stood up. "My father is doing a great work, sir," she said, "for humanity. *I* don't care so very much about humanity, but I shall be very glad if he is to become famous." She was always a woman of such few words, that now being moved to speech, there was a certain slow, stately force in what she said that for the moment struck Ware dumb. "I never met a woman so lovable or so infernally stupid," he confessed to Laird afterward. "I went on my knees to her at first sight."

It was all because she thought the coarse, blatant fellow held the trump of Fame ready to sound for her father: she always had known the world sometime would recognize with her the colonel and Braddock as demi-gods in it; it was no wonder therefore that Ware was impressed with his welcome; Isabel of Spain could have given no more royal one to the discoverer who had opened to her the treasures of a marvellous unknown world. Ware, who had been quizzing the colonel unmercifully outside, turned to Mr. Laird, flushed and stammering, bowing humbly.

"I am glad to have the honour of meeting you, sir; I hastened up from Gray Eagle as soon as I heard there was a chance of meeting Mr. Laird here. I—I am really going to illustrate Colonel Latimer's process," with an uneasy side glance at the old man's radiant face, "for the Critic. It will make a most readable article—practical, statistical, embellished with fanciful descriptions of scenery—such as the ore drifts and shafts, and charcoal hearths."

"I know very little of the cookery of such literary messes," drily, turning indifferently away. Indeed, an odd change had taken place in Laird since Ware entered. Alone with Bell, he had been an ordinary blunt, outspoken man on the same level as herself. Now, from the glossy curl in his red whiskers to every puffy roll of his stout body he asserted himself a prince of millionaires. Money and the power of it hinted itself, from the comfortable crossing of his feet to the cool gleam of his blue eyes. He had put on the armour before which the average American is always worsted. He held Ware off at a distance, as one does a dangerous dog which may spring, we know not when.

However, the dinner was hearty and pleasant enough. Diogenes himself would have warmed into a tolerably good fellow at Thomas Latimer's table. The old man, when money was plenty with him years ago, had delighted to give splendid banquets to his friends, but none of them had ever paid him then more deference and sincere homage than this Laird, whose soul was popularly believed to be made of money, or this poor reporter known everywhere as a "dead beat," did now, although the cloth was coarse cotton and the forks but plated. How blind they were too, to the homœopathic size of the roast of mutton which he pressed on them so anxiously; how they passed and repassed the bottle of execrable sherry (the colonel never had been a judge of wine), and ate and drank so heartily that he whispered, delighted, to Bell as they went back to the other room, how that the dinner had been a thorough success, that those fellows thought everything delicious and choice—searching in his pockets for the last fifty cents for Oth because the right hand of that famous cook had not lost its cunning.

Bell, happy in the present dinner and future fame, was disposed to be less silent than was her habit. Her father and Ware sat out on the dilapidated old porch to smoke.

"This Mr. Ware appears to be a most discriminating person," she said sententiously. "You were certainly mistaken in all you said about black-mail. It must have been some other Ware."

Mr. Laird was watching him with half-shut eyes, as he had done all evening. "What could have brought him here?" he said.

Ware leaned in the window just then, his big body crushing the honeysuckles. "I found your confidential clerk, Andross, at Gray Eagle, Mr. Laird."

Laird's face suddenly cleared. "Ah-h! Now we have it!" he muttered. "Yes, I understand he is in business here," carelessly.

Ware drew leisurely long whiffs from his cigar into his mouth, and then emitted it in blue rings; Laird leaned back in his chair as leisurely, fingering Bell's tools, but the eyes of each man were fixed on the other without faltering. "What does he know? What will it cost to buy him?" Laird's would have said if they had been suffered to speak, but they were dull and unmeaning; Ware's were eager to articulation. He had almost probed a secret, and a secret of Houston Laird's or his Ring was equal to a good "business connection."

"It was young Kenny who discovered him," he said at last. "He met him accidentally while trouting up in these hill streams."

Laird nodded civilly. The matter apparently did not interest him so much as the sharpening of Miss Latimer's pencils. "Another, Miss Isabel," pausing, penknife in hand.

But Ware was not so easily bluffed. "Kenny," knocking the ashes from his cigar on the sill, "came back to town flush with greenbacks. He's usually as impecunious

as the rest of us. He said he had found the Nittany
Range a lucky ground for speculation. He put five thousand in Erie the day after he got back."

"Ridiculous!" growled the colonel from outside.
"What chance for speculation is there among these trees
and boulders? Must have been trading in Lock Haven."

Mr. Laird thought it time now to face the reporter
deliberately. The fellow held a checkline and knew that
he held it. But what did it amount to? He had discovered that Andross was a confidential agent of the Ring,
and was trying to shake loose from their hold. But the
man knew that every such organization had such agents,
and that once used, for them to be turned loose to chatter
and blab was—not expedient. That was all. Andross
was not the man to chatter secrets to Ware, however he
might loathe and hate the Ring. Laird saw that Miss
Latimer also had turned her steady attentive eyes on
Ware. But she was too slow a woman to suspect anything.

"Ware," he said gravely.

"Yes?" The big handsome head was thrust eagerly
forward.

"I am afraid your cigar ashes will be blown over Miss
Latimer's moss; be more careful, pray. That is all."

The protruding brown eyes stared defiantly at Laird a
moment, then Ware laughed. "He forgets," he thought,
"that when a man lives by his wits, the wits are apt to
be a tolerably well managed capital. But," he said aloud,
"don't you think it remarkable that Kenny in two days
should have turned such a pretty penny among these
woods and boulders, as the colonel says?"

"I suppose," said Laird, "that seeing Kenny's big
yield of grapes of Eshcol, you hurried up to pluck a
bunch from the same vine."

"Precisely." He was suffered to puff away in silence
so long that when he spoke again he went directly to the

attack. "It is no doubt inconvenient for the company to spare Mr. Andross so long?"

"Very inconvenient," calmly.

"He is acquainted with the routine in the office, with your peculiar—system better than any other man could be."

"Undoubtedly," smiling. "But what would you have?"

Ware stared again, perplexed.

"These are not the days of thumbscrews and heated gridirons, remember, Mr. Ware. The Company is a New York business association, not a hierarchy of the dark ages which could compel men to serve them by such secret means. We left those things behind us with the donjons and moats of knightly times. Mr. Andross was a superintendent in our pay, and a very efficient officer he was, by the way. Now he is a clerk in the pay of Judge Maddox. That is all there is of it."

Ware forced his features into a miserable similitude of a grin, and nodded significantly once or twice. "Talking of fires in donjons, Miss Latimer," he said abruptly, "you ought to hear that fellow Wachtel, as Manrico. I saw him in Paris last December," etc., etc.

A moment afterward he took the colonel by the arm and strolled with him down to the creek bank, deep in the mystery of lumber and ore.

Mr. Laird waited for Miss Latimer's curiosity respecting Andross and his antecedents to pour itself forth. He knew that she had not known of their connection. The fellow would have kept the history of it, to which Ware had adverted, a secret. But Miss Latimer worked on quietly, as though she had not noticed their conversation. Mr. Laird admired her the more because she was a dull woman, as he thought, who left him to ask all the questions.

"By the way," he said presently, "who is the lady

whom our young friend Andross wishes to marry? I have heard such a story."

Miss Latimer answered slowly, as became a dull woman: "I do not believe he wishes to marry anybody."

"What sort of woman is Maddox's little daughter? Pretty? Refined? Andross would not choose a wife who was not both, any more than he would choose to drink out of a tin cup."

Bell laughed. "Miss Maddox might be reckoned among the fine porcelain of womanhood. She even looks like a bit of alabaster."

"It is she, no doubt, then." He rose hastily as if he had finished successfully some task set for him, tossed over the books on the table a minute, and then went out to the men outside. Miss Latimer's steady eyes followed him. "He never heard that Andross meant to marry. He guessed 'the woman!' in the story," she said to herself.

She laid down her work and stood by the window. The night, a dark and threatening night, was settling down upon the far ranges of mountains full of impending storm, but about the house and in the gorge a clear twilight made a singularly bright calm: the near objects came out distinct as photographs. It was home. Some unuttered tumult in her mind made this real to her as never before. Old Nittany and the nameless height at the other side walled her and hers safely in; a late bird or two pecked hurriedly at the vegetables in the garden before flying home to shelter; the bees buzzed gladly into their hives: on the clean stone steps of the kitchen, the fire glowing red within, old Oth sat and smoked and sang a plantation song with which he had many times rocked her to sleep; the water lapped the gray stones below the window, telling its mysterious message; near the barn she could see the colonel's thin stooped shoulders and gray hair as he went about, shutting up for the night, his cow-skin boots sinking deep in the soft, brown mould.

She could smell the fresh mould and grass on the damp air. There was not an inch of it which was not dear to the quiet, affectionate girl, simply because her father's feet had so long trod in it; the stars hung burning between the mountain shadows overhead—so near that it seemed to her that happy other life into which she and her father were going some day, was close at hand. But the dark figures of Ware and Laird down by the creek were alien; they did not belong here. This little mountain gap, her father, Braddock—this was her share of the world. What had these men, with their schemes of politics and plunder, to do with it? Isabel, as anybody might know from her firm flesh, square jaws, and large, sweet-tempered mouth, was subject to none of the poignant little loves and hates of Anna Maddox, but a chance word dropped to-night had caused her to put both men into her scales of judgment; and, her mind once made up, it was not likely that any reason would change it.

She looked steadily at the two figures, measuring her strength against them. They should go out of this place and away from her father.

Just then their voices, raised so as to be heard over the rippling of the water, reached her.

"You have a hold on him, then?" said Ware.

"Yes. But I doubt its efficiency, if there be a woman in the case. If he have a fair prospect here, with a chance to marry, the line I have held him by so long will not be strong enough to bring him back."

"But you forget the money he paid to Kenny?" eagerly.

"He did pay it—in cash. It is impossible that he could have earned that amount since he came here. There's a thumbscrew for you ready to use. And I'm here to back you. The press, sir! Next to a jail-cell there's nothing a guilty man dreads like the daily newspaper. We reporters are the unpaid police of the country. You had better let me bring Andross over to-night. What d'ye say?"

"I shall see him in the morning," coolly.

The money king however apparently appreciated the power of the unpaid police, and had chosen in the last five minutes to use a much more civil tone to Ware, even while he snubbed him. The fellow had his influence, as he reflected, and it might as well be secured for the company as not. Nothing could be more annoying to a man or a corporation than the incessant barking of these smaller dogs of the press.

"Take a cigar," said Ware confidentially, pulling out a curious Turkish case. "They were brought to me by a friend straight from——"

"Thanks, no." drawing back coldly.

"Now this old fellow, the colonel?" anxiously. "What a queer party he is, anyhow, eh? With his mixture of intelligence and stupidity, and his big bones and flying hair, and then, going hungry to make us eat his bit of roast mutton—a very unusual sort of person, it seems to me. What an excellent figure-head he would make, Mr. Laird."

"I don't understand you."

"In your business. For the company. Agent, say. The kind of man in whom everybody puts confidence; why, his word would go as far as the sight of your securities. Upon my word, sir, he somehow put me so in mind of my childhood and of some that are dead, sitting at the table yonder, that I could hardly command my voice. It would be a capital thing for the company to bring him into their employ, and a capital thing for the old man, too."

"Yes, very probably," but in a tone which dismissed the subject.

"A hold upon Andross? A rod to drive him to their work when he chooses to live and marry here?" Women reason by hints, not syllogisms. Bell saw as though she had heard all the facts. The life-long struggle for freedom which drove Andross first to coaling, half naked, up in the gorges, and then to theft, perhaps, and to hiding half mad like a beast among the rocks. The secret of his struggle might be found quite as much, perhaps, in his own weak jaw and uncertain womanish eyes as in any power of Laird's, but Bell made no allowance for such side issues or reasons.

Did money then rule? Did this man Laird, dull and uncultured, and a liar at heart, think because of his foundation of solid dollars that her father and Andross were to go under his yoke and become part of his machinery? To her heated brain it was as though she had heard the very words of the devil as he stood plotting in the garden; but beyond the circling mountain range, everything bent to Laird's money. She knew well the world to which he belonged—fashion, false show, plunder—gambling in stock by the pennies or by the millions. Were her father and Andross to go back and take part of that?

"Does he think there is nothing in this world but greed and money? He forgets who will take part against him." The words came out slowly on her tongue. It seemed to her as though He, the great elder Brother, stood on the bank of the creek, brawling yonder down the gorge, as ready to help poor Andross, as he had been to stretch out his hand, eighteen hundred years ago, to any poor Jewish cripple or profligate.

Bell's religion, being a woman without fancy or sentimentality, was as real and hourly a matter of thought to her as the work which her hands fingered. She stood in the unlighted room now until the darkness closed in over the gorge and the house. Laird and Ware had disappeared. She did not know by what strategy or tricks they would attack her father or Andross. The danger was actual and imminent to her. But what was danger, or Laird, or that awful invisible power of evil lurking everywhere? One benignant presence, of all men most a man, was here, close to them all, to bring, as he had done for ages, right out of wrong. Bell never had been sure whether she believed in Apostolic Succession or Pædo-baptism or Predestination or not. She used to toil and tug with her illogical brain through doctrinal books every Sunday afternoon in order to make out a proper creed for herself, and they only wreaked upon her utter confusion of spirit. But she knew Him and trusted Him; and she was so sure now that He would make it all right that she went about the room, closing the curtains, and lighting the lamp, singing at first a hymn, but very soon a song with a merry ringing burden, of which she and her father were both fond. Indeed, she heard presently his cracked voice as he came in from the barn joining in the chorus, and went out to hold the light for him.

"That's right, my dear. Our friends have strolled along the creek; they'll be in presently. We must be up early to-morrow morning; Mr. Laird is going over to the Works."

"Mr. Laird's business here is with Jack?"

"Yes, I suppose it is," in the guarded tone with which the colonel always warned women off the sacred precincts of business. "I am glad Laird knows Andross. He can give him a lift in the world as few men are able to do."

"You think Mr. Laird a good man then, father? honest, fair dealing?"

"Bless my soul! Houston Laird! Why, he is the very centre of commercial activity in this state, and head of religious clubs and—what are you thinking of?"

"I had an impression——"

"Oh, an impression? No, I never knew a woman who would not throw a man's character to the winds, and all the testimony of the world in his favour to boot, if she had 'an impression' against him. You are all alike, Bell!"

Isabel smiled and held fast to her opinion. Her father, she saw, would be no ally on her side.

CHAPTER XI.

DR. BRADDOCK drove Tom back at a spanking pace.
If he talked at all, it was of the buckwheat crop
or Buck's heifers or pig iron. The little creature beside
him was no less Una and Godiva than the night before;
but somehow this sublimated homage would not find
words in common daylight, and it occurred to him to
wonder what Isabel would think of it with an irritated
feeling of being in a jail of which Miss Latimer kept the
key.

Anna ran up to her room after he had left her (stopping to kiss and hug her papa into good humour on the
way); then she prepared to receive Andross in a white
frilled wrapper, laughing to think how silly Braddock's
scheme was to keep them apart. She knew Jack would
follow her in half an hour. Then she ran down to coax
Miss Shanks (the " help ") into making her favorite pud-
ding for dinner. She was so pretty, and so overflowing
with love and wilful baby ways, that that young lady laid
aside a sacque she was braiding for camp-meeting and
humoured her. Anna having only nibbled a little breakfast, then ate a slice of pound-cake and some pickles, and
filled her pockets with nuts, and went back to her chamber to write in her diary. Then she cried over Andross's
hard fate (she was really very fond of Andross and her
father and Miss Shanks and anything else that came in
her way), and slept sweetly until dinner-time. After
dinner she dressed again, and it was while she was eating
an orange or two in the seclusion of her own chamber,

that she finally resolved to marry Andross. Her new
poodle, Puck, was there, and she had nursed and kissed
and made him beg for cake, before she was led to reflect
that one could manage men quite as easily as poodles. It
was so absurd and priggish in Dr. Braddock to interfere,
when Andross really loved her! It was so absurd in men,
at any rate, to wrap themselves up in the dignity of their
political schemes and business plans, "when I can do
with any of them what I please—just what I please!"
nodding her little head. This poor Jack now? What a
big, stout fellow he was! and how much more he knew of
the world than Dr. Braddock; and yet—Anna stroked
and kneaded the fluffy little ball on her lap with her
white hands, thinking that Jack was in their grasp more
absolutely than this little beast. "Whether he goes up
or down in this world or the next depends pretty much
on me," murmured the rosebud lips aloud. "He'll be a
Christian or a sinner, as I choose to use him, I'm sure.
It's a great responsibility!" and she sighed and put Puck
down and went for some more pound-cake.

Andross, meantime, at the Works had appeased the
curiosity of the men as he best could, and worked steadily
at his desk all day. The fingers that held the pen were
the fingers of a thief, and Laird was at his back. It
would be better he should never look in Anna's face
again; and in this mind he remained until evening; then
he shut his desk, flung on his hat, and with Braddock
looking him sternly in the face, nodded to him, and going
out of the door went directly up the path to Judge Maddox's.

Long afterwards it seemed to him that if Braddock had
stretched out a kind hand to him at that minute, spoken
a single word to him as a friend and a Christian, it would
have made his life different to the end. But Braddock
could give all his savings and make no sign; yet he could
not greet Andross heartily, or keep from snappish answers

or suspicious looks.   It is very likely, however, that nothing he could have done would really have had any effect.

Jack had every reason to be a miserable, despairing man that evening; but in fact he was reasonably happy. Except in the cleared acre or two about the Works, the great Nittany forest crept down from the mountains and choked all the valleys to the creek's edge.   Jack's way lay through it.   He could not help noticing how full of rainbow-glimmering dust were the wide beams of light which the low westering sun struck through the aisles of oaks and chestnuts, and how the thick trunks stood out in it, painted green and yellow and crimson with lichen. His feet sank deep in the leaves, rotting for years; he stooped to untwist a creeping vine of morning glory from about his legs, its pink blossoms yet open in the shade. He halted to look down into the strange, green funnel-shaped hollows which the people called witch's holes; at the swarming ant-hills higher than his shoulder; at a fungus standing like a scarlet star on a dung-heap; at the brilliant blue butterflies which he had never seen elsewhere, that darted across the tan-coloured mountain stream; at a saffron night-moth with a white cross on its back, that, shaken from its bough, hung in the air dazed with the late daylight.   The air was damp, heavy with wood-scents.   He could no more help forgetting himself to notice these things, than the ant could help its poison-ous bite, or the moth its blinded eyes.   He lay down for awhile on the thick layers of leaves, and actually forgot all about money or the avenger coming, or Anna, in feeling that his clothes were warm and comfortable, and his bed soft, and the air deliciously light to his lungs.   There was too, under all, a vague assurance that the Power who had made the world such a delight and comfort, must know that he, Jack, was not a bad sort of a fellow after all, and would have done right if—if——

At any rate it was not hard to do right now.   He

sprung up and walked buoyantly along, his hat in his hands, that were clasped behind him. His womanish, brilliant eyes glowed with the great thought that had come to him in some way out of the slanting beams and the floating moth and wood-growths. It was the easiest thing to be right! He would own the theft, and if he were allowed to do it, go away to some obscure part of the country, where Laird and his father were unknown, and work until he had paid the money. When he came back with clean hands Anna would marry him. Her love was like that of some redeeming saint—it would be most tender to the sinner. If she did not——he stopped. at that suddenly. No matter; he could live alone to the end. "I will lift up my hands unto Thee, O Lord!" he repeated, remembering some of his mother's hymns or psalms. He hurried on; his pulse throbbed; the tears came to his eyes. He reached the judge's house, opened the gate and, crossing the garden paths, came to the window where Anna, after writing in her diary that his doom was hers, and giving her hair a crowning touch of halo-like fluffiness, sat and waited for him.

He tapped at the pane. "Won't you come out?" humbly. "There is a thunder-storm coming up the valley, and the air really takes hold of you like live, damp fingers."

"He looks excited as though he had been drinking," thought Anna, but she only raised her white-lidded eyes to his and put out her hand.

Andross did not touch it. "Come out. I feel as if I could not breathe in-doors to-night. See, old Nittany has wrapped himself in mist already; it is lightening beyond the Muncey mountains." He leaned his elbow on the window-sill, his eyes wandering up and down the valley, while Anna pouted that they could leave her face. "Look at that bird with the flash of red on its wing; how low and straight its flight is to its nest. I knew the storm was coming as soon as any swallow of them all," with a boyish exultation. "See how the hollyhocks burn red as the sun goes down! And this clematis about the window; its mass of feathery green makes the right framing for your pale-tinted face."

Anna's rocking-chair was comfortable, and she had her usual fear when lazy of taking cold. But she was that ideal of all men, a yielding woman; if her lover had felt his mission to be a journey into Africa or to the North Pole she would have gone with him with effusion, though if he had left her behind to pack the trunks, she might have married another man before the ship sailed.

She shivered but wrapped her lace shawl about her head and came out. Andross was waiting. He looked at her furtively from head to foot, and then turned away.

"Come to the seat under the chestnut. You can command the valley there. It won't rain for an hour," going before her hastily.

"Won't *you* take cold?" touching his arm softly; once, no more. Jack laughed from sheer delight. There was something immeasurably exhilarating and delicious to the big, stout fellow in the idea of being taken care of by this feeble mite of a creature. Samson found Delilah, without doubt, a little, gentle woman; who petted and coddled his strength out of him. "I forgot," chirped she, like a sweet-voiced bird, "that you were used lately to the night air. Oh! where *did* you go, Jack?" clasping both hands about his arm and looking straight up into his eyes, "Oh! how could you vex and frighten me so?"

"Did I vex you? God knows—" Jack stopped, pulled her hands from his arms roughly, and walked away.

The chestnut stood over a spring, that bubbled out with a sleepy whisper over the mossy rocks.

"It's easy to be right," Andross said to himself, again and again. But the sleepy, lapping whisper seemed to drown the words. If it had been Bell who sat there he could have grappled with his trouble, told it to her in plain words as to a man, and she would have helped him. But Anna was only a delicate child; he must never forget that.

"Yes, you did. You always do vex me," she moaned. She had seated herself on a knob of the trunk; thick trees shut them in, except where, in front, the valley opened in a gash through the hills, to the gorge in the west, behind which the sun set. Clouds walled this far-off gorge; you could see that it was already raining there; but the light struck up behind the clouds, and filled the upper sky with fervid warmth and colour. The mountain spring sparkled in it, the leaves, with that still shiver of a coming storm, grew darker green in it, but to Andross, the woman, with her reddening cheeks and parted lips, the brown snaky blossoms of the chestnut dropping down on her loose hair and uncovered shoulders, was the centre and meaning of all the heat and brightness—the meaning · of life.

"You did vex me," her eyes following him, compelling his to turn. "I knew you fled from here because you were in trouble or shame. Yes, I'll speak the truth. *I* knew you had committed a crime!"

"What do you mean?" Jack said, drawing farther away.

She sat quite still, her hands held out towards him. "Did I ever ask what it was? Did *I* care? You are my friend. I would have shared your trouble. I would have gone with you." Still Andross did not take the begging hands. She clasped them over her burning face. "I did what I could. I followed you. I forced Doctor Braddock to take me with him to search for you."

Then a hot drop of water or two forced its way between the little fingers, and rolled over the back of her hand. At that Jack gave a groan. No thought now as to whether it was easy to do right or not. He dragged the little fingers from the flushed, lovely face and looked at it. Her eyes were wet, but laughing. Was this whole dreadful business only a comedy then?

"You can't deceive *me*," she said; "Spillen says you were out fishing. Papa says the moon had something to do with it, that it affects people who are not quite right," touching her forehead, "and that no man can be quite right and care so much for ragged books and cracked pottery. It was the change of the moon did it, he says."

Jack laughed.

"But I knew it was neither the moon nor fishes. What is this dreadful mystery that hangs over you?" She peered closer into his face, with the ready pout on her lips, when she saw thoughts there that lay deeper than any love for her.

"There's no mystery," said Jack. "I've not been a lucky man. I've never been able to go straight on a beaten road, like Braddock or the colonel. I've been hampered by business relations, dragged this way and dragged that. I've been handcuffed, hobbled. I didn't mind it for awhile. But it seems to me now as if the hold on me was turning into iron, and was going to drag me down always;—after I'm dead, even into that place they call hell, if I can name such a place to you safe, comfortable people."

Even Anna could feel the bitterness under his joking tone. Her responsibility as to his soul's safe conduct flashed upon her. Now was the time to take charge of it.

"I think you're very irreligious, Mr. Andross. You ought not to use such language at all. And besides, it's all nonsense to say any man out of a jail is hampered in this free country. You are free. You can go into business and marry, and vote, or go to housekeeping, or be sent to the legislature, or any of those things. And you can go to church regularly and so on, and then there's no danger of going to that other place. It is all plain and easy, in my opinion."

The words from anybody else might have seemed silly and unfeeling to Jack. But from Anna—the way opened before him in them plain and easy, as she said. The way to safety, to love, to heaven.

"Don't hold my arm so tight. You hurt me!" she cried. "Why do you look at me in that way? You know it's all true what I say. It doesn't matter what you have done, even if it's murder——" shivering with excitement. "God will forgive you. And——" she looked away, "if there is any woman in the world that loves you, she would forgive it too."

"Do you mean——"

In the sudden silence Anna looked up. She started back with a little cry, as if she had thrust her hand into the fire.

"I'm afraid of you." In a moment she controlled herself. "Why do you frighten me so?" patting her wet eyes and burning cheeks with a perfumed handkerchief.

"Oh!" groaned Jack, "for God's sake don't say more than you mean. It's life or death with me to-day. I misunderstood you, may be. But I thought you meant that even if I had committed crime, you could forgive me, and—and love me, Anna."

He did not make love as she had planned it many a time; that was certain. He did not tremble at her touch, nor touch her at all, indeed, but walked off and stood by the spring, with his back to her, grinding the bits of rotten wood under his boot-heel, his hands thrust deep into his pockets. But she felt somehow that the body and soul of the man, both bigger than her own, were undergoing some physical or mental torture. She remembered how Gertrude Von der Wart stood by her dying husband on the rack and put water to his lips. She was sure she loved Jack enough to do that.

"I can't tell you what I mean if you turn your back to me."

He came back slowly.

"If I were a man of honour, I would never look you in the face again."

She drew back.

"Your secret has nothing to do with another wife?"

Jack laughed.

"No. There is no woman in the world who has come into my life in any way but you. You must know that."

Her head dropped on her heaving bosom.

"Then you—you do care for me a little?"

"Care for you?" he cried, still standing off and looking at her as banished Satan might at his lost crown.

After all, why was it lost? This girl, this wife, was his crown of manhood. He was a man like other men; why should he let it slip from him? If she went now, she would never return.

At whatever risk, then—. He put out his hand, but uncertainly, as she saw.

"Why can not he be funny or agreeable when he comes a-wooing, as he used to be?" she thought, impatiently. "A person don't want tragedy all day."

This young Lochinvar came wooing with a mortal sickness at his heart, apparently. All the gayety and electric vigor that had made Andross, Andross, was gone.

He drew her slowly toward him.

"God knows whether I care for you or not. Did you mean just now that you would be my wife? No matter what I have done—that you would marry me?"

"Oh, indeed yes, Jack," she whispered.

Her head sank on his breast, the soft perfumed hair was blown against his mouth, her arms were around his neck. Anna's frail body always exposed every feeling within. Her skin was pale, her eyes languid, her breath came slowly. Nothing could seem more weak or loving or loyal than she, lying there. John Andross had never kissed a pure woman's lips before. When he touched them the warmth and brightness of the day struck home to him. His face glowed, his eyes flashed. What was Laird or stolen money or Rings? He kissed her but once, and then placing her gently on the rock, sat down before her. He had such a reverence for her—such tenderness, akin to pain! He held a bit of her muslin dress in his hand; if he let her go altogether, it seemed as if he should drift away, he knew not into what abyss. That old dreadful life of a minute ago was gone as far as past ages. The time when he doubted, was guilty——. He remembered quickly that she had no mother to guard her now, that love was coming to her. It was quite in the nature of the man to feel, above the hot passion surging in his blood for this woman, an unspeakable respect and awe for her, and all women through her—such as a mother feels for her maiden child. He would take good care of her, from even his own love. Anna put her hand shyly again into his.

"What do you see yonder, Jack? Why are you so quiet? Why, your eyes are wet! I thought a man was glad when he was loved, and did not cry like a woman."

Jack put the little hand on his eyes.

"I never thought this would come to me," he said quietly. "It seems as if——" He stopped. He could not say even to her that he felt as if Christ had forgiven him, and laid His hand on him through her. "I've been a worthless dog," forcing a laugh. "I never thought, since my mother died, that God or man took much account of Jack Andross until now."

It was very disappointing! She had flung herself into the abyss of his despair, and he began to talk about his dead mother! She had never, in opera or tragedy, known a situation which was more dramatic, and Andross always used to look so delightfully like a brigand; and yet he made nothing of it; he was as quiet and respectable in his wooing as Braddock would be, or that old deacon who said grace when he kissed his wife. And she had always known she was a frail, lonely creature! She did so need to be protected by an engrossing, warm passion!

The rising storm concentrated the heat and light about them; the lapping of the brook grew more drowsy, the shiver of the oaks audible. Oaks and low swooping birds, and the water, red in the oblique light, grew distinct, as the world seemed to Andross to stand off and regard this woman and himself. Her eyes were lowered, her crimson lips apart, her soft hands held one of his between them. He dared not look at her.

"Anna," he said, rising and standing before her, "I'm going to do what's right in this thing. If you are really given to me, I'll take you with clean hands, so help me, God. I'll have no deception about it. I'll go to your father now and tell him my whole story, and then ask you for my wife."

"Yes, Jack," she whispered.

"I know he will give you to me," earnestly. "I believe in myself to-day as I never did before, and I am sure he will believe in me."

"Yes; but papa's such a practical man," cooed Anna, "he is not apt to be influenced by people's moods. I'm afraid he would wish for some indorsement of the future beyond your faith in yourself."

Jack's face fell as if he had received a dash of very cold water indeed. "Then I must prove my faith by my works," smiling. "At least my honest confession of the past will argue in my favour. It would with any man, Anna," he urged as she shook her head, "a practical man, especially."

"W-ell, of course you know. Won't you sit down?" pleadingly. "Keep the sun from me with your broad shoulders—there. And when must you go to papa with this story?" nestling closer, and picking the threads from his cheviot coat.

"I shall not wait a day." If he had stopped there, Anna would have persisted no further. Silence was an unknown quantity, a sign of masculine will which puzzled and daunted her. But there was no argument, however logical, against which she would not fly bird-like, to peck a flaw in it. Andross began to give a reason for his faith to himself. "I never felt what my life was worth until to-day. I must act like a man."

"If it was winning me made you feel that, you are in strange haste to lose me."

"Lose you!"

"Of course, lose me! You go to papa with a crime in one hand, to ask for me for the other! Just as I thought all was so pleasant and nice! I've been so lonely! I thought I had you to care for me and to protect me!" sobbing and cowering close to his side.

"What would you have me do?" He put his arm about her, looking down with stupid dismay.

"Am I to conceal the past from your father? Win you like a thief?"

"Oh! dear, dear! What *has* papa to do with the past? Of course you must tell him, but not to-day. Let me have one hour of sunshine. To-morrow will do."

Why would not to-morrow do? Why should not he, too, have an hour of sunshine?

The sunlight grew dimmer, the light rose and rested on the tree tops; Andross saw nothing but the face upturned to his.

"Now," she cooed, "tell me your plans for us."

Plans for us? Here was his very dream of a wife! How could a man go wrong who could bring all his practical work-day thoughts to this little fair woman, whose soul within her was meant to be a pure counsellor—a messenger of God?

He spoke more cheerfully and confidently than he had ever done in his life. "One thing I know, I'll never go

astray from the right with you to guide me, Anna. I
have not decided on any certain plan, except that we will
go as far from the seaboard cities as possible—to the West,
probably."

"Chicago? There's a great deal of style in Chicago,
I've heard."

"And you want to still hide in the woods, Maud Muller? But you must be practical, darling. I could earn a
living more readily in a large city. I could get a position
on a paper in Milwaukee, I'm sure—news editor or something—until I looked about me; that would keep us in
bread and butter."

"About how much would that pay you?"

"Pay?" a little surprised. "I don't know. Say
fifteen or twenty dollars a week."

Anna's cheek was very hot. She sat quite erect.

"But you quite forget papa, Mr. Andross. Of course
I don't care for money. I'd be glad to live with you in a
hut or a cave. But papa is a very practical man."

"And he would not be willing for me to try to support
you on twenty dollars a week?" anxiously.

"Oh! it is absurd to talk of that!" the ready, vexed
tears on her lashes. "Heaven knows I would go with
you if it was in the dead of night, and you had nothing
but your steed and spurs, like the old knights. But papa
has refused me to two gentlemen because their incomes
were less than his own."

Something very like an oath choked Jack's throat.

"I've neither steed nor spurs," he said. "Nor is there
any way for me to gain an income equal to your father's,
that I can use—even for you."

"But there is such a way, you mean?" her head
dropped plaintively on his bosom.

"Yes. But I shall not use it."

A long silence followed. Anna raised her head at last,
and looked at him with swimming eyes.

"I don't blame you, God knows!" cried Jack vehemently. "But you're the only thing in this earth untainted by the greed for money, money! Surely," after a pause, "you wrong your father? He would not insist—when he knew you loved me——"

"Oh! but indeed he would!" hastily. "If he knew it would kill me to forbid it (and I wouldn't be surprised it would drive me into a decline) he would never let me marry even a reasonably poor man. But twenty dollars a week! Why, he would think you mad!"

"I suppose I have been mad."

"I really must go now," rising. "There are some people coming for supper——"

"Anna! Can you talk of supper and people now? There, there! Don't look at me in that terrified imploring way," calling her in his passion and rage a white dove and an injured angel, and himself a brute, walking beside her to the gate, frightened into silence when she resorted again to tears and the handkerchief.

"You—you must not be unjust to poor papa," she sobbed. "It isn't greed. But he's so foolishly fond of me, he thinks nothing good enough for his Nannie——"

" "Nothing is good enough! If one of God's angels came down, I couldn't find clothes or lodging fit for it, and that's the way I feel about you. But—I've loved you so! It seems as if my love ought to be enough——"

"And so it would to me," softly. "But poor papa! Those gentlemen were very worthy men, and of the very best position in society, and quite wealthy. And then if you went to him and said I am John Andross, and I have twenty dollars a week, and, and——"

"In danger of the penitentiary. No," with a loud laugh. "You reason correctly; my recommendations are not of the best."

They had reached the gate now. The light was gone. The sycamore trees in front of the house swayed wildly to and fro, and a few large drops fell from the darkness overhead on Anna. "Go, go!" she cried, hurrying under the porch and holding her hand to Jack without. "I can not ask you to come in. Your agitation would betray all."

The door and windows were open, the house was brilliantly lighted: it seemed as if the warmth and light were about to absorb the fair little creature in her fluttering curls and lace; he, without in the rain and night.

"I don't wish to go in. Why should I?" wrenching her hand in his pain until he hurt her. "I may as well say good-by to you now, I suppose, and be done with it all, as any other time."

She leaned a little farther out. "It must be good-by then?"

Andross was silent.

"There is no other way?"

"No," sharply. "There is no other way."

"Because," her breath was warm against his cheek now, "if there was another—— If I could be your wife —oh Jack! I do love you!"

Her lips touched his and she was gone.

Andross went down the mountain, not knowing that the night had come, and a drenching rain was falling. It seemed to his excited brain as if the hell of which Braddock talked lay below, and that he was walking steadily and purposely into it.

Anna hurried to the kitchen to see that Miss Shanks had the best napkins out for tea, and then went to dress. She wore a rose-tinted silk, while lace and tags of ribbon and tiny gold chains made a soft shimmer all over her. She fastened some blue stars of the succory weed in her curls of pale gold, and then stood back from the mirror.

"It is precisely like the pictures of the French marquises that one sees painted on porcelain. He will be sure to notice that."

"He," was Mr. Ware, who was coming for tea.

CHAPTER XII.

SPELLIN, who came into the office next morning for the monthly accounts, was particularly friendly to Jack. "Andross is pulled down as if he'd had a tug with the typhoid," he told the judge that evening. "I had a capital joke on Jake to tell him, and he laughed (he'd laugh in the jaws of death), and then looked at Dr. Braddock as if scared that he'd done it. He's got into some devil of a hobble, Judge. You ought to see to it. I think it's a pity a good-natured, jolly fellow like that can't have his laugh out in this world. Now the doctor—he rayther enjoys trouble; what with his civility and his backbone and religion, he knows how to meet it."

The judge hurried Spellin off, as two gentlemen were going to walk over with him to the Works to see a casting by night—Colonel Latimer, who stood smoking by the stile, and Mr. Laird from Philadelphia. They were waiting on Mr. Laird, in fact, who was lingering beside Miss Maddox in the little parlor. You could hear, now and then, Anna's sweet little pipe of a voice from within and bursts of musical laughter.

"I must go, now," Mr. Laird was saying, as he bent over the piano by which she sat. "There is a young fellow, Andross, at the Works, whom I wish to see. I'm going to tempt him back with me to seek his fortune," looking closely into her face.

"His fortune? Oh! Can you——? But it is no affair of mine," dropping her eyes.

"Can I——?" smiling. "Well, I am no magician with old lamps or magic purses for the young man, Miss

Maddox. But I can promise him work suited to his capacity; and if he has that, a brilliant career is before him. It is absurd to see such a man as that at a clerk's desk."

"Yes, indeed!" said Anna warmly, though she had always looked on Jack as necessarily a weak, illiterate fellow, owing to the coaling hearth where he originated. She pinned a rose in Laird's button-hole, and stood by the window waving good-bys to him.

"Your daughter, Judge, is the freshest and sweetest creature I have seen lately! She reminds me of—of strawberries and cream," said Laird gallantly, as they walked down the hill. "She is a good deal interested in young Andross, I find."

"Mr. Laird has promised me to do something for Andross, Judge," interposed the colonel.

"Ah! that's clever of you, Mr. Laird. Yes, Anna's interested in him. We're all interested in poor Jack. If you hold out your hand, the young man's fortune is made, of course."

Maddox was secretly annoyed, and showed it. Where was he to get a clerk who would do Jack's work for such wages?

Andross saw them coming down the side of the hill, picking their steps, for last night's rain had made the ground wet and clammy as a sponge.

He laid down his pen and looked back at the door.

"Mr. Andross!" called Braddock.

Andross did not answer.

Nothing was easier than to go out of that door, and in the gathering shadows of evening take the hill-road to Millheim, and somewhere, in some corner of the world where Laird was unknown, live an honest life. But then he should leave Anna behind him.

If he waited, in five minutes Houston Laird would be in the office. He would offer him the way to win her.

He got down from the desk-stool and took his coat from the peg, being at the time in his shirt sleeves.

"Andross," said the doctor, coming in, "I wish you would notify Spellin that Forbes's account is overdue. There were five loads of slag against flour and——"

He stopped. Jack had not been drinking? His face was livid, his eyes blazed. Braddock tapped on the table.

"What is the matter with you? What are you laughing at?"

"I was thinking how you were bringing me slag and flour to balance just now," wildly. "I beg your pardon, Braddock," after a moment. "I'll attend to it. I am a little worried about—about——"

His coat was on, and he had taken up his felt hat, and was brushing it without looking at it.

"You are going out?" said Braddock. "I'll make out the account for Spellin at once, then. Or will you wait until the judge is gone? I see him at the gate yonder with some men."

Jack stood one moment, then he laid down his hat.

"I'll not go," he said.

He sat down and took up his pen, dipped it in the ink. The gate slammed behind them. He could see where their umbrellas shook the rain from the old cedar by the fence. Their heavy boots creaked along the wet boards; they came into Braddock's office; the door was ajar enough for him to hear them as they stood talking and joking with him.

How was this? Laird was not only a companion of Colonel Latimer's, but Braddock met him as an old friend; Braddock had dined with him in Philadelphia; was urging him to go up and see his mother. Had he been mistaken? What if Laird were the genial, honourable man and Christian they held him to be, and he a morbid, suspicious fool?

He shook his head. No. No need to try to hoodwink

himself. Right was right, and wrong, wrong clearly
enough before him to-night; he knew the man. What
he was going to do would be done with his eyes open.
He lighted the lamp, stirred the fire which the chilly rain
had rendered necessary, until the little office was in a glow
of light, then turned to pull down the window shade and
shut out the mountain, that filled the melancholy twilight and lowered down on him like an accusing ghost.

While his back was to the door, it was pushed open,
and turning he met Houston Laird, the light falling full
on his stout, well-dressed figure, his pleasant blue eyes
smiling, his fat white hand held out. The other men
were behind.

"Here is another old friend! Why, Andross, how hot
you are here!" adroitly covering the fact that his hand
was not taken, by lifting his beaver hat off, and wiping his
forehead. "Jack always had something tropical in his
nature," looking back to Maddox. "He has that love of
colour, music and the like which we Americans lack. I
never ventured on buying a piece of furniture, much less
a picture, without consulting him. The fitting of our
club-house was left to your taste altogether, you remember, Andross. He's more daring in his effects than most
men would venture to be, simply because he knows his
ground."

"Yes, I remember the old club-house," said Andross
stiffly. "I suppose there is a different set of men there
now?"

"No. Very much the old clique: on Friday nights at
least, excepting Noyes, who is married, and is given over
to literary lectures and family dinners, and poor Fanning,
who was sent to Nice on account of his lungs. But they
don't make the gap your going did."

Jack smiled. He knew the men had missed him; they
were good genial fellows, alive with that ready energy and
wit and every-day wisdom which belongs to the present

generation of cultured young men in towns; in the club too, Jack knew he was an authority, while Laird, who had nothing but his money, was admitted on sufferance. He warmed insensibly. "And Noyes is married, is he? He was in love once a week. How did the battle about the reading-room end? There was some money to be spent there, and Stewart wanted to put it into a couple of Hamilton's marines, and Fetridge to buy some old historical relics of his family."

"I suppose blood carried it then. There are some rusty swords and chairs and such lumber there."

The bell of the Works tolled.

"That is for the cast, I believe, Mr. Andross. Bring your friend in. Come, gentlemen," said the judge. There was an odd change in his manner to Andross, just as Laird intended there should be. The intimate friend of Honston Laird, a fashionable club-man and diner-out, was a totally different person from Braddock's protégé, picked up at a coaling hearth.

"There's a queer story going now about Fetridge, by the way," said Mr. Laird, taking Jack's arm as they went out of the office. They stood apart by the furnace, while Laird told it, and when it was finished, Jack shouted with laughter. It brought the old pleasant times vividly before him. Half an hour ago he would have said that this man on whose arm he leaned came there to lead him back into hell; he forgot all about that now. The men gathered in at the tap of the bell: they were covered with grime and naked to the waist. The furnace threw uncertain red gleams through the large wooden shed, on the heaps of cinders and green glassy slag out to the pitchy darkness without, where the rain was beginning to fall and the wind to sough ominously through the mountain gorge. Andross stood apparently watching, like the others, the men draw troughs in the wet sand of the floor. How like the winking eye of a beast of prey the furtive dull gleam of the fire was! there was a fierceness, a homelessness in the moan of the wind which the invigorating breezes in town never had; the men, too (good fellows every one, Jack had thought them in the morning), there was a savage quality in their ignorant faces, due doubtless to the solitude of the huge mountain fastness about them.　Fetridge and the others just now were at dinner together somewhere; the gas burned softly; there were flowers on the table; the talk was of the old pictures which Whitten had brought back after the siege of Paris, or of Tom Pool's book, or of any other trifle; but with the subtle free-masonry under all which gave to every word a fine unspoken humour and meaning. After dinner they would drop into the Walnut, or go to listen to Nilsson as Gretchen in the great cathedral scene. The opera with its lights and tier on tier of beautiful women, and music that uttered all passion and pain— that was different from this dingy shed and the slag and rain!

"Very picturesque thing, a casting by night," said the judge, coming up to Laird.　"At least so Mr. Andross thinks, and he has a good artistic eye, as you say, sir. Known him long?" lowering his voice.

"Since he was a boy," promptly.　"He belongs to a good Delaware county family—none better."　For he was determined to smooth all obstacles between Jack and Anna.　There, he saw, was his future hold upon him.

"Queer now, his going out to burn charcoal?　Braddock found him at a hearth in the mountains.　Fact, sir; how do you account for it, eh?"

"Pooh!　A boy's whim.　He fancied himself tired of excess of civilization, and tried solitude, just as we older men change our liquor, when the taste of one palls."

"You intend to take him back with you?" anxiously.

"If I can.　We need a man of just such qualities. There's a high ladder ready for him to climb.　But perhaps some mountain beauty has made him too much in love with solitude," with a significant smile.

"Tut! tut! Nothing of that!" But the judge bent anxious looks on the ground. What if this handy, clever fellow, who had been so ready to fetch and carry, should turn out all that Laird prophesied? Where would he find such a match for Anna? "Even if there were such a thing," he said aloud, "it would be better for him to go earn a social position for his wife than to stay drudging here on a sub-clerk's pay."

"Certainly! certainly! Did you speak, Latimer?"

"They are going to draw, now. The melted metal has accumulated behind that iron flap, and the firemen will let it out into the wet troughs of sand."

"I see, I see."

There was some delay, however, in the drawing, and Laird meanwhile went back to Andross where he stood alone. "Jack!" he said, with a certain blunt friendliness in his tone. "Jack, I came up to the mountains purposely to find you."

"I know you did."

Neither of the men lowered his voice. Latimer and Braddock, with some of the workmen, were within hearing. Now that the hand-to-hand struggle had come which was to end in a mastery for life of one over the other, nobody who heard them detected any deeper meaning in their words than an ordinary business parley.

"Yes," said Laird carelessly; "I heard you were here, and I ran up from Harrisburgh to see you. What the deuce is that fellow with the ash-rake doing now? I want you to drop this folly, Jack, and come back to your desk in the office, and to the club, and to your old place in every respect. It will pay you to come."

"And you," quietly.

"And me, of course," smiling. "What else should I come here for? I am not acting as a philanthropist in the matter, by any means." Whatever covert threat lay under Andross's words lost half its force when thus coolly met as a plain, practical argument. "I know your value to the company in a business point of view. You know our routine, our secrets—every company has its secrets;" nodding to Maddox, who stood by attentive, "eh, judge? We have found nobody to take Mr. Andross's place; and, in fact, we want to find nobody. We're ready to bid high for him again."

"'Pon my word, I wish such a chance had been put before me at your age, Jack," chuckled the judge.

Andross spoke as deliberately as Braddock would have done, when he did reply, which was after the pause of a minute or two. "You overrate the necessity of my return. Whatever tricks of the trade I may know are safe with me. I shall not disclose them. It is only fair, before you bid, to tell you that."

"As if he expects me to trust him," sneered Laird to himself, "when ten words from him could ruin the business for years," applying inwardly, as he never failed to do, the salving reflection that the business was honest, though it chanced to be run counter to popular preju-dices. "Why! you talk as if you were gray-headed!" aloud. "Where is the old headlong Jack gone? You used to be ready to tumble into whatever pitfall offered; but now you mean to pick your steps?" meaningly.

"Yes, I do. I fully expected you to make some offer to me to-night, and I mean to stand quite free-footed in considering it. None of the old reasons which induced me to remain in the employ of the company will weigh with me now."

"One moment, Andross," beckoning him aside but not altering his pleasant voice, and nodding confidentially; "ten words can settle this matter between us now that we are out of hearing of these people. I want you. You know how and why. I am willing to pay you your price.

You want me just as much. The company were naturally indignant at your defection; but no exposure has been made by them of that old business concerning your father —stop; hear me out—nor shall be made, if I can prevent it, whether you return or not. Revenge is not business. But look at the matter in the light of your own interest. You remain here, an underling of that prig, Braddock; obscure, poor, unknown. Suppose you wanted to marry (every young man ought to marry, and that early), what chance have you?" eyeing him sharply, and quite aware when he had touched the quick. "Whereas, if you come with me, in one year, I assure you, not a competency, but what even in town would be called a large fortune. The opportunities thrown in your way of turning over money are treble what they used to be. In addition, I intend that you shall be elected to the state senate this winter. You know what that means. Sheffield, of our district, is dying. A man must go in for the remaining six months. You have the certainty, at option, of reëlection. There is not a mercenary father who would not bestow his daughter as cheerfully upon you as upon Aladdin with his house built out of jewels."

"Now, Mr. Laird," called out the judge, "you observe the man withdraws that block against the hearth——"

"Yes, I'm watching. What do you say, Andross?"

Andross thought that he had made up his mind before he met Laird, and that the struggle was over. But for a man worthy the name to give up his manhood forever, costs more actual pain usually than the physical loss of life.

"What do you say?" Laird repeated, coming close in the darkness to look up to him. At the moment there was a flash of blinding light from the furnace, and seeing Jack's face close beside him, Laird drew back appalled.

"Poor devil! I wish I'd let him alone in the beginning!" he thought to himself, and walked hastily away.

Braddock and Latimer came up to explain the process. The melted iron, like white fiery serpents, crept through the troughs drawn in the wet sand, flinging off myriads of burning sparks.   The sooty overhanging roof, the men standing about, the shining glitter of rain in the outside blackness, the far off mountains, were suddenly illuminated with a red, angry glare.   Laird could have seen Andross distinctly, but he kept his back turned to him. He was heartily sorry for him, and if the actual existence of the Company had not been involved, would have "let up on him," as he said.   But what would become of the National Transit Association, if Andross chose to disclose that it was, in fact, a band of distillers?   And where would Houston Laird be in church, or the "Christian Brotherhood," if it crept into print that their president was head of a Whiskey Ring?   As for Jack's religious or honest scruples that was balderdash.   But Laird could appreciate a young fellow's dislike to the weight of a yoke about his neck; it appealed to his sentimental nature as would a strain of music.

"It's cursedly hard lines on Jack to have a lot of men say 'go' or 'come' at their pleasure!   I wish I could turn the thing for him!   But he knows too much.   No padlock will serve on a man's mouth, but death or money. Yes, very fine, Judge, very fine!   I should like to have seen the effect from a distance through the rain.   Ah! Mr. Andross, did you speak?" turning sharply as Jack touched his shoulder.

"I'll go.   On my own terms."

"Very well.   I'm heartily glad for the sake of the Company," rubbing his hands with congratulation.   But he had not the bad taste to offer one of them to Andross. "Our friend Jack has consented to go with me, Judge," in a loud voice.

"Aha!   Well done, Andross!   Your fortune's made, my lad!" coming up.   Latimer and Braddock followed

"MOTHER! MOTHER!" HE CRIED. HE WAS TURNING FROM HER
FOREVER.

him. But Jack was gone. The momentary illumination was over, and but for a dull glimmer the shed was in darkness.

While the men in a cheerful group took their way to the judge's, a dark figure lagged dully along toward the mountain in the rain. "All for love and the world well lost!" he said aloud with a laugh. But it was not a pleasant laugh to hear. He knew it was his last night in the mountains, where he had tried to be honest and courageous.

God had weighed him for the last time in the balances, and found him wanting.

He could not keep his mind on Fetridge and the club, nor on Anna. He found himself chanting in his rolling baritone, "*The Lord is my shepherd, I shall not want.*" It sounded like a devil's voice mocking him. It seemed but an hour ago that he lay, a little fellow of eight, on his trundle-bed, his face chapped with the wind and his hands black with bruises, and his mother sat beside him on the foot of the bed teaching him that psalm. A little pock-marked woman with a coarse brown stuff dress; but no face in the world had ever been to him as fair and dear as that one.

"*The Lord is my shepherd.*" Why could he not drive the cursed words out of his head? "He is the shepherd of a lot of pious people in church," he said, walking faster, "but I don't see but that the rest of us have to shift for ourselves as best we can. The ' green pastures ' of this world belong to them who can pay for them. It is men like Laird who sit beside the ' still waters,' " with a bitter chuckle.

But even as he said it he stopped on the side of the mountain, looking to the one gray break in the rain-drenched sky.

"Mother! mother!" he cried, though his dry lips made no sound. He was turning from her forever. Was there no help for him? Was it all money—money? Was this talk of the Lord a lie with which weak women fooled themselves?

When Jack was a little fellow learning his psalm, his mother knew that the next day at school he would be wholly ruled by whatever boy sat nearest to him. It was with the old boyish affectionate eyes and uncertain mouth, he stood now choosing his way of life. If he could go to Braddock for help? But he was afraid of Braddock and Braddock's God. To Anna? He shook his head. Anna's only thought, dear child, was a good salary for him. Salary and clubs, work, here was enough to reach for. He went on to meet them, but he did not look back to the gray break in the sky. A chance for another life lay behind him in the mountains, which should never come to him again.

CHAPTER XIII.

IT was in the middle of December when Mr. Laird came up to the mountains again. Colonel Latimer met him at the Lock Haven station one nipping, bright winter's day, and rescued him from two local editors, who were taking notes of every word, wink, and garment, of the "Great Railroad King," for their next issue.

"Why don't you ask what the deuce brought me here in such weather? I know you think it," tucking the buffalo skin tightly about his knees in the sleigh as they drove off.

"I did think it. Nothing wrong?"

"For one thing, I felt qualmish; I don't know whether it's an inactive liver or disgust at trade, and the town and life in toto, but I do know there's something in the mountain air and the solitude, and—well, your daughter, Latimer—that acts like a tonic or galvanic battery on me—keys me right up. When I go down from here I always am resolved to turn over a new leaf for both soul and stomach; forswear late suppers, and money-making, and—all the rest of it."

"Morbid, morbid! If every man could have your record!" said the colonel gravely. "Why, look at the Christian Brotherhood you founded, and the homes for——"

"Yes, yes," uneasily. "Never mind that now. I was joking, of course. My other reason for coming was to bring you back with me, Latimer. I want to convince you what folly it is to bury yourself and Isabel here in snow and ice doing nothing, while you ought to be laying up a snug sum for her future."

"You will leave nobody in Nittany. First you took Andross, and then the judge and Anna, and then Braddock. Bell will think of you as the spider with the flies, if you tempt me down into your web."

The colonel's attempted pleasantry was not successful. "I am aware that Miss Latimer has a remarkable religious prejudice against towns," said Laird irritably. "She refers most of the usual ways of earning a decent livelihood directly to the devil. As for Maddox, he was selling his iron at a loss after October; he consulted me, and I advised him to stop the Works, unlock his capital, give it to me to invest for him and to come down to town to keep an eye over it, as I might say. The change has certainly been of advantage to him pecuniarily. As for that brilliant little girl of his, she needed society—she opens in it like a flower in hothouse air. I certainly had nothing to do with young Braddock's desertion of Nittany. It seemed a sensible move enough when he was thrown out of employment here. Even Miss Latimer, surely, could not have objected to that."

The colonel was silent. He jerked the reins, glancing

anxiously at his companion as they hurried over the icy path. Laird, he knew, was ignorant of the right Isabel had to a share in Braddock's movements. He did not want to tell him the whole story; how the marriage had been arranged for August, and postponed by Braddock without farther reason than lack of funds on which to support a wife. Part of the matter, however, he could lay before Laird with advantage; but just as he was planning how to begin, his companion abruptly turned to him:

"The fact is, I should like to explain what it is I wish you to do before encountering Isabel's prejudices. There's an end, I understand, to your experiments here?"

"Oh! altogether. When the Works stopped there was no chance for me. I could afford to hire the hands now and then for a day, but not to run the furnace. Well, to tell the truth," laughing, "Bell and I have to draw the lines tolerably close, even in the house."

Laird nodded gravely. "I thought so. Now listen. You know a man in my business—railroads, transportation, etc.—has a good deal of surplus capital. I have put it into a business about which I say little because of a popular prejudice against it. This is all sub-rosa, of course?"

"Of course."

"Well, since the government put that absurd tax on distilled liquors, thousands of barrels are secretly made in Philadelphia in Irish cabins; poison, sir, sheer poison! Made out of the vile deck-scrapings of sugar vessels, and seasoned with vitriol or strychnine. But the profits are e-normous! Well, to prevent this sort of thing, respectable men have gone properly into the business on a large scale, and they have induced me to invest a good share of capital in it!"

"In distilling whiskey!"

"Now, you're not a teetotal fanatic. I'm sure of that,

Colonel. You take wine. Can't you see the propriety of giving the poor devils who *don't* take wine a pure article to drink instead of liquid death ? I may have been wrong," with an anxious frown, "but I did it for the sake of humanity. Of course I only draw my dividends. I never was in the distillery in my life."

"But I don't see," evasively, "what I have to do with this ?"

"Oh," eagerly, "now we come to the point ! There is a certain office vacant in the city—Collector—and these gentlemen—this organization for putting down illicit distillers——"

"The 'Whiskey Ring,' Andross called it, I think ?"

"Very probably. Mr. Andross's imagination is a fertile one. Did he tell you that *I* belonged to it ?"

Now the colonel, dull as he was in such matters, saw that Laird was in a smothered white heat of rage at the bold, coarse name of his business. He stammered out, "No;" that Jack had not spoken of him as one of the Ring, but continued to ponder and eye him like a confused owl, with some vague remembrance of Andross's story, and a notion that there was a mystery and disgrace with which Laird had had something to do, under the matter, which he ought to be able to understand. Braddock, no doubt, if he were here, could see to the bottom of it in a minute.

"This organization," said Laird, after a moment's pause, "have, as I was going to say, a good deal of power in city affairs. We can give this Collectorship to whom we please ; and as soon as I heard of it on Friday, I said, 'Latimer's the man !' Pontifex—the banker, you know—wanted it for his brother-in-law. But I said, 'No, Latimer's the man !' So I determined to take a holiday, and run right up about it."

"It was very kind in you, Laird, I'm sure."

"Not at all. But it's a snug thing, I can tell you,

Colonel. Why, Prideaux, who had it before, built a ducal palace out Broad street, and lived in it like a duke, too!"

"I had no idea that government paid its civil service officers at such rate. Now, in the army we——"

Laird shot a doubtful, keen look at the colonel. Ware had hinted that the "innocent old patriarch" would not only make a fine figure-head for the business, but would soon be wide enough awake to all the tricks of the trade. But Laird knew better. The very invincible integrity of the colonel was the capital they needed with which to face the public. It must be genuine, or it was worth nothing. He had made a misstep in hinting at bribes.

"There are some perquisites attached to the office," he replied quietly. "The salary is not large in itself. Probably they were larger when Prideaux held it than at present."

"Oh, I shall not object to the size of the salary! If I take the office, the money will be my only object. If I sell my birthright, let the mess of pottage be as large as possible."

"You mean by your birthright—— ?"

"Bell and I have been very happy here, and contented. I doubt whether money would bring us either happiness or content."

"Yet you want it—like the others?" laughing.

"I've a reason for that," anxiously. "The man who was to have been Bell's husband has different notions from mine about dollars and cents. I've gone through the world head over heels. He has Scotch canniness; you understand? Very praiseworthy, no doubt. He is afraid to marry, unless, as he says, he can feel the ground under his feet. So, for the child's sake, if I had a few hundreds ahead——"

"Quite right. I did not know that Miss Latimer's choice was made," drily.

Mr. Laird remained silent after that. Certainly his

pangs of disappointment at the knowledge that Miss. Latimer could never be his wife could not be extreme, his passion for her having been of the most leisurely and well-bred description; they quite equalled, however, the anger and annoyance he felt when his friend Patterson outbid him the week before for a Gérôme which he admired. Neither Bell nor the Gérôme would have been in keeping with his drawing-room furniture, perhaps; he was not quite sure that he really wanted either of them; but why should any other man have them? The other man in this case, he guessed at once to be that pious prig, Braddock, who had been afraid to trust him with his paltry savings. He would take care that the course of true love did not run smooth in that quarter.

"I am sure that Isabel's choice, whoever it may be, is a wise one," he said presently. "Better, perhaps, if he had not been of so practical a turn; if she lacks anything, it is imagination. But as for you, Colonel, it is your business to enable them to marry. Experimenting for humanity is all very well; but if a man has children, he is bound to furnish them with a solid foundation for happiness."

"In the shape of money?" smiling.

"In the shape of money. I want you to think over this offer of mine to-night, Latimer. I've a paper in my pocket with the details set down. Hillo! here we are at Millhall already."

———•◦•———

CHAPTER XIV.

"BUT, Bell, there is no reason in what you say."

"But it is true, father." They were waiting in the supper-room for Mr. Laird, and had been talking in an eager, low tone for some time. A red heat had come into Isabel's cheeks as they talked, and her eyes burned.

"You talk as if the earning an honest livelihood were worship of the devil. For my part," said the colonel, stretching his long legs before the fire, "I feel that dabbling in philanthropy and science has been too lazy a business for me. It's high time I went to hard work. I don't understand your objections. I can see no sin in a large salary any more than," glancing at the supper-table, "I can see the grace 'of God in cheap meat and no butter."

"I don't like dry bread either," with a shrug, "but nobody here thinks the worse of us that we eat it. I suppose it is because the mountains are so huge, and the sky so near, but you know it is a fact that money or the want of it is a trifling matter here. We take so little account of it, that we have time to think of other things. But in town, one smells the dollar everywhere. People are not ranked by their birth, as they were down in Virginia, or by their creative power, as they used to say up in Concord, but by their moucy. Very soon, papa, you and I would take the fever with the others. We would spend one half of our lives grubbing for the money, and the other in displaying it to shame our neighbours."

"Here is a moralist!" laughed Mr. Laird, who had come in unseen behind her. "But I'm inclined to doubt the effect of your huge mountains and sky as a cure for that fever, Miss Latimer," placing her chair behind the urn. "You must remember that I know your modern Arcadias tolerably well: I've not had the luck to find Cincinnatus at the plough, or Una at the churn. Take your Berks county Dutchman, for instance—who lives on the refuse potatoes and pork of his farm, and hoards his penny savings in the clock-case; and his daughter has just as keen a zest for fashion as any city belle; she loops up her calico into a panier, and strings wax-beads in her hair instead of pearls." Isabel laughed, but Laird was in no humour for jesting. "I did not know," turning sharply on the colonel, "that you proposed telling Miss Latimer of my proposal immediately!"

"Oh yes!" calmly. "Bell and I are partners."

Mr. Laird sat down at the table, disarranging the napkin and plate while he leaned forward to renew the argument with her; suddenly silent again when he remembered that she never argued, and had none of the modern glibness of women. He knew her to be as slow of speech as Moses, except to her father. She had no brilliancy, no accomplishments, no beauty such as was possessed by a dozen girls in New York, who would not be unfavourable to his suit, and who as wives could bring both influence and money. What was there in the girl that always made him, when near her, feel how shabby a thing his life was, of how little import his money? He certainly had never felt any love or passion for her; it was rather an overwhelming conviction that as his wife she could and would lift him to a higher level than any man would have thought it possible for Houston Laird to attain.

"It's maudlin sentiment," he thought, staring meditatively at her from under his red eyebrows. "I've had the same sort of impression looking at old Nittany or listening to the vesper anthems, yet Houston Laird is hardly the man to spend his time mooning about mountains or churches. Yet what could that priggish bigot Braddock do with such a woman?"

Isabel, meantime, quite unconscious of any element of sublimity in her akin to Nittany or church music, was yet aware of the storm in the air, and wondered what had put their guest in such ill-humour, while the colonel carved the tough meat with chagrin. The game suppers he would give to Laird and the other boys when—that is, *if* he took the office!

"There can be no doubt," said Laird suddenly—"yes, coffee if you please—no doubt, whatever, that American

society is corrupted to the very root by this greed for
money. Yes, to the very root, sir! Chicanery and bribery
in the very highest places, truckling and toadyism in the
lowest, and, all to make a little more show than our
neighbour. What else makes our men bilious dyspeptics
and the women nervous wrecks at middle age? Yes,
Colonel, you, passing your life in a farm in Virginia or
experimenting here, have no idea of the rottenness of our
social life. Isabel was right, sir! Her fine instinct showed
it to her. The boy is trained from his cradle to make
money, and the girl to marry a rich husband. It's all
push, climb, heat, and struggle from the beginning to——
I swear, I'm tired of it, Latimer!"

He spoke with vehemence, stirring his cup hurriedly,
and keeping his eyes down. Bell was silent, turning carefully away from him with a queer feeling of having surprised him undressed. "There's something in the air
here," trying to recover himself with an uneasy laugh,
"that forces these things home on me. I always look
down from this place on that gang of jobbers and gam-
blers at Harrisburgh, and think what cursed folly it all
is—drive and cheat and steal for a handful of greenbacks
more or less, and in a year or two—lie down in a wooden
box in a cut in the clay, and there's the end!"

Isabel met his blue eyes fixed on her. Their rims were
red, they were altogether off guard.

"Why do you tempt father down into the crowd then?"
she said gently.

Some far-off thought crept into his eyes, shrewd, wary,
humourous. "Don't take me at disadvantage, Miss
Latimer," quickly, with a total change of tone. "Your
father is incorruptible. I mean to serve him; I mean
that, honestly. Besides, what would you have him do?
His experiments here are stopped."

"My father," earnestly, "is a great inventor, Mr.
Laird. He has something better to do than to make

money. You have certainly heard of his new hygrometer ?"

"Yes," respectfully. "What became of that, Latimer?"

"Some fellow in Boston was beforehand with me, I found when I went to patent it."

"And the machine for surgeons to use, and the plough, and the attachment to sewing machines?" she held the cream-jug suspended, speaking so fast as to be scarcely intelligible.

"Bell only finds speech when defending me," said her father laughing. "Every one of those were really great inventions, Laird. But the difficulty was they were too intricate: the attachments cost double the price of the original machines."

"There is no reason why you should not go on inventing until you achieve something of use," with rising colour. "When my father," turning to Laird, "is in the army, or when he is experimenting, I go to bed every night, thinking how he is fighting or working for others. Never for himself. Some day the world will know what he is. I have known it always. I can not make you understand," stammering. "But he is the only great man I have known. I don't mind hunger or cold as long as there is a chance for him to do his work. But I will not have him go down to grub for money with the rest." She put both her hands suddenly on her father's shoulder, and looking at Laird, tried to smile, but her chin trembled, and the water stood in her eyes.

"I only hope," said Laird lightly, making a sudden flank movement of argument, "that he may be as successful as the rest who have come from Nittany. Andross is one of the luckiest, gayest fellows about town. Whatever he touches turns to gold. The judge, too, is on the high road to fortune ; and as to Braddock, if he keeps to legitimate business," significantly, "I have no doubt of his success."

"What do you mean by legitimate business, Laird?" said the colonel, while Isabel sat down quietly.

"Well, Braddock is, I fancy, in haste to be rich. The fever," glancing furtively at Isabel, "which Miss Latimer dreads, has attacked him violently; it was in the blood, you know: Scotch-Irish."

"I never knew any man," she said composedly, "who was less disposed to overrate money than Dr. Braddock."

"I really ought not to differ with you, for I don't know the young man," carelessly. "I offered for his mother's sake to be of use to him when he came up to town last July. He had saved some money, a mere pittance, but his all, and I proposed one or two safe and profitable investments——" He paused, noticing the eagerness with which she followed him. It was part of Bell's dulness to have no curiosity, but it was not in woman's nature to refuse to listen now. She had known how every dollar of this pittance, which seemed to her so large, had been saved. How many hundred times had they consulted over its investment! Secretly Bell would have been willing to marry long ago without a penny, and to trust in the Lord; but Braddock had not been so minded. When the seven thousand were secure, however, he thought the future was safe. He had gone from her full of hope, meaning, as she knew, to put the money in Laird's hands for investment; the Nevada mines, or National Transit Stock, as everybody knew, were sure ground on which to grow dollars out of pennies. After he came back he never had once named the money to her; he had not, in the anxiety to conceal the real disposition he had made of it, even told her the different opinion he had formed of Laird on reaching town. She only knew that the money was not to be the basis of their future; that her lover had cooled and hesitated, and finally postponed the marriage on the plea of want of funds. She sat motionless as Laird went on.

"I proposed these investments, but he would have nothing to do with them ; carried his money off to turn over according to his own judgment. I hope it was a wise judgment, I am sure. But there are so many sharpers about town ready to seize on a credulous fellow like Braddock, and so many ways of risking money——"

"Do you mean dishonest ways ?" said Isabel, from the lofty height of her lover's innocence.

"Well—not precisely. Young ladies hardly understand financial operations clearly enough to comprehend technicalities. Without being gambling, strictly so called, there are certain ways of making money which are not clean, while legitimate brokerage is clean. I can scarcely explain it to you without——"

"It is not necessary. Dr. Braddock never invested in any dishonourable undertaking knowingly. And he is not at all ' a credulous person,' either," tartly.

"I am very glad to hear you speak so positively of the young man, Miss Latimer. Your judgment is, of course, unbiassed," heartily. "For his mother's sake, I should be sorry that he lost his little savings."

An awkward silence followed. "Laird," said the colonel, leaning over the table anxiously after taking council with himself, "the truth is that I wished to speak to you about this very matter. Braddock *is* a friend of ours. There is a reason why I am interested about his conduct in regard to that money. A business reason, you see ?" feeling himself a very Talleyrand of diplomacy. "But there have been very unpleasant whispers about that affair of the money in the neighbourhood. People in a sparsely settled place know each others' business, and are the very deuce to gossip. Braddock took the money away, and came home without it ; began to save and stint himself in every way. There was talk of his having been drawn into a gambling-house, or to a race-course ; but the lad is a professor of religion. I could not credit that. But now that you speak of those other modes——"

"Papa," said Bell, in an unnecessarily firm voice, "You may be sure that whatever disposition Doctor Braddock has made of his money was the very most honest and wisest disposition that could be made."

"That settles the question, Latimer." Mr. Laird forced a laugh.

"Not to my mind," eagerly rubbing both hands along his thin knees. "Heaven knows I have no desire to meddle in his or any man's business affairs. But this concerns—concerns a friend of mine, a woman whose future depends on him. Her happiness——" he glanced at Bell, wishing that she should understand, and quite sure that Laird would never penetrate the inscrutable mystery in which he wrapped his meaning.

"Of course," said Laird cheerfully, "he gave an account of his disposal of the money to anybody who had a right to such an account. Neither you nor I have that, Colonel. The natural supposition for us outsiders, when a young fellow from the country lets six or seven thousand slip from him in town, and makes no explanation about it, is that he has lost it in some disgraceful way. Miss Latimer must not think us harsh."

"That rule would not apply in this case," interposed Isabel calmly. "It would be simply impossible for Clay Braddock to be concerned in anything disgraceful."

She stopped, swallowing once or twice. Mr. Laird paused, his cup in his hand, looking at her in astonishment. He had always thought her a plain woman before. Something about her at the moment startled her father also. His wife had possessed a rare beauty which had made her everywhere a woman of mark, and it had often vexed him that her daughter had not one of her features, and passed unnoticed through life. But now——. It occurred to him also suddenly to think what the child must have suffered during her lover's long neglect and silence, about this same cursed money on which their future hinged. If he could but cure her of her love for the fellow!

"It looks badly," he blurted out. "And there is more than that which looks badly. Nobody knows it but Maddox; God forbid it should be whispered about—but I can tell you two. Braddock's books did not turn out right—the judge detected altered numbers, for years back. He said nothing to Braddock, because he could not find where the money was missing exactly; but the numbers were undoubtedly altered——"

"This is too much!" rising. "Mr. Laird, you do not know Dr. Braddock. *I* assure you it is all false. I wonder my father allowed Judge Maddox to hint such a thing to him! Clay never wronged a man of a penny."

"You have proof of that, of course, Miss Latimer."

"Proof? why, I know it is not true. That is enough," haughtily. "And as for any woman, papa, whose future is in his hands—you need have no fear for her whatever. Her future is safe. Perfectly safe."

She walked across the room, while the two men, not exchanging a glance, watched her as if mesmerized.

Laird drew a long breath. "To think," his thoughts ran, "that pride in such a respectable stick as that Braddock could lift her out of herself into that wonderful woman. It's just the difference between a scrawny flannelled race-horse in its stable, and the creature as it bounds into the goal, full of fire and beauty from head to foot. If she had loved a man, now—*a man.*" His blood was strangely heated, but he helped himself to bread, composedly choosing a soft piece.

She took up her fur mantle, and began to hurriedly button it about her. Her father went to her. "Bell, where are you going?"

"I—I don't know, papa. If I could tell him"—with

a bewildered look around her, the tears coming slowly up to her eyes.

"It's not like you to be nervous, child. Your hands are as cold—come to the fire." He began to take off the mantle; but in a minute she was herself again.

"I am chilly; I think I'll keep it on," going back to her chair. "I beg your pardon, Mr. Laird. Dr. Braddock is a friend of ours, and——"

"There are no half-way measures in your friendship! I only wish I had so loyal an ally. There must be a very genuine worth in that young fellow," he added with heartiness, "to gain such genuine friends as he has had the luck to make here and in town."

"I did not know that he had any friends in town," said Isabel quickly, "or even acquaintances."

"Why, you would not have the boy turn hermit, Bell?" her father interposed impatiently.

"He told *me* that his time was fully occupied in his work and study," she said.

Oth came in to remove the supper dishes. At Laird's proposal they sat still about the roaring fire of pine logs.

"I have taken a fancy to this room," he said lazily; "to the broad hearth and the red curtains, and the white hills without, and the deer's heads on the wall, and the bear's skin under foot."

The truth was, he did not wish to disturb Isabel; he wanted to watch her as she sat, her head bent forward from the fur, looking moodily in the fire, her hands folded idly in her lap.

"These suspicions of Braddock are having their effect on her," whispered the colonel, quite forgetting that he was keeping Bell's secret from Laird. "It's time she demanded an explanation from him, as Maddox said. The whole business has an ugly look. Clay ought to set it right, sir."

"She would not believe if she saw him pick Maddox's

pocket. It would only be a pretext for exalting him into a more honest hero," laughed Laird. "Tut, tut. You don't know women, Latimer."

Oth piled up fresh logs and swept the hearth; the two men plunged into a discussion of the internal revenue tax, but still Miss Latimer's gray eyes were fixed immovably on the shifting blaze.

"Now, if it is the intention of the government to wipe out the debt——" said the colonel, pointing his argument off with his forefinger on his scuffed trousers.

"How many evenings in the week does he give to his friends, as you call them?" she said, looking up suddenly at Laird.

"Who the deuce——?" cried the colonel.

"Very nearly all, I judge," said Laird readily. "I meet him at Judge Maddox's every time I drop in there, and I see him at concerts, in opera boxes, and so on, constantly."

"Miss Maddox's opera box?"

"Yes, I believe so. That is—well, I have seen him with them twice this winter. What a charming creature that little girl is, Latimer, by the way?"

"Yes, very pretty. Not regular enough features to please me, however," absently, and glancing at Isabel, whom he felt, with a dog-like sort of instinct, was in fresh trouble of some kind.

"Anna Maddox's face has not a fault!" she said energetically. "I am sure, papa, you never saw such exquisite form and colour."

"Tut, tut. Nothing of the kind. The child is very pleasing, to be sure. The most innocent, ingenuous little creature——"

Mr. Laird laughed.

"On the contrary! I don't know a shrewder little practitioner in society."

"You are perfectly right, Mr. Laird," said Isabel,

rising hastily. "She is full of art. I never knew any-body who was more persistent in laying her plans, or showed more skilful duplicity in carrying them out."

"Why, Bell, you certainly used to laugh at Anna as a silly child."

"Then I was very much mistaken. She has had sense enough to choose the man best worth any woman's choice for her husband, and she has succeeded in winning him, that is plain. Oh, that is quite plain!"

The face within the dark fur had suddenly lost its colour, and showed how thin and worn it had grown in the last few months.

"It is intolerably hot in this room!" pushing off the mantle. "I must go out for some fresh air. I'll see if Oth has—has put Rosy in her stall."

"Rosy! What the deuce has she to do with the cow? God bless me! the ways of women!" ejaculated the colonel, hurrying after her, while Laird, thrusting his hands in his pockets and stretching out his feet on the fender, laughed.

Her father found her pacing up and down the back porch, only prevented from pacing in the yard by the snow, which was up to her knees.

"Bell!" trying to part her hands, shut on each other.

"Yes, papa."

"This is unlike you. This is abject folly. Doctor Braddock——"

"Don't name him to me! Never again. That he could be so weak—as to be deceived by that—that miser-able little creature! And then to deceive me! Oh, to deceive me!"

"Bell, you have no warrant for even accusing the man. Be reasonable. You have heard nothing except that he visits sometimes at the judge's, and was twice in their box at the opera. Could anything be more natural? And you go off at a tangent, and believe him in love with her."

"I believe more than that," with solemn calmness. "I believe that I have now the key to the whole mystery —he means to marry her. He meant it from the night she tricked him into wandering through the mountains, pretending she was searching for Andross. He has invested the money with a view to marrying her. Why should he not tell me what he had done with it else? It's just as clear——. He went to town to please her— followed her——."

"Because the Works stopped and left him without a dollar, Bell. Be just, child. You are not lacking in common-sense."

"Papa, my instinct told me all this long ago. It is all perfectly plain to *me*. He is married, very likely, by this time. I knew by instinct, the very day her cunning eyes turned on him and her wiles began to tell on him."

"Oh! confound instinct!" muttered the colonel. But Isabel's hands were beginning to feel cold and limp, and her forehead like fire; in spite of her low voice and swift steps he felt that she very likely would fall the next minute like a rag in his hands. "And what am I to do with her then?" said the bewildered and imbecile colonel. She had always been like a son to him, a ready staff on which to support his vagaries or griefs or rheumatism, and now at this first touch of idiotic jealousy she crumbled as it were into a senseless, helpless dead weight on his hands.

"Bell, dear, won't you at least come to your room? You'll certainly have the influenza again. And as for poor Clay——"

"If you think," with slow emphasis, "that I care about Clay, or that his going will cost me a single tear, you are mistaken, papa. If he could be beguiled by such a painted, shallow actress as Anna——"

"I thought," slyly, "you considered her beauty without a flaw?"

"Ah ! *you* are laughing at me ?"   She stopped, looking up at him ; her wrists which he caught trembled, the
pulse was gone ; she began to sob in a noiseless, stifled
way.

"Laugh at you ! God help you, my darling, no," cried
the colonel, picking her up in his arms like a baby.
"But you're such a fool ! Come to bed directly."   He
pushed open the door of her room, and laying her in a
great easy chair began to build up the fire, blowing it
vigorously.   "They're all alike—every woman of them !"
he muttered half aloud.   "She'd love him all the better
if he'd committed burglary, but let him speak civilly to a
pretty girl and there is no forgiveness for him.   There,"
glancing over his shoulder, "she's crying comfortably,
thank heaven ! It'll all come right now."

The colonel wisely left Isabel to her tears.   When he
was going to bed a tall white-robed figure beckoned him
to her room door.

"Papa, I've been considering Mr. Laird's proposal,
and I think we had better accept it.   There's no need
that we should worship Mammon, if we do live in town."

"No," looking at her dubiously.   "I thought we
would take a month or two to talk it over.   When would
you wish to go, Bell ?"

"To-morrow, papa."

"Oh !" said the colonel, and. in that exclamation
buried both his difficulties and amazement.

Bell went back to the clear fire, and the bear's skin in
front, on which she had been sitting, and the low stool
set on it, with the lamp, and her little old Testament
open beside it.   She had read it every day since she was
a child, but so cheerful had been her life that this was
the first time that its pages were wet with tears.   Perhaps
because she had had no mother, this Elder Brother of
hers was more real and nearer to her than to other people.

She could not read to-night, though she tried. No common-sense, no argument would have comforted her. But when she pushed away the lamp, and kneeling down laid her head on the stool, and cried without any words, she knew that He understood all of her story; how dear this old home was, and how innocent; what the man was to her who had loved her there, and how she had lost him.

He knew.

When she rose at last to get into bed it was with the quiet, almost happy, face of a child who has sobbed itself to sleep on its mother's bosom. She laid her cheek on her hand on the pillow, thinking with a smile that He would bring it all right, and that this world was a happy one after all, and full of good, friendly people. "Excepting one," she murmured, as she closed her eyes. "Artful little creature!"

———◦◦◦———

CHAPTER XV.

MR. LAIRD passed most of that winter in New York, because, as he said, he must supervise the business of the National Transit Company in person, but in reality, to keep the Whiskey Ring at a distance from which none of the ill-odour of their doings could cling to his garments. The best chess-players are those who do not need to see the board.

One evening in March he dropped in as usual to the Century Club, which gave a reception that night to a distinguished English poet who had just arrived. Mr. Laird carefully avoided the public apartments, however, and hurried to a window where, half-hidden by the lace curtains, a small, fair-haired young man was alternately looking out at the moon and down at his dainty feet.

On every Saturday evening he found this same fair-haired little man waiting for him at the same window.

"Ah, Willitts, you are here?" drawing up a chair.

"Yes, I've been here for an hour," balancing his eye-glass on his nose. "Perrott came over from Philadelphia with me, and we've been surveying the crowd. Some most remarkable faces there, sir," waving his little ringed hand to the mob of men who, in full evening dress, were gathered about the stranger. "But I doubt if the poet gets a fair glimpse of them through the cigar smoke. Tell him this is an æsthetic club, and then stifle him in their own parlour with the smell of tobacco and whiskey! It is simply indecent, nasty, as I tell Perrott."

"If you had not come I should have run over on the 12:20 train," said Laird heavily. There was an intentness in his manner, a rigidity in his solid features, which showed a marked departure from his usual easy indolent bearing when discussing business. "No additional news which could not be trusted to the wires, Willitts?"

"No," carelessly dropping his glass. "Good type of John Bull, that fellow yonder—of the lean, smug kind! No, nothing tangible. But a certain uneasiness and a good deal of talk about a tornado coming, nobody knows from whence. Pity somebody had not a nose for a financial crisis, as Jack Andross has for a thunder gust. That fellow scents it days beforehand! It is remarkable to find such magnetic sensibility in a healthy, stout man."

"I am not particularly interested in Mr. Andross as a barometer," drily. "Has he attended to that matter at Harrisburgh?"

"Well, no," beginning to take off his gloves. "The gentlemen down on Franklin street—your partners," hesitating.

"Very well, go on."

"They bade me tell you that the crisis is too imminent

to risk anything. At least three votes are needed in the House to pass the bill——"

"I know all that! I told you last week that those votes could be bought as easily as any others. It is only a question of price. I told you to charge Andross not to spare expense. It's no time for haggling!" He got up suddenly, throwing up the window; the March wind, wet with sleet, rushed in, flapping the curtains.

"Ugh! Allow me," gently, closing it. "You forgot the hail. The difficulty," taking the dampened tea-rose from his coat, "is not with the legislators, but Andross. The gentlemen think it advisable to ask somebody else to negotiate the matter. Jack has some scruples, it appears. Heaven knows what they are," laughing. "Those fellows are for sale, and why not buy them as you would a pound of sugar?"

"No one can approach them so well as Andross," thoughtfully. "I don't wish to compel him—— But we shall need his vote also."

"Oh! That, of course, will be a debt of friendship. Jack has done nothing for us since you gave him his seat in the Senate. No price to pay there."

Mr. Laird was silent. "Andross is a working member of the Senate, I hear?" he said presently.

"Yes," laughing. "He has laid the axe to the root of the tree with a vengeance. No bill passes unquestioned, Perrott tells me. No snakes creep in with them this session. Some of the men think Andross is another name for honesty; and some, that he is only making a reputation to command a higher price presently!"

"He is quite sincere." There was a marked respect in his tone.

"Oh! yes. I've no doubt of it. I'd trust Jack's honour as I would my own. Now, if he makes any difficulty, I think I could go down and manipulate those fellows, Mr. Laird?"

"No, Ned. They are gentlemen and statesmen—for their constituencies. Transactions with them must be strictly under cover. It would not do to have you buzzing too much about Harrisburgh. You'd tell your errand everywhere, like a mosquito."

"All right," good humouredly. "But I think you've overrated Andross's possible usefulness to you. A man of business for the company he will never be, that's certain."

"No. But there's something about Jack that attracts people, and that's what I want. To me he has always seemed a weak, vacillating fellow, but his influence over the poorer classes is simply incalculable. No man could serve me better if he chose. But to make him choose—"

Ned Willitts twisted the waxed ends of his fair mustache meditatively, bending his little brain to the solving of this problem. At home Ned was a harmless, kindly, light-hearted fellow, ready to escort his sisters to ball or opera, and a famous referee iu all matters of dancing or ball etiquette; in the office he had been taught since he could speak that man's duty was to make money—to "get on." In his neat little body, from feather head to feather heels, there was no troublesome monitor to ask meddling questions as to the "how."

"It would not be easy to reach Andross through his pocket," he said. "He has gone into a set who are so cursedly independent as to pretend to have souls above greenbacks; a lot of journalists, actors, and the like; very nice fellows really, but full of whims. I don't see but that they charge full value for their wares, though," laughing.

"What women does he visit?"

"Oh! a dozen. He's a social fellow, you know. But he's a perfect slave to that little girl of Maddox's. He does not care who sees that."

"And she will rate herself at a high figure when it comes to marriage."

"Very possibly; she's not a fool. She's worth it. But social position is of more weight with her than money; though *I* should not be at all surprised she'd make a love-match some of these days without either. She's an affectionate little thing."

"You seem to be quite behind the scenes, Ned."

"Well, yes. It's only a sisterly sort of friendship, but she really gives me more of her confidence than anybody else." The sentence ended in a conscious giggle. "Of course," he resumed gravely, "she depended on Andross a good deal to get into society. She's not the sort of woman to wait five or ten years of probation according to Philadelphia custom, so she began by going to all the public balls, meaning to pick up acquaintances there, but Andross soon stopped that. She has made her way into a certain fashionable set, however, to his great disgust. Girls who lead in petticoats and bonnets, and who are noticeably *décolleté* at the opera. Jack is fastidious about women."

"Yes. She will lose her hold on him." If she did, Laird had lost his hold on him.

For the moment a rash impulse seized him, to let the gallant young fellow go. He was now doing an honest man's work honestly; saving money, as Laird knew, to replace that which he had stolen; well-clothed, light-hearted, going among all kinds of people, carrying a cordial cheerfulness with him. Everybody who met him, like Spellin at the furnace, had the feeling that Jack was a man who ought to have his laugh out in the world; and Laird was no exception to the rule.

But this was no time for generous impulses. He had educated and reared this man to serve him, and now when this service was needed to stand between him and ruin, it was no time to take off the yoke.

"I'll come over on Wednesday and see how matters stand."

"You mean in the Transit office?"

"No. That business is clear enough," gloomily.

"No trouble ahead, really?" nodding and smiling, as he stood behind Laird's chair, to his acquaintances in the crowd. Curious glances were thrown now and then at the great Railroad King and his jackal, as they called Willitts, but they were not disturbed. Laird made no reply to the last question. Certainly the business was clear to him! Destruction waited for him on every side. He remembered the old story of the prisoner inclosed in a cell with movable walls, which each day shut in upon him with inexorable steadiness, until he was crushed between them. There was no chance except in the relief which ought to come from the profits of the distilling business in Philadelphia, and if the bill he had drawn up did not pass the Pennsylvania legislature, these profits would be diminished one-half. To pass that bill, Andross's help was necessary. It was plain enough!

"That is the Rev. Dr. Hyde, under the chandelier," said Ned over his head. "No better brain in the city than that fellow's. He was coining money in trade, and threw it all up to preach to drunken sailors. By George, a thing like that makes me believe in religion! Ah, how'reye, Whalley?" winking with his eyelids and mustachiod upper lip at once; a familiar frisky recognition for which he was known on Chestnut street. "That bald man was Whalley, leading gentleman at Wallack's. By the way," lowering his voice with gravity, "that ballet-girl I told you of, and for whom you gave me *carte blanche?*"

"Yes."

"Well, it was worse than I thought, though when I heard her coughing in her tulle and tights in the cold flies, it was so horrible it fairly sickened me. I told you about that, though. I found she lived with her mother in a squalid little court—Melon alley. They had nothing but what the girl made—mother was crippled; the girl actually crept out of bed, night after night, with the death sweats on her, to go down to the Varieties to dance. Perrott went with me; we had them both taken to the hospital, and put in one room together. All comfortable. I got Roberts—he's a clergyman, a friend of mine—to go at once to her; his wife took jelly and things——"

"You ought to have sent fruit. The fever is intolerable in that disease sometimes."

"Yes, I did. So did Cram, the Varieties manager; he's not a bad fellow, Cram, but careless; he ought to have seen to the girl before. Oh! it was all very comfortable for them, and Roberts told me she—she felt ready to go at the last. Roberts was quite satisfied with her state of mind, sir. The poor thing only lived two weeks."

"I am glad you attended to the matter so well, Ned," earnestly. "Any other cases of real want that come in your way, remember to call on me."

"Well. I generally keep out of sight of such things, but sometimes they force themselves on one. As for street-beggars they never get a rap from me."

Mr. Laird drew out his watch, and said something about supper, when Willitts stopped him.

"Oh! I meant to tell you, there was the very devil to pay in the distilleries."

Laird's dislike was so great to being openly identified with the business, that he affected indifference, even to this confidential messenger; who had for so many years been a go-between for the actual distillers and capitalists who furnished the means, that he had dubbed himself the Mercury of the whiskey-barrels; and who knew just how deeply he was involved with them.

"Ah! what is the trouble, Willitts?"

"An old officer named Latimer is the trouble, and a tolerably obstinate one, too. He is the new collector, and

Wilkins and Brady and every other whiskey manufacturer are up in arms against him, and inquiring how the deuce he got the appointment. But he has it, and is likely to give them a Waterloo defeat before long, if all accounts be true."

"I gave him the appointment," coldly.

"I beg your pardon, Mr. Laird. I did not know that."

"Now if you can lay aside jesting for awhile, perhaps you will explain the business so that you can be understood. I gave Colonel Latimer the place, because he was a brave, honourable man; the party has not so many of that kind in its service just now in Philadelphia."

Ned shook his head, listening attentively.

"Latimer" (Mr. Laird continued slowly, choosing his words) "is a man of invincible integrity. No bribe can touch him. He needed the place, and the place——"

—"Needed him," supplying the pause. "I understand. One such man will strengthen the party in public estimation, beyond the power of any Citizen's Reform Party to damage it. A cloak, like charity, to cover a multitude of sins. But, confound it, the old fellow need not have made honesty an epidemic! It's likely to prove more fatal to the distillers than the small-pox."

"In what way?" Laird motioned Willitts to come in front of him, and leaning both hands on his knees, looked steadily—not at the flippant young man, but at the disaster behind him.

"Well, hitherto, the distillers and officers have been as one family—brethren dwelling together in unity. Now— but to make you understand, Mr. Laird, I must enter into details, which hitherto you have avoided."

Laird coughed doubtfully. "I don't like them, Ned," frankly. "The tricks and the air of the distilleries are something totally alien to my habits or nature. When I put my money into the business, it was with the proviso that I was to have nothing to do with them. Still there seems to be brain-work needed now, and I must understand the situation. I have no doubt, now, that there is a good deal of deception practised on the government officers !"

"I am afraid there is," dropping his eyes to hide their twinkle. "In a dozen ways. If there were not, the profits would be small indeed. The most common trick is the sending out twenty barrels of liquor for one on which the tax is paid. The detectives, under controul of the collector, have been in the habit of taxing, every day, only the barrels on which they found no greenback laid. Neither of your distilleries have been taxed for one-tenth of the article they sold."

."I did not know how the thing was done. But the tax is really too exorbitant," said Laird calmly. "My distillers, I believe, are reckoned exceptionally honest. because they pay a tax at all."

"They will have a chance to grow in grace under Colonel Latimer's discipline, then," laughing.

"What do you mean? Nobody attempted to bribe him?"

"No. But his man Bowyer, special detective, has taken the collection of the tax in his own hands. Wilkins himself sent him in last night to count the barrels, having left on each one a crisp new note, and found them untouched. This morning Wilkins was arrested on charge of illicit distillation. In fact, that was the news I came over to give you. The other distillers are looking for arrest on Monday morning. Their houses will be closed if that be done."

"If they close now I am ruined," Laird said, so calmly that Ned rejoined lightly: "Not so bad as that, of course. What is to be done? Latimer can not be removed. There has been too much gratulation on his honesty. To behead him, on any pretext, would be for the party to plead guilty, in so many words."

"Tell the men to pay the tax on every gallon. We can stand it—for a week or two."

"You will not throw Bowyer off his guard in that way. The fellow has the eye of a lynx. And he really seems to do his duty for the duty's sake. A dull kind of fellow, I suspect, with no idea of making his way in the world. In case he is as wide-awake as ever, after this spasm of honesty in the distillers, what are they to do?"

Mr. Laird got up and walked impatiently down the room. Coming back he beckoned Willitts. "It is quite time for supper," he said, as though he had forgotten the subject altogether. It was not until, with his napkin spread over his portly chest, he had discussed the bill of fare with the waiter, and settled himself to wait for the first dishes, that he replied, leaning back and directing his eyes to the chandelier overhead:

"This part of the matter I have nothing to do with, Ned. Isn't it enough that I furnish money to those fellows, but must I furnish both brains and hands? Wilkins ought to know how to manage such obstacles as this Bowyer. He used to have a way—and tools with which to force such obstacles to stand aside."

Willitts nodded, poured out a glass of sherry, sipped it and nodded again. "Y-es, I know," he said deliberately. "It is a good while since anything of that kind was done though, and it is risky, always. I don't know, exactly, how the thing was managed, but Wilkins could engineer it, no doubt. There was a fellow called Rourke or Voss, or any other convenient name, who was a useful person to have about, Wilkins said. The fighting manager, they called him at the distillery. Andross had the man under his thumb, they said."

"Jack got him out of the penitentiary four years before his sentence ran out," Laird said, with ill concealed irritation that he was obliged to answer. "I can send him back to-morrow if I choose. He fought with Mace

last week in Brooklyn. Wilkins knows where to find
him, if he wants him. Now, let us be done with this,
Willitts.   It's not a subject I fancy."

"That's true.   It spoils digestion.   Though if the
worst come to the worst, it can only give Major Bowyer
a month or two of seclusion in which to mend a broken
head, and meditate on his own virtues."

" Try this salmi ? Whatever is done to Bowyer, let it
be effectual. Don't let there be any bungling. Don't
let him be attacked and made more furious, like a beast
half mangled by dogs."

"That is the objection to using that kind of men.
You never know how much they will do, or leave un-
done.   I object to coarse tools always."

Laird did not answer.

" By the way," asked Ned presently, delicately wiping
his mustache with his napkin, " in case Wilkins is obliged
to have recourse to our friend's aid, what is to be done
with him afterwards ? There will be no difficulty in
bringing him through a trial scot free, if you choose the
judge and counsel, or would you prefer to have him
locked up for a few years ? "

" Time enough to discuss that hereafter.   He may not
be needed at all.   But if he is," stooping forward with a
suddenly startled face, " remember Colonel Latimer is to
be held as safe as I am.   Bowyer is the point of attack.
If one of old Latimer's gray hairs are touched, every man
concerned in it shall suffer as for murder. Make Wilkins
understand that."

" Very well," composedly disjointing his bird.   But
secretly he thought the blow had better be aimed at the
real cause of difficulty, and he had little doubt that
Wilkins would agree with him, and follow his own
counsel.   In fact Wilkins, infuriated by his arrest, had
threatened this very morning to take matters in his own
hands in future, and hinted that Laird's capital did not

counterbalance the personal risk run by the actual distillers, or give him the right to dictate.

Willitts was forced to hurry his supper to catch the midnight train. Mr. Laird walked with him to the door of the club-house. He detained him a moment at parting.

"Ned, if you know any means which can be brought to bear on Andross to induce him to vote with his party, I wish you'd use them. I have a sure hold on the fellow, but I'd rather not have recourse to it, if possible. The fact is, I like Jack."

"Everybody does. I'll think of it."

Ned, stretched at ease in his sleeping berth, had leisure to think of it seriously. Andross used to be an easy fellow, ready to turn this way or that at anybody's beck or call. Since he came down from the mountains he had been wholly changed—economical, plodding, obstinate in trudging on his own path. "It's partly religion, and partly love for that little witch that ails him," shrewdly guessed Ned. "He thinks he can pass through the Harrisburgh legislature like Shadrach and his friends through the fiery furnace. Every time he turns his back on a fee, or plumps an honest vote, he thinks it brings him nearer to heaven and Anna." He lay quiet for a minute or two, and then whistled, his merry, good-natured faced twinkling.

"Aha! that will do! We can put a ring through any bull's nose in that way. Master Jack will find he can't slip the party traces. I wonder we did not think of that plan before. But Anna must manage it." And he composed himself to a balmy sleep.

CHAPTER XVI.

MR. WILLITTS had an early opportunity of carrying his plan into effect, as he found a note with Anna's monogram in daintiest pink and gold on the seal, inviting him to dine with her father the next evening. Miss Maddox usually controulled her father's efforts at hospitality.

As the church-bells were ringing for evening service, Ned found himself in the hall of the judge's gay little house on Spruce street. Every gas-burner that could give a light was blazing at its full head from garret to basement; frescoes and brilliant chromos and gilding, Axminster carpets and brocatelle curtains sent back the light all over the house; from the open parlor doors came a buzz of voices, amid which Anna's sweet, shrill little pipe cut the air incessantly. Ned drew off his overcoat quickly; he liked the house and the overdressed manner of it; it was like a brassy opera of Verdi's.

In the hall he met Ware.

"Is Andross here?" hurriedly asked Ned.

"No, but he is coming, I believe. He runs down from Harrisburgh every Friday to pay his court here until Monday, they tell me. What chance has he, do you think? Maddox will want his daughter to marry for money or position, I fancy."

"I do not know," said Ned coldly.

Ware was a good fellow, but in danger of forgetting the anvil from which he dated, if he was not snubbed now and then.

There were half a dozen men for dinner, but no women excepting Mrs. General Ralston, one of those ponderous matrons so common in Philadelphia, whose bulk and black velvet and hook nose and turrets of shining white hair atop symbolize a sort of social Gibraltar, commanding any position. Mrs. Ralston was there as a chaperone for

Miss Maddox, who held herself, however, carefully aloof from her, having her own business to transact with every man present.

Anna, grown thinner, her complexion more delicate, and dressed by Worth with a regard to her peculiar style, was a much finer study of Simplicity and Youth than in her crude state in the mountains.

Willitts secured a seat beside her at dinner, and on somebody regretting the absence of "our young senator," remarked carelessly that he heard that Andross was determined to slip the party yoke, voting as he pleased, according to his conscience.

"Yes, by George, sir !" said General Ralston, a little, lean, bewhiskered man, with a bass voice ; "the young man forgets himself, sir ! We don't send representatives to Harrisburgh to exercise the right of private judgment, but to serve their constituency. It is lucky for the district that his term expires so soon."

"The meaning of which is," whispered Ware, "that Ralston took an axe up to Jack last week, and brought it back unground."

"An axe ?" said Anna, bewildered. "But will not Mr. Andross go back to the senate after this term ?" turning to Ned.

"I'm afraid not," laughing. "His tactics are not popular with the drum-majors of the party, as you see."

"But really, Mr. Willitts," said the judge, lowering his tones, "it is very wrong in Andross, as well as impolitic, to oppose the men that elected him. It's ungrateful ! Ralston tells me he refused—absolutely refused point-blank a position to his son-in-law, on the ground of incompetency. Now, without Ralston, Laird never could have got that seat for Andross. No use for Jack to butt his head against customs in force before he was born. It's cursedly Quixotic."

"Do you really think he will not be sent back next

term?" persisted Anna, as soon as the voices drowned her whisper. Her fair forehead was knit, and there was an angry glitter in the blue eyes which Jack called saintly. "He has not so much social rank or money, Heaven knows, that he can afford to throw away the little his friends have got for him! What is the matter with his tactics? How does he offend these men?"

Ned was idly speculating, as she talked, how this shrewish tone would sound thirty years hence, when the nose and dimpled chin were sharp, and crow's-feet had come into the neck.

"Tactics?" he said hastily, catching himself. "Well, Andross has set himself against these men in every way; he is a rigid impersonation of virtue. He might be as honest as he pleased, but not run counter to every man's prejudices. Apropos to prejudices, I am glad to see that you are not a fanatic about temperance," glancing at the half empty champagne glass which she had absently raised to her lips.

"Do you think it looks unwomanly for a young girl to take wine?" looking sharply at him.

"I? Oh dear, no! All fashionable girls take it. You ought to see Netty Ford after supper! By the way, that is one of Jack's delinquencies. He is abstinent to an absurd degree; makes himself a sort of living sermon at every dinner or card-party in Harrisburgh. Now," leaning closer, as he saw how intently she listened, "he is precisely one of the men to whom wine in moderation would be an advantage. A glass or two would make him more genial, pliable—popular; you understand?"

"I shouldn't like," shaking her head gravely, "to see him a drunkard."

"Am I a drunkard? Is your father? Be reasonable, Miss Maddox. It is your duty, as his friend, to advise Andross for his good; and you see the imminent danger he is in of losing his seat."

"Oh, if he loses that little bit of respectability, he need not count me as his friend, I can tell you," tossing her daintily coiffured head. "Let us talk of something else. I'm tired of Andross!"

Ned obeyed. But he saw that she only meant to gain time to make up that bundle of small particles, her mind. There was a slight bustle in the hall presently, and Andross's voice, loud and hearty, was heard. A pleasant stir passed round the table, as though a fresh wind had suddenly come into the room. "There he comes!" said one to another, smiling. Even Ralston relaxed his scowl: he could not help but like the fellow in spite of himself.

"Why, Jack my boy!" cried the judge, going to the door as Andross in full evening dress, his handsome face glowing and ruddy with the frost, came in. He shook hands with everybody, joked with Ned, touched Anna's hand with a furtive look, which Willitts caught, and thought how like a woman the.man was, with all his tremendous muscular power. Ned had never seen a woman's eyes so brilliant and tender.

"You think if he would be friendly and drink moderately with those people it would bring all right?" breathlessly whispered Anna.

"He would undoubtedly become more ductile. The party complain he won't work in harness, as you heard."

"He ought to work in harness or in anything they give him," irritably. "What right has he to oppose the party, when they can take his salary from him?"

"I would not argue with him on political grounds if I were you," cautiously suggested Ned.

"Oh, I never argue!" quickly. "Nothing disgusts men with a woman so much. As for politics I owe all I know to you, Mr. Willitts," with an upward confiding glance, which for the moment rendered Ned dumb. "But if the wine is a remedy I will administer that," smiling across the table to Andross who, unable to hear her words, was watching her lovely, mobile face with delight.

"I went into Holy Trinity church, Miss Maddox, as I came up," he said, "and heard Phillips Brooks lecture. I am glad you have chosen that church."

Anna bowed and smiled. Her care in choosing a church had been to find one in a fashionable neighbourhood, and when found, to secure a foremost seat in it.

"Yes," responded Mrs. Ralston, "one comes out of it with a new faith in humanity."

Andross felt as if he did not need Phillips Brooks to give him faith in humanity to-night. Life was so different with him from the best which he had hoped, when he put on Laird's yoke. Nothing had interfered with his resolve to be honest. To-day he had seen a chance where by a lucky stroke he might honestly earn the money to replace to the Gray Eagle account. That done he could look God and the world in the face again. As for this depravity in mankind, to which Mr. Brooks had referred, that was a far-off matter for theologians to deal with. No doubt there was truth somewhere in those old symbolic legends of a pilgrim soul beset in its dark and lonely way by tempting fiends, which, when it was vanquished, dragged it down to abodes of unknown, unutterable woe. But what place was there for tempted souls or evil spirits in Judge Maddox's drawing-room? Jack's heart was light as he walked by Anna's side into it; his eyes full of laughter. These men, all the men he knew in the city, in fact, were such a cordial lot of good fellows! sensible, practical, attaching too much importance to money, perhaps, but ready to help on with any useful work of science or knowledge; charitable, too, and supporters of churches and asylums. Ned Willitts, for instance; why, that featherheaded fellow had a heart as easily moved as a girl's by a fine poem, or a touching song, or a tale of suffering. And then there were the women—with their beauty and tenderness, as if God had sent them purposely to help a poor striving fellow back to Him.

He paused by the door, holding it open for Anna to pass through. She halted one moment uncertainly, and then motioned to a servant:

"You did not take wine with me, Mr. Andross," smiling, the glass in her outstretched hand. "We must drink to your reëlection."

Jack held it carelessly, watching her with kindling face. "I care very little about my reëlection. I shall have no trouble in finding work out of Harrisburgh."

"The toast ought to take a wider range, then, Miss Maddox," said Ned. "Your success, Andross; you can't refuse that."

"No," draining his glass. "To my success."

Anna blushed shyly as she took his arm, having caught the look with which he gave the word significance.

"I wish I could think wine or anything else would help me to speedier success," whispered Jack, as she leaned upon his arm. "But you are so far removed from me now."

"You must act differently," eagerly. "You must keep your position if we hope to marry at all. Papa is a prosaic, practical man, as I have told you before. And to keep it, you must be more friendly with the leading men of your party; join their parties—play cards—drink with them. You are not afraid to do it?"

"Why, who has been filling your little head with politics?" laughing. "As to those men, they know me, and what I am worth, tolerably well. I am no hero in their eyes as in yours," softly; "and as for drinking, of course, I'm not afraid. I never cared for liquor in any shape, and never shall. It is rather disagreeable than otherwise. Tobacco is the fatal temptation to me."

Yet at the time he felt strangely warmed and heartened, whether by the wine or the fervour of Anna's repeated soft glances he could not tell.

CHAPTER XVII.

WHEN Andross left the judge's house that evening, he saw a man crossing one of the squares, and waited under a lamp for him to come up.

"It looks like Braddock; but it can't be the old fellow, surely?" he muttered anxiously. Braddock had been for the last three months in Washington, which had prevented their meeting. This man was just off a journey, carried his satchel in his hand; but where was the immaculate broadcloth, the glossy shirt-cuffs, the high hat by which Clay was wont to be known afar off to all men? Andross noted the stooped shoulders, the worn coat, the general air of shabbiness and depression. The change startled and touched him so sharply that he stood still instead of hurrying forward.

"What trouble can he have had? What can he have done?" He always had thought of Clay, with his firmness and virtue, as one of the people who jog safely along a straight but pleasant path from the baptismal font to the gate of Heaven; very much with the unutterable envy with which the prodigal come back from feeding the swine, regarded the elder brother who never had left home or respectability behind him. Yet there was something of the hungry and disreputable air of the prodigal in Braddock now.

Perhaps nothing could have made it plainer to himself that he was "going down hill" than the scuffed trousers and unblackened boots; but it would have been hard for him to explain what was the trouble. He had been barely able to earn bread and butter in the city, was one thing. When the time came for him to dispatch his weekly remittance to his mother, he had more than once been driven to a pawn-shop to obtain it. In Washington it was worse. One young fellow after another said to him, "There's no room for patient, honest effort in a city. You must have capital, or influence, or cheek, which is better than either. Money-making is a great game of grab, and a modest man stands no chance. Look at Fisk or Tweed, in New York, or——," naming two or three Philadelphians, whose liveried and gold-mounted equipages dazzled the street. "Did they achieve success by modest industry?"

He could not but remember that he had put Laird's influence and his own little capital away from him for the best motives; and where was his reward? The wicked were exalted and the righteous man cast down. Clay, standing with his empty pocket at the street corners while these carriages flung mud from their wheels in his face, was tried by the old problem which thousands of years ago vexed David. And what chance had he to marry now?

As for Andross, he heard of him as rich and prosperous; a touch from Laird's sceptre had opened every way to him. Now although Braddock had carefully hidden from Jack the sacrifice he made for him, he was galled that he did not know it, and angry at his ingratitude. He had heard in Washington this morning that he was to marry Anna Maddox, and had come on purposely to stop it. It was a righteous errand, and justified the Sabbath travel, he told himself. It was his own fault if this marriage took place. His mawkish feeling for Andross had kept him silent—made him shelter him when he should have warned Judge Maddox against him as a thief. It was not yet too late. The innocent child could yet be saved. He would be silent not a day longer.

And under all this disappointment and bitterness and
rage there was another feeling at the remembrance of the
innocent child, which gnawed at Braddock's conscience,
and made him more wretched than them all.

It was in this mood, hurrying to deliver himself of his
message, that, looking up as he came under the lamp, he
faced Andross.

"Braddock?" He caught him both hands on the
shoulders. "Have you been ill? Don't you know me,
Clay?"

The light shone full on the erect, gallant figure, the
fine, sensitive face. There was a peculiar warmth, a
gayety about Andross in these his happiest days which
stirred even passers-by into momentary cordiality and
cheerfulness. Braddock resented it; he resented the upright, prosperous bearing of the man; the very rose in
his button-hole, the anxious, alarmed scrutiny of himself,
which seemed to assert their friendship on its old footing.

"No. I have been quite well," settling his hat on his
head and forcing a civil smile. "I ought to have known
you, Andross. You are not altered."

"I did not know you were coming up," he went on
eagerly; "I asked Miss Latimer to-day when you would
be at home, but she did not expect you."

"No;" with the old mannerism which Jack remembered he had used to others. "Since I was obliged to
postpone our marriage I have not written to her as regularly as I ought. My resolve to come up to-night was
sudden, prompted by some news that I heard."

"Where are you going now, Clay?" walking beside
him and holding his arm as an affectionate school-boy
might.

"To Judge Maddox's."

"I came from there just now. The house is closed by
this time. Come to my room. You can see them to-
morrow, but I must be gone by the early train. Come."

Braddock went.   There was something in the manner and touch of the man which he could not resist.   He walked slowly, angry at himself for yielding to the old unaccountable influence.

Andross talked on, too excited and eager to be conscious of the chilly reserve.   There was nobody, not even Anna, who came as near to the headlong fellow as Braddock.   Other men were his friends, but a brother might have done to him what Clay had done.

"Were you sorry to leave old Nittany? And how does it go in Washington? Miss Latimer tells me she thinks you have been successful there."

"I have succeeded as much as I had a right to expect, probably," coldly.

"Every time I came up from Harrisburgh I hoped to find you here.   I wrote, you know, but you did not answer.   I knew you were too busy; don't think I minded that, old fellow."   They walked on in silence for a square, when Jack broke in : "It's odd, Braddock, but whenever I think of you, it is as you looked to me that day out by the coaling hearth, you remember? My going there was a mad freak, and yet to go back seemed madness, and when you, a gentleman, spoke to me, half naked and covered with ashes, as your equal, it was like a voice calling me out of the pit.   You remember you bought clothes for me at Bellefonte, and took me straight into the office.   No man ever trusted another as blindly as you did me."   He was so much moved that he did not notice Braddock's unbroken silence.

They stopped at a modest little house on a narrow street.   Andross opened the door, and led the doctor up to a small room plainly furnished.   An open fire was the only sign of comfort.   "Come in," cried Jack heartily.   "This is my boarding-house while I'm in town.   It's clean, at at events.   Put your feet up to the fire," wielding the poker vigorously.

Braddock looked curiously about him. "I certainly expected to find you in more luxurious quarters. I thought you were on the high road to fortune?"

"Not precisely," carelessly. "The salary's fair enough, but I'm sailing close to the wind, you see. By George, I turn a penny over twice now, before I spend it."

"May I ask why?" standing eagerly before him. "You are going to marry soon?"

"No. It's not for that," colouring, and beating a tattoo on the bars of the grate. "It's a debt that I want to pay. Six thousand dollars. It was a terrible criminal piece of business—God forbid you should know anything about it, Clay. I've had the weight of it to carry until sometimes I thought I never could rise under it. But, God willing, I'll clear it off by spring."

The doctor, shabby and thin, stood looking down at him for a minute. "Stop rattling that poker, Jack," he said, laying his hand on his shoulder. "You behave like a school-boy."

Something in the touch of the hand made Andross look up, and the two men laughed.

"Why, I forgot. You've had nothing to eat!" cried Andross jumping up. "I'm as hungry myself as a Nittany wolf. I was at Judge Maddox's for dinner, but I never can eat in that house." He had thrown off his coat, and was hurrying from the table to a little closet. "Pull off your boots—there are slippers. We'll have supper in no time. I board myself, you see. Oh! I'm a model miser, Clay," fastening a wire stand over the gas-burner, from which presently came a whiff of stewing oysters and coffee. Dr. Braddock put on the slippers and toasted his feet before the fire with an odd sense of comfort and good fellowship which he had almost forgotten was in the world. It was not possible for him to show affection by words and glances like Andross, any more than he could have laid aside his dignity to stew oysters in his shirt sleeves. But the man who could took his heart and fancy by storm.

"You said it would have been madness in you to go back from the coalings to Laird and the Ring again. Yet you have gone back, Andross?"

"Yes, I have," sitting down beside him while the cooking went on by itself. "Laird offered to put me into Sheffield's place—you know how two or three men here controul the election. When I accepted his offer that night at the furnace I felt as if I had sold my soul to the devil."

"Yet you did it?"

"Yes, and like the first man, for a woman," with an attempt to laugh. "I was mad, I suppose. But I am not cured of the madness," going uneasily about the room to hide his agitation. "I supposed," after a pause, "that I would be the tool of Laird and his clique. But as yet I have been wholly untrammelled. I have voted and spoken in the Senate in every case out of my honest conviction, in the best service of the party—*not* the Ring. They have not once interfered with me."

"It is an unusual result," said Braddock drily, "that the yielding to temptation should help you on the way both to honesty and success. My experience has been different."

"Yes. I don't know how it is. I'm tempted to think sometimes there is not such a strict watch kept over us above after all. It really seems as if there was no devil nor special—Providence ; just a lot of fellows struggling together to get ahead of each other. God knows, Braddock, I have yielded—sunk about as low as a man could. Yet here I have the chance to win back my own self-respect—to be a rich man, honestly, and to marry some day the only woman I ever loved," his fine face heating again.

"You mean Miss Maddox, of course !" with such

marked reserve in his manner that Jack became more anxiously cordial. "Yes, I think there is no doubt of the judge's consent if I am reëlected. There are three or four men madly in love with her : Bislow and Hoar, the diamond dealer. Hoar has enormous wealth and is well preserved in spite of his age. But the judge would prefer me, provided, as I said, I go back to the Senate."

"And Anna?"

"Oh, I have no doubt of Anna !"

Doctor Braddock turned in his chair and scanned his face ; his own curiously haggard at the moment. But Jack's countenance was so bright and genuine ; the man himself, affectionate and hopeful, looked out of it so frankly that Braddock turned away. How could he tell him that his errand to-night was to take this woman from him by proclaiming him a criminal ? He clasped his hands behind his head again, and leaned back in his chair.

"You were born for success, Andross."

"It looks like it now ! It really looks like it ! Come Braddock, come ; supper is ready."

About midnight, Andross left Braddock in his room and started to take the one o'clock train. The doctor stood at the door of the little house and watched him go whistling down the street, his springy step ringing on the pavement; the policeman touched his hat and wished him good night, cheerfully; the driver of the street-car woke up and brightened into a human being as he jumped aboard with a hearty, Hillo !

But the charm was off of Braddock when his back was turned. "Uncertain as water, thou shall not excel," he muttered.

Jack at the same moment was summing up his own future. "When I am clear of this cursed theft, I'm safe," he thought. "No danger that I should ever slip again. I'll be successful, as he says, and deserve success."

CHAPTER XVIII.

DOCTOR Braddock called on Miss Maddox before finding Colonel Latimer's the next morning. He told himself the reason for this was that the house lay directly in his way; yet he despised himself for the lie, as he did it.

Anna, when his card was brought to her, was especially in need of the soothing influence of friendship: love, she felt this morning, was harassing beyond endurance. If she had to begin manœuvring for Andross as a lover now, to keep him up to a decent grade of salary and society, what would she not have had to do had they been married? Had he not invited her once to a blissful union to be founded on honesty and twenty dollars a week? In the vexation caused by such blind pig-headedness, the advent of Doctor Braddock, who regarded her as a bewitching saint, was opportune and refreshing: she hurried down to meet him.

Outside, the sky was thick with fog, a heavy rain falling; streets and pavement deep with mud; the jarring of carts and cars, the patter of rain on umbrellas the only sounds heard; inside, the gay little room was filled with flowers, birds sang, a delicate Italian grayhound slept on a Turkish rug before the sparkling fire, and Anna, in white, her fair hair flowing about her shoulders, was the personification of summer. Doctor Braddock had but little imagination; but that small share was taken captive by the scene and the actor. He was guarded to dulness in his manner, however, through his fear of betraying Andross's secret, which he knew she already suspected, and perhaps from some deeper reason. But the morning was too wet for her to go out or to expect visitors, and the stiff, pale man in his unfashionable suit of black, and green necktie, on the other side of the fireplace, was the only support offered for Anna's clinging nature.   Scuffed trousers and green necktie were trifling drawbacks compared to the stupidity which would make a man fly in the face of his salary.

She did not propose, however, to confide this individual grief to her friend. She gave him very clearly the general idea of her lonely and isolated condition in the fashionable crowd ; of her homesickness for the mountains ; he penetrated to the depths of her nature, he thought with delight, as one would look into a clear forest spring—she all unconscious of his gaze. She was Maud Muller—without the desire to be the Judge's bride, decked in silken gown. Then she concerned herself gently for his well-being ; was sure his feet were damp ; ran to feel his overcoat as an anxious mother might, brought him a cup of hot coffee "to take the chill off," and stood, her innocent eyes upturned to his, holding the saucer while he drank it.

A mother ? *A wife.*

And Andross, with all other good fortune, was to have this lovely creature to wait on him, to be waited on, cherished, held in his arms.

"You are chilly—you are so deathly pale ! Will you have some more ?" drawing back in unfeigned fright.

"No, thank you. I saw Andross last night, Miss Maddox," forcing a smile. "Faithful to his allegiance still ?"

Unmistakable sadness clouded her fair brow. She was silent a moment, and then her confidence ebbed slowly forth. Her father and Mr. Andross looked upon their marriage as a certainty : she herself felt as though she were tangled in a net which drew her in more closely every day. Mr. Andross was a dear friend to her, he was a dear friend to everybody. "But, oh ! Doctor Braddock," her head sinking on her breast, "there is something in him that I dread ! He is in some points totally alien from me !"

"Ah! I believe that, Miss Maddox. And yet Jack is a loyal friend, and he would be a most faithful husband."

"I know by your voice you are forcing yourself to say that!" without looking up. "You know he is a grown-up child, and so am I. I ought to have a stronger guide than he is. I have fancied that when I married——"

Doctor Braddock set down the cup. Why should he not listen to her innocent talk? She was but a spoiled child, as she said. "What was your dream of a lover or husband then?" with an awkward laugh.

"I hardly can put it into words," gazing with absent eyes into the fire, while the tall figure in black stood stiffly before her. "A man strong in principle and piety. Yes, of all things, principle would be first in my eyes."

"You would respect such a man; but would you love him?" Doctor Braddock passed his forefinger over his mouth once or twice after he had spoken; a most ungainly, stupid gesture, but some motion must break the intense strain which he had put upon himself. The rain pattered hard upon the pane, the cat purred and turned sleepily over, but Anna was silent. Her fingers pressed closer on each other until the delicate tips sunk into the pink flesh.

"Love and friendship," the doctor's harsh voice broke the silence, "are such different things. You—you could not love such a man?"

She suddenly raised her dovelike eyes to his, a fiery red dyed her face and neck and bosom; she started up and shyly began twisting the dried fern leaves in the vases.

Braddock made a hasty step towards her, and then dropped into a chair by the table, covering his eyes with his hand. What fight he fought with himself in that minute no one ever knew but himself and God. He stood up again angular and stiff, wiping his pale face with his handkerchief; "precisely," as Anna told herself, "like a Presbyterian elder beginning an exhortation."

BRADDOCK'S MENTAL ANGUISH.

"Your idea of what married life should be coincides with mine, Miss Maddox," he said formally; "I chose a wife whose principle of actiou is higher than—than mine. God help me!" with a sudden break, "I love her very truly. I respect her too as I do no other human being," emphatically, and talking as Anna well knew, to himself.

"Ah! but we can not all deserve her happiness!" with a tearful smile. "There are few Bell Latimers among womankind!"

The magnanimity of the lovely child! How she struggled against her pain lest she might trouble him; struggled against—could it be? her love for him?

Again a sudden silence fell upon the room, the dreary beat of the rain again grew audible. For one rapt moment Doctor Braddock saw only the mellow tinting of a delicate cheek turned from him, across which a bit of fair hair had fallen; then he began to pull on his worn gloves, took up his hat, and muttering he knew not what, stumbled out of the room and the house.

"The awkward wretch!" said Anna, "he almost fell into my jardinière. His feet are such scows—like coal barges. To think me in love with him—of all the conceited——" But seeing at that moment his umbrella pass the window, with his stern, thin face under it, and realizing how much more picturesque it was than Jack's merry phiz, and that he was gone from her forever, she sat down and dribbled out some of her ever-ready tears.

A few minutes later, Doctor Braddock, seated in Andross's room, without taking off his overcoat, wrote the following letter:

"Dear Isabel: It is with the most thorough trust in your love for me that I ask you to prove it. There is no need of our waiting longer for more money on which to marry. You do not care for it, and God knows I have need of that which no wealth can buy just now, but which you may give me." He stopped, dipped his pen

in the ink once or twice, conscious that he had strayed
from the main subject into one which it was not easy to
pursue further.   Doctor Braddock was suffering from
none of the mental agony expressed by cold sweats, pallor,
etc., common to Anna's imagined heroes; he felt as if
he had been struck a blow from which he would never
recover; the feeling he had for Anna was so different
from any he had known that he fancied it deeper and
truer; but was he not playing the Christian hero by con-
quering it?   He had never felt better satisfied with himself than as he wrote "Dear Isabel" upon the blank
page, and his self-respect and complacency increased
with every word.   He ended by asking her to set their
marriage-day a week hence; he would come up from
Washington on Wednesday morning, and the wedding
could take place that evening; begging in conclusion
that it might be as quiet as possible; and was always hers
sincerely, H. Clay Braddock.

Was he not hers?   He thought, as he directed the envelope, his whole life would be given to her service, and
she never should be troubled by knowing that he might
have married a woman of such different mould.   For
there was the difference between them of fine porcelain
and plain Delft.   He was very fond of Isabel, and would
give her the homely, domestic love which her homelier
nature craved.   So resolving, he put the letter in his
pocket-book, to be mailed at Washington, and started to
catch the southern train; wretched enough at resigning
Anna, but with a comfortable enjoyment of his own mar-
tyrdom.

CHAPTER XIX.

"I DON'T see, Colonel Latimer, what we can do to them if they pay the tax. It's only a trick to throw me off the watch, but they certainly have been ordered to pay it on every gallon since Wilkins's arrest, though it hasn't been done, as yet."

Colonel Latimer, at one side of his office table, sat watching the speaker, who stood at the other—a broad, fat man with a queer cast in one of his eyes and a stubbly crop of iron-gray hair and whisker.

"These distilleries, you tell me, are those in which Houston Laird owns a share ?"

"He is the principal owner, sir."

"Then I have no doubt, Bowyer, he has been apprised of this rascality, and ordered a stop to be put to it ; so that it is no trick, but a permanent reform. You'll have no further trouble, Bowyer. Laird is a man whose orders must be obeyed. I know him. I know how outraged he would be by such villany under his name."

"I don't know him," rejoined Bowyer bluntly. "But them that do, say Wilkins is the honester man of the two."

"You make a mistake in repeating that to me," said the colonel with peculiar mildness. "Mr. Laird is my friend and a gentleman."

Bowyer took off his hat. He had forgotten before that it was on his head. "In case, sir, however," he said in a subdued tone, "that I find Wilkins and the others are at their old practices, I'm to close in on them without consulting Mr. Laird ?"

"Certainly. Why, I tell you, Laird will be as hearty as any man in the town in his approval of your energy. It's a personal stigma on himself, d'ye see ? The fact is, he

went into the distilling business from good motives—
mistaken, but good."

Bowyer bowed, fixing on his employer the puzzled,
amused scrutiny with which he often favored him.

"I shall not be able to come down to the office to-morrow," said the colonel rising. "I have left schedules
for Joseph to fill. We have a wedding up at the house,"
colouring as though it were his own. "My daughter
marries. A gentleman from Washington."

"I hope he is good enough for her," energetically.
Bowyer had a Westerner's disregard of social distinction.
"Sudden, is it not, Colonel?"

"It has been a long time under consideration," turning
the key in his desk. "Now I trust to you, Bowyer, to
keep a sharp lookout on Wilkins and his confederates. I
wish we could change work for awhile. You're hardly
fit to deal with those fellows; it's a sheep among foxes.
They'd never deceive *me*. I know the ways of them."

Bowyer came down the stairs after him gravely; but
at the bottom met one of his aids and winked to him to
wait. "Houston Laird is pulling the wool over the old
man's eyes. He'll have no more trouble about it than if
he were a baby. I mean to play my own game after this.
Laird will find he has met his match. I'd feel as if I'd
done one good job in my life, if I could have a wrastle
with that tremendous humbug, and throw him."

His deputy said nothing. Nick Bowyer's honesty was
all very well; nobody ever had doubted that or his pluck
either; but what was your honesty or your pluck against
Laird's money? "Millions!" gasped the fellow, thrusting his hands deeper into his pockets.

Colonel Latimer hurried home. His house was on one of
the quiet side streets; a large, many-windowed dwelling,
set in an ample garden, which gave to the passers-by the
idea of comfort and a home. It had a wide reputation
already as one of the pleasantest houses in the city in

which to visit. The Latimers were originally from Virginia, and descendants of the Fairfaxes and Pages had started from all corners of the city to claim cousinship with them; old army officers gathered about the colonel; Andross had brought his friends, artists, a few well-born and bred women, and three or four gray-haired old gentlemen, who adopted Bell, after one visit, and transferred their chess-playing and musty-flavored gossips about dead Shippens and Duanes, from the Athenæum and Historical Society to her quiet library. The young girl lacked the beauty of the belles of their youth, they thought; but she had a simple high-breeding which had belonged to them. It brought back the days of their love and gallantry, as did the faint perfume which hung about the long empty flagons on their dressing-tables. The artists laughed with her at her designs; the women declared to her she followed the fashion of two years before. She had no especial wit or wisdom or ability on which to hang a compliment, yet her house was besieged every day, and all who came were friends. Of all houses it was the most hospitable; guests dropped in at breakfast, dinner, supper—the colonel and Bell coming and going with the rest; Oth presiding loftily downstairs, the meals well or ill served as it happened. By and by a certain peculiarity developed itself in the majority of the guests; people came there who went nowhere else. Lonely old people, morbid young ones, everybody whose life was stinted and bare, coming once into the warm, sunny, disorderly house, and having once shaken Bell's large, healthy hand, came again and constantly. Andross called the house a moral pool of Bethesda, and came himself, as often as he could leave Anna, to be cured. A certain cousin Arabella Morgan had established kinship with the Latimers a few weeks ago. Out of sheer pity for them, she gave up her rooms in her respectable boarding-house, and came on a winter's visit. Her arrival was immediately followed by the rebellion of every servant in the house; but Cousin Arabella had by this time conquered a peace.

Bell, as usual, was waiting that afternoon for her father, by the church. "I did not think you would come for me to-day, sweetheart," touching her hand slightly as she took his arm. Neither of them would say to the other that it was the last day she could come. The Latimers seldom expressed feeling that was deep.

"Cousin Arabella," laughing, "was outraged at such a breach of decorum. I ought to have been in-doors for a week, she says. There she comes! These are happy days for her; she finds so many loose ends, as she calls them, to tie up."

"She ties them a little too tight," said the colonel, shrugging his bony shoulders. "I wish we could have had our walk alone. But she is a kind soul," smiling and bowing as the little plump woman bustled up, her jetty fringes and little bobs of glossy ringlets and cheap purple feather shaking and dangling together.

"My dear Bell, it is not usual for a young girl to be rampaging the streets at such a time. Heaven knows I scorn etiquette; the Morgans are well known as the only family among old Philadelphians who can dare to be Bohemian, and that is solely owing to their literary achievements. *I* can set society at defiance. But it is a very different case with you."

A man muffled in an overcoat came quickly up abreast with them at the moment. "I beg your pardon," nodding, "but can you give me the time?"

Colonel Latimer stopped, and, with anxious courtesy, took out a ponderous old watch. "Just six o'clock, my friend."

"Thank you; I'm making a train." The man had eyed the colonel eagerly from head to foot; his build, carriage, height, while he stood in front of him; he hastily turned now, and disappeared down an alley.

"I hope the poor fellow won't be late," said the colonel, looking after him. "He seems to be laboring under some excitement."

"That fellow had no train to make," snapped Cousin Arabella, shaking her head. "He followed you for two squares, walking slowly. I saw him as I came to meet you. He had some sinister purpose, Colonel Latimer. He has the worst eyes I ever saw."

"Tut, tut! It was the milkman that you suspected of being a heavy villain yesterday, wasn't it? There are not half the burglars and rogues in the world that you good people suspect, Cousin Arabella!"

"But this man I know to be a rogue!" triumphantly. "I knew I had seen him before. It was down at Cape May last summer, and when an excursion came down, Brother Ben told me to come out, and see some of the worst roughs in the city. I declare to you, Bell, they were in broad-cloth, the latest fashion; this man's wife wore a brocade silk flounced to the waist, and a white Rabagas bonnet and rubies; yes, I assure you, rubies, a full set—on that creature—and very fine stones they were, for I made Ben take me past her to be sure about them. And this fellow—what was his name now?—Ben said was the ringleader of all the ruffians in town; just out of the penitentiary, where he had been sent for burglary, and curiously enough, Colonel, it was either your friend, Mr. Andross or Laird, who got him out. They called him Laird's protégé. Voss—yes, that was the name, Voss. Now, what grudge can the fellow have against you?"

"Mr. Laird's position draws that kind of idle slander upon him," gravely. "As for me, set your mind at rest. I haven't an enemy in the world."

They walked on in silence. Bell and her father forgot

the incident the next moment; the coming day weighed heavily on the old man, and Bell knew it. But Cousin Arabella fell a step behind, and eyed the colonel with a vague notion of keeping watch over him. She had a presentiment of danger; and the Morgans' presentiments were by no means to be despised. They had dabbled in spiritualism, mesmerism, etc., with gloves on, as one might say, and, according to Cousin Arabella, had acquired thereby a sense beyond the legal five.

She intercepted the colonel as they entered the house, and drew him aside to the library.

"Now here's the paper of 'day's duties,'" drawing it out. "You know I always make one out every morning, and tick off each as it is done. You'd find such a system invaluable in your business, Colonel."

"I don't doubt it."

"First, Bell's clothes. Of course a proper trousseau is a hopeless matter with a week's notice, but everything essential is in now but stockings, and as for bonnets—"

"That will all come right. I really wish to talk to Isabel——"

"About the supper? Oh! that's all arranged. I have the bill of fare regularly made out. But what I wanted to speak to you about was the guests. Half a hundred people will feel hurt if you neglect them."

"I'd like to have them all—everybody I know," and the colonel's hospitable soul heaved a sigh. "But, you know, Dr. Braddock especially requested a private wedding."

"That is the point. *Why* did he suggest it? Heaven forbid I should suggest an unworthy doubt, but the young man's course is exceedingly suspicious. I love Isabel, Colonel," her florid face growing redder—"the child has no mother, and you know so little of the ways of the world——"

The colonel bowed laughing.

"Oh! it's true! Why, everybody down to rats and

beggars were devouring your income till I came. You're no more fitted to take care of yourselves than the babes in the wood. It behooves me to keep a sharp eye about me, and I've fixed it on Dr. Braddock. This marrying at a week's notice—none of the Morgans would risk offending public opinion to that extent, much as they trampled on conventionality. Such haste and secrecy! It looks as if he were afraid. What story was that Judge Maddox told about a missing six thousand dollars?"

"Braddock referred to that most satisfactorily in a letter which I received to-day. He had lent the money to a friend, and was in hopes it would soon be returned."

Miss Morgan began to untie her bonnet strings with a jerk.

"Of course it's all right! I've no wish to wrong the young man. I have never even seen him. I've no right to exact more for your daughter than you do; but the present generation of men make love and marry in a free and easy manner—throw the handkerchief I might say, in a way unknown to our days, Colonel. Bell, foolish child, in her joy at his letter, showed it to me. *I* thought it arrogant; taking it for granted she was waiting, with all her spring dresses made, for the sign to marry him! I should never have consented without time to send for a proper veil, at least."

"You did not consider that the letter showed proper affection for Bell?" anxiously. "I thought the young man was deeply moved. Clay is not demonstrative."

"Moved by something else than love for Bell," nodding shrewdly. "I have given you warning. You ought to make inquiry as to his habits; to keep a sharp watch on him if they are married."

"Where the Latimers trust, they trust wholly," the colonel said quietly. "I can not give my daughter to a man as his wife one day, and follow him like a policeman the next."

CHAPTER XX.

THE southern train halted in the Philadelphia depot the next morning long enough for an erect, prim man to step off, which he did, deliberately. It was Braddock, who, as we know, in his normal condition, was a cheerful, business-like fellow; but now he looked about him as if ready to offer to the sun or wind or even the freight-master a cowed, miserable apology for cumbering the earth. He had been talking to himself all night, recounting his generosity toward Andross, his honourable dealing with Bell, assuring himself that he loved her—loved her purely, tenderly as he did his mother, the mountains where he was born, his religion—that his passion for Anna was a mad, unclean frenzy.

But all would not do. He felt dishonoured in every drop of his blood; he had no relish for his mother or the mountains or domestic bliss just then; he had not drunk the cup of passion, and he wanted to do it; he was the Prodigal, forced back to the tedious elder brother and insipid fatted calf before he had tasted of the riotous living, or proved how bitter were the husks which the swine did eat. All night, Anna, her cloying amiabilities, looks, and gestures that had brought her beauty close to him, the very tones of her shrill voice, had been present with him, clung about him, stifled him like a delicious nightmare.

Outside of the car the keen wind of dawn woke him from his passionate torpor; the night mists yet lay on the river and shipping as he crossed the bridge; the wind blew in his face, full of gusts of glistening frost; he passed down the vacant street through stately rows of silent dwellings, their brown stone carvings greened and softened by the winter's damp. In daylight this street always taunted Braddock with his poverty; it was aggres-

THEY FLUTTERED FEARLESSLY ALL ABOUT HER.   SHE AND THEY SEEM-
ED TO BELONG TO THE BRIGHT, PURE MORNING.

sive with wealth. Now there was nothing in it but noble form, and the beauty of the coming day. The bare trees of Rittenhouse square lengthened in the shadows into interminable aisles with black, high, fine-lined arches; where he had been used to plough through dust, lay the white sheet of untrodden snow; where liveried carriages had wheeled mud in his face only the mist rolled, full of golden light. There was but a solitary figure in the distance, a lady, tall and slight, and of singularly noble carriage. She had stopped below the trees near the hundreds of sparrows which were pecking the grain that some kindly soul had sprinkled on the snow. They fluttered fearlessly all about her. She and they seemed to belong to the bright, pure morning, Braddock thought, in his heated fancy, and when she came up to him out of the golden mist, he thought so still. Surely in all these multitudes of people there was not another face so clear or happy. It succeeded Anna's as did the morning air to the hot atmosphere of the car. He hurried to her.

"It is you, Bell! What are you doing here?"

"I came to meet you, Clay," holding out her hands. "Are you not glad to see me?" after a waiting moment.

"Certainly; how can you ask such a question? Only I did not expect to meet you here," with a grave hint of rebuke in his voice. "Is it usual——? What will people say?"

"How can I tell?" laughing softly. "I know that I am here."

He drew her hand in his arm. When he did not speak of his errand, she began to talk—to cover her shy happiness.

"See the birds, Clay—how hungry and tame they are! They were brought from England for these trees. They are not our great Nittany trees. But look at them how they glitter in the frost."

"I can only look at you!" energetically. "You are a woman that I never knew!"

"I can not have changed so much in four months," hastily.

Miss Latimer had her own feeling about love; how that it was a fine, subtle kinship; how that no change of body, even the going to another world, could touch it. Yet here was her lover criticising her precisely as a stranger would! She knew that every thought of a true wife and husband were known to each other, their very souls became as one; yet now her husband stood apart as though totally alien to her, with a half alarmed inspection of her face, her very dress. But Bell never had yet put her theories or her love into words for Braddock; she walked on in almost unbroken silence, often replying to him only in a sudden, sweet little laugh, which meant far more than words, and was, like her dress and her look, new and startling to him.

When they reached the house she ran up the steps before him, throwing back the fur hood as she looked down. "I hoped that perhaps you would ask me to go wandering about all day in search of adventures; there are such queer solitary places about Philadelphia; and then all our lives we could say, we went here or there on our wedding journey; and in the evening we would have come in and been married. I should have liked that! But now there will be veils and supper and trunks instead!"

"You always had a drop of vagabond blood that I lacked, Isabel," smiling with a good deal of his old fondness down on her. But at heart he regarded her with something very different from that humdrum affection; a surprise and alarm which drove the thought of Anna away for the moment. This was not the Isabel he used to know; something about her impressed him as a fine strain of music does a man who is not educated to understand it, or a wide landscape one whose eye would grasp it all, but can not.

"You, at least, I thought, belonged to me," following her into her sewing-room.

She seated him in her own chair; the fire blazed on the hearth; the morning light shone in at his back; his feet rested on the bear skin she had brought from Nittany. There he was at last, her household god, her own private and particular joss, safe from any other woman's worship than her own!

For how many years had she prayed for him every morning, blushing, though she did not utter his name! There was no need for her now to blush; this morning her Master had answered her prayers. But Isabel, like other big-natured people, had no petty coquetry of lids and lips; there was no way to guess at the deep delight of the loyal creature except the kindling of her slow fine face. She stood off at the other side of the fire-place, not looking at him.

"There is one thing I ought to confess to you, Clay," a laugh trembling about her mouth. "I doubted you, once. It seems absurd to me now. Just like a child!"

"You heard some story about money?" frowning.

"Yes, but that was nonsense, of course. My trouble was about Anna. I absolutely hated the poor little creature. I was so long alone, and you wrote so seldom. I know you had not time," eagerly.

Braddock stood up. "Miss Maddox is nothing to us now, Isabel."

"I knew that when your letter came," gravely.

But it never entered into his head to go into the confessional, and never would.

There were no tea-roses in this room, no canaries nor faint perfume; only the big fire burning briskly, and the fresh daylight and the woman with an unfamiliar fine face standing apart from him. If he could get out of this fog that was about him back to the daylight and Bell again!

He went across the bear skin presently, and took her
hand. "I have been but a dull lover, Isabel."

"I did not think that, Clay." At his first touch a
soft warmth reddened her firm flesh.

There was a knock at the door. Oth came in, a pre-
ternatural solemnity struggling to overcome his delighted
grin at sight of " de bride and groom."

"Doctor Braddock, sah—yes, sah. I'se quite well;
town agrees wid me fuss-rate—it's a telegram foh you,
sah."

He tore it open. " *Come to me at once. A great danger threatens me which you can avert.—A.*"

"Is it bad news? is it from your mother, Clay?"
watching him as he refolded the paper and slowly put it
in his pocket.

"It is—a poor woman who is in trouble which she
thinks I can help. I can not go to her. This is the day
on which I came to marry you."

"How far would you have to go?" asked practical Bell.

"Only a few squares. Do not speak of it again."

He took her hand again mechanically; but there was a
strained unwonted look in his eyes that startled her.
"If the poor creature needs you, go to her, Clay. I can
spare you for an hour or two, as you are going to be mine
all of your life," smiling.

"I shall not go," almost fiercely. "I am here now.
What do you drive me away for? This is our wedding-
day. I think you are mad to drive me from you."

Poor Clay! No doubt, she thought, he was nervous
from overwork and loss of sleep. "Very well," she said,
cheerfully. "We will hope that she exaggerates her need
of you. Only do not look so anxious about her."

"She is not a woman who exaggerates; I know what
I can do for her, but my place is here."

He might sacrifice himself, but Bell should not wrong
the little creature who loved him so hopelessly.

"COME TO ME AT ONCE. A GREAT DANGER THREATENS ME WHICH
YOU CAN AVERT.—A."

Another knock.   Oth again at the door.

"A lady, sah, to speak with you.   Won't leave de carriage, sah."

Doctor Braddock followed him hastily to the street, where a close, shabby hack stood before the door.   In five minutes he came into the room again, labouring under some uncontroulled excitement.

"She is there.   I must go, Isabel," stopping short on the other side of the hearth.   "There is danger—of—danger——"

"Danger of what?"

"Oh! God knows.   It is all a horrible—horrible muddle."   He held his clasped hands up to his mouth, and stared at her irresolutely over them, then turned suddenly to the door.

"When will you be back, Clay?   In an hour?"

"Yes, in an hour," vacantly; "but why should I go at all?   What can I do?"   He went out without a word or look of good-bye.

Poor Clay! thought Isabel again.   Never was there so sensitive a nature; the grief of this poor creature, whoever she might be, had made him half crazed, as though it were his own.   She rang the bell, and ordered Oth to keep back the breakfast for an hour.   Doctor Braddock had been called away by sudden business.   When they were married, she would stand between him and such appeals—so she went on with her revery—and take the brunt of pain from him.   As she sat alone for the next hour looking in the wood fire, she smiled once or twice to herself, thinking how jealous she would have been a few months ago if any woman had so carried off her lover.   She had outgrown such notions since she came to town, and had been drawn out of her shell, as Miss Morgan often put it; adding that a change of food and air was as wholesome for the brain as the digestive organs.

Breakfast was served and eaten.

"I thought," said Cousin Arabella, marvellous in the freshness of purple ribbons and jet fringes, "that Doctor Braddock, probably, would have been here on the early train."

"Bless me, I forgot the lad!" cried the colonel; "He'll be here by noon, all right!" He talked so fast and energetically of a dozen things at once, that Bell had no room for explanation.

The baggage must be ready for expressage by five, as they would go through this tomfoolery of a wedding journey; the old Virginia customs were best, etc., etc., his eyes fixed on Bell, with a quiet sadness and hunger, oddly belying his jerky, impatient sentences, which often ended half spoken. He was losing Bell. Baggage or wedding journey or Braddock himself were mere surface trifles in the colonel's brain compared to that. When the noon train was in and Doctor Braddock did not appear, however, he became, as usual, immeasurably anxious and restless, and coming bustling in to console Isabel, was amazed to find her composedly mending his old coat, her cheeks unusually rosy, and eyes clear.

"I knew Cousin Arabella would forget it, and you would miss it before I came back," snipping off the threads.

"Thank you, my dear. I'm exceedingly anxious about Clay, Bell. The train has been in for an hour. I'm going to telegraph."

"Clay is a more impetuous lover than you think," with a shy smile, telling her story as she folded up the coat, and ending with, "Now I shall go and dress, so that we can all be together when he comes." She pleased herself with thinking how impatient he would be with the poor creature, and her grief which detained him. What other man would make such a noble sacrifice on his wedding-day? If the Women's Club, whose president

Mr. Ware had introduced to her, only knew Clay Braddock, they would hold very different opinions on the marriage question, and the proper authority of a husband over a wife !

The day had proved rainy, the golden mists going down into clammy fog that clung to the outside of Isabel's window, as she bathed and made herself fair for her lover; nothing could be heard but the dull patter of the rain on the panes, and the jingle of car bells, and tramp of the horses in the muddy street.

Miss Morgan bustled in. "Well, well! Here's four o'clock. The supper's all arranged, and the carriage ready to go for Dr. Croly. Why, Bell, how bright and sweet your room is, and you——" surveying her from head to foot at arm's length. The little old maid had a mother's heart in her bosom; she put her hands softly on Bell's head and drew it to her breast. "There, I'll leave the kiss for your husband. I'll not take it."

She went out, moved in spite of herself. She could not utter a word of her suspicions of Braddock, or her wrath at the disrespect implied in his delay, or the other thousand remarks with which she effervesced; she was usually a little afraid of Bell, as a woman of stronger brain and better culture than her own; but the girl to-day, in her simplicity and happy faith in her lover, was so like an innocent child, so different from shrewd city women, that Miss Morgan had not the heart to hurt her.

She went down to the parlours and supper-room, already lighted and filled with flowers, and there hid her rage.

An hour later, Oth, the delighted grin quite gone from his mouth, and his wrinkled face under the gray hair as grave as his master's, tapped softly at the door of the room, where Colonel Latimer sat waiting for Isabel. She came in by another door, as she heard the knock.

"Has he come?" glancing from one to the other.

The old man lifted both hands. "De Lohd bless de

chile! When I used to ride de little gull on my knee to Babylon, neber tought to see dat lubly face and de bride's dress, all train and lace!"

The colonel, whom Miss Morgan had driven to dress in his full uniform, stood up straightening his cuffs. "I thought you came to say Doctor Braddock had arrived."

"No, sah," lowering his voice and carefully closing the door. "Fact is, when I saw de lady in de car'age dis mornin' I mistrusted somefin. She was veiled, but I knowed her. It was Miss Maddox, and *I* neber put no stock in dat ar, sah." He turned his back to his young mistress, with a delicate wish not to see her face, and went on hurriedly. "Dis af't'noon I escaped from Miss Arabel's sight and I goes down to Judge Maddox's, and dey tells me dar dat Doctor Braddock wid Miss Anna took the noon train to Harrisburgh. De judge am out of town too, an' not to be back until to-morrow."

"Doctor Braddock left a message?" said the colonel.

"No, sah. I inquired particular, but dah was none."

"He has telegraphed, and it has been delayed at the office. You can go, Oth, I'm very much obliged to you, my good fellow," said the colonel quietly. He had no intention of subjecting his daughter to the pity of even this old servant. When the door closed again he took her in his arms: "You've come back to me again, child; that is all."

CHAPTER XXI.

MISS MADDOX had not ventured on her errand to Dr. Braddock alone, or without premeditation. The judge had had his usual whist party the night before. Anna had chosen to set up her work-table in the corner of the room, where she could listen to the political discussions which interrupted the game, toy with her silks and crewels, or grow confidential with the two or three men lounging about her, at her pleasure. When the cards were thrown aside and the voices about the table grew more eager and repressed, she got up, fluttered over to her father, and perched herself, blushes, lace, tags of ribbon and all, on the elbow of his chair. M. de Millé, the French journalist whom Ware had in charge that evening, hastily rose and would have led her to the piano.

"They talk but of affairs," he earnestly assured her; whereat Anna shook her head saucily, and sat still. Her whim that evening was to understand these very "affairs"; as she had already heard Andross's name once or twice in the discussion.

"There is no staving off the bill later than to-morrow evening," said General Ralston, tapping with the pack of cards on the table to mark his words: "and do what you will, the vote on it will be, if not a tie, the closest this session. One vote will probably win or lose it."

"Mr. Laird knows that," remarked Ware, drawing out his thick beard through his hand admiringly. "He has had Ned Willitts up there lobbying for a week."

"It behooves him to lobby," said the general. "If the bill is lost, Laird's great Transit scheme will shrivel up like a bladder that has been pricked. He ought to have drilled the tools of his Ring better than he has that fellow Andross, before he allowed his fortune to hinge on their votes on a single measure."

"He can do as he pleases with his own money; but he had no right to drag other men into such a hobble," said Judge Maddox. Something in the judge's tone made the other men look at him, and then glance significantly at each other. He had been noticeably quiet all evening; his usual leaky dribble of talk having ebbed down into an occasional curt, snappish sentence. They noticed that

his daughter, too, sitting poised like a pet bird beside
him, turned quickly at his words, with an odd change on
her pretty face, and put her hand on his. The rumour
was true, then, that Maddox had risked all he had in this
scheme of Laird's, and would in all probability be ruined
by the non-passage of the bill?

There was an awkward silence for a moment, which
nobody was able to break with tact, when, to the astonishment of M. de Millé, at least, the bird-like little girl
began to chirp.

"If I understand this tiresome talk, you all want a
bill or an act or something to pass to-morrow night?"
looking at General Ralston.

He nodded gruffly.

"And one vote will count for a good deal? I think *I*
can manage it for you; ah, papa?" putting her arm
about his neck.

General Ralston threw down the cards impatiently. "I
would not encourage my child in that style of talking,
Maddox. We've enough of it from petticoated brokers
and reformers. You ought to have sense enough to keep
your little head steady on your waltzes and dresses, Anna.
A woman's strength lies in her feminity."

"Nevertheless, I shall pass the bill for you, General,
while you sit growling at home," clapping her hands and
laughing like a baby. "Be good enough to ring for me,
monsieur;" and when the servant appeared at the door:
"Order a hack to be at the door by seven o'clock to-morrow
morning," she said, with a sharp little nod of command.
"No, papa, my own carriage would *not* do; this is a
particularly private business of mine. We will have some
music now, if you choose, Monsieur de Millé;" and in a
moment she was rattling over the keys in a fashion
which made Ware—who had a sensitive ear—shiver.

M. de Millé left the house with him soon after. "But
your American women take the breath from me every

day !" he exclaimed. "In France this young lady would be with the good sisters, learning the music or bead-work, and here she sets out alone to cajole the state Chambers !"

"Not so bad as that," said Ware uneasily. "She has one or two lovers there whose votes she may influence."

"Ah ? I understood from the Judge Maddox that his daughter was, as you say, betrothed to that Monsieur Bislow ; a man of large estate, as I heard. It appeared to me a very suitable marriage. The young lady could expect wealth ; she has a good dot, they tell me, and, without doubt, great beauty."

Ware's usual fluency had deserted him ; he made no reply.

"Probably you do not recall this, Monsieur Bislow ? A fat man, with the hair quite gray."

"I know the fellow well enough. He is old enough to be her father."

"So much the better," lifting his eyebrows. "He will be the better guardian. Madame Bislow shall not hire the hack and go away to cajole the Chambers, that I will bet with you, if you please. But these things are not incroyable to us of Paris, monsieur. We know the American ladies. Why, one, I shall not say her name, finds her husband unable to yield the support to her, and she buys of a poor Berliner the patent for an engine which he invents, sells it again for sums enormous to the city governments in France, England, here, to use in the water works. Young—a mere child, monsieur ! With cheeks like the rose ! Peddles her engines here—there ! Talks ? Ah ! *mon Dieu !* how she talks ! how they all talk !"

But Ware made no defence of his countrywomen ; they had reached a street corner, and he bade the garrulous Frenchman a curt good-night, and turned off uncivilly enough. The case was clear to M. de Millé ! Ware was one of the victims of this insatiate little huntress, whose game was man. She might have spared this poor wretch, he thought, with an amused smile; empty pockets were hard enough to bear without an aching heart.

Ware was in reality so much discomposed by some chance word of de Millé's, that he went back to Judge Maddox's, and entering the hall abruptly, caught sight of Anna sitting in a shaded corner, blushing and sweet, with all the weight of Mr. Bislow's ponderous and amorous regards upou her. Mr. Ware walked directly to her side, and stood there in the attitude, and with the gravity of a footman. Oddly enough, Miss Maddox did not flutter into one of her pretty vixenish passions at this marked rudeness, but became suddenly speechless and motionless, with an expression on her face of a much older woman than she had ever seemed before. It startled Mr. Bislow as much as the advent of the very uncivil young man at his back, and as he was a man who carefully shunned both emotions or uncivility, he rose and took leave of Anna; the leave-taking being no less impressive or affectionate for Ware's presence.

Ware, who was in one of the dumb rages which his fellow-workmen in the blacksmith shop used to dread, did not break the ominous silence, and Anna, for the first time in her life, was apparently ill at ease, and insecure of her pecking, chirping self. She fidgeted on the sofa, pulled at her lace sleeves, glanced up at him timidly.

"Mr. Bislow was remonstrating with me about my bringing votes for that bill: such a wise, fatherly old man as he is! The principal idea I used to have of him was, Fat. Yes, indeed," giggling, "but when one is intimate with him, his good qualities come out. Internal qualities, I mean. I really never think now how much he weighs."

"I was told just now that your father had promised you should marry him."

Anna made no answer; the colour went slowly out of her little pinched face, her mouth stood weakly open as she looked up at him. Whatever secret hold or power the man had over her, he was not moved, apparently, to relax it, by any pity or sympathy.

"I believe in my soul you are sincere in your feeling for that mass of flesh," scanning her coolly. "I used to think you were only a clever little actress, when you led a dozen men to believe you were in love with each one of them. But you mean it; you are like an oyster. You cling to the first solid substance that touches you. And you are just as bloodless and as cold."

Still no hint of resentment from her; her red lips opened and shut once or twice, irresolutely, before she spoke.

"Then you don't think as Mr. Bislow does of my trying to pass that bill?"

"The bill! I'd be very glad if the bill was passed. I have some shares in the National Transit myself. But what can you do? Wheedle that poor fool, Andross?"

The very tone of Ware's voice, coarse and direct, was so different from the caressing softness with which all men addressed Anna, that it attracted curious glances from the other side of the room. She looked up at him scared, imploring, trying to don again her poor little tricks of archness and coquetry.

"No, no, I will have nothing to do with poor Jack. I have a better plan than that: I will bring Doctor Braddock to work upon him. Braddock makes up the larger half of Andross's religion. Oh! it's a very complete plan I have, I assure you!" nodding complacently.

"You can do nothing with Braddock," he growled. "He's to be married to-morrow."

"I know that!" Her whole face and figure dilated and glowed radiant. "I mean to bring him here to do as I wish, if he has been married but an hour! That log of a woman shall see what power I have, silly child as she calls me! You, too!——" rising with a feeble little cackle of defiance. "There are men who would not hold me in this miserable bondage, even if they had the power. They serve me as slaves—they are glad of one kind look. They do not guess what I am!" The always ready tears stood in the beautiful eyes, but Ware was unmoved, stroking, as usual, his curly red beard.

"Are you tired of your bondage?" he said quietly.

"No, Julius; oh! no," with a half sob. She put her hand on his arm, and led him to the farther room, where they walked up and down talking earnestly.

Miss Maddox had usually an affectionate manner, more pleasing to her companion of the instant than to the envious lookers on; but it was observed that her attitude toward Ware to-night was unusually clinging and vine-like; in fact, General Ralston commented to the judge on the familiar footing which the young journalist had obtained in the house.

"I know little about the fellow," the judge replied gruffly, shaking off a moody fit. "Anna admires his courage, I believe, in this last move of his. He has given up his profession and taken to preaching. Some New Light of his own—Spiritualism, Broad Church, Ritualism, I don't know what. He goes about from town to town, and is having great success, Nannie tells me. Come out, Ralston, and have a bite of supper," with a sigh from the depths of his fat paunch. "There's some comfort left in well-cooked terrapin, however the bill may go."

CHAPTER XXII.

WHEN the hack drove to the door for Anna, the next morning, the servant handed her a note. It was mysterious and melo-dramatic enough to tingle her small soul with delight.

"My own, you are at liberty to carry out your plans to-day, as you choose; remembering only that a day of reckoning will come, and that before long, and for every misstep, you will be held strictly to account."

It was without signature.

But neither Anna's soul nor body tingled with delight. She read it over again and again, and then tore it up, leaning back against the shabby, ill-smelling cushions, with a sick and miserable look of uncertainty.

The stoppage of the carriage at Colonel Latimer's door, and the sight of Dr. Braddock's agitated face at the door, however, roused her as the first view of the audience does an exhausted actor.

"Yes, it is I," she sobbed excitedly, leaning forwards. "I must not keep you a moment. I know it is your wedding-day. But we are in such imminent peril——"

The predominant feeling with Braddock was that the great temptation of his life was before him; he summoned all his Scotch-Irish grit to resist it; a quality which certainly does not dispose its possessor to suavity of manner.

"It is my wedding-day; but if I can serve you, Miss Maddox, I am ready to do so," bowing stiffly.

"A word from you will serve—serve to save me from a fate worse than death!" her imagination kindling with the words. "But it is such a long, miserable story," glancing distractedly around the awakening street, with the curious glances of the passing milkmen and bakers on each side.

Braddock hesitated a moment, then he opened the hack-door. "Drive slowly around the square," he said to the coachman, and then sprang in. "Now tell me this miserable story, you poor child!" he said, and, in spite of himself, his voice softened. But he did not take the place beside her, and sat upright on the opposite seat, his gloved hands resting on his knees.

Anna's story, in brief, was simply the fact that her father's whole fortune was involved in Laird's scheme, and dependent on the passage of the bill that night at Harrisburgh. "If it is lost we are penniless," she added. "Will you use your influence with Andross to vote for it?"

"It is a question of money then? How can I ask Mr. Andross to vote against his conviction? Men have convictions and a conscience in these matters, Miss Maddox;" and after a pause, "I did not suppose it was for a mere matter of money you brought me here."

For money just now seemed to economical Braddock the vile dross that church phraseology held it to be. He had always been in the habit of believing that long ago he had withstood the powers of darkness in a mysterious, secret conflict, and made his calling and election sure forever. But during the last five minutes, sitting opposite to this woman, who tempted his flesh so sorely, striving to keep his thoughts on the woman whom he had loved in his best days, it seemed to him as if he were going through the old fight again, in another more actual fashion. Jack Andross, in his profane way, had talked of real living devils who fought you in commonplace matters hand to hand——

But Braddock's soul told him that he was impregnable. Very different from poor Jack! The more his narrow imagination kindled into a strange delight and heat with Anna's every look, the more stiff and harsh became his manner. This was the buckling on of armour which should save him. But he felt as if the living man was being crushed under it.

"I am sorry if your father will lose any of his income. But the loss of money is a small matter, and easily borne —easily borne. There are other temptations that weigh heavily beside it."

"It weighs very little with me," rejoined Anna, with a certain tone of desperate calmness, which unconsciously impressed him more than her wonted tears could have done. "My father—you know him, Doctor Braddock— would be a most miserable poor man. But I——"

"How can it affect you?" leaning forward and as suddenly drawing himself back. "You have too many friends, child. Poverty will never come near you. You do not need *me*."

"It affects me in this way," with the same air of cold restraint. "My father is largely in debt to but one man. If he is not pressed by him for payment, he can have time to recover, even if this bill fails to pass."

"The man is a friend of Judge Maddox, probably. If the matter was stated to him fairly——"

"He is more," hastily, her face dyed with blushes. "He is a friend of mine—my father intends that he shall marry me."

Braddock started, and then smiled. "Such things never happen in real life. Cruel parents do not sell their daughters to save themselves from ruin, except in magazine and Ledger novels, and Judge Maddox is the last man to play such a rôle. You have let your fears deceive you."

"I think not," quietly. "I have given you all the facts. Mr. Bislow is the creditor. My father has never influenced me to accept him. But I know that if I refuse to marry him, he will push his claim at once; as my husband he would never push it. If this bill passes to-night, papa could set him at defiance. But if it is lost

——I promised to give Mr. Bislow my answer to-morrow." She stopped.

"And you will marry him to save your father?" in a tone of wondering homage. Common-sense and judgment fled. That pale, lovely face in its dark hood opposite him, was capable of any heroic sacrifice. So Jephthah's daughter looked, he thought, dying for her sire. Nor was his enthusiasm the less because he was too shrewd a man not to see the folly of such sacrifice. Bislow, no doubt, had been secured by mortgage or good names, on the paper, before he had disbursed a penny to Maddox. But what did this foolish, romantic child know of securities or mortgages? Her head, he knew, had been so stuffed with fiction and poetry that this immolation of herself appeared the only natural, feasible means of saving her father, and fond as he was of her, the judge would be but too willing to marry her, under that deception, to a man of Bislow's solid character and income.

He took up one of the little bare hands, which were clasped outside of her cloak, and warmed it between his own. "And for your father's sake, you will give yourself—*yourself* for the whole of your life, remember—to a man whom you do not love?"

"What can I do? What does it matter what becomes of me?" the blue eyes looking wildly up into his. "I never can marry the man I do love."

"You—you mean John Andross?" Braddock's voice was hoarse; he turned his head away from her as he spoke. Her little heart beat and thumped against her delicate tight corset. Here was passion—tragedy in her life at last! There was silence for a moment, then she said:

"No; Mr. Andross is a dear friend to me. There have been times," her upturned face growing grave, "when I fancied he was more. But——I know myself now," with a shy, swift burning glance into his eyes. In fact, the child did fancy that she knew herself now for the first time. Here was her real soul's mate. All men besides this pale, cowed, yet stern man opposite were but as actors in a pantomime. Besides, what fun it was to think of Isabel Latimer, with the pride of a hundred women, waiting for the husband who did not come! He should not come to her—never! The hand he held trembled and struggled to be free, as a heroine's always does at the supreme moment. And much to her surprise Doctor Braddock promptly dropped it, and began fumbling with his dog-skin gloves instead. Assuredly, there was nothing melo-dramatic in the school to which he belonged. Yet the one thought surging through his brain, with a wild exhilarating throb, was—"It is *I* whom she loves! I!" Being, however, preëminently a logical, practical man, he mastered the situation, even in this ecstacy. In her love and despair, this impulsive child would throw herself away to rescue her father. He, Braddock, must be cool, save her, himself—Isabel. Isabel ——, he stopped there with a twinge.

The hack stopped, the driver's head appeared: "Am I to droive around the squoire wance more?"

"No," said Braddock promptly. "To Judge Maddox's. I will set this matter right with your father," he said to Anna. "Ten minutes' rational explanation will be enough. Miss Latimer will spare me so long."

"You know best," in a submissive whisper. She knew that her father had gone to Harrisburgh an hour ago.

There was no matter in these words which required that they should carefully avoid meeting each other's eyes, nor that their voices should be scrupulously formal; yet they were so.

"I have always found," he resumed, "that in the difficult places of life, Miss Maddox, we must take common-sense and duty as our only guides."

Anna's reply was a little sob.

Dr. Braddock straightened the fingers of his glove, and looked steadfastly out of the window. Andross, poor fellow, had suffered his love for this girl to lead him out of the paths of rectitude. How different it was with himself! It was well for Maddox, for himself, for poor Anna in this strait, that he, at least, had a clear head and a trustworthy conscience. By the aid of common-sense and duty he would make her life's path straight before this loving child, and then return to Isabel and strive to forget all that which might have been. His soul was in this heroic mood, and a scrap of poetry running in his head about a "future of work, calm, approving conscience, and a smiling heaven," when an odd thing happened.

They drove past an old shop full of queer, second-hand furniture. A year ago he and Isabel, wandering about town in her idle, vagabondizing way, had passed the place, and he, stopping her at the open door, had chosen prettily carved bits of furniture for their house that was to be, a book-case for the parlour, a lounge for the cozery. How proud and glad, into his very heart, he had been to see the warm, bright blushes creeping into her cheek! He had gone back, time after time, just as he could save the money, to buy one piece after another, and had stored them away to surprise Bell some day after they were married. Could he be the same man as the happy, embarrassed fellow who drove those bargains with the Ridge-road dealer? That was the true Braddock, a real man, loving and hating heartily, who had stood chaffering there; this was a weak, morbid fool in the hack, not fighting a real temptation, but paltering with a sham passion, as one who stands doubting on the brink of a sickly tepid bath. For one brief moment Braddock saw himself with clear eyes. Andross loved this woman; but did he? He knew he did not. In the next moment he

might waken from this unhealthy dream. But the next
moment they stopped in front of Judge Maddox's door,
and Anna chose to alight alone and walk in unassisted,
but trembling visibly. The little creature was frail, indeed! sent into the world to be supported, protected;
yet, with what a noble moral strength she had put him
aside! though she felt he should have been that pro-
tector! He hurried after her; all his self-confidence returned. Truly, he thought, caressing his thin whiskers,
this was a difficult part given to him to play!

Miss Maddox having penetrated into the house, came
back to meet him.

"We are too late! My father has gone to Harrisburgh! Mr. Andross will vote against the bill. It is all
over—all over!" she ejaculated in broken sentences, leaning against the wall. "Go, Doctor Braddock. Leave
me to my fate. You have been very kind," she added
faintly, the lids closed on the white cheeks.

"I begged of you, Miss Maddox, to leave this matter
to me," he said, pacing up and down the hall. "I will
bring order out of confusion. You shall not marry Bislow."

She shuddered, her eyes still closed.

Braddock stopped, looked at her, and choked back an
oath.

"Everything is bartered for money in this accursed
town! But, God willing, you shall not be!"

"If this bill could pass, all would go well," she murmured, half unclosing her eyes.

"Bill? What is the bill? A subsidy, or grant, or
some kind of privilege to the Transit Company, is it not?
Why does not Andross vote for it? I don't see what
moral question can be involved in it! If he knew what
results hung upon his vote, surely——"

"But how *can* he know? Who is there to state the
whole case plainly to him?"

"I will write. I can put the matter so forcibly that,

if his conscience is not opposed to it ——. If I may
ring for pen and ink ——"

Anna did not move.

"It is very uncertain whether a letter could reach him
in time. The bill may be put upon its passage this afternoon. Besides," with a shiver, "it is hard to think of
my story being put into a cold, written statement. Do
forgive me. I'm a foolish, spoiled child, I know."

"No, it is not foolish. I understand you. But what
am I to do?" He paused irresolute, then drew out his
watch hurriedly, and rang the bell. "Bring me a paper
with the time-table to Harrisburgh," to the servant.
Anna had sunk upon a chair; a faint rose flush was stealing into her cheek as she watched him glance over the
paper. "I find that a train leaves in half an hour. I
can run up and be back by five o'clock."

"And leave Isabel all day? Never! For me, too?
Oh, no. Leave me. I shall be always alone. What
does it matter for me?"

"It matters this much: that I will at least ensure
your safety from this wretched marriage!" vehemently.
"I can leave Miss Latimer alone for a few hours, surely,
for that. So much of my life, at least, I may devote to
you. But I will telegraph to her why I am absent."

He sat down and hurriedly wrote a message. When it
was finished, and he was about to summon the servant
again, she held out her hand.

"Give it to me. I will have it sent up at once to the
house. Dear Bell! she will be so glad to help me!" and
hurried out to read the paper, crumple it in her little
hand, and deposit it, with a shrug, in her pocket.

When she came back a moment afterwards, she had
changed her cloak and hood for a most becoming travelling suit and hat.

"You are not —— ?" hesitated Braddock.

"Going with you? Oh, yes, indeed. I, too, may

have some influence with Mr. Andross," with a sad, be-witching smile.

Braddock would have argued, but he remembered the ride up the mountain by night. Argument, he had reason to know, never deterred this yielding creature one inch in the road which she had made up her mind to take. He followed her in silence, with a countenance by no means heroic, but ill-tempered and harassed in the extreme. What would people say, who saw who was his companion on this, that was to have been his wedding journey? When they were seated, Anna's pleading little face was turned to him wistfully, all its sweet, passionate meanings ready for him to trace. A sudden glow of heat passed through him at the glance, but he put his head out of the hack window, instead of returning it.

"To the Pennsylvania Central depot," he said, and then leaned back, grimly silent.

----•♦•----

CHAPTER XXIII.

THE train to Harrisburgh had scarcely passed out of the city limits on to the flat, cheerful farm-lands of Chester county, when Braddock was sensible of a sudden uneasiness on the part of his companion. She had made one or two efforts to draw him into a whispered colloquy, but in vain; the jolting of the cars, the dust from the engine, the momentary attacks of news and gum-drop boys were all antagonistic to any expression of that relation of suppressed affinity, which it is to be supposed they held to each other. Braddock felt that the clatter about them would render it necessary to shout out in her ear his tender sympathy, if he spoke it at all; such shouting would rob the emotion, for him, of its bloom and charm. Anna, most probably, would rather have heard it through an ear-trumpet, than not at all. Souls such as hers exist but on supplies of sympathy from hour to hour; and they are the ones most likely to receive it.

Finding it impossible, therefore, to broach any but commonplace subjects, Anna had sunk into silence at his side, and beguiled the time with studying the face of the conductor—a most picturesque face, in her opinion, and one which indicated a peculiar heart-history. But presently Braddock observed that she sat erect, her breath came hurriedly, and she turned her face steadily to the window.

"What is wrong?" he asked.

In fact, he was beginning to tire of this perpetual emotion of one sort or another; he felt like a theatrical walking gentleman going incessantly out of one second-rate tragedy into another. There was a certain comfort, after all, in Bell's large, easy, sunny-tempered ways.

"Nothing is wrong," said Anna sharply. "Are you afraid of being followed and watched? Why should anybody watch us?"

She had not turned her head, or she would have seen Mr. Ware, who had lounged up the car as though he had just bought it, and now stood beside them, portly, smiling, assertant, from his flowing red mane to his glossy patent-leather shoes.

"Ah! Going to Harrisburgh, Doctor?" throwing himself easily into the seat in front of them. "Good morning, Miss Maddox. I did not recognize you at first."

"I have some business with the legislature," said Braddock, in haste to render account of his proceedings to anybody, "and am taking Miss Maddox to her father."

Ware nodded indifferently, gathering up his flowing neckerchief in his hand, and looking at it.

"If you stay over to-night, Doctor, come down to the town-hall. I hold forth there."

"I am going back on the next train. You speak on the crisis?" forcing himself to be polite. "I did not know you meant to take the stump this campaign."

"No," said Ware gravely; "I have given up politics entirely. When one considers with any attention the Infinite Forces of Good and Evil contending for humanity——"

"You mean God and the devil?" said Braddock, who had a habit of interrupting.

"You may put it in that way, if you choose. *I* call it old-fashioned and narrow. But when one considers these Forces, all questions of municipal reform, the tariff, etc., appear very petty; very petty, sir."

"Y—es." Braddock was confused at being hoisted so suddenly into such lofty regions of thought. "But I supposed the tariff and such matters were the especial business of you newspaper men?"

"I've done with newspapers." Ware's voice filled the car; and as soon as people began to lay down their papers and listen, it rose and rolled with fine emphasis. "I thought you knew I had given up the disjointed thinking of journalism, as Dr. Rush called it, and had ranged myself among the moral teachers of mankind."

"Gone into the ministry?"

Braddock perceived at the moment the close attention which Anna gave to every word of Ware's, although she kept her head turned from him.

"I certainly have *not* entered the ministry. Priests, Protestant, and Catholic, sir, are the incubi upon humanity. I look on them as barnacles that clog the progress of the—the vessel. Disposing of the water of life for filthy lucre. I belong to no sect, Doctor Braddock. I have gathered about me a band of like-minded men with myself—free, progressive thinkers—and we meet in an upper hall, like the disciples of old. I pray and preach for them. They think I have a little gift that way."

Braddock was galled with impatience, but it was necessary to keep Ware's curiosity and attention away from himself and his errand.

"You are the founder of the sect, then?" he said. "I—I hope they pay you a good salary?"

"None at all!" triumphantly. "I have had calls to three Broad churches—very broad—where the salary was large and assured. But I told them, 'No, gentlemen; the truth is not to be sold. I receive no wages—not a penny!' I would not go!"

"Very praiseworthy, indeed. You propose to work at some trade or business, and give your services to the Lord. Just as St. Paul made sails——"

"I think it very questionable whether St. Paul did anything of the sort," testily. "No, sir. I shall not henceforth labour at all. I have higher work. I have been called to pray and preach, and for the means of livelihood I throw myself upon the unfailing Love in the bosoms of mankind. I throw all care to the winds and live sure of support from day to day, like the lilies of the field—the birds of the air——"

"But I really don't understand——"

"I simply live a life of faith, like Jung Stilling. I receive such gifts as the faithful send."

"Taking care that it is known you are ready to receive them," said Braddock, laughing.

"It *is* known. So far, I have wanted for nothing. One sends me a board bill paid in advance, and at a good hotel—very good; another a dozen of fine handkerchiefs —each according to his ability. Now, this suit—notice the quality—that came only last week from a Chestnut street house—receipted bill. Oh, I have no fear; a life of faith is the surest life."

"Now, that might answer for a single man," said a shrewd-eyed Jersey farmer who had been listening. "But how about your wife? How does she meet the

butcher's and grocer's bills at the end of the week? How
do they appreciate this talk of lilies and birds?"

"If I had a wife," said Ware loftily, "she should at
the outset devote herself to some ennobling pursuit and
effort for humanity, like myself—the teaching of the
Freedmen, say, or civilizing friendless children. That
one great thought would blot out lesser matters, such as
occupy other women. Butchers' and grocers' bills!"
with a contemptuous wave of his hand. "You agree
with me, I am sure, Miss Maddox?" turning suddenly
on her.

"Oh, entirely!"

Ware nodded triumphantly, and rising, sauntered down
the car.

"You do not actually endorse that fellow's crazy pro-
jects?" Braddock said, turning to her.

"Crazy! They seem to me the fruit of a very noble
enthusiasm," she replied.

The doctor looked at her keenly. There was a strange
tartness in her dove-like cooings at times. But what
could it matter to him what her feelings were to Ware or
to any man? She could be nothing to him. He sank
back, looking moodily out of the window, and the silence
remained unbroken until they reached Harrisburgh.

———◦◦◦———

CHAPTER XXIV.

"I WILL leave you in a room at the hotel, and send
your father to you, Miss Maddox, while I find
Andross," said Braddock as they left the cars.

"And if you can not find papa?" looking about the
unfamiliar streets with the timid eyes of a hunted doe.

"He is up at the capitol, no doubt," soothingly. He
bestowed her safely in the hotel, holding her trembling

hand tenderly one moment at parting. What manner of man would have the care of this poor, clinging woman for life? Only to hold her in his arms one moment! to protect—— Then he clapped on his hat, and left her without a word. The truth was, the charm in Anna was in this matter of protection. Isabel was so healthily tough and sensible, was either stupidly blind to trouble or else joked it so resolutely aside, that Braddock never had found anything about her over which to play champion. He looked at his watch; he had but an hour. He almost ran through the streets up to the capitol; nodding hastily to such acquaintances as he met. They did not know what an heroic fellow he was; which of them would do the like? Which of them would give up this queen of women, if she loved him, to keep his word of honour?

Into the lobby rooms, the restaurant, the senate chamber, with its dirty floor and gaudy frescoing; but no sign of Andross, nor even of Judge Maddox. As he was leaning over the gallery partition, anxiously scanning again the senators' seats, Wilson, a lumber dealer from Lock Haven, tapped him on the shoulder. "Looking for Andross, Clay? That young man has had a lucky boost out of your furnace into this room. Why had you no friends at court?"

"I make my own way. I do want John, immediately. Do you know where he is?"

"Gone out, Maddox told me, to dine with some friend in the country; the judge did not say where. He had urgent business with Jack, too, and had hired a sleigh to follow him. Jack's not in any difficulty, eh?" curiously.

"No. You do not know when they will be back?"

"I haven't the slightest idea; but if I can be of any assistance——"

"No, no."

"Your errand is of too delicate a nature to bear any

interference," broke in a rich, rolling voice behind, and the doctor turning, met Ware, coolly looking over his shoulder at the men below. "At least I infer it must be so, when it brings you here in company with a pretty girl, whom you are *not* going to marry, on your wedding-day."

"On your wedding-day, Clay?" asked Wilson eagerly. "Miss Latimer?——"

Braddock bowed.

The old man lifted his hat from his gray hair.

"I hope you deserve her, my lad. If she had been a man she would have been like her father. I can't say more for her than that. But what are you scouting about the country at this time of day for? and with a woman, did you say?"

"It is a matter of delicacy, as Mr. Ware said, and one which will not bear even his interference," said Braddock irritably.

Ware laughed aloud, and shrugged his broad shoulders as Braddock hurried off, a scowl on his face. It occurred to him for the first time that he might seem to others to be playing a mean and ignoble part, to-day. And old Wilson lifted his hat at the mere mention of Isabel? He laughed with a sudden glow of pleasure. Well, Bell was precisely the kind of woman to command that involuntary sort of homage. The hour was nearly over; he was walking rapidly toward the hotel when he met Anna.

"I fear I must leave you, Miss Maddox. I have not been able to find Andross. I shall leave a letter for him and a message for your father to come to you;——unless you will go back to Philadelphia on the same train that I do?"

"No. *I* will not leave my father, Doctor Braddock, in this crisis of his fortunes. What I can do for him I will do."

"You do not mean that you will marry Bislow? you

can not mean *that?*" What with his brisk run through the cold air, and Wilson's mention of Isabel, matters had put on a hearty, healthy aspect. This possibility had escaped him; it yawned before him with a sudden horror like death.

"What else can be done?" said Anna. "Every help is gone—even you have deserted us —— But go to Isabel, she expects you."

"Yes, I telegraphed her I would be back in the five o'clock train." He took out his watch, looked at Anna, at the engine in the depot, already puffing blue wisps of smoke into the frosty air, up and down the vacant street. When Andross had talked once of being netted in invisible cords, and dragged down into commonplace, every-day evil, how easy it had seemed to escape; there were none of Macintosh's demons to fight. But now——

"Thank God! There is Andross at last!" as a sleigh filled with men dashed past them, going towards the capitol. "I will follow them. I will be in time yet to go back on the five o'clock train. Good bye."

"You are going back to Isabel?" her eyes on his.

"I must go. Oh, dear child! Surely you know——" he broke forth, but what more he would have said she never knew, for at that moment Mr. Julius Ware lounged in his lofty manner into sight around a corner.

"Good bye," she said with sudden admirable self-possession. "Go, and do what you can for us with Andross."

———◦◦———

CHAPTER XXV.

BRADDOCK, directed by a member in the rotunda, hurried to the private committee room, where the friends of the bill had been waiting for Andross. When he reached the door he stopped, looking among the men for him. The short winter's afternoon was nearly over; the dull remaining light fell, in a melancholy fashion, through the bare windows, on the gray plastered walls of the square room, the hacked table in the centre, the gaudy carpet, with an earthen-ware spittoon set here and there. There was a heavy smell of dead tobacco smoke over the whole. It was all dingy and dispiriting; even the groups of men talking earnestly were grave and anxious. But in front of the blazing fire stood Jack, his furred overcoat thrown back, his hat in his hand; gay, flushed, handsome, absorbing all the warmth and light of the room. His eye was more brilliant than usual, his tongue more ready. Braddock guessed, though unjustly, that he had been strengthening himself for the coming struggle with such courage as could be found in champagne.

"There, there; now, boys," waving them off, laughing. "One at a time. But you might as well have left me to eat Shreve's dinner in comfort. It was hardly worth while to bring me here to tell you how I shall vote, when you know it already. Besides, the bill is lost without me by a majority of two."

"No, McElroy and Spinner have come over," cried a dozen voices. "But Waite, who votes with us," added one, "is going to fly the track. So it rests with you, Andross, after all."

Braddock, meanwhile, unnoticed in the confusion, was vainly trying to push through the eager crowd to him.

Jack felt his overcoat getting heavy and threw it off. "So they've deserted me?" with a laughing shrug. "How did you manage it, Willitts?"

"'Pon my word I had nothing to do with it," protested Willitts with an innocent smile, which produced a shout of laughter.

"They do say," interposed a lean, carefully dressed man at the table, who was jotting down something in his

note-book, "that Mrs. Spinner has become violently interested in the rise of Lehigh Valley stock since last
night, and that Willitts here presented McElroy with a
basket of champagne of a rare quality this morning."

"No harm in that, I hope?" drawled Ned. "No,"
said the other, "nor in making it true Green Seal with
a five hundred dollar bill in the wire of each bottle."

Willitts laughed. "Never listen to gossip. Major
McElroy has a costly taste in wines, that's a fact."

"At least, Mr. Willitts," said Andross sternly, "I
hope you did not intend to offer me champagne of that
brand. I am obliged to end the matter abruptly, gentlemen," raising his voice, "but it has been thoroughly
discussed before between us. I am sorry to vote in direct
opposition to my party. But I believe this bill to be a
fraud upon the people of the state for the benefit of a few
rich men. Even with its face meaning it is a dishonest
trick, an attempt to bolster the National Transit Company, bankrupt now for four months; and the snake
hidden under it is, as every one of you well know, the
rider intended to give extraordinary powers to the Whiskey Ring of Philadelphia. If I am annoyed further in
the matter, I shall not only defeat the bill by my vote
to-night, but I will expose fully the real intent of the
Ring, and the Transit Company." He pulled his gloves
off nervously, his eyes half shut, and mouth set. It was
so like Jack, thought Braddock, to pass from his careless
gayety to angry defiance! So like him, too, to exaggerate
the evil purpose of the bill! At this moment Andross
caught sight of him, and hurried eagerly forward.
"Excuse me," nodding to the others. "But I see a
friend who has some personal business with me, no doubt.
Why, Braddock, old fellow," excitedly, "what drove you
among us money changers and thieves? If old Diogenes
should only chance to come along with his lantern to-
day, he'd find at last one honest man in Harrisburgh."

"Tut, tut, Jack!" under his breath, "that's but a poor joke, and a rough one," glancing at the men, who were going slowly out into the hall, but not yet out of hearing.

"Bah, they're used to it. It's a rough place, Clay. We talk of bribes as we would of bread and butter. That Willitts could tell you the price of every man who is in the market, to a dollar. He'll find there's one man he can't buy," tossing his head contemptuously. "But what are you doing here? Anything gone wrong?"

"Yes. Wrong enough to bring me away from Isabel, although this is our wedding-day. It's this bill, Jack. This Transit Company bill." Its connection with any whiskey ring he secretly supposed to be one of Andross's imaginative additions.

"The Transit bill!" with astonishment. "What can you have to do with that, Braddock?"

"Nothing, personally. I should have nothing to do with it on the part of any one else if I could believe it to be as iniquitous a matter as you assert. But your fancy is easily heated, Jack," with an indulgent smile. "I have read over the draft of it, with all its clauses, carefully, and can detect nothing objectionable in it."

"I differ with you. Even in its expressed significance, it is a piece of wholesale swindling. But like one third of the bills passed this session, it is designed to cover another and totally different measure. The important victories of the Ring have been gained in riders, and——"

"I don't understand such matters," impatiently. "But this bill appears to me to be all right. And I came to ask you, Andross, to vote for it."

"*You* came to ask me to vote for it!"

"Not if you have any real conscientious objection," quickly. "Surely you know I would not urge you to a wrong act, Jack! But you do exaggerate ordinary things to yourself so frightfully! I really can see no connection with whiskey in this Transit matter, and if you could vote for the bill it would bring order into a terribly confused business."

He insensibly had fallen into the dogmatic, didactic tone which he ordinarily had used to Jack. With all his success and manly strength and beauty, he was in Braddock's eyes but an overgrown school-boy, full of whims, before his tutor. The bill was honest enough. Surely he was the best judge of that; he could not forget that he was a member of a church, and that poor Jack was —— no matter. But it was certainly presumptuous in Andross to oppose him on moral grounds, especially when he was making such heroic sacrifices to-day.

Meanwhile Andross stood silent. The unnatural heat had gone from his face; he was quite sobered. "I wish you had not asked me to do this thing, Braddock. I've had a hard fight for it; but I did not think I should have to refuse you. May I ask for whom you are acting?"

"For Maddox. I did not intend to tell you, or to compromise the poor child. I thought my request would be enough."

"What child? What do you mean?" coming closer.

"I mean Miss Maddox," without looking at him. "The judge is involved in this Transit Company, besides owing Abel Bislow a large sum. Anna has conceived the idea that the only way to save her father is by marrying the man. Some mortgage or note of hand is due, which Bislow would not press as the judge's son-in-law. Or if this bill passes, the judge is safe. Her account of business matters is very unintelligible, as you may suppose; but I understood enough to show me that between actual pressure and her romantic notions of self-sacrifice, she would, in all probability, marry Bislow if her father loses his fortune with the defeat of this bill. So I left everything to come to you. I thought," meaningly, "you would be as anxious as I to save the young girl from so horrible a fate. But I have laid the matter before you; that's enough. I must go now," drawing out his watch.

"Stop, Braddock," holding him by the shoulder. "You are bewildered, man. Somebody must have been playing a stupendous practical joke on you. I don't know what you mean by this talk of her loving or marrying Bislow."

"I never said she loved him," colouring violently and trying to disengage himself.

"But you think"—it was Jack who was on fire now and breathless—"you think that her father will drive her into this marriage, and she—she, poor child, has appealed to the man she loves for help?"

Braddock saw the mistake that Andross had made. But the poor fellow, he thought, would soon find out that Anna did not care for him; and in the meantime it was not for him to betray the hapless secret of her love for himself.

"I have no time to discuss the matter with you, Andross. I only say to you, vote for the bill if you can. Nothing you can do hereafter will serve her as that one act to-day will do."

He shook himself loose, and without a word further hurried out of the capitol, and down to the depot, just in time to see the express train to Philadelphia steam down through the cut between the hills.

"When will the next train go up?" he inquired of the station master.

"Not until eleven to-night."

Braddock turned and walked down the street, not knowing where he went. The raw air was cutting; his coat was thin; he was hungry, too, although he did not know it. He had failed to meet Isabel, failed in his effort with Andross. He felt himself a most uncomfortable, miserable man; his only consolation being the cer-

tainty that he had done his duty religiously and showed
the gratitude of devotion to the service of a woman who
had thrown away her whole life's love upon him. The
sense of his own heroism grew so strong upon him that
he presently rallied from his depression. He would go
back in the late train. Isabel might be disappointed,
but she would forgive him. The wedding could be cele-
brated to-morrow just as well as to-day. It was curious
that with all this tenderly-nursed passion for Anna, he
never anticipated any other end to his romance than a
marriage with Bell. That was a solid entity in his life,
like bread and meat or decent clothes or church-going,
the absence of which he had never conceived. With the
assurance of his own merit thus strong within him, he
went and ordered a comfortable dinner.

CHAPTER XXVI.

BRADDOCK had scarcely left the committee room,
when Willitts entered it. "Alone here, Andross?
It's so dark I can hardly see you," he called out famil-
iarly.

"Yes," rising from where he sat looking in the fire.
"I'm going up to dinner now. Those fellows brought
me home from Shreve's just as the soup was taken off,
and on a wild goose errand. They had nothing but the
old story to tell, after all."

"I have something else to say, now that we are alone.
No, no, Mr. Andross," lifting his hand deprecatingly.
"I am not going to insult you by putting you on a level
with such men as McElroy. But I only want to ask you
to give a hearing to a friend of yours and mine about this
matter. No man can be so cool and dispassionate as you
in deciding on action, or so little influenced by feeling."

"Yes, I think you're right, Willitts; my judgment and action are usually pretty cool. Well, who's your friend? Though I warn you it's of no use. Doctor Braddock, an old friend of mine, has just been here urging me to change my resolution too. If his reasons were sound I would have yielded. But he's mistaken——" an anxious cloud coming into his face. "It is the most absurd story, he tells, that I ever heard! He's certainly mistaken."

"I don't know Dr. Braddock. It is Judge Maddox who wants to see you now. He followed you to Shreve's, and missed you. Maddox," keenly noting Andross's startled look, "is deeply involved in this Transit business. It is either the passage of the bill or ruin with him."

"So Braddock told me, but I did not credit it. Stay! one moment before you bring him in. Do you know whether it is true that Bislow holds any of the judge's paper?"

"Yes, and a good deal of it, too." Willitts hesitated a moment, and then played a card which he felt to be doubtful. "I suppose you know that Bislow—the old porpoise—would be glad to marry Miss Maddox, and in that case there would be no trouble. But of course she would not consent."

"No," said Andross. But there was a marked change in his manner after that. He had a stunned, bewildered air, moved uneasily and aimlessly about the room, a different man from the ready, gallant fellow who faced the crowd but half an hour ago.

Willitts, drying his dainty boots turn by turn at the fire, watched him with an amused twinkle in his eye. Of all that little witch's victims, John Andross was indubitably the worst hurt, and fancied himself the favoured man, no doubt, he thought complacently, for he was quite certain that if Miss Maddox really had a *ten-*

dresse for any man, that man was Ned Willitts. "I'll tell the judge you're ready to see him; shall I?" he said at last, going to the door.

"Yes, I'll see him."

A moment after Judge Maddox, more portly and redder about the jaws for the town's high-seasoned living, rolled and puffed into the room, not an object, surely, for veneration; but in Jack's eyes it was Anna's father who came, and even Anna's dog was a thing to be regarded with care and solicitude by him. He hastened anxiously to place a chair. "I am sorry you have had to search for me, Judge," he said respectfully.

"Yes. I've had a chase!" blowing and panting more than was necessary, while he tried to determine the proper relation in which Andross and himself could meet. This fellow before him had been his clerk and handyman, a few months ago; now he was a leading politician, a senator, with every chance of putting his hand into the money bags of the Ring when he chose. The average American, however, readily accommodates himself to such metamorphoses as these, and yields homage where homage is due. Besides, the judge never forgot who could or could not be of use to him. There was no trace of familiarity in his manner as he resumed, coughing deferentially. "It's worth a little trouble, however, to find a friend, Mr. Andross. That is, a friend a man can depend on. Like yourself. Huh! I'm out of breath with these plaguy stairs! Well, sir, I came to talk to you about this Transit bill. It's to go on its passage to-night."

"Yes."

"They tell me," again coughing and hesitating, "that you are opposed to it? I was surprised to hear that. Very much surprised! Mr. Laird is your—your friend. What has he got to say about it? He hardly expected you to fly the track in that way."

"You have heard quite right. I have intended to vote against the bill," said Jack gravely.

"Friend or no friend, eh? Well, sir, thanks to this man Laird, whom you can afford to put out of the question, the bulk of my property is in that Transit stock. If the bill fails, my financial credit is not worth that!" filliping his thumb.

"I did not know until to-night that you were involved with the company."

"And if you had known, you would have thought differently about your vote, eh?" eagerly. "That's what you were going to say? I knew you would not fail me! I said to Ralston this morning (Ralston is in it up to the ears), 'Don't be alarmed. I've got a friend at court!'"

The ordinary spasmodic vehemence of Andross's manner was gone; he stood relaxed, his back against the table, and spoke in a dull, quiet voice.

"I had some principle involved in the question. There seemed to me objections to the bill, founded on simple honesty. I have fought against it for weeks for that reason. Though that may seem an unlikely thing for me to do," bitterly.

"Oh, not at all unlikely! It's a very Quixotic thing to do, and very characteristic of John Andross!" betrayed into a momentary tartness. "You always were too chivalric for old-fashioned fogies like myself, you know," with a hasty, cringing smile. "But the chivalry in this case would be to come to the relief of your friends, it appears to me."

If it were only Colonel Latimer, Jack thought as he looked at him, how easy it would be to explain! But although this was Anna's father, he felt it was useless to utter a word in self-defence. The old man sat trotting his foot impatiently, nursing the other leg on his knee, the black beady eyes, which gave cunning to the round, red face, fixed with a slow deliberation on Andross.

"Well," smoothing the oily black mop of hair down over his forehead with an air of sudden determination, "I suppose my errand's done! I may go hunt Ralston, and tell him the game's up. If John Andross is the man to turn his back on an old friend when it's life or death with him, I was mistaken in him. That's all there is to say," rising.

"Stay," lifting his hand to detain him, but not looking up. "I have not said that I would turn my back on you."

The judge sat down again. The defeat of the bill, as he well knew, would not ruin him, but it would cramp him enough to make the matter serious. He had brought all the powers of his brain (a Machiavellian brain, in his own judgment) to bear on this manipulation of Andross. He meant to accommodate himself to the flighty, high-toned notions and language of the fellow, as far as practicable.

"I don't wish to hint," breaking the silence presently, "that I've any claim whatever on you. That's not my way. When I remind a man of an obligation, I cancel it. When I took you into the Works, Mr. Andross, without any reference or introduction but young Braddock's word, I certainly never expected the day would come when I should beg a favour in return of you. I had no ulterior motive in it. I don't bring that into consideration at all."

"I know," interrupted Andross harshly, "what my debt of gratitude is to you. I am not apt to forget a kindness."

Both men were silent again. Once or twice Jack raised his head as if to speak, but when he met the gross, shrewd countenance before him, he shut his mouth more firmly. He burst at last into an angry, feeble laugh.

"Braddock, now, could settle this matter with a word. When he knows what's right, he puts his foot down, and there is the end of it. I don't know why I should be

more unlucky than other men. I never made up my
mind in my life, but a dozen considerations interfered to
pull me this way and that——"

"That's because you've a heart. Braddock's a dry,
sapless sort of a fellow. I'd never expect *him* to be
moved by gratitude or friendship."

Andross walked nervously to the door—back again,
stopped by the table.

"They tell me, Judge, that Bislow holds your paper.
Is he disposed at all to press you ?"

"I don't know who has been so busy in gossiping
about my affairs," irritably. "No, Bislow is not going
to disturb me. He's too anxious to stand well with me
just now," with a significant chuckle. "The truth is,"
his eyes gathering a sudden intelligence, "Bislow wants
something from me worth more than money."

"And you intend to give her to him ?"

"No, sir; no. I can't entertain such an idea as that.
Of course, looked at in a mercenary point of view, it
would be a good match; but——. Well, the truth is,
Jack," with a sudden outburst of frankness, "I know
how the child's fancy turns, and I always meant to in-
dulge it. You and I have talked of this matter before,
and when I came up to see you on this Transit matter
to-day, I really felt as if I were approaching a—a member of my own family. Well, I may as well be frank,
and say—a son."

"I thank you, Judge Maddox." Andross's eyes flashed,
his breath came quickly, the hand he held out burned.
He did not remember that when they talked of the matter but a week or two ago, the judge had undoubtedly
been exceedingly cool about receiving him as a son. It
was not Jack's habit to remember, or to reason.

She was his—at last ! He was conscious now of how
long he had waited for her—how hard the struggle had
been. He held the old man's hand tight clenched a

minute.   It did not occur to him that he ought to say a word more.   The flood of joy swept all thought away.

Judge Maddox was fond of Anna, and had really a warm feeling for Jack.   "Why, why, boy!" looking at his face not ill-pleased, "I did not think you cared for my little Nan in this way! God bless you both, I say. Why, certainly! The wedding can be arranged as soon as you two choose, and we shall all be comfortable together."   Jack would vote for the bill; his own money would be saved, and Laird, being satisfied, would no doubt find a permanent place for Andross, which would make Anna a rich woman for life.   "Yes; we'll all be comfortable," he repeated.   "Well, shall we go down and have some dinner at the Lochiel House? You young fellows can live on raptures, but I must look out for my stomach.   I've been fasting since seven o'clock."

Jack laughed as though the judge's wit were of the finest order; helped him put on his coat, and held his cane while he buttoned it.   The square room, the dull fire, the tobacco-stained carpet, the vacant desk waiting for him in the senate chamber yonder—all had vanished out of the world; instead, the dreams for years which his delicate fancy or warm passion had by turn conjured to make his dull life brighter, were suddenly reality to him: glowing, nearing, ready to be grasped.   He followed the judge mechanically; the old man taking his arm when they reached the lighted rotunda.   Maddox liked to be seen leaning on the arm of the young, popular senator; he scanned the fine mobile face and gallant bearing, and even the well-fitting furred overcoat approvingly.   He would have every reason to be proud of his son-in-law— when Laird should have given him a permanent place.

"You'll come down to town with me to-night?" he whispered confidentially as they passed through the groups in the hall.   "I'll wait until the one A. M. train. They will have voted on the bill before that."

"The bill?" Andross stopped short. He looked at the judge as if awakened from a sleep. "I had forgotten the bill." He stood without speaking so long that Maddox dropped his arm.

"You certainly do not mean to refuse me *now?*"

Andross looked him straight in the face, without answering.

"Ah, you've finished your quarrel?" said Willitts, leaving a group of men, and tripping gaily up to them, "or was it a friendly bargain? How is it with the Transit Company, Andross? 'To be, or not to be?'"

"I'll vote for their bill, of course," said Andross, with a sudden burst of loud heartiness. "I can't turn my back on my friends; can I?"

"Well done! well done, Judge!" whispered Willitts, as he passed them with ill-concealed excitement.

He had no mind that Jack should know how imminent were the issues that hung on his decision. Without a word farther, he hurried off to telegraph to Laird and to the Philadelphia stockholders. As he passed the attentive, waiting crowd that he had just left, he nodded significantly to them. The next moment they had surrounded Andross, joking and congratulating him.

"All the better for us," said one squeaking voice, rising above the din, "that you turned your coat. But the speed with which you turned it—that was re—markable!"

"At least, Mr. McElroy, there was no padding in the lining!" retorted Jack. "That will do, gentlemen," motioning them aside haughtily. "There's no room for congratulations; every other corporation has its hand in the public pocket; why not yours? As for me," turning to the judge, "Jack Andross has his price now, like the rest of them," with a laugh which Maddox felt to be unintentionally discordant and insulting.

CHAPTER XXVII.

BRADDOCK, when he entered the lighted depot to wait for the express train for the West, ran against Ware, who was walking up and down, wrapped in an ample cloak, and in a certain loftiness of purpose so apparent as to attract the admiration of the row of working women inside, ranged against the wall, their satchels at their feet. Every one of them, principally on the basis of his light gloves, set him down as an aristocrat, and eyed him with the good-humoured envy or wrath which the individual penniless American cherishes to that class. Braddock, lean, anxious, shabbily clothed, whose arm Ware took and leaned on in an airy magnificent way, they recognized at once as a poor dependent.

"So you go back successful in your errand, Doctor Braddock?"

"No. Andross gave me no definite promise."

"You know he has promised somebody to vote for the bill?"

"I heard so at the Lochiel House just now. But it was in answer to no solicitations of mine," coldly.

"Of your companion's then. It is all the same."

The doctor noticed now that Ware's thin skin was reddened, and his manner irritated, either with liquor or some suppressed emotion. "I saw Mr. Andross," he continued, "a few moments ago, going into a private parlour of the hotel, where Judge Maddox and his daughter were waiting for him. There was a fine supper ready for them; the young man was to be summoned to the capitol when the bill was called. Probably that young lady's affections were thrown into the scale with whatever bribe was offered him. There's a good deal of speculation to-night as to how he was bought."

"No bribe was offered to him." Braddock stopped and drew off from Ware. "And no manly man," lower-

ing his voice, "would bring Miss Maddox's name into
this discussion. If you knew her you would feel the
grossness of your suspicion."

"Well, no need to be ill-humoured about it. How
should I know the young woman?" with a coarse laugh.
"Ah! here comes Laird's whipper-in, Willitts. A nice
fellow. You ought to make his acquaintance. Something's wrong. He's going to telegraph Laird, I'll wager
you a dollar."

He waited until Willitts came out of the telegraph
office, and then clapped him on the shoulder with a loud,
"How goes it, Ned?"

Willitts shrugged his narrow shoulders. "You've a
playful touch, like the blow of a sledge-hammer. It's
going well enough, or will to-morrow."

"What? How's that?" eagerly. "Postponed?"

"Ford and his party, who oppose the bill, as soon as
they heard Andross had come over, determined to shove
it off until next session. They may talk it down to-
night, perhaps. But it shall go through to-morrow."
He hurried past them.

"He talks as if he had the whip in his hand, and the
dogs yelping about his heels," said Ware. "Did you see
my bills?" pointing to a flaming poster. "*A Life of
Faith. Jung Stilling. Lecture by Julius Ware. With
Songs!* The songs were an idea of my own. They draw,
I find. No charge at the door. People like anything
which costs them nothing. Rev. Catharine Small introduced me, and after the lecture last night she got up and
stated that *I* was the modern Jung Stilling. I never was
so astonished in my life. I felt as if I could sink into
the ground with confusion," pinching and fumbling his
white bull's neck, smilingly. "But these women! One
never knows where to expect them! After that, of
course, came a collection, and a very nice sum it was!"

Braddock bade him a curt good-night, and hurried

down to meet the train, whose bright, red eye of light
he saw approaching through the darkness. He felt an
indescribable nausea for the whole affair—Ware, Maddox, bills and bribes; the very air about him was unclean,
sickening, heavy with the smell of stale tobacco smoke
and decayed fruit. He was out of humour with everybody
but himself.   He, at least, had done his duty nobly; and
he began to be glad that he was going back to clean ways
of dealing, and to Isabel.   After he was aboard of the
train, he tried to bring Anna back as she had seemed to
him lately. Marry whom he might, that gentle womanly
presence must abide with him spiritually, a priceless possession.   But he could not; she somehow made a part of
the sickly, unpleasant whole. He could not separate her
from her atmosphere.

Isabel was a reality; she would recognize the courage
and prudence of his conduct. Isabel had always been
foolishly inclined to make a demi-god out of him; he had
a suppressed conviction that now she would have reason
to do it.

While the train bearing Dr. Braddock to his postponed
nuptials was steaming into the suburbs of Philadelphia,
Colonel Latimer and Miss Morgan were seated at breakfast.   The door opened, and Isabel came quietly in and
took a seat. Miss Morgan, who had not gained admis-
sion to Bell's room all night, was discomfited; it showed
in her wandering eye, in the very knot of her purple
necktie. In all her experience she had never before
passed through the crisis of a wedding deferred by an
unwilling bridegroom. No such supreme disaster had
ever occurred to a Morgan.

"When any calamity *did* happen to a member of my
family, that member of my family never was able to eat
anything whatever," she said emphatically, after declin-
ing an egg and eyeing Isabel with mingled alarm and in-

dignation. "But the Morgans have very acute feelings—very acute. You may see that I am too sensitive for my own good, even now. No, Colonel; no waffles for me. Hand them to Isabel; I have no appetite. After my sister Ann's husband—Mr. Stemson—died (he was a judge of the supreme court of this state, you remember, Colonel), she had the window-shutters hung with black for two years, and Ann herself lived on oatmeal mush for that entire summer. Wholly on oatmeal in different forms! I used to tempt her with sweetbreads and jelly and things; but she would cry: 'Take it away! Leave me to my sorrow.' But if Mr. Stemson had not married her at all—if he had disappeared on the wedding-day—I am sure not even oatmeal——"

"For heaven's sake, Cousin Arabella, don't nag the child any longer!" cried the colonel under his breath, desperate even to incivility. "The miserable morsel she has eaten need not offend your sense of propriety. Can't you see that she is keeping up for my sake?"

"Then don't keep up, Bell, darling. I do see it! There's not the colour of blood in your face. Go to bed at once," fussing and clucking affectionately about her. "There's nothing so unwholesome as keeping up. Besides, it's absolutely indelicate under the circumstances. Go to your room, and I'll bring up a foot-bath and a cup of tea directly.

"I would rather take chocolate now, thank you," said Isabel, pouring out a cup with a steady hand. "Why should I go to bed?" smiling. "I am not ill, nor a widow."

"No, dear child! Would that you were!" shaking her head mournfully. "Heaven knows I care little for the opinion of the world, and yet one can not but reflect ——. The very milkman and baker ask questions. And that censorious Mrs. Lamping——she will assuredly be up before an hour."

Miss Latimer listened, calmly sipping her chocolate, and then touched the bell beside her. "Otho, is the fire burning brightly in the library? Doctor Braddock will be here presently, and I shall see him there. Papa, the flue in that chimney needs repairing. The room is seldom warm enough."

Miss Morgan stared in astonishment. "It is not possible, Colonel Latimer," she said, when the door closed behind Otho, "that you will allow her to meet this man again? Hush, child, this is a matter for your elders. You will treat him as an army officer and a man of honour should do, Thomas?"

"Patience, Arabella, patience!" begged the poor colonel. "I will treat him as a man should a man. My daughter"—he stopped, passing his bony hand hastily over the high-featured, thin face, in which all sign of agitation had been held down and mastered that day— "my little girl, if Doctor Braddock comes again to the house, it does seem best to me that you should not receive him."

Isabel turned, and for the first time that morning her father looked fairly into her face. There were certain lines in it which never had been there before. The old man, leaning forward on the table, read them as open letters in a book.

One day, at the taking of Vicksburg, it had fallen to Thomas Latimer's lot to recognize, through his field-glass, in the ensign of a rebel company, his nephew; a lad whom he had brought up with Bell as his own son, but who had gone to join Beauregard at the beginning of the war.

The young fellow, colours in hand, stood on a broken wall surrounded on every side. There was no chance for him. The colonel could neither help nor hinder; he sat on his horse immovable, while Dick, steady and cool as ever, braced himself against the wall and waved the torn flag defiantly until he fell, when he shook it feebly up with his last breath. The colonel gave a tremendous shout of triumph, but his jaws lost colour under the gray whiskers as he put up his field-glass.

"It was a young fellow that I saw shot yonder," he said by way of apology to the general. "He belongs to a family that I know. They don't make much show in the world, but they've got staying power in them."

As he looked at Bell now, he suddenly remembered Dick, going down into death, waving his poor rag; his eyes kindled, then he touched her hand gently and pityingly, as her mother would have done.

"Do as you think right, child. You are a better judge than I," he said. "Come away, Arabella. I wish to speak with you."

Miss Morgan followed him with a jerky solemnity; but before they had opened the door, Isabel interposed with the same steady, tranquil voice.

"Whatever opinion you may form in this matter, cousin, I wish you to understand that Doctor Braddock is not at all to blame. He doubtless went to Harrisburgh to serve Miss Maddox. She is an old friend of—of—our family, and Clay was only doing his duty to me in serving my friend. Very probably when he comes he will think it necessary for me to go down to Anna, to aid or comfort her. If he does, I shall certainly go."

"And I will certainly not obtrude any of my old-fashioned notions of decorum upon you, Isabel," said Miss Morgan gently. But when she was alone with the colonel, her purple ribbons fluttered, her beaded tags jingled with her excitement, and the tears were in her eyes. "She makes an idol of the man still," she cried. "Oh! the weakness of the silly child!"

"Does she?" said the colonel doubtfully.

"She worships him! It was always a blind infatuation, and it is just like one of our sex to persist in it. Always loving, trusting! 'To build up idols, and never to find out they're clay,' or however the poem reads. Nothing will open Bell's eyes, nothing ever opens a true woman's eyes to faults in those she loves, but death."

"I don't know about that," thoughtfully. "But we'll not interfere, Arabella. Do you know I'm really sorry for Braddock? He was a good fellow, and such love as Isabel gave him would have made a man of him. It's very unaccountable, this behaviour; but still I think he very likely could give an explanation that ought to satisfy a rational woman."

"Bell does not want any explanation! She will ask for none!"

"No, I don't think she will. Well," with a smothered sigh, "I must say I liked the lad. What is it, Otho?"

"Mr. Bowyer, sah. 'Pears in great haste."

"I'm coming." But the colonel was a long time in coming, going to his chamber and exchanging his slippers for boots; whistling snatches of what seemed to be some miserable, tuneless dirge, and meditating on the amount of "staying power" of the Latimers—women as well as men. As soon, however, as he was out of his morning-gown, and installed in his stiff office-suit, these lax domestic feelings were sent to the right-about. "Ask Mr. Bowyer to come up, Otho," he called, going down the stairs with his most rigid, military air; "I am ready for business."

Oth hurried back, with a scared glance behind him. He had just convoyed Doctor Braddock to the library, and had noted, from the immaculate neatness of his scuffed clothes to the complacent smile, the indomitable virtue which asserted itself in that hero, from head to foot.

"Neber do to let Mass Thomas see him look like dat!" thought the peace-loving Oth.

Miss Latimer was seated by the fire, her work-basket

beside her and sewing in hand. Miss Morgan had already visited the room once or twice out of interest in the flue, scrutinizing the quiet face sharply. Oth, opening the door for Braddock, turned his woolly head carefully away from it.

Doctor Braddock laid his hat and gloves down on a table as he passed it, and came up to her. "I am here at last, Isabel."

"Good morning, Clay. There is a chair near the fire." She put aside her work, as she would have done courteously for any stranger. Braddock, as he came up the stairs, had for the first time been conscious that Isabel, who had loved him faithfully for years, might have cause to feel herself insulted and aggrieved. There might be tears and reproaches and trembling of the Anna kind, he thought, with a qualm, for, in fact, he had enjoyed tears and trembling to satiety during the last day or two. Or Bell might receive him with indignant hauteur, or a cold disdain, which would speedily melt away into her old blushing, tender manner. The possibility never entered the man's narrow brain that she could love him less. Braddock imagined thus hastily his probable reception, taking scenes out of the few novels he had read as the basis of his guesses. But Bell had not learned the manners of novel heroines, and would not fit into any melodramatic scene of real life. Whatever processes of pain or resolve had gone on within, she was the same outwardly—slow, downright, simple. She lifted some muslin from the chair to make room for him, and stroked the dog with a good-humoured laugh when he stumbled over it.

Yet Braddock, after an awkward remark or two upon the morning, sat silent, oppressed by an alarm and dread such as he had never felt before. He quite forgot the magnanimous part that he had played.

Neither anger nor tears, nor shy blushes from Isabel,

for this common-sensed woman, habitually grave and
slow of speech, had been shy and blushing with her
lover, and garrulous sometimes as a child. He had unconsciously been flattered until his vanity burned high,
by the indescribable difference in her manner toward
other men and himself. Laird (of whom he had always
had an indefinable jealousy) had spoken of her once as a
white house rose, or some tame domestic bird, to be held
sacred beyond all others, because it made home more
homelike. Laird might make such fantastic compliments, but she was his; it was only for him the flower
opened its inmost leaves, and the bird sang its song.

But to-day she met him precisely as if he had been
Mr. Laird. There was the matter-of-fact hospitality, the
ready courtesy, the kindly smile—everything but love.

"Isabel," rising, so great was the effort he made to
speak in his usual didactic manner, "I see that you appear both grieved and surprised that I did not return
yesterday. You have not heard any explanation. You
—— Well, I consider that I did my duty to you, and—
and other friends honourably and—I really expected,
Bell," giving way to a little snappishness of tone, "that
you, at least, would approve of my conduct."

"Very probably it deserves approval; but," with a
feeble smile, "I may not be Spartan enough to judge
fairly. I shall not try." He noticed as her face came
between him and the light its utter lack of colour. She
suffered then; she was not insensible. She would come
to him for strength and comfort, as Anna did. If he
could ever once, for one half minute, have been mor-
ally certain that he was Isabel's superior, how fondly he
would have loved her! The thought of her actual pain
now gave his heart a real pang and wrench, very different
from the mawkish sentimental sympathy he gave to Anna's
woes. But if Isabel needed comfort, it was not he who
could give it to her. She turned her eyes to the window,

where the snow was falling softly, as if she had forgotten
that he was in the room. It was the first minute since
he knew her, that he was sure that this strong woman,
at heart, was weak and clinging, and with the knowledge
came the certainty that he never would be the man who
should give her what she needed. Who then ? Perhaps
Laird. Doctor Braddock grew hot with a jealousy which,
under the circumstances, was hardly just.

"You treat me unfairly, Isabel," he broke out angrily.
"I tell you that I have done my duty, and you refuse to
hear me. You never loved me, or you would not mis-
judge me. I went, as I sent you word in my message,
with Miss Maddox, on business almost as urgent as
death."

"I received no message, Clay. Probably," looking up .
at him gravely, "you entrusted it to Anna."

"Yes, to ensure its coming with more certainty.
Listen to me, Isabel." He sat down beside her ; he
shifted his feet, crumpled his gloves, talked with sudden
spurts of energy. He was alarmed, nervous from head
to foot. Could Anna have delayed the message ? Tricked
him through all this affair ?

"Bell, do not speak to me until I tell you the whole
matter—all of it." And he told her Anna's sad di-
lemma, and his own heroic effort to rescue her, omitting,
as we may be very sure, all mention of the semi-passion
which had inspired his heroism, the rewarding moon-
beam smiles and glances of the rescued maiden, and all
the hot-house, unhealthy fervor which had made his ex-
ploit appear like a romantic deed of derring-do to him,
instead of a trip on the Pennsylvania Central to Harrisburgh. He was quite conscious as he talked, of the baldness of the narrative without this impalpable colouring,
and saw his adventure himself through the very commonplace medium in which it came to Isabel. She was so
slow and short-sighted, he remembered, comforting him-

self, that she would never suspect the hidden romance
which the bare facts did not translate. But there is no
microscope like jealousy; his haste, a sudden catching of
the breath now and then—there was the whole truth laid
bare. He waited, looking on the ground when he had
finished; he had not courage to face her.

"It was hardly worth while to tell me this story," she
said quietly. "I knew much of it before. I could have
told you years ago that Anna Maddox had her poor little
brain filled with cheap romances, and even as a school-
girl had a certain aptitude at assuming the rôle of heroine
in them."

"You are unjust beyond belief! But no matter!"
suddenly cooling into irony, and waving his fingers with
a gesture of indifference. "Go on. She is a woman.
We all know the mercy women have for the one of their
sex whose beauty men value!"

Isabel waited patiently until he had finished. When
she spoke, her voice never had seemed so simple or
earnest before to him: it cowed and shamed his weak
rage in spite of himself. "I knew what Jack Andross
was before now, too; how the man has struggled to serve
God, and to play the part of a man, while Anna has
tempted him to serve the devil. I know how easy it has
been for him to fall, and how hard to stand alone. I
never told you or anybody, even papa, how, or where I
found him in the mountains that day, nor the words he
spoke to me in his misery. After that I understood him
well, and that poor creature that he loves. I am not
surprised that she has dragged him down. But——"

"But what, Isabel?" Braddock's lean body grew fixed
in his chair. What if she were right? What, if she,
young and fair and innocent, were indeed a righteous
judge, and he, the poor weak dupe of a weaker, wicked
woman?

"I almost know what the end must be for him," she

said. "He was ready to give up his manhood or his soul any day to that lightheaded, vicious child. But I never thought that you would be the tool which she would use to drag him down at last. I never looked for that! I—I trusted you so, Clay!"

"And you don't trust me now?" with a spasmodic effort to feel wronged and indignant. "I tell you, Isabel, you know nothing about them, or human nature, either. Andross! Andross is a——. But no matter for that! Only I will say that at the very time he was winning your pity and tears, hiding in the mountains, he was a felon, and might have been marched off to a convict's cell if it had not been—if it had not been for some people who never will be thanked for what they did! As for Anna, the poor child is as pure and artless as one of God's angels—I'll stake my life on that! And I consider, Isabel," finding his courage and self-approval oozing back by degrees, "that you are hardly as good a judge of the moral issues involved in this bill, of which you do not even know the name, as I, a man, supposed to know something of politics, and who have read it carefully clause by clause. It is a habit with most women," in a lofty tone of patronage towards "the sex," "to elect themselves moral censors in matters whose bearings they can not possibly understand. But I hoped you were superior to such—such inconsequent weakness. You are not listening to me?" sharply. "You look out of the window all morning as if I were not here."

She turned quickly, the tears rising uncontrollably into her eyes.

"You are not here! You are not the Clay Braddock that I knew. I lost him yesterday; and he will never come to me again—never—never!"

"Isabel?"

He did not dare to touch her, or to put his arm about her, although he thought she would fall. Could it be

that he had ever come near enough to her to do that?
She stood in the cold gray window, the snow falling behind her. This was the fairest and noblest woman he
had ever looked upon! He knew that now, when there
was danger of losing her. He would *not* lose her, of
course. Why, what would he do without Isabel—without
Isabel? The very idea staggered him with an unreal ab-
surdity, as if somebody had said that he must henceforth
live out-of-doors, with no roof over his head, or that
there was to be no air to breathe.

"I can understand that you have cause to be hurt with
me——"

She turned to him with a tired sigh.

"Don't let us say anything more. I am not hurt. I
was only mistaken."

"In me, Isabel?"

"Yes. I thought I knew you, and—I loved you very
much, Clay. No, do not touch me," quietly. " That is
all over. You allowed a woman whom I—I do not
respect, to cajole you into the belief that you loved her,
and for that love you left me on our wedding-day to
obey her whims, feeling that you played the part of a
hero when you came back to me to keep the letter of
your promise. You would have given me your name,
when you had given her all beside."

"As God hears me, Isabel, it is you that I love," protested Braddock. "I confess that I admired poor Anna
—her beauty and gentle ways—I felt tenderly——"

"The man *I* marry," said Isabel, fixing her slow-mov-
ing eyes, which at the moment had certainly a very ox-
like persistence and obstinacy in them, "must give me
all the tenderness he has to spare. There is no use of
any farther discussion between us," changing her tone.
"I will never marry a man whom I know as little as I
do you."

"You mean to throw me off as you would a garment

you were tired of!" cried Braddock, in as bitter a rage of disappointment, as though he had been a martyr of constancy. "You mean that there is to be an end to all between us? Do you remember your letters, Isabel? Do you remember the day I told you I loved you, and asked you to marry me—by the mill-race—down there at Lost Creek? You've forgotten that? And now you throw me off?"

She threw up both hands to her face, and cried passionately for a minute, but spoke presently as steadily as before.

"You do not understand. I was deceived in you. Some women would marry you, feeling as I do to you, and could live with you perhaps comfortably. But *you* are not the man I loved. I shall not find him again."

"I have no wish to marry you without your love." He stepped back from her. "You will live certainly more comfortably and luxuriously in your father's house than in mine. I am a poor man, and likely to remain so; I had nothing but you, and that I have lost."

"It has been my fault, perhaps," after a pause. "I should have known you better before I allowed myself to love you. As for money," quietly, "I have not been used to value it very much."

Something in these words stung him as nothing else had done into certainty that she had put him from her irrevocably. It was not her own abandonment or the love she had given him, and which he had trifled with, that she mourned for with that white face and monotonous, weary voice. It was *he*, Clay Braddock, the meaner, weaker man than the one she had loved. Was she right? Had he been simply dishonourable and sensual when he thought himself a Christian hero? Had the tempter come to him as to poor Andross, and his fall been more sudden and deep, because he stood secure on his own vain-glory and confidence? Even in that su-

preme moment of pain and loss, loss even of himself,
came a wonder why the deuce old Macintosh preached
against the dead Satans of doctrines, when here were living devils in the shape of friends and a woman to drag a
man down, and make him vile and wretched in this
world, at least.

But this was folly. Anna was no devil, and he, Braddock, was a consistent, humble-minded church-member,
who neither swore nor drank, nor even smoked. No man
had a cleaner record. And if Isabel, out of sheer stub-
bornness, refused to make any allowances for margins in
a man's nature, larger than her own, and to cast him off
at the very moment when he was most faithfully doing
his duty to her—let it be so! There were other women
who took him on trust—women incapable of criticising
and carping over his character. At the remembrance of
Anna, the sudden sensuous emotion crept over his mind,
as an August wind or heavy perfume might over the
body.

He stood irresolute a moment, his elbow on the mantel-
shelf. It brushed against an old silver candlestick with
crooked leaved branches, which Bell had always set in
the window at night to light him over the ford. It was
an idle trifle to remember; how, as Tom's feet plashed in
the brawling water, he always looked for the three lights
in a certain sash, and the glitter of the leafy silver below,
and knew that Bell with her work-table was waiting by
the fire, with the great bear-skin stretched in front of it.
He looked slowly now at the fire and the shaggy old skin
at his feet and the work-basket he had given her, and
then at Bell, waiting—to drive him out!

Then without a word he went to the table and took up
his hat and gloves, opening them methodically.

"I think you are right," he said. "I have no claim
to stay here longer." He did not go, but waited for her
to answer.

"No ; you have no claim," said Miss Latimer.

"Then good-bye, Isabel."

Was she a log or stone? Was it possible that she would let him go ? Without a word ?

If she had been a man, when she said all was over, she would have held to that resolve ten minutes at least; but it never was a woman who cried,

> "Hin ist hin,
> Verloren ist verloren."

unless she thought the cry would bring her lover back for a few more last words.

Instead of a quiet good-bye, Isabel came up to him, her honest face ablaze.

"I have but one request to make of you, Dr. Braddock, at parting, that you go straight from me to the woman who has taken you from me."

"Anna will give me a kind welcome, I am sure," composedly.

The angry red died out of her face suddenly. "Yes, go to her.   I wish you to see the full value of the goods for which you have sold your life and—— "

"And yours, Bell? Does it cost you something then to give me up?" trying to take her hand. "If I thought you suffered at all—— But you are made of iron," angrily pushing away the cold, nerveless hand.

"I have not spoken of myself," quietly. "It is all said between us, I think," ringing the bell. "Otho, Dr. Braddock waits for you."

Braddock stood feebly a minute looking at the old black man's averted, pitying face, and the tall, stately figure by the window. He had a fierce mind to rush to her, to drag back by some means the love he had lost— to show her—— What? How mad and weak he was? She knew that already.

"I am ready," he said, nodding to Oth, and followed him down-stairs.

He stopped on the door-step, the driving snow wetting his pinched face and blue lips. The door closed behind him.

"I'll go to Anna, as she bids me !" he said. "She, at least, loves me, poor child."

CHAPTER XXVIII.

AS the hall door shut behind Braddock, Mr. Bowyer, in the study, rose from his chair after a long colloquy with his chief. The colonel, pencil in hand, was in deep reflection over some papers, and Bowyer had leisure to look around him, and wonder whether it was the pipes and tobacco pouches hung on one side of the wall, or the guns and swords and big ears of corn from Nittany on the other, or the boxes of tools and models heaped pell-mell in the middle, that entitled the room to the name of study.

"About as fit for a study as Old Tom is for a collector," thought the detective, standing on one leg, which was cramped. His deputies already had dubbed the colonel "Old Tom," just as his regiment had done. He was going over some accounts slowly, running his finger up the page, his forehead knit sternly.

"I never could make a column tot up the same amount twice over," looking up anxiously. "Neither can Miss Latimer, or she would help me. It's very annoying. I'm afraid that Joseph sometimes is not accurate."

"But about these distillers, Colonel ? I had, as I told you yesterday, certain information that Laird directed the full tax to be paid on each barrel. But it has not been done for a single day. The working distillers are small owners of stock, it appears, and have taken the matter out of the hands of the capitalists."

"I told you Houston Laird was an honourable man," glancing down again at the unruly figures.

"'So are they all—all honourable men!'" muttered Bowyer, who had been drilling his boy as Marc Antony lately for a school exhibition, and who had his head fuller of strategems and assassinations and fiery eloquence than was Sam's. "Well, sir, what am I to do? Put the screws on at once, as you directed?"

"Now, Bowyer—eighty-nine, just remember eighty-nine, if you please," holding his forefinger on the spot. "Now, I would not be too hasty. You're sure they have not paid the tax since they received orders from Laird?"

"Not a dollar, sir. Wilkins, in fact, has said openly that if Laird interferes further he will throw up the management. They could not spare Wilkins, so Laird will not interfere."

"I think you're mistaken there. You'll find Laird is a man who will rule his own household, even if it is made up of distillers. Wait until to-morrow before you use stringent measures. I'll find Laird to-day, if he is in town, and if not, telegraph him. He'll set it all right. Eighty-nine and eight——"

Bowyer regarded the colonel attentively a minute.

"Wilkins," he said, "has boasted openly, too, that he can carry on the business just as he has done it in defiance of you or any force which you can bring with you."

"He—what?" cried the colonel. "Why, do you know, sir, that I could arrest that miserable scoundrel and put him to trial, sir? Try him like any common thief! The proof's so plain that there's not a judge nor jury in the land that would dare not to convict him, if I once order his arrest."

"I don't know that. Wilkins is an influential man in his ward, and judges and jurors would want to know what the Ring had to say before they move in the matter. They always do."

"Confound the Ring! What else does the fellow say? It's really amusing to me! Now, I want you to keep cool, Bowyer. You're too hasty. I'll manage this affair myself. He'll sell his infernal whiskey under my nose, in spite of me! Why, it's—it's insubordination, sir!"

"They've had a gang of roughs from the fourth ward on the premises every night for a week in case of a seizure."

"They have, have they?" shutting the ledger, and pushing it back until he upset the ink-bottle.

"Armed, I suppose?"

"Oh! armed, of course!"

"'Pon my soul, this looks like business," laughing, with a red spot burning on each cheek bone. "Go down at once, Bowyer, and levy the tax due on every gallon in the warehouses. Give them until five o'clock this afternoon to pay it. If it is not counted down then, to the last dollar, I'll collect it in person."

"You'll consult Mr. Laird in the meantime?"

"I'll do no such thing. Do you suppose I'm going to manœuvre and honeyfugle a lot of thieves to get the just dues for the government?"

"Very well, sir," gathering up his papers. "If the money is not paid by five o'clock, I'll have the gaugers in force at the Sixth street Station?"

The colonel's countenance fell.

"Gaugers? I—— Do you mean to say we must call in those fellows?"

"Why, we could hardly attack the distilleries single-handed, Colonel," keeping his face grave with an effort. "And you can't call out the military on such an occasion."

"More's the pity. Even the volunteers—— Why, when Baltimore was under martial law, Bowyer, with the guns of Fort McHenry turned on her, there never was such order known there. It was peace, sir, peace;

a perfect dream of Arcadia. But for an old West Pointer to go into a fight with a troop of revenue men at his back—making it a legal affair—it's like taking a mean advantage of Wilkins. I don't relish it at all!" in a tone of chagrin and vexation.

"Well, sir, it is a legal matter, and you are an officer of the law. So it seems appropriate, somehow, to say the least."

"Oh, of course. The law. Now do you know, Bowyer," lowering his voice, "I have very serious doubts whether the law ought to be the highest authority, eh? There's a deal of red-tape injustice in the law, I can tell you, sir; and the judges, as you acknowledge, are sometimes tools of the Ring; and what are the juries? A dozen dunderheads picked by chance because they know nothing of the matter in hand. Down in the army, in the days when the duel was permissible, the code of manners and morals was fixed by gentlemen—educated men of honour. Look even at your Lynch law; it's a rough justice, but it's not for sale. I don't mean to say that I want Lynch law in its extent—— What the deuce is the matter with your leg, sir?"

Bowyer emerged from behind the table with a red face and twinkling eyes. "Nothing but cramp—asleep. I'll run over that account, if you choose, Colonel, and see if Joseph is correct. I used to teach school, and got the knack of figures."

"All right. I never did. I wish you would." The colonel had suddenly grown grave and anxious. He had just recognized Braddock as he passed the window. "I must go now, Bowyer. Let me hear from you at five, sharp."

The detective seated himself at the blotted ledger, and Colonel Latimer hurried across the hall to the library, and pushed open the door. He fancied Bell was lying back motionless in her chair at first, but when he came

up to her she was sewing industriously, her cheeks red,
and eyes bright and cheerful.

"He has been here, Isabel?"

"Oh! yes, papa," rising hastily. "It's all right.
I've postponed the wedding—no, that is a lie. I have
given him up altogether. But it's all right. I'm quite
happy. Don't fret about me, papa. We won't worry
about it. Nor talk of it any more, will we?" breathlessly.

"Not if you do not wish it, my darling. Did——But
I will not ask any questions," checking himself. He
stooped and kissed her softly again and again on her
forehead, her hair, her closed eyes. She let her head rest
on his breast awhile and then looked up, smiling again
persistently.

"Why, what has happened? I have not seen you look
in that way since you used to try a new casting at the
Works, or when you were going into battle."

"Nothing, my dear, nothing you could understand.
Business, business. Shall I drive you out, Bell? Is
there anywhere you would like to go?"

"To go?" with a dreary glance out of the window.
"Nowhere, papa."

"Anybody you want to see then, darling?" anxiously.
"I'll take you to any of your friends in town."

"No; there is nobody," the lids falling dully over her
heavy eyes. "I don't want any friends but you," holding up her mouth to be kissed. "Now go, and let me
finish my sewing, dear; I'm very busy. When you come
back to dinner we'll be as happy as if there were no—no
business in the world."

"I hope so, Isabel," said the colonel gravely. "I trust
in God so, my poor baby!" He kissed her once more,
and putting on his hat hurried out of the house. If the
child's mother had only lived! He was hard and coarse
—he could not come near enough to her, even to show
how he loved her.

As soon as Bowyer saw the colonel go stalking past the window, he jumped up, seized his hat and crossed to the library, tapping at the door, and then pushing it hastily open.

"It is only I, Miss Latimer," not noticing in his haste a certain confused and dazed look of the young girl as she rose.

"Good morning, Mr. Bowyer. Colonel Latimer has just gone out, this moment."

"It wasn't the colonel I came to see, ma'am. It was you. Yes, I'll take a chair, thank you, though I'll hardly warm it. I'm a good deal pushed for time to-day, and I've idled away a half-hour in the chance of seeing you. You're attending, Miss Latimer?"

"Certainly."

At this moment, there rushed upon Bowyer's remembrance the fact that this young lady was to have been married yesterday, and that evidently no such marriage had taken place. He was silent a full minute, and then proceeded quickly. There had been a hitch somewhere, he thought, it was none of his business where. The wholesomest thing for the young woman was to give her something else to think of.

"Now, I'm not like the colonel," he said aloud. "*He* says keep women and business apart. But I say find the right cog for the wheel, and put it in—male or female. Now that case of Julius Cæsar's—if he'd taken heed to Calphurny, it would have ended differently all round, especially for him."

"Cæsar? Calphurnia? I'm afraid I don't follow you," said Isabel anxiously.

"Oh! never mind. It was just an illustration of mine—on account of teaching it to our Sam, and it really *is* a case in point, if you know all the items. Now, here's the items, Miss Latimer," his voice changing from its embarrassed vacuous hesitation to sharp decision. "I'm

·going to trust you, because you don't talk. I saw that, and you struck me as a solid, sensible woman the first day I came here, and because your father's not to be trusted in this matter at all."

"What do you mean?"

"He's too headlong. To warn him of danger would be like holding a peck of oats before a mule's nose. He'd walk into it, like Cæsar into the senate-house. I'll trust this Calphurny to manage better," nodding affably.

"Is my father in danger?" Being a soldier's daughter, used to danger and to seeing it warded off, she asked the question with a composure at which Bowyer was ready to applaud.

"I knew I was not mistaken in you, ma'am. Yes, he is. There's been some difficulty with whiskey distillers: collecting the taxes—you wouldn't understand."

"No. Don't stop to explain."

"The gist of the thing is, your father's too honest a man for the place, and interferes with their profits, and they want him ont of it. The party that put him in are afraid to remove him—it looks too badly—see? So there he is, a fixture. He (and me) we've been running a gang of distillers pretty hard, this last week or two, and they've taken means of getting us laid on the shelf. I can take care of myself. But the colonel—he won't, and that's the truth of it. I haven't thought best to mention it to him."

"You don't mean that they would assassinate my father?"

"I mean just that; perhaps not kill ontright: shoot or stab. Pistols are handier than daggers nowadays, and a job of the sort don't need as many slashes as Brutus's gang had to make. Especially air-pistols."

"Mr. Bowyer," said Bell smiling, "you've been reading of Brutus and the rest until you are unnecessarily alarmed on the subject of assassination. Such things are not done nowadays. This is not Rome."

"Who shot John Ford, Miss Latimer?"

"I—I'm sure I do not know. I did hear something about a man of that name."

"I'll tell you. He was a special, like me. He was shot down in daylight, two months ago, and the Ring had so bought and paid for judge, jury, and press, that though everybody knew the men who had hired the assassins, they could not be touched; only their tools were punished."

"And you mean that my father has provoked these men?"

"Yes. I know they've threatened us both, and that I've been dogged night and day for a week. But I go pretty well protected by daylight," touching his breast-pocket, "and they know it. And at night I've just had to keep in-doors. It's cowardly. But it'll only last a few days. Before another Wednesday there'll be an end of Wilkins's trade or mine."

"There was a man named Voss?" remembering their encounter two days before.

"One of their 'men,'" said Bowyer, "out of the Penitentiary a year ago. You've got your finger on the right spot." But he asked no explanation, and she volunteered none.

"You could never persuade my father to remain in-doors." Isabel sat erect, intent now on every word of Bowyer's. He saw that she had forgotten all else.

"Of course not. I know the colonel. If I'd hint this to him he'd march the streets, like a war-horse smelling the battle. That's why I come to you; for you to take care of him."

"I understand."

Bowyer scanned the young girl's grave, steady face for a minute, as a mechanic would a tool he was about to use, and then continued: "I can depend on you, Miss Latimer, not to mention to the colonel one word I have said to you. I wish you to detain him with you in-doors, as far as that is practicable, unless when he is out with me on business. This difficulty will only last for a day or two, while Wilkins and I and the law are settling which is to rule."

"If my father and you gain your point," Bell said in her slow, meditative way, "there will be more danger for him. They will want to be revenged on him. I think he and I had better go back to Nittany."

"No. These men of the Ring and their tools don't care to put a man out of the way unless it pays. A murder for revenge, now, there'd be something respectable in that. These fellows only work for hire. You needn't trouble yourself about the colonel, ma'am, after I tell you he's safe."

"I think we had better go back to Nittany."

"There's a good proportion of the mule in the Latimer family," thought Bowyer, but he rose and bowed respectfully. "I've got to go now, ma'am," setting his chair back carefully against the wall. "Don't be over-uneasy, so's to get your nerves unhinged."

"I have no nerves, Mr. Bowyer," smiling.

"Glad to hear it, ma'am. And on the other hand, when you think the matter over, don't pooh-pooh the whole thing, as your father would do. I'm not an alarmist."

"I do not underrate the danger." She had risen, and was leaning on the back of the chair. "My father is out now. If I go after him—— But there he is," as the colonel's shadow passed the window.

"Yes, and I must be off the other way. Take notice of all messages he gets, ma'am. We don't live in Rome, as you said. But a man dies as quick from a bullet fired by Rafferty, or any of the other bullies of the Fourth ward, as if it was a 'rent the envious Casca made!'" Bowyer bowed again, and went out, feeling that he had turned the last sentence neatly, with that scrap. A little book-learning was a very convenient thing; he was glad Sam was to have the advantages he had missed. That girl of the colonel's was good grit, yet she had broken terribly in the last day or two; the detective's eye seeing what her father's had failed to mark.

CHAPTER XXIX.

THE opponents of the Transit bill managed, as Willitts had foreseen, to talk it down that night, and showed such skill in manœuvering, and such strength of resources in exposing the open bidding for votes, that the embryo statesman was alarmed, and by daybreak the next morning hurried down to the depot to telegraph to Mr. Laird to come on without delay.

"I feel there's a collision of the worst sort inevitable," he said to McElroy, "and let him be here to engineer it himself. I've been acting partly on my own responsibilty, and if matters go wrong he'll call it meddling."

"Hardly so bad as that, Ned." McElroy was very cool about it, having his greenbacks safe in his pocket; he had leisure, therefore, to wonder why Laird trusted so much to such a leaky fellow as Willitts, any how? Having nothing better to do, he lounged beside Ned on to the depot, and paced up and down that ill-smelling place of resort, kicking the pea-nut shells and orange-peels from the platform while Willitts ran up to the office. A crowd of men with pick-axes and tin-cans were waiting on one side; a crowd of women with the inevitable dirty-faced, plumed babies, and little boys in tawdry knickerbockers on the other; a mulatto girl with gilt ear-rings and pink bonnet flaunted up and down, all of whom McElroy eyed as though he saw them not; but he suddenly stopped, looking closely at a stout, short, red-bearded man in a shaggy overcoat and travelling cap, who stood amongst the workmen, and about whom they had gathered with eager deference.

McElroy ran up the office-steps breathlessly, and hailed Willitts. ".Here's your chief, Ned, Laird. He must have come up on the eastern Express. What can he want with those men ? You don't think he'll go back on your arrangements, do you ?"

"Your champagne is safe, Mac. I see him. Yes, that's Laird," coolly, nodding his companion out of his way.

"You'll introduce me ?" anxiously.

"Another time, Mac, if you please. Business now."

Willitts was as much astonished at Laird's appearance as McElroy, and as curious about his business with the labourers ; but he picked his steps over the platform and stood swinging his cane, waiting for him nonchalantly, as though it were a ball-room and they were both invited guests. Mr. Laird touched his hat to him, but finished, his colloquy.

"You'll go back to your boarding-house then, Mr. McGuire," he said to the foremost of them, "and desire Mr. Smalley to come to the Lochiel House immediately, and ask to be shown to——. What is the number of your room, Mr. Willitts ?"

"Eighteen—first floor. Better write it down."

"You hear ? No," putting back Willitts's card, on which he had scribbled the number. "You will remember it, sir ? You will miss the train—lose the day's work, I suppose. When you bring Smalley, I will pay you double for the loss of your wages. Go at once, if you please."

"You manage that sort of people better than I. I am too familiar with them," remarked Willitts, as they turned up the street. But Laird only nodded. There was something gloomy and oppressive in the silence, which annoyed Willitts. "May I ask," he said after a pause, "who is Smalley?"

"Voss."

Ned gave a silent whistle of dismay and glance of alarm at his companion. "You find it necessary to call him in?"

"Yes. He fights shy of Wilkins, it appears. I ascertained that he came here, found out his last alias yesterday, and by luck stumbled on these men, who knew him, just as I left the train."

"I thought——" Willitts hesitated. He approached the chief with cautious touches, just as the jackal would the lion, finding him in ill-humour. "I thought Wilkins would be able to attend to this matter?"

"Wilkins?" Mr. Laird never swore, but he had a habit, when under great excitement, of closing his lips, more emphatic than any oath. "Wilkins has broken the traces completely."

"Yes. He refused to pay the tax as you directed."

"You should have notified me of that," quietly.

"I came on to attend to what I considered more important business here," said Willitts. "I did not really suppose," deprecatingly, "that the losses in the distilleries could seriously affect your business."

"It is not the loss in, but the loss of the distilleries. That fellow Bowyer has determined to expose the whole scheme, and ruin it. You know how extended it is, and that it has no foundation but secrecy. It is toppling to destruction to-day. Payment or non-payment of taxes is a trifle—it is the exposure that is fatal."

"Andross," cautiously, "before he gave in, spoke to me of the National Transit Company as bankrupt for months."

"He was quite right, as you know," meaningly. "If this bill is choked off, and the distillery revenue stopped —the bubble is burst."

Ned gnawed the end of his rattan, and wet his dry lips.

It was very well for Laird, who had made enormous failures once or twice before (paying twenty cents on the dollar), to the great improvement of his fortune, to be calm about the matter. But this gigantic sham, had given to him and dozens of other young fellows, its architects, not only food and clothes, but all the luxury of the town. He glanced down at the Paris made trousers on his little legs, the blazing solitaire on his white hand. He had no trade nor profession. And there was his mother and sisters to think of—Gertrude unmarried yet.

"What is to become of me when it bursts? I know nothing outside of it," with a laugh, dreary and pathetic enough, had there been any one to take in its full significance.

"'Go West, young man!' as Greeley would tell you," with a sardonic laugh. "Dig, plow, eat bacon. How long is it since Andross promised us his vote?" abruptly changing his tone.

"Last night."

"He has changed his mind by this time, then—once or twice. I'll nail him this time. There's no room for risk now."

They walked on in silence until they had reached the pavement in front of the hotel.

"You will see Voss in my room when he comes, sir. Do you wish him brought up with any regard to secrecy?" asked Willitts.

"None whatever. Why? The fellow knows his business. He'll not be caught; and if he is——. It is Mr. Voss who will suffer, most probably. Nobody else."

Ned laughed. He was more reckless about offending Laird than he had ever shown himself before.

"Even in Italy, which is the land of banditti, there is some show of secrecy about hiring assassins," he said. "But you are right. Even the press will help hush the matter up, when Bowyer disappears."

"Bowyer is not going to disappear. Voss may probably give him a drubbing or broken head, to teach him to attend to his own affairs. Brute force is the only means to use with such fellows."

Mr. Laird spoke civilly, but Ned saw that he was in a dangerous mood. The truth was, that this brute-force part of the transaction disgusted and chagrined Laird's finer nature inexpressibly. He had the same loathing—absolute nausea—at the idea of meeting Voss as he felt once when he had inadvertently been present at the dissection of a dead body. He added presently:

"My only business with Voss is to secure him. Wilkins will give him his directions in detail. I must trust him so far."

"Wilkins?" Willitts looked thoughtfully at the knob of his cane. "The point of attack is Bowyer, you said, sir?"

"Certainly. Who else would it be?"

"Oh, I'm sure I don't know, Mr. Laird," hastily. It was no business of his if Wilkins meant to go back of Bowyer to his principal. Latimer was nothing to him, not even an acquaintance; and if the thing had to be done at all, the more securely it was done the better.

———•◦•———

CHAPTER XXX.

MR. LAIRD, on entering the hotel, retired to make a careful toilet, and without taking time to order breakfast, sent up his card to Miss Maddox.

"You are sure the girl is still here?" he asked Ned, with the disrespectful tone in which he always spoke of that charming woman.

"Oh, quite sure. The Governor gives a state dinner this evening, and Anna has telegraphed for a trunkful of finery."

"She'll wait an hour to dress now, I suppose."

But Anna, who usually lay in bed until noon, had been up and armed for action in flowing ribbons and crimps since early morning. In the very heat of the fray of her love-affairs, the last act of the drama—it was no time for lying in bed. Mr. Laird was therefore promptly ushered up to her parlour, the door of which was ajar. He ran against a man in the dark passage.

He was gallant and tender, as was his wont, with Miss Maddox, while she, in the innocent frisky gayety with which she received this middle-aged admirer, was quite lamblike. She chattered unceasingly as he placed her chair nearer the fire, wondering if she could have produced any real impression on him? He was a little too stout for a lover—but—no, not considering his enormous wealth. With his portly build and millions to back it, he was really quite—quite ducal, according to her ideas of a duke. She did not see her father come into the room behind her, and looked around when she heard him speak, her fair lashes snapping irritably, and then ran up to kiss him.

"I don't know whether we shall admit you, papa, or not. Mr. Laird and I were just going to be cosy and confidential, aud have a cup of coffee together. I'm sure you have not breakfasted, Mr. Laird? We really did not invite you, *cher* papa!"

"There, there, Anna, don't be a baby. I'm glad to see you, Mr. Laird," pushing her aside and dropping heavily into a chair. "This business has told on me, sir. I'm too old a man to venture into such doings. I thought it was all up yesterday."

"There's a strong opposition to the measure, I know," calmly.

"I should say there was! The whole state is roused. They've enlisted what they call the honest element of both houses against us. Chadwick yesterday denounced

it as a swindling trick to support a gigantic swindle.
And the worst of it is—he told the truth!" glaring
angrily at Laird. "If I had my money once out of it!"

"Of course, my opinion is not that of Major Chadwick, or I should not be in favour of the bill," calmly.
What, bonbons! No, thanks, Miss Maddox! You will
not keep these lilies and roses long if you eat candy so
early in the morning. I ran up," turning composedly to
her father, "to look after matters. But I find it all arranged. You have secured Andross's vote?"

"Yes, I secured it. At a pretty price, too," muttered the judge, glowering in the fire with a certain
shame creeping into his angry face. "I don't mean a
price, exactly, of course. But the fellow, as you know,
has wanted my little girl here for years; and to keep him
in a good humour I was forced to consent, that is, conditionally. Conditionally, of course. There are several
other better matches which Anna could have made; very
brilliant matches, so far as money and position go. But
if the girl's heart is set on Jack—and to make sure of
his vote——We could not have done without his vote."

Mr. Laird, still standing, leaning on the mantel, had
been watching Anna during this slowly spoken speech,
for the first time puzzled by her. Was there really anything in the girl beneath her shallow trickery? That
was assuredly a real pallor on her pinched features, and an
actual fright in her eyes, which were fixed on her father.

"The judge does not misstate the case for you, Miss
Maddox?" said Laird gayly. "Your heart is not cold to
poor Jack? You will reward him for all that he does
for us?"

Anna's little mouth opened and shut weakly, once or
twice; she did not turn her eyes from their terrified
scrutiny of her father. "I—I am very much attached
to Mr. Andross," she simpered at last; "I'll do what I
can to help you, I'm sure. Is it so bad, papa?" her

voice growing shrill. "Are we going to lose everything? the house and horses and my things and all?"

"It is very bad," interposed Laird gravely. "I wish you to realize all that depends on you in the next twenty-four hours. That was what brought me here. Other men we can buy; but you must hold Andross. Keep him with you; humour him to the top of his bent until it is time for him to vote. Don't give him time to think. Whenever Jack thinks, he is sure to change his opinion," smiling. "You understand what you are to do?"

"Oh, quite," her eyes sparkling. "I have been told I had a very good head for politics, and I'm so flattered that you think so, Mr. Laird. The French ladies used to do that sort of thing in their salons, you know—; they quite ruled the nation. Now, papa, dear, go find Mr. Andross, and tell him I want to go out sleighing in this lovely snow."

The judge rose. "If the bill passes we're safe, Mr. Laird?" holding him by the sleeve.

"Yes, if we are successful in one or two other little arrangements," drawing back, so that the judge's hand slipped down.

"And if the bill passes, you see, Anna"—her father meditatively hitched up his trousers and pulled down his waistcoat—"if it passes, and Jack is reëlected, his fortune and ours are made. I don't see that you could do better than to marry him. His income will be nearly equal to Bislow's, and considering that you're fond of Jack——"

Again the insignificant little face was strangely distorted by some powerful emotion. "Too powerful to belong there," thought Laird.

"It will all be right, papa," she cried, pushing him toward the door with an effort at archness. "Send Jack to me. We shall sleigh this morning, and go to the dinner, and I will be in the Senate gallery as soon as it opens, and keep my eye on him," turning to Laird.

"We all know the magic of that look. By the way, Miss Maddox, who was the man I met as I came in? Julius Ware, was it not?"

"Yes," turning away from him to warm her hands at the fire. "It was Mr. Ware. He came up yesterday, to lecture here."

"He has turned street preacher, or something of that kind, I hear."

"He has adopted the faith of Jung Stilling," quickly as a parrot reciting its lesson.

"Oh? Well, Miss Maddox, take my advice, and leave Mr. Ware to his life of faith for to-day. Do not bring him in contact with Andross. Just for to-day, until the vote is taken. You understand?"

"I understand," quietly, the curly lashes dropped timidly on her cheek. She scarcely lifted them as she returned Mr. Laird's bow and farewell.

On leaving her, Laird went to his own room, and sat patiently by the window until he saw a gayly caparisoned sleigh draw up at the side entrance. Andross, after tenderly lifting Anna into it, and tucking the skins about her, sprang to his own seat, and shaking the reins loose, drove rapidly away into the soft mist of falling snow.

"There he goes!" he said to Willitts, who was waiting beside him. "The snow and the bells and the pretty face are enongh to keep all thoughts of honesty or remorse out of Jack's head. He's safe—for an hour. Now bring in your man Voss."

CHAPTER XXXI.

NED WILLITTS, escorting the champion of the P. R. along the corridors, eyed him askance, and entreated him respectfully as to precedency, with very much the same kind of cautious gentleness with which he would have handled a bull-terrier that he was about to muzzle, but which might turn on himself some day. He told Gerty, his sister, about him, afterwards, as he would of a strange beast in a menagerie. "I met the creature once by chance," he said. "He has blue eyes and fair hair, and a very pleasant, agreeable laugh; and a hand as small and nicely kept as a woman's. You'd have taken him for a genteel mechanic, if it wasn't for a big emerald pin in his shirt, vulgarly set, of course. But a very nice stone—very nice."

When he had shut him in with Laird, he came away with a sigh of relief. The colloquy was a long one. Andross had returned with Anna before it was over, and Willitts, passing the door of her parlour now and then, could hear her merry voice and Jack's ringing laugh; the tones growing softer and almost inaudible at times.

"He has forgotten there is such a thing as a bill or legislature on earth," he said to Laird, meeting him as he came out of his room.

"All the better. But I must remind him of them now."

"What is wrong?" For Laird, for the first time in Willitts's knowledge of him, wore a haggard, uncertain look.

"Nothing that can not be easily set aside. This fellow," pointing his thumb backward over his shoulder, "is disposed to be contumacious, that is all."

"Asks too much?"

"It is not probable I would stop to higgle on a matter of a few dollars to-day. No. He wants his safety ensured after the thing is done."

"Hasn't he your word?"

"My word," laughing, "is not enough for him. He says, 'I'd take your name for any amount of money. But this is honour, Mr. Laird. And I'm not so sure about it there,'" and Laird laughed again with a full appreciation of the joke. "He prefers Jack's. Andross got the fellow's pardon some years ago, you remember, and he looks upon him apparently, as a power in the land, and the real type of an aristocrat. He will not be satisfied unless Jack assures him it shall all come right at the end."

"Which is impossible," after a pause. "You can not expose this thing to Andross."

"I must do it."

"He'll kick the traces then altogether. He is an honest, humane fellow, at bottom, sir."

"What am I?" Mr. Laird's manner was almost bland in its civility, but a heat fairly purple spread up from his throat. "If he kicks the traces, as you express it, I shall be forced to let him feel the yoke on his neck. Where is he?"

"In Miss Maddox's parlour."

Laird bent his steps thither, taking no heed to the obsequious clerks and porters who crossed his way for the purpose of bowing to him; while Ned patrolled the hall, his thin lips angrily shut. "Laird," he thought, "ought to let that poor devil alone." If it had been himself, now—— he—Ned, would as lief have set Voss on Bowyer as not; one ratter on another; hit or miss—uppermost dog, win! But Jack was different. Jack was cursedly gentlemanly in his feelings! It was an infernal shame! He went down for some brandy to soothe him; but he avoided passing through the corridor in which Anna's rooms opened, where Laird had already met Andross. He had a dull feeling that a man was being done to death there.

Mr. Laird, finding a room unoccupied opposite to Miss Maddox's, entered it, gave directions that he should not be disturbed, and sent to Andross asking for an interview of a few minutes.

"Mr. Laird?" Jack looked at the servant bewildered

when the message was given. "Is Houston Laird in the house?"

"Yes, sir." For Houston Laird's face and name were known to every man in his fief of Pennsylvania.

"I will come, certainly." But he waited irresolute after the man had left the room. He had been standing with Anna by the open window; while she thrust out her little rose-leaf of a hand to catch the snowflakes, holding them to him, to see if he could trace the tiny stars and angles before they melted on the warm pink; to be kissed away—always to be kissed away. The fire burned low and clear, the room was quiet. The steady white fall of snow shut out the view without. It did not seem to Jack that they were in a hotel parlour, playing like two children, but in some far, lonely corner of the world; just they two together. Here the fire was warm : there the snow fell, and she was beside him, the one woman on all God's earth. Her soft luminous eyes looked into his ; her breath touched his cheek, her warm moist palm with the drop of snow-water on it, was pressed to his mouth. He had waited so long for her—years and years. Now she was his. Bills and legislatures were, in fact, as things in a dream. If he thought of his fall at all, it was to vaguely remember that Anna had showed him an hour ago, how when this one sacrifice was made—her father saved, and the marriage once over, they could live and act just as Jack pleased. Be as honest and honourable as missionaries or martyrs, as he chose, and live on a crust. "What shall we want with money? I have plenty of things to wear, and do I care so much for eating? now, do I?" she had lisped, clasping his arm and looking up in his face with an arch solemnity that drove him wild with delight. His face burned and his eyes shone, as though with wine.

Just at that moment the man had announced Houston Laird, and Jack being, as we know, a full-blooded sen-

sitive fellow, felt a sudden chill at the name, as though
in the heat of a summer day death had touched him on
the shoulder.

"I'll go, certainly, Anna," he said again. "I shall be
back in a few moments. Mr. Laird can have no business with me that need detain me from you. Good-bye,
darling!"

It was with the soft pressure of her arms about his
neck, and the touch of her lips yet on his, that he crossed
the hall and entered the room where, for the last time in
his life, Laird waited for him.

A shallower man, or one with less kindliness than
Laird, would have greeted Andross with a show of excess
of friendliness. But the struggle was to be one as for
life and death, as Jack would know; fair words or sham
courtesy would count for nothing. Besides, Laird was
sorry for the lad; he was fond of him in his way; would
have spared him—if he could.

There was a grave sincerity in his manner, therefore,
which warmed Andross's heart to him at once. But the
whole world was so warm to Jack that day! It was so
full of delight and friendliness, that if the similitude of
death could have met him, the happy fellow would not
have known him, but with his glamoured eyes had
clothed the skeleton in comfortable flesh and blood.

"Come in. How are you, Andross?"

"I? Oh, very well. Never was better in my life,"
hesitating a brief moment, and then holding out his hand.
It was years, as Laird remembered, since Jack had shown
him this proof of confidence. It embarrassed him for
the moment.

"Sit down, John, sit down," with an uneasy hospitality.

"No, thank you. I am engaged, particularly, this
afternoon, and must go back as soon as we have finished
our business. What can I do for you?"

Laird, who was much the shorter man of the two, looked up at him, while he hesitated for a word. The youth, the finely cut face, the personal presence of the man, strangely affected and agitated him. He could understand, while looking at him, without a reason, why this brute Voss was ready to put his faith in him, even to risking his neck on the gallows. He reminded himself that he had a sure yoke about the fellow's neck; yet he himself could not credit it.

"What can you do for me?" he said meaningly. "I'll tell you, Andross. But sit down. It will take some time."

"No. I prefer to stand." A look of doubt began to creep into Jack's eye; he followed every movement of Laird's closely, as he walked up and down the room, forcing himself to appear at ease. Laird never had been at ease with Andross, as with other men, even when Jack was but a boy; he always remembered not only that the lad had come of a different race from his own; had been born to culture and gentle manners as his birthright; but that the money, which other men worshipped him for, counted for absolutely nothing with this serf of his, whose aims, ambitions, tastes, were all pitched at a higher level than his own. It was not a pleasant thing to be forced to remember that these aims and tastes might have been his also; that he had made a meaner, more vulgar man of himself for the sake of this money; a man whom Andross, penniless and with the lash on his back, despised.

Judge Maddox, in his place, with all his good-humour, would have used the lash now unsparingly to save his money; but Laird was galled by all this old self-reproach. When they stood face to face, he remembered that he, with all the weight of middle age and power on his side, was going to drag this young fellow from the clean, honest path he had chosen, down to a way from whose foulness he never could escape.

Maddox would have put "the job" in the plainest speech, but something in Laird responded so faithfully to the honesty of Jack's purpose, that he could not find words to cloak his own. Although Voss was waiting, he thought moodily through two or three turns, how, if it were not for this money and the constant fight to keep it, he might have been a man whom Jack or his own son could respect ——

"But, to business!" He stopped, reminding himself of his position in Wall street, and that Jack was penniless. But that did not put him at ease.

"You ask what you shall do for me?" plunging suddenly into the middle of the subject. "I must remind you, Mr. Andross, that you have, as yet, done but little for me. I procured you Sheffield's seat, in order that you might repay me by at least a just consideration for my interests. You have not done so by word or vote this winter."

Jack was fully on guard now.

"Pardon me, while I amend your statement," courteously. "You gave me the seat, because you were afraid that, once out of your trammels, I would betray your secrets. You brought me here just as the unruly slave of the gang is placed near the overseer."

"Tut, tut! Don't use such strong language. You always do use too strong language, Andross."

"I owed you no debt of gratitude. I do owe"—he stopped abruptly, his countenance fell, "that is, until last night, I thought I owed some duty to the people and some respect to myself; and since I came into the Senate I tried to pay both. As far as I was capable of judging, I have voted and acted honestly for the service of the people I represented."

"Forgetting, apparently, that your very salary was a perquisite from me."

"My salary," continued Jack, "I have saved, with

other earnings, to pay a debt which I owed at Nittany.
I was forced into that—that debt by your agents.　They
drove me to the wall——" again he broke off, confused
and excited.

But Laird, apparently, saw nothing of his agitation.
"I have no wish to quarrel with you," he said, coldly.
"I had a service to ask, and I preferred not to ask it as
a favour nor a right, but to put it on the ground of a
simple business transaction.　Work, for which you had
already received the value."

"What is the service?　I have already promised my
vote to the Transit bill.　The very newsboys and pages
are speculating by this time how much it cost to buy
me."

"Pah, nonsense!　You are morbid.　This is nothing
as serious as a vote," adopting suddenly a confidential,
friendly tone.　"It is only a word or two I want from
you, Jack—your influence with a man with whom you
have influence, and I have none.　I want to hire his time,
and he refuses to give it, unless you—will endorse me."

"Endorse you?　As to your ability to pay?　How absurd!" laughing.　"Certainly, you shall have my recommendation.　Why did you introduce such a trifling matter so formally?　Where is the man?"

"Here.　Just round the corridor.　In my room,"
hastily.　"I'll send Willitts to bring him.　It is not precisely endorsement," with anxious hesitation.　"I want
to employ the fellow on a rather troublesome business,
and he requires to be assured that he shall suffer no loss
by it—bodily or otherwise."

Jack looked up at him, a doubtful suspicion gathering
in his frank face.　"I don't understand.　What have I
to do with his bodily loss?　What bodily loss can ensue?"

"'Pon my word I don't know what absurd whim the
fellow has!　All I do know, is that he has taken a fancy
to you, and refuses to clench the bargain without your

counsel to do so. You need not be annoyed by seeing him—a most importunate fellow. If you will write a line or two assuring him that in our business transactions I will care for his interests as my own—— ?"

Jack, after a moment's pause, drew a chair forward and sat down. "I will look into the matter a little first. What is the man's name?"

"He calls himself—Voss. I think. Yes, Voss. You procured his discharge from the Eastern Penitentiary a few years ago, and the fellow has made a sort of demigod of you since."

"Voss? Yes, I remember." He sat silent for a minute, and then looked up at Laird quietly. "I understand. You intend to use this poor ruffian in some way which will bring upon him the punishment of the law, and want me to assure him that you will protect him from it."

"You state the matter baldly. But that is about the gist of it. There's no use of any circumlocution farther," coming up and looking fully at Andross, with very much the look of a bull-dog driven to a corner.

"No. Not with me. I know that you will not protect him," calmly. "The Ring have usually found Moyamensing or Sing Sing the safest places to keep their tools after a job—until they needed them again."

"There is no need of any crimination or recrimination passing between us. I told you I did not mean to quarrel with you. You refuse to serve me in this thing?"

"I certainly refuse. If the poor wretch has a good opinion of me, I assuredly shall not use it to drive him faster to the devil. If that is all of your business with me, Mr. Laird, you might have known that it was hardly worth while to disturb me," rising.

"One moment, Andross. It would be better for us first to look at this matter in a business point of view, without any loss of temper——"

"I am not losing my temper," flushing hotly. "I will not look at the matter from any point of view whatever. I am under the yoke of your accursed Ring myself, but as God sees me, I'll not drag any other man under it to perdition!"

Laird laughed coolly. "It would be hard to increase Voss's chances for a good long stay in purgatory, I fancy. Now, Mr. Andross, this is a sheer Quixotism on your part. The man is a ruffian, in the grain. I want, I frankly confess, to use his ruffianism against a fellow of his own sort; to punish him temporarily—that is all. Voss has no religious scruples—his only fear is of the Black Maria and Moya. I give you my word, he shall escape both. Will you give yours to him?"

Jack had been watching Laird with an astonished pity as he spoke. "I knew this kind of business was done by the hirelings of the Ring," he said gravely. "But I would not have believed, unless I heard it from his own mouth, that Houston Laird would take part in it."

Laird made a hasty step towards him, then paused. "One is driven by necessity to many disagreeable things," he said calmly. "I think you will find, before we have ended, that it will be to your interest as to mine, to take part in this."

His calmness was more dangerous than any rage. Andross felt that the decisive moment had come. He laid down his hat, bracing himself unconsciously. "I am ready to hear all you have to say."

He had never struggled with Laird before, except when the right was on his side; and he had always been worsted. Always. But he would not be worsted now! Was he to help drag this man down to hell? Did they dare to come to Jack Andross with such a job? Though he had sold himself last night——

"Go on, Mr. Laird."

"I need not remind you, Andross, of your position

here. You are a prominent leader, beginning to be known as a brilliant orator, handsome ——"

"What has that to do with Voss? Keep to the subject —— This poor bully whom you wish to hire ——" The rage and scorn which he repressed flashed in his eyes, and made him stammer.

"You will see the connection presently. There is a straight road of success open for you. I need not mark it in detail. In a month you will marry the woman you love —— if you serve me in this matter."

"You can not hurt me there. She is mine. Nothing can take her from me."

"It is necessary," continued Laird quietly, "for the very existence of the Ring, that this Voss should serve me; will you compel him to do so?"

"I have told you, I will not!" with a loud emphasis.

"Then it will be needful for me to go into a committee room yonder," nodding toward the State-house, "and show an affidavit which I have in my pocket-book, signed by Shortlief Kenny, which proves that on last July, John Andross—"

"Kenny —— For God's sake! ——" Andross staggered back to a chair, his fingers tugging at his cravat, the blood leaving his ruddy face livid.

Laird paused for a minute. "The Legislature is lax enough as to morals. But we can not reëlect a known thief to his seat; or, would Maddox, do you think, give his daughter to the man that had stolen from him?"

Andross got up at last. His chin trembled like a woman's. "Let it come. I deserved it. But I had just got the money ready to pay into the Works —— Oh, God! These are hard lines!"

"You will not give Voss the order then? Think better of it, Andross," laying his hand on him soothingly.

"No!" pushing him violently back. "I'll never do it!"

Laird hesitated, eyeing him thoughtfully, and then left the room for a moment, unnoticed by Jack. There was a little tap at the door, after he reëntered, and Anna's face, showered over with golden curls, was thrust in.

"Recall yourself, sir," whispered Laird. "She knows nothing!" The judge came puffing in after her.

"Why, dear me, have you two been quarrelling? Why don't you look at me, Jack?" touching his sleeve. "You've been here an hour. I thought you were never coming back to me."

He looked at her with a smile; the poor wretch could not keep the bitter tears out of his eyes, ashamed of them as he was. "I never will go back, Anna."

"Never!" with a terrified little scream, holding by his arm and looking round to Laird for her cue.

"There is a difficulty, Miss Maddox," Laird said, "which I can explain to you. I require of Mr. Andross a service that costs him nothing, but on which my financial credit and that of your father depend. In my anger at his refusal I was so rash as to threaten that Judge Maddox would not give his daughter's hand to a man who disobliged him in so important a matter, and who," glancing significantly at the judge, "could no longer be considered the favoured organ of our Company."

"And you were quite right, sir," cried the judge. "Nothing for nothing's my motto. Are you going back in your vote on the Transit bill?" turning fiercely on Jack.

But Andross did not hear him. His eyes were fixed on Anna. All the love, all the long struggle of the man's life were in them, if there had been anybody who chose to read them.

"Anna, you shall decide for me." He took her hands, and drew her in front of him. The judge would have interfered, but Andross motioned him away. "Stand back, sir. You have no right to come between us."

Anna sobbed, and looked over at Laird. "Why certainly, dear Jack, I'll decide," she cried. Secretly, she wished he had a glass of wine to bring some colour into his face. It was quite ugly. So sallow and contracted!

"This work which this man Laird gives me is vile. I can not even name it to you. But if I refuse to do it, I lose you. If I consent—they can not take you from me. What shall I do? I—I can not give you up!" His hold of her was so heavy that she could hardly bear the pain. But for once the woman showed a certain strength. The same incomprehensible expression of perplexity and terror which Laird had noticed before, came into her face; from some secret under-current of thought, as he plainly saw.

"It would be wrong for you to do it, Jack?" she said gently. "It would be a sin, and you would do it to keep me? Then I think"—withdrawing herself slowly from his hold: but she stopped, with a little quiver. "But then, if you don't, poor papa will be quite ruined! The house and everything go—and—"

There was an absolute silence through the room. "Dear Jack," she said at last, her puny features contracted like an old woman's; "I think you had better be obliging, and be governed by Mr. Laird, and then—" she lifted his hand so as to press it against her lips.

"Then—you will not desert me? When I pay this price for you, you are mine for life?"

It was noticeable that it was not Laird's faith for which he required a pledge, but Anna's.

She gave an hysteric, exhausted scream. "How can I satisfy you all? Poor papa's fortune, and—— Oh, I dare not, I dare not!"

"But you love me, Anna? If I have not that——"

She caught Laird's eye, and was suddenly calm. "Of course I love you," looking beyond him at her prompter like a whipped child. "It's not fair to lay such burdens on poor little me! I think—I think I am going to die!" sinking down.

Andross carried her as he would a baby to the sofa, and laid her down, stopping to lift a lock of hair gently back that had fallen over her face ; then he turned his back on her. "It was not fair to ask her to decide. I will do as you wish. Is the man—Voss—here?"

"In one moment, Mr. Andross." Laird hurried to the door. "Willitts!"

"I don't know what this Voss matter is, I'm sure," said the judge ponderously. "I hope you're not offended with me, John. I really thought you were going back on us about that bill business."

But Jack did not hear him. Anna, her faintness past, looked at him out of the corner of her eye unseen.

In a minute, Willitts ushered in Voss and speedily disappeared. Andross hardly waited for the door to close.

"Mr. Voss, I understand that you require my advice before you close with whatever offer Mr. Laird or his agents may make you. I do advise you, to accept their terms."

"Well, you see, Mr. Andross, it is a ticklish and unpleasant kind of thing ; to begin with——"

"We will not discuss business before the lady," hastily interposed Laird.

"You had better come to your own room, Anna," said her father.

"No. I'll stay. I want to see this gentleman."

"I'll be careful." Voss removed his hat and ran his hand through his oily hair. "I have a great regard for the fair sex myself, ma'am."

Anna, on the sofa, nodded and smiled sweetly on him. Voss, who had as shrewd a sight as one of his own terriers, perceived that the men before him were strongly moved by some discussion which he had not heard, and the consciousness of this embarrassed and checked his garrulity.

"I'm quite satisfied with Mr. Laird's terms," he said gruffly, turning to Andross, "as to money. But it's what we call a fancy job, and I'd rather have nothing to do with it, unless I spoke to you first, Boss, and you'd give me your word it ud be all right, and no backing down on me in the end. As one gentleman to another."

Mr. Andross did not answer readily. "I advise you to take the job; as one gentleman would another," breaking into a loud laugh. "We are all gentlemen here together," still laughing, with what Voss thought unseasonable gayety.

"Well, sir; that's all right, then," he said, confused. "I needn't have made such a p'int of it, I suppose. But I knowed you, and I wasn't acquainted with your friend Mr. Laird. When I heerd in New York, this fall, you'd been run into Billy Sheffield's place, I just remarked to the boys, ' There's one man in the legislater is a friend of mine. *He's* a man you can tie to.'" He had come up close, with an assumption of intimacy. With all his fastidious tastes, it never annoyed Andross to "fellowship" with the dirtiest or most vicious ruffian; he answered Voss as though they had been equals, with a wild, uncertain wandering of the eye.

"You're quite right, Voss. If I have a virtue, it's firmness. All my friends, and God, too, I suppose, know how far I'm to be trusted," laughing again, until he caught Voss's bewildered look, when it occurred to him that there was but little manliness in jibing or whining over his fall to this bully. "You can go now," he said abruptly, nodding to the door.

Voss was used to the changing moods of people who trafficked with him; he made a cringing bow. Andross was none the less to him the finest gentleman he had ever seen, because he ordered him out like a dog.

"Well, sir?" he whispered, passing Laird.

"Go at once to Wilkins, I have no more to do with it,"

turning away and coming up to Jack, while Voss went out, feeling as if he had hardly clinched the bargain securely after all.

"Mr. Andross," said Laird aloud and formally, "you have obliged me greatly; so greatly that I wish you to understand that this is the last favour I shall ever ask at your hands. The burden of obligation is hereafter on my side. I will make a pact of friendship with you, if you wish," smiling pleasantly. The smile faded when he met Jack's eye. The poor fellow, he felt, had been driven now a step too far; he was dangerous.

"I do not wish it," said Andross in a low tone. "I only want to know that we are done with each other. I've paid the price of your secrecy. You will not play this game again on me?"

"No, no," earnestly. "Take your own road now. I'll do all I can to make it successful. I wish you could understand, Andross. It was very unpleasant for me to push you so far. But there's an enormous amount involved. You've no idea—"

"Successful!" said the judge, who had caught a word and was anxious to make the best now of Anna's bargain. "Oh, there's no doubt of Jack's success now. The party will refuse you nothing after you've settled this Transit matter."

Anna gathered herself up weakly from the sofa. "Jack, will you look for my slipper? I've lost it," thrusting out the point of one tiny foot in rose-coloured stocking. "Let us go back," she whispered, as he knelt to put it on. "You've made an end of this business here, haven't you?"

"Yes, it's ended," rising.

"Well, then!" sharply. "Don't look so haggard and ghastly about it! That Mr. Voss is the only cheerful man in the party. What a lovely emerald pin he had! I do love emeralds!"

"Do you? Jack will hang jewels all over you, Puss, no doubt," said her father. "He'll be a luxurious, indulgent fellow for a husband!"

Jack smiled, as the judge meant he should. "You should only wear pearls," he said, looking down fondly into her eyes. The poor little woman, how could she know the price he had paid for her? Why should she not chatter about emeralds? He heard her chattering still as they crossed the hall, but did not understand her. That Jack Andross that he was yesterday—how far off he was—dead and gone! All that scraping and saving of dollars to pay Maddox : what folly that had been! And that incessant old-fashioned talk of honesty and serving Christ, which his mother had harped on perpetually —that was folly too! There was nothing in it when you looked at it. If he was elected again, and could buy a house for Anna, and fill it with rare furniture and old china : could dress her as she should be dressed——that was all there was real for him in life, after all; just as with Laird and the others—it was a struggle with all of them for emeralds, or houses, or stocks.

In the hall they passed a gray, venerable, old man, a judge of the criminal court, with two or three young lawyers, all from Philadelphia. They bowed deferentially to Andross, the judge shaking hands cordially with him.

"I hear, Mr. Andross, you are going to support my friend, Mr. Laird, when his bill comes up this afternoon. The party will not forget it," meaningly, bowing again low to Anna.

"That is a member of the Christian church, and he knows that I was bought like any other chattel," said Andross quietly when they had reached the room, whereat Anna began to cry.

"It is impious in you to talk that way of Christians and religion, and I don't choose you to do it," she sobbed.

The Christian religion, just then, seemed worth as much to Jack as the traditions of the Parsees.

"I want to be alone, anyhow," she said when he did not reply. "I shall go to my own room for an hour or two." She lingered, the knob of the door in her hand, waiting to be coaxed, but he made no effort to detain her.

"I will wait here for you," he said dully.

"But if the bill comes up—?" anxiously. "Your vote, you know?"

"They will take care to find me," with a shrug.

Anna hurried into her chamber, and when she had shut the door, burst into an uncontrollable hysterical spasm of weeping, throwing herself upon the bed. Her suffering was unmistakably intense, and real.

"It's too late!" she cried. "No emeralds, no pearls for me! Oh! Never, never!"

—•◦•—

CHAPTER XXXII.

MR. VOSS did not go farther from the hotel than to the telegraph office, where he sent a laconic message to Jabez Wilkins, at his residence in Green street, Philadelphia, signing it by another name than his own, and then returning to his boarding-house, to tranquilly await the result.

The message, received by Mr. Wilkins about noon, was at once carried by him to one or two other distillers who had formed "a ring under the Ring," which, as they said, "meant not talk but biz."

"Voss tells us to send the party to him. He won't show in Philadelphia, and he's about right on that," Wilkins explained to his colleagues, who were more thick-headed than himself. "The party must be old Latimer first then: Bowyer 'll not budge from this town any more than a hound when the slot's gone into a hole."

After further discussion, though the words were few and to the point—for Wilkins was clear-sighted and a man of action—a plan was determined upon, which was to pay the tax imposed by Bowyer within an hour, when the colonel would be relieved from any duty of watchfulness ; and then, as Wilkins explained, "to summon him to Nittany immediately by a bogus message. The old patriarch can be fooled by a child. Barry, as he don't know you, you can run up with him on the train to Harrisburgh and give Voss his instructions, to go on with him to Lock Haven. Let Voss manage the rest himself."

"You've not—— There's no intention of inflicting any permanent injury on the old man, Wilkins ?" asked Job Follet, the youngest of the party.

"Why, certainly not. Do you think we are brutes ? Only a sufficiently severe lesson to teach him to attend to his own business, and keep from meddling; that's all."

"Permanent injury ? Of course not," repeated Barry, shaking his head emphatically. "But the bogus message, Wilkins ?"

"I can manage that. I've got the run of the colonel's antecedents pretty thoroughly. He's a Virginian, with cousins by the score. I'll draw on his family affection. Let me alone. I'll manage it. Do you be ready at the depot, Barry, to go aboard whatever train he takes, and keep him in sight until Voss has him in charge. Follet, take this check up to that thief Bowyer. It's the last."

"Voss is not as large a man as the colonel," said Barry, in an undertone, when the door closed behind Follet.

"I've seen Latimer. He's a rheumatic old rackle of bones," grunted Wilkins, "and Voss has the muscles of an ox. Besides, he'll be well armed. Sam Voss is not going to risk anything to a hand to hand fight, when a pistol will do the job better. He knows his business."

"Yes, I suppose so," said Barry, uneasily.

By one o'clock, Follet tapped at the door of Colonel Latimer's private office, and came up to the square opening in the railing, behind which the old gentleman sat at his desk poring over his inscrutable accounts, while Bowyer, newspaper in hand, kept watch and ward over him.

Follet, a smug, light-haired little Irishman, laid down the check on the desk. "For the distilleries named in this list. Monthly accounts of taxes, paid up to date," he said, scrutinizing the old colonel eagerly.

Colonel Latimer threw down his pen, and rubbed his spectacles clear, before examining the check, with an as-

sumption of great keenness. "Ah—h; quite right,
Mr. —— ?"

"Follet, sir."

"Mr. Follet. Here, Bowyer," with a triumphant nod,
and muttering, "I told you Laird would make his men
deal fairly. Your receipts, Mr. Follet."

"That makes us square, I believe? " said Follet, hesi-
tatingly, as he took them. He had a morbid curiosity
about the man on whom Wilkins and the rest were going
to let slip their dogs before night. A soldierly looking
old chap, he thought, eyeing the colonel's ungainly lean
length of build: if he were to be at the fight, he'd take
the old man's part, he believed, though he was running
the distilleries down to blue ruin.

"Yes, that is all right!" said Latimer, cheerfully.
"I'm very glad "—stopping to dip his pen in his ink once
or twice, not being sure how far he ought to be civil to such
scoundrels, and changing his cordial tone to one of grave
dignity. "I am pleased that you have perceived how
much more advisable it is to conduct this business in a
legitimate and open way. Because, sir, the law will have
its course. The authorities are aroused, and are determined to enforce honesty and justice in small matters as
in great. They will speedily put an end to all underhanded dealings, Mr. Follet."

"I am rejoiced to hear it, Colonel," said Follet, coolly,
putting his receipts smoothly in his pocket-book. "And
so should you be, I am sure. Good morning," stopping
at the door for another quick, grave inspection of the
colonel.

"A very agreeable, shrewd young fellow, apparently,
Bowyer. Who is he?"

"One of the gang."

"I was a little uncivil, I'm afraid, eh? The man came
to deal honestly, and it was no time to read him a moral
lecture. Well, there's no need for a raid on them to-
night, you see?"

"No, I suppose not," gruffly.

"The men always meant to pay. No doubt of it;
might have been a little hard pressed for a few days. But
Houston Laird's an honourable man. I told you it would
come out all right. You don't know him, Bowyer ; and

you're apt, do you know, to be a little censorious? You ought to guard against that. I ought to guard against it myself; in fact, I'm apt to judge human nature pretty sharply, I tell you. But then I'm an older man than you, and have had more experience of the world."

"Yes. I think I have retained the ingenuousness of my youth, Colonel," said Bowyer, gravely.

"Then you're convinced these men are going to deal fairly, now?" anxiously.

"I don't know how they are going to deal," angrily. "They're a trick ahead of me this time."

The postman came in at the moment. Now, just around the corner, the postman had met a boy running breathless to intercept him with a letter, which he had left by mistake the day before at the wrong house. Such accidents had happened to him before. He glanced at the letter, in a yellow envelope, directed to Colonel Thomas M. Latimer, Collector, etc., and with the written postmark of some obscure country village—Nittany Hall, Centre county. He thrust it into the bundle of the colonel's letters, and laid them a moment after on his desk, not thinking it necessary to make any explanation of so trifling a mistake.

In a few moments Bowyer was startled by the colonel's loud "Tut, tut!" followed by the slamming of his ledgers and locking of his drawers.

"What is wrong, sir?"

"Oh, the deuce to pay up in Nittany! Hale Latimer, a cousin of mine, is up there, ill—worse than he says, I suspect. He thought I was there still, and went up from New York to finish out the winter, and stayed at old Van Meter's, hunting on the range. Now he has pneumonia. Just like him, to go there without knowing where I was. The most unpractical, head-over-heels fellow! The other branch of the Latimers are all just that sort of people. Here, Dick!"

"May I ask what you propose to do, Colonel?" said Bowyer.

"Do? Why, go to Hale at once," scribbling a hasty note as he spoke. "Take this note up to Miss Latimer, Dick, with this letter. Tell her I'll be back to-morrow evening with my cousin, if he is able to travel. I forgot to mention that." He was buckling on his overshoes and his old military cloak, twisting them all awry in his haste. "I'll just be in time to catch the up train. Lucky those fellows paid their taxes, or I should have had to stay to fight it out—with the gaugers at my back! Confound it, Bowyer, I didn't like that! Where the deuce is this cape? Well, I'm off now."

"Had you not better take Miss Latimer with you, Colonel?"

"Such weather as this? I have to ride from Lock Haven across the hills on horseback. Besides, Miss Morgan would load me with baggage, if I went near the house: dry socks and mustard plasters and a portable bed for Hale, very likely—no, no. Always keep clear of women if you want to attend to business properly, Bowyer."

Bowyer walked with the colonel to the depot. He thought it best to see him safely out of town, not knowing what the game of Wilkins and his men might be. Laird might have interfered, as Latimer said. But nothing could be luckier than this sudden summons of the colonel out of town.

"How do you propose to carry a man ill with pneumonia across the hills on horseback, Colonel?" asked Bowyer as they waited for the train to start.

The colonel glared at him for a moment. "That's just like a woman, to raise feeble difficulties. I'll find the way, sir. You'd have me leave Hale there to die, would you? Of all men he's the least fit to take care of himself: the most headlong——"

At that moment the bell rang, and the colonel jumped aboard. Bowyer, seeing his gray head disappear in the car as it moved off, sauntered across the bridge again with a long-drawn breath of relief. Mr. Barry, unseen by him, had entered the other end of the train, and before Bowyer had reached the office, was seated by the colonel exchanging vehement opinions with him on the corruption in their own party, and the urgent need of the Citizens' Reform. A more intelligent man, or one more awake to the needs of the hour, the colonel thought, he had never met.

.　.　　.　.　.　.　.　.　.　.　.　.　.

Dick made unusual haste with his message, as it was to Miss Latimer, who had been kind to the boy. He lingered after it was sent in, in the hope of being sent for, and when Oth summoned him, hurried in.

Miss Latimer was standing in the middle of the floor, the open letter in her hand. She had a stupid, terrified look in her gray eyes, which enlisted even the boy Dick as an instant champion.

"Colonel Latimer says he is going to my cousin Hale. This letter is not from my cousin Hale."

"I don't know about that, ma'am. The colonel is certainly gone to the mountains. By the 1:20 train. He's off now," glancing meditatively at the clock, "some fif—teen minutes."

"Did Mr. Bowyer know he was going?"

"He 'companied him to the depot. So it must be all right. Mr. Bowyer's sharp, I tell you now," in a consolatory tone.

Isabel turned the letter over again—held it to the light. She had not seen Hale Latimer's writing for years, but as with most slow people her memory never failed her. This was a forgery. Her father had been decoyed out of town by a trick, and Bowyer had been tricked with him.

When she turned toward Dick, the lad jumped from his seat. "What has happened, Miss Latimer? I'll run for Mr. Bowyer."

"Stop; there will be no time. When does the next train go to Harrisburgh?"

"In half an hour. The Pittsburgh express—— "

"Bring a carriage and I can reach it."

Dick ran like the wind, and seated by the driver, speedily brought the hack rattling up the street. Isabel was standing in the door, Miss Morgan wrapping her fur mantle about her. "If I knew where you were going! If you would only let me go with you, Isabel," she cried again and again.

But Isabel heard and saw nothing. An animal on the track of the hunter who had carried off her young could not be more deaf and blind to all on either side of her.

People hurrying past her to go into the train as she crossed the depot, paused to look back at the girlish face, with its unnatural pallor, and the stern-set gray eyes.

Not a handsome face, but very like to old Tom Latimer's when he was going into battle.

For the first time in her life the full power of the woman was awake and in action. She meant to save her father. God only knew how. But he was all she had.

"Shall I tell Mr. Bowyer to follow you?" said Dick breathlessly, waiting by her seat, although the train was in motion.

"He will know what to do. Tell him that the letter was a forgery, and that I have gone to my father. I have a friend in Harrisburgh, who will help me, John Andross."

But Bowyer had left the office when Dick returned, and it was not until ten o'clock that night that the boy succeeded in finding him, and delivering the message. Bowyer received it in absolute silence and without the change of a feature. Then he drew out his watch, and looked at it.

"A telegram to the police at Lock Haven an hour ago," he thought, "would have been enough. But it's too late now. They've dealt with the old man by this time."

He went down the street, looking about him as though stunned.

"Tricked Nick Bowyer, eh?" he said. "Tricked Nick Bowyer?"

His vengeance, he knew, would be sudden and swift. But of what avail was vengeance?

———◦◦◦———

CHAPTER XXXIII.

IF Andross was troubled by remorse or despair when Anna left him to take measure of himself, such unwholesome megrims were suffered to haunt him but for an hour or two. Whatever might have been her private grief, that heroine (after a nap and lunch), returned to her task with the zeal of a soubrette actress, about to play for the first time a leading part. She had no lack of assistance. The issues dependent on the final action that day of this impulsive young man, were too great for him to be trusted to the manipulation of any woman. Every advocate of the bill was ready to join with her in fooling him to the top of his bent. It was not known precisely how his vote had been bought, but the coarsest lobbyist understood that it had not been a matter of dollars and cents, as with McElroy. It was expedient, too, that Andross should be kept out of reach of the opposition, which was led by Hetherington, and included every man of honesty and integrity in both houses. Jack, who, as Laird's tool, had on his election been received with suspicion by these men, had slowly won for himself a place among them. The report of his defection yesterday had been received by them at first with an indignant denial, and then with an amazement and anger with which their liking for Jack had almost as much to do as their interest in the bill.

"Andross," said the leader (a gray-headed old champion of unpopular honesty for years in Harrisburgh), "Andross was tricked into this, not bought. There are some men who have not a price, and that lad is one of them. If I could talk with him for five minutes, I'd set the matter straight."

But Laird's plans were too well laid; neither Hetherington nor any of his followers could gain the five minutes. The state dinner was given up, and Anna, with Andross, spent the short winter afternoon at the house of a woman whose whole fortune was risked in Transit stock. There was no more talk of stock or bills in the house than if they had been encamped in Arcadia. There were rare engravings, natural flowers, a few men and women, well-bred, gentle, and witty, whose lives seemed to have been spent in the pleasant places of the world, and who had come to idle away an afternoon here together as the pleasantest of all; there was a dainty lunch, with an incessant flowing of champagne. Jack, who came among them, haggard and silent, could not but be touched and pleased, at first, by the delicate homage which Anna received. That too often garrulous child had learned, since she came to town, when wisely to be silent, and took the rôle now of a lovely listener. Jack knew these cultured men and women could properly recognize her rare beauty and innocence, which he could not bear the common herd should look upon, and was satisfied that they should appreciate her, and glowed with delight at being able to claim her as his own. He was referred to, constantly, also as an authority in some disputed points in the matter of engraving, and grew interested in explaining them, and then he sat down with one or two of the pictures before him, whose feeling had touched him nearly. Whatever sharp pain he had felt had dulled down into a vague melancholy.

"Stay, Anna," holding her rose-coloured drapery when she would have left him. She would so much rather have gone to the fire where those gentlemen were; but the bill—the bill! She would not, however, have long to sit stupidly watching his pale, grave face bent over a lot of yellow prints. The clock was on the stroke of four: she had just heard a whispered message sent from Laird that the bill had passed to its third reading, and the Ayes and Noes were about to be called. Andross might be summoned any moment.

Meanwhile, the snow outside fell tranquilly; some one in the next room, with a voice full of power, was softly singing a ballad of Schubert's. The music lifted his mood unconsciously. He had no especial thought of Vosses or Lairds or vile sales of a man's honour; it was the world—life itself—which was full of an infinite sadness and longing!

There were some prints of the antique statues before him. "There is the same meaning in this Psyche's face," he said to Anna, as though thinking aloud, "as in the song. It tries to tell us that it has found nothing better —nothing higher in the world than material beauty. It was quite right in the old Greeks to give to the faces of their gods of Beauty and Strength, a certain sense of loss—of a something beyond themselves, never to be attained. I suppose men in the days of Phidias, just as now, grasped and groped for a virtue, or religion, or a God which they never reached, and had to be contented with poorer things which they could see and handle."

"I don't know anything about Phidias, I'm sure," pushing the print away. "I think those nude figures are very immodest."

"I did not notice that it was nude."

The simple, noble faces might have a sense of loss in

them, but they were expressions of the highest thought of a nation whose thought and action moved on high levels: they could not fail to quicken for the moment the man's sensitive nature, to ennoble in his fancy the meanest things he looked on. The electric fire of that ancient time and people kindled answering, latent heats in himself.

If it was pain or a sense of loss, it was a keener enjoyment than any other man's pleasure. Yet Andross could not have told in words what it was he enjoyed. He leaned against the window-frame, looking now at the red in the sunset sky, burning behind the snow, now into the heart of a crimson rose which was growing beside him; the music, lofty now and soaring, seemed to engross all life and feeling. Yonder across the sea those wonderful statues carried their white beauty from age to age: from day to day the red burned in the sky; the roses bloomed each year the same; the wind that blew on his face had swept since the days of creation on its given path; music incessantly over the world told its mysterious messages. It was one of those moments in Andross's life when a sudden perception of the inexhaustible beauty and strength of the material world about him seized and rapt him and held him dumb.

What did he or any man count for in this vast whelming force and life? If he voted Aye or No for the Transit bill, or if Voss pummelled his fellow bullies, would the sun burn less red, or the winds alter their awful courses?

Anna observed that his cheeks were heated and his eyes dim with tears. "I never knew a man so easily affected by music," she said, thinking it was no wonder Jack was turned to this side and to that by any men who chose to play battle-door with him. "*I* think that voice is too flat. Mr. Ware has taught me a great deal about music this winter."

Their hostess, Mrs. Norris, who had shrewder eyes than Anna, came to lead her away to the lunch-table. "You have not tasted any champagne, Mr. Andross?" chirped Anna, who had a fervid conviction there was no sure hold on any man but liquor.

"That is not one of his tastes, I am sure," said Mrs.

Norris, hurrying her away. She looked at him attentively over Anna's shoulder, as she stood heaping the young
lady's plate with cake and sweetmeats. "No, wine
would not touch him," she repeated. "*You* are his
coarsest temptation, I suspect," with a bow and smile
which converted the words into a compliment. But she
felt a disgust at herself, remembering that the wine had
been provided especially for Andross. This man was not
the sensuous fellow whom Laird had described to her;
her heart warmed to him: she wondered if he had a
mother living. Long afterwards, when Andross's career
was spoken of before her, she felt the same twinge of self-
contempt, remembering how she, on this last day, had
helped him to his undoing.

The gentlemen were beginning to cluster gaily about
Anna at the lunch-table, when a slight stir was heard
without, and the jangling of sleigh-bells halted suddenly.

"Is it so late?" said Mrs. Norris nervously.

"They will reach his name in twenty minutes," whispered one of the men.

"It is a message for me, I suppose," said Andross,
coming forward with a curious change of countenance.
"I must vote on a certain measure, Mrs. Norris; you
will pardon me for deserting you and Miss Maddox."

"Oh! But we are all going with you!" cried Anna.
"Everybody is anxious about the bill; most of these
gentlemen must vote on it too!"

These people, with whom Jack had established a certain Freemasonry, ventured to show now their gratitude to him. These men regarded the bill as the salvation of the state. This widow would be penniless with
her orphan children if it was defeated. Jack, with a
secret consciousness that he was being duped, could not
resist the pressure. He answered the men cordially,
listened sympathetically to the black-robed stockholder,
and then sprang into the sleigh, where Anna blushed
and beamed on him out of white furs and snowy plumes.
It was not in his nature to forget, as he dashed through
the street, this creature beside him, rosy and warm as
the summer dawn. He knew the crisis of his life was
upon him, and there was a certain exhilaration in the
very knowledge.

"As for the bill—what of it ?" he said in a loud voice to Anna. "As many good people defend as oppose it, it seems to me." Whistling the whole matter down the wind as a trifle, he lifted her from the sleigh at the door of the Capitol.

The red heat had left the West. The evening was ominously gray and dreary. But the old many-windowed building blazed with light; the lobbies, every entrance were alive with excited, eager crowds. He passed through the Rotunda, with Anna clinging to his arm; groups of men, who had been watching for him, hurried before them into the Senate chamber; he remembered, with a boyish thrill of excitement, that his coming would bring chagrin or pleasure to every man in the house. But he had no mind to subject Anna to the view of the crowd.

• "I shall take you to a committee room, my darling," he whispered, "and send your father to you. The other house has crowded into the Senate chamber to hear the vote on this bill; there is a great deal of excited feeling; it is no place for you."

"Don't ask me to leave you, Jack," pressing closer to his side, and he, smiling tenderly at her childish devotion, led her to a seat in the gallery by Mrs. Norris, and lingered before taking his place on the floor. Anna, indeed, detained him beside her; each moment was precious to her in which she could be seen by the multitude beside the hero of the hour; she appeared to be looking up in his face with eager, innocent questions, but she saw with delight the eyes of the whole house upon him, noted the anger and scorn of the opposition, the triumph of his own party.

The clerk was slowly calling the Yeas and Nays, each member, as he gave his vote, choosing to state his individual reasons for it, more for the benefit of his far-off constituents in Philadelphia or Westmoreland than for the anxious, silent crowds about him.

Mr. Laird, in the impatience of his now certain triumph, pushed his way through the throng, and came up to Andross in the gallery, where he still leaned over Anna, returning the salutations of those who looked at him with a flushed, defiant face. He stood erect when

Laird touched him, bowed coldly, and walked down the aisle to his place.

"I ought not to have come near him just now," said Laird with evident chagrin. "It was ill-advised. I never shall be able to conquer that man's antipathy to me."

"What does that matter?" said Anna, who could not understand why so rich a man as Laird should care for the good opinion of any penniless fellow. "Why does the opposition make no effort, Mr. Laird? They do not even seem to listen to the voting."

"All they have to do is to bear defeat stoically. It is too late for any effort. Every man's vote has been canvassed and known for days. Our success was a foregone conclusion when Andross came over, yesterday."

"They do not try to influence him. See, those are all members of your party, who are crowding about him."

"No; he is safe at last, thanks to you, Miss Maddox," lowering his voice. "Nothing would have brought Andross over but the certainty of winning you. Your promise——"

"Ah—h!" She drew her breath sharply through her teeth, half rising and looking about her with an unmistakable terror.

"What is it? Are you ill?"

"No, no," with an hysteric giggle. "It's all right. Jack's vote will save you, and papa's property, and all. It's all right."

Laird looked down at her through his cynical, half-shut eyes, but made no answer. The girl was always a bore to him. Now, too, he was anxiously watching Andross's tall, stately figure, about which Ned Willitts was buzzing like an uneasy fly. He saw Jack laugh with him once or twice, and his countenance cleared. Ned had tact, and Andross liked him.

Willitts, in fact, never had felt sheer, downright envy until now, and expressed it frankly.

"No man in the country has such a chance before him as you, Mr. Andross," he said, "to be one of the leaders of the most powerful moneyed ring in the East—at your age—— It's not easy for a hard-working drudge like me to laugh at the sight. Some men are born for luck."

"I wish to Heaven you were in my place, Willitts!"

But he was not quite sure that he wished it. Every face in the massed crowds told him of his power; in the future he saw only a life of luxury and command; of burning passion; of tender love gratified. It was early in life thus to reach the top and crown of things. He turned his agitated, glowing face to Anna across the great lighted hall—— It needed but to stretch out his hand to grasp the marshal's bâton—Success.

At that moment a page touched his arm, and laid a slip of paper on the desk before him.

He rose hastily.

"Where are you going?" cried Willitts, detaining him. "Your name will be called in a few minutes."

"It is a woman, a friend of mine, who is in great trouble. Where is she?" to the boy.

"In the first committee room."

"But your vote——for Heaven's sake, consider, Andross!"

"I shall be back in a minute. The vote is safe. Don't detain me. It is Miss Latimer."

The next moment he pushed open the door of the room where Isabel stood waiting for him. With a woman, or any one who suffered, Jack instantly took the place of adviser and helper with indescribable tenderness and quickness of insight. He gave but one look at her face.

"Whatever the trouble is, you are unnecessarily alarmed," he said, taking her hand gravely, without pausing for greeting. "You say your father is in danger. Take time to think, and then give me the plain facts—without your fears."

He was not alarmed. The colonel had no doubt gone headlong into some difficulty, and Isabel, practical as she was, exaggerated it, according to the manner of women.

Isabel looked at the clock; there was only an hour in which to do her work; she paused, choosing her words. "My father left Philadelphia for Nittany, tricked by a forged letter. He is now one hour on his way to Lock Haven. On the train there is a man who has been paid to murder him."

"Murder! my dear Miss Latimer! You are terribly nervous and tired. Tell me what the colonel's difficulty really is.   But murder?   We don't live in the dark ages, or days of assassins," trying not to smile.

"My father has made enemies.   They are the same men who paid for the killing of John Ford."

The smile left Andross's face.   It was quite true—there had been such a wretched business last winter. Ford had been shot by the order of the Whiskey Ring, and when the actual murderers threatened to betray their employers, the poor wretches had both been killed, and all inquiry hushed speedily.   But Colonel Latimer——

"What object could they have in attacking your father?"

"A plain business object; he was ruining the profits of all the distilleries, and can not be removed.   The man who threatened him was a distiller, Wilkins; employed by Houston Laird."

"Wilkins?   Yes, go on."   Andross came a step nearer, his countenance altering strangely.

"When I found the letter was a forgery, I followed my father here.   I was but an hour behind him.   He was alone when he left home.   The station master here, who knows him, tells me that he left the train in company with a distiller named Barry; that Barry was in close converse with a man who was waiting for him at the depot, and whom he introduced to the colonel as a friend who was going up deer shooting in the mountains; and that both men went on the train with him to Lock Haven."

Andross was silent.   Some question hung on his lips which he dared not ask.

"There is no danger for my father on the train," speaking in the same monotonous, unnatural voice. "But he will be cordial and friendly with this man. He will offer to ride with him across the mountains—it will be night.   It is nearly night now," looking wildly out of the window.

"What manner of man was this friend of Barry's?"

"Short, broadly-built, light haired."

"Did—did the station master hear his name?"

In all her own agitation, Isabel was startled by the sudden ghastliness of the man before her as he asked the question.

"He knows him. His name is Voss."

Andross threw up his hand, and turned away from her. In all the grief or pleasure of his life he had been used to give vehement expression to his always stormy emotions. Now, he uttered neither word nor cry; yet something in the very air held Isabel dumb and motionless, awed by the presence of a more terrible pain than her own.

"If your father is murdered," he said, with unnatural quietness, "it is not Voss who has done it—it is I."

"I do not know what you can mean. But you will go with me? I was sure you would go with me to follow them."

"Follow them? Is there time? to save him?"

"The train will not leave for nearly an hour," speaking distinctly and slowly, as she observed his vacant, bewildered look. "We may not be in time, but we can follow them. Can anything be done here?"

The words woke him as from a stupor. "Something can be done—yes. I can repair my mistake here. My whole life has been a mistake. Oh, my God! I see that now!"

The agony of this strong, cheerful fellow was more than Isabel could look upon; she felt dully that he should always be just the old merry Jack, fun-loving, affectionate; she offered no sympathy nor comfort. In his pain he was far apart from her. No one but God could help him.

She turned away and stood quietly by the fire. It was noticeable that in this hour of delay, she gave no sign of impatience, or made no moan to intrude her suffering on others.

"You will wait for me here, Miss Latimer?" he said at last. "I shall not detain you long;" and closing the door he crossed the rotunda again. Willitts met him.

"Thank Heaven! you're here!" too eager and excited to observe his silence. "Hill, when he voted 'no' just now, hinted that you had dodged at the last minute! It fairly took the breath from our people. Hark!"

"John Andross!"

The harsh, nasal voice of the clerk could be heard outside of the Senate chamber.

Andross shook off Willitts's hold, and went slowly down the middle aisle to his seat.

"The honourable member from Philadelphia," drily interposed a member (who had just voted with the opposition), "probably requires to be informed that the bill now before the house is for the relief of the National Transit Company, in which he is said to be, of late, largely interested. The question is, in fact, left for him to decide—shall it pass?"

"John Andross!" called the clerk again.

"*No.*"

There was a moment's pause of amazement, and then a burst of cheers from the younger members of the opposition, mingled with a few hisses from the other side.

But astonishment soon hushed the house. Andross remained standing, waiting for silence. As soon as he could be heard he said, in a low voice, "I shall not offer any reason for the vote which I have just given. But I wish it recorded as my last public act while a member of this body. I tender my resignation to you, Mr. Speaker, from the Senate of Pennsylvania, to take effect from this day. I resign, because —— " he stopped, his eyes wandering uncertainly from face to face; to Jack they all seemed friendly faces—they had met him from day to day with kindliness, and jokes, and laughter—"because I—I know myself unfit to hold a seat longer among you."

From any other man the words might have been followed by jeers or indifference. Legislative bodies are suspicious of anything that savours of the melodrama. But Jack Andross was known to every man there; the terrible sincerity of the few words moved them.

"It was like the death cry of a woman," old Hetherington said afterwards.

It was in the midst of absolute silence that Andross walked, alone and degraded, out of the chamber which he was never to enter again.

Not altogether alone; for as he passed through the middle aisle, a thin, black-a-vised man, shabby yet prim as to clothes, came eagerly down to meet him and, taking his arm, went out with him.

"Was this necessary, Jack?" he said when they had reached the Rotunda.

"Is it you, Braddock? I have but an hour——" looking about him as if the light blinded him. Braddock, seeing how he was shaken, asked no questions after that, but followed him with affectionate zeal, glowering fiercely at every passer-by who looked askance at Andross.

It was so like Jack, he thought angrily, in this outbreak of remorse, to humiliate himself before the world! Why could he not quietly have slipped out of the Senate? —— "Unfit to remain with them?" A gang of bribe givers and bribe takers! He followed Andross until he pushed open the door of the committee room. The gas burned brightly within. The room seemed crowded to Andross, as he stood on the threshold. Isabel stood waiting. Houston Laird was there and the members who had sat in caucus night after night, to push his bill; Judge Maddox and, nearest of all, her blue reproachful eyes fixed on his—— Anna. The blue eyes, perceiving Braddock behind him, it is true, wandered occasionally; but Braddock, although he had come to Harrisburgh in the desperate hope of finding comfort with Anna, avoided her now and drew back into a dark corner, out of sight.

Judge Maddox, in the excess of his wrath, could scarcely wait for Andross to enter the room.

"It is hardly worth while to tell you that you have ruined me," he stammered.

"Mr. Andross has a right to vote as he chooses," said one of the members; "but if he will explain why he deceived us during these two days——"

"Why should he explain?" hastily interposed Laird. "Why need there be any farther recrimination? I came here to beg there should be none. The vote is given. Mr. Andross has resigned his seat. There shall be an end of it."

"No. I have a word to say," said Andross. He had come up to the square table and stood leaning on his knuckles, facing them, the light full on his pale, bearded face. There was silence for a moment. The crowd about him were so many shadows; he saw only the woman that he loved, and whom he was going to put away from him forever.

"I am sorry if I have caused you any loss," turning dully to Maddox. "I ruined myself first of all. I've been playing a sham part long enough. I'm going to end it now."

"You are going to act like a rash, headlong Hotspur, as usual, Andross," said Laird, laying his hand soothingly on his shoulder; but whether prompted by kindness or policy he could not himself at the moment have told.

"When I was a boy," continued Jack, without noticing him, "I learned the meanest tricks of trade and practised them, through fear of—of a man who held a rod over me. When I was in your office, Judge Maddox, I robbed you of six thousand dollars to rid myself of him: to-day I was accessory to a murder to buy his silence about that theft. I do not blame him. It is I who have been the thief and the coward."

"Six thousand? I never missed that money!" stammered the judge. "It's very remarkable!"

"Now, gentlemen," said Jack, turning to the men, "you know the worst of me. "I need buy no man's silence henceforth. I always thought myself a strong man," his chin quivering, "but I've been weak—weak as water."

There was an embarrassed pause. One or two of the legislators went quietly out of the door, nodding to the others, who, after a moment's hesitation, followed them without a word.

Judge Maddox broke the silence. It was the time, he felt, to adjust all matters definitely that concerned this young man in the future.

"This is an astounding disclosure to me! Truly astounding!" after a preparatory cough. "You can hardly expect, Mr. Andross, that after you confess yourself guilty of theft (though I can't, for my soul, see when that six thousand——) guilty of theft, as I say, that you should retain any pretension to my daughter's hand."

Andross looked at her in silence; but the soft blue eyes went wandering to the ceiling, the floor, everywhere but his face.

"I do not expect it," he said in a low tone.

"Come, my daughter, we will go then," rising and drawing her hand into his arm.

Andross made a quick step between the pink-robed figure and the door. He held out his hands; "*Anna!*"

"What is it, Jack?" calmly.

"If I have sinned, it was for you. It was because I loved you that I turned my back on my God. It was to put away all obstacles between us that I took the money; that I came here as the tool of the Ring. They bought me for the worst purposes to-day, with the promise that you should be my wife, and *you knew it.*"

"Oh, yes, I knew that," with an arch little nod.

"I never deserved you as I do to-night, when I am ruined and disgraced. I have left myself nothing but you. Can you give me up?"

"You have no right to distress my daughter in this way," blustered the judge.

But Andross only held out his hands to her with the look of a drowning man asking for help. "Come to me. I have only you. And I—I loved you so!"

"Don't hold my arm, papa," composedly. "He does not distress *me* in the least. I can not marry you, Mr. Andross, even if I wished to marry any gentleman whose social position would be so uncertain, because——" she grew a little paler, and her pipe of a voice quailed slightly, "because—— It's quite time that I told you about it, papa——I am a wife already. I have been married for two months—to Mr. Ware. Oh, dear!" beginning to cry. "Where *is* Julius? He never is near when he is wanted."

She began to cry more vehemently in a minute or two. There was something awful even to her shallow soul in the face of the man whose life in this world and the next she had trampled down: there was such a blank silence about her too: it was not at all the delightful dismay and melodrama to which she had always looked forward in this denouement. "Take me home, papa. Why don't you take me home?" she cried irritably.

The judge, who had dropped into a seat with his purple face buried in his hands, groaned aloud: "Married! To a starving preacher! How in Heaven's name am I to meet Bislow's mortgage, now?"

Anna turned from him to be confronted by Braddock, lean and stern and black-coated; fit, she thought, for a judge in any lugubrious Presbyterian Israel.

"Do you mean to tell me," catching her by the pink

bejewelled wrists, "that you were another man's wife a
week ago?" He dropped his hold of her with a gesture
which, in a less religious man might, she felt, with a delicious excitement have been a curse. He turned his pale
face to Isabel. He saw now what he had lost for this
poor creature—saw how weak and guilty he had been ;
how that he in his immaculate strength had fallen as far
as Andross. "To think that a woman—a member of the
Christian church, should drag men so near to hell!"
he cried.

"And for Ware!" muttered the judge. "A fellow
without a penny!"

"You shall not speak harshly to her, Braddock," said
Jack. "Poor child! poor little child!" looking down
at her as she crept up to him, with infinite tenderness and
pity in his sad eyes. He even saw the red marks on her
wrists, which she rubbed and held to her cheek; remembering, as he did it, that it was the last time he should
ever be so near her or touch her.

"Nobody was ever so good to me as you, Jack!" she
sobbed.

He put her gently away from him. "I loved you for
a long time, Anna. I wish you could have found it in
your heart to care for me. But you were right to marry
the man you loved. I don't blame you." He hesitated
a moment, and then raised the reddened little wrist to
his lips. "Good bye," he said simply, and went to the
door, whence Isabel followed him.

When they were gone, and Anna was left alone in the
gaudily dismal room with her fat, groaning father, and
Mr. Laird, who began to button up his overcoat, as if the
play were over, she felt as if the anti-climax was indeed
flat—the conclusion of her long-projected romance both
lame and impotent. Both Andross and Braddock were
gone now out of her life forever. Nobody was left but
Ware, and fond as she was of Julius, she had long ago discovered that he would never play up to her in any of
her little dramas of passion.

"Shall we go home now, papa?" she asked again,
shivering drearily, and looking at the flaring lights, the
hearth covered with ashes and tobacco-juice, and her pink
silk skirt drabbled and wet.

"You will go with your husband as soon as he comes to claim you," said the judge.

"Julius lives a life of faith. He has no settled home," she said, shuddering, as she remembered the cheap boarding-house in Philadelphia in which he made his abiding place.

"Then you can live a life of faith together," coolly. "There he comes across the Rotunda," as a large figure striding grandiloquently, came in sight.

"At least," she cried shrilly, looking up at Laird, "nobody can deny that I made a love-match."

"No," bowing gallantly. "Who could accuse you of mercenary motives?"

"They might have done so," shaking her head solemnly, "if I had married that poor Andross. Only see how he has turned out! It would have really been a judgment on me. He reminded me just now when he went out into the night, of Cain driven forth a vagabond and a wanderer."

"Yes," looking gravely out into the gathering darkness, "poor Jack's punishment is heavy enough. 'Bad has begun, yet'"—with a shrewd glance over the drabbled pretty figure, "in my judgment, 'worse remained behind.'"

"I don't understand you," lisped Anna, innocently. "Ah, here is dear Julius, papa!"

* * *

CHAPTER XXXIV.

THE journey to Lock Haven was made in the midst of a driving storm. The hail beat on the car-windows and ran down in glittering drops outside. Isabel sat quite erect, holding her hands together, looking steadily out as though she could penetrate the darkness.

They would be riding side by side through the mountain gorges now. It was dark—dark—— There were gaps and crevices at the side of every mountain road where the snow lay deep all winter. A man could drag a dead body there and it would not be found for years——.

Once or twice Andross, who paced up and down the
car as though he would have urged it on by his motion,
stopped and said to her: "Do you think we will be in
time?" It seemed to her as if it were a boy or a child ·
who had asked the question : he was so unable, dependent, restless.   Yet there were times when she read in his
ghastly face some pain worse than her own, and wondered
vaguely at it.   It was not his old father who was to be
done to death to-night.

When they had almost reached Lock Haven, they were
alone in the car, and Jack sat down beside her.   He was
a man who could not keep even the extremest pain hidden in his soul without groping for some man or woman's
hand to help him.   He began talking to her in a slow,
incoherent way that she could not understand, of the boy
Jack Andross long ago, whose mother used to sit teaching
him at night; and of some psalms ("The Lord is my
Shepherd," was one of them), that she had taught him:
and then he repeated that verse, "Though I walk
through the valley of the shadow of death, I shall fear no
evil; for Thou art with me."

Isabel dully was conscious that Jack had had a good
deal of trouble to bear to-night, and was sorry for him;
but she could not understand any one who made this incessant moan when in pain.   The whole matter dropped
speedily out of her mind, together with the crimes im-
puted to Andross to-night.   Isabel having once accepted
man or woman, had an incurious habit of shutting her
eyes and ears to all reports, or even facts, concerning
them thereafter.   She might hear it proved, on the clear-
est testimony, that her companion was a thief or a murderer, but in five minutes she would swing stupidly back
to her old conviction, that it was only Jack Andross, who
was her father's friend up in Nittany, a good shot, full of
fun, and altogether a loveable sort of a fellow.

If she had not been so slow, she would have seen where
he stood to-night, and not have left him so utterly alone.
Andross was not a man who could stand alone.

She turned her face mechanically to the window: the
range of rolling hills which her father must cross was
now in sight, mere gloomy shadows against the unlighted
horizon.   Lonely even at noonday; but at night who

would hear a solitary pistol-shot? The man had chosen his ground well; there was no chance of interruption when he chose to kill his victim.

Jack, when she turned away from him, had gone out and stood on the platform as the train slackened its speed, rushing toward the sleeping town. He had been certain (according to his habit of boyish, irrational hopes), that Colonel Latimer would have stopped in Lock Haven, and would come up to meet him with his usual Hillo on the platform. It was not in nature—God couldn't mean it, that the old man should die! That he—Jack Andross —should have his blood on his hands!

"Why, I'm his friend!" he cried. "I wanted to be a friend to everybody—and an honest man!"

He felt in his heart, too, even now, that he had not been a bad sort of fellow: that he had had a friendly, cordial feeling toward God: there was not a day when he had not thanked Him for this beautiful world, and wished he could live closer to Him, and yet—— Because he had been weak now and then—this had come upon him! He looked wildly up and down the familiar, silent streets as the car rolled on. It seemed incredible to him that all these sleeping people, whom he knew, should be innocent —and he out in the night, a thief and a murderer.

He opened the car door and came up to Isabel as the brakes grated, and the train rumbled heavily up to the station. When she looked up at him, she took his hand hastily in hers. She had been selfish to forget the poor creature in his misery, she thought.

"If your father is not here—— if he has gone on —— and is dead, it is I who have done it!" he cried. He could not have helped crying out thus to her. He was so utterly deserted by God and man that, with his temperament, he would have gone mad, if some human being had not broken the silence into which his life seemed to have fallen.

Isabel, at last, understood how the case stood with him. She waited a moment to think what she should say. She had never come near a soul in such straits before. "I shall never reproach you with what you have done. I know how you have tried to do right, and—— *God knows. Come, let us go,"* rising.

He followed her slowly out of the car, afraid to look at the group of figures on the platform, dimly seen through the falling snow—lest Latimer's should not be among them.

Now there was in fact a reasonable chance for this most unreasonable expectation; for Andross had forgotten that, as they waited in the depot in Harrisburgh, Braddock, who had followed them from the Capitol, had drawn him aside, and obtained a full account of the purpose and meaning of their journey. Braddock had gone promptly into the adjacent office, and telegraphed to Lock Haven that the colonel should be detained there until his arrival, and then had taken a seat in the rear car. He had—he knew in bitterness of soul—no right to offer help to Isabel. Andross, of course, had never thought of such matter-of-fact aids as Braddock or the telegraph. The only chance to prevent the murder was for him to follow Voss, and, in a hand to hand struggle kill him or be killed. But the telegraph office in Lock Haven had been closed for an hour, which fact Braddock, with all his business-like readiness, forgot was the custom in the little town until he was on his way.

It seemed, indeed, as if Jack's were to be the only way of rescue. He followed Isabel to the half-dozen dark figures on the platform. She looked at them, and turned away. Her father was not among them. But Andross took her place, speaking rapidly and with decision. Since Isabel had shown some sign of interest in him, his veins seemed to be filled with new blood.

"Has Colonel Latimer gone on to Nittany?"

"Yes, sir; him and another gentleman—— By George! Mr. Andross! I didn't know you!" The station master knuckled his hat which, like his caped cloak, was heavy with snow.

"Were they on horseback?"

"Yes, sir. You're not going on, surely. It's a monstrous rough night to be out on the mountains, as I told the colonel. But he said there was a sick lad waiting for him in Nittany, and his friend determined to pull through with him. That's never Miss Latimer!" going up to her, for Andross had left him after the first word and had already bargained with Joe, from the Fallon House, for the sleigh and horses, which he had brought down to meet the train.

"How far are they in advance of us?" was Isabel's only reply to the station master's bows and questions.

"They've been gone an hour. Quite an hour I should say, Joseph?"

"About that. No, Mr. Andross, you'd get no better team than that if you tried every stable in the town."

Some mystery was abroad which Joe would fain have discovered. He hung about Andross until he disappeared into the station, where by the lamp he hastily examined the priming of his pistols, buttoning them in his breast pocket more carefully, to keep them dry. When he came out, a tall man was feeling in the darkness the girths of the horses, loosening a strap here, tightening a knot there.

"There will be no time for stopping to do this on the way," he said when Andross muttered, impatiently, at the delay.

"You, Braddock? Now, Miss Latimer, you will go to the hotel. I shall come back as soon as —— as I can bring you word, what the end was."

"I? I am going to my father, Mr. Andross."

"That is impossible; —— Braddock?"

"Let her go," whispered Clay. "Lift her in and wrap the buffalo-robes about her." He stood apart, while Andross obeyed him, and watched them disappear in the blinding snow. Isabel had heard him, and leaned from the sleigh, trying to see his face, but she could not. Her strength left her then for the first time. There seemed to be nothing before her in that whirling gray night but death. If Clay could but have come with her—if she could only have heard a word of advice from him, it must have ended differently!

That strength-giving hero meanwhile, according to his systematic habit, had gone to a livery stable and hired a stronger horse than either of Joe's, and was rapidly following them up the road that led to the hills, gaining on them with every mile: the echoes of his horse's feet lost in the soft, deep snow.

CHAPTER XXXV.

ANDROSS stopped at a toll-house; afterward, three or four miles further on, at a cabin in which a light was burning. At both, the same report was given. The two men had passed on horseback an hour before, riding side by side, the gate-keeper said. The man in the cabin, Leftwik, an old Swede, who lived by trapping, had been summoned to the door by the colonel to bring a light.

Something had gone wrong with the saddle: a girth cut, which the old colonel had tied up. It was Colonel Latimer, of course; Leftwik had known him this many a year. He had his joke and laugh as usual, in spite of the sleet which beat in his face. The other gentleman had fallen a few paces behind the colonel, and seemed grum and quiet. Thought he was disheartened with the weather. It was the worst storm of the winter. They would not put up till morning? with a curious glance at the cloaked woman's figure.

A few paces behind? Andross did not turn after this to look at his companion. He felt that the end was at hand. They were nearing the higher peaks of the range now, where the road ran through long gorges to gain the valleys beyond. These mountains were lonely, untraversed even in summer by the most adventurous hunters; the defiles deep and drifted now high with snow. Their progress was slow. Andross could do no more than sit wet and half frozen, patiently urging forward the unable horses, that had showed signs of exhaustion an hour after starting. The heavy sleigh more than once had balked, in the wet, clogging snow. If he could have run or have fought his way through the night and snow, this dead weight would not have settled on his body and brain. But to plod, plod, step by step, when the gain of a minute might save the old man's life and leave his soul clear of murder! More than once he fancied he heard, echoed in the depths of the interminable leafless forest, a pistol shot, or cries; and then the horses would drag more slowly than before.

"I've been in a hurry all my life," thought Jack, with

a forlorn laugh. "I suppose the end is to be measured off for me."

For unconsciously, and without regret, he knew this was the end. To-day his past life had closed, and barred all its highways to him : left him without work, wages, a friend, or purpose in the world.

They had reached that toll-house which stands on a high level at the entrance of the chain of barren peaks, or rather massed rocks, heaped, height on height, as for a rampart in some old war of the giants. Even in summer they are utterly destitute of vegetation : lichens and the tender moss, which hide all unsightly things, never had essayed to shelter their savage rudeness; but now the snow had frozen in the gorges between, and coldly whitened the darkest crevices, throwing into bold relief the full meaning of the mountains. It seemed to Andross, standing on the height, that they turned to him the unfeeling solitude of a dead face, with the white cere-cloth loosely fallen from about it. The snow had ceased to fall, the moon had risen, and threw a ghastly light upon the farther peaks on the horizon.

Jack shouted and pounded on the door. It was a relief to hear his own voice and that of the old one-armed gate-keeper. "Colonel Latimer had passed through the gate. The man with him was a stranger. They might have gone two miles by this time."

"I thought it would be done here," Jack muttered, looking down the long defile before him. He trudged along by the horses' heads; any motion was better than to sit idly holding the reins.

As the mountains rose higher on either side of the road, the shadows fell more heavily. The deep snow penetrated his clothes, icy-cold. He could fancy the old man, lying helpless, buried in it, the life-blood oozing away in it. If Voss attacked him before he reached Nittany, it was here that it was done. And he, Jack Andross, had counselled and sent him to do it.

As Jack ploughed his way through the narrow chasm, one hand on the horse's bit and the other on his pistol, he no longer glanced warily from side to side. Latimer and Anna and Laird slipped away from him, and he seemed to be alone, face to face with the God whom his mother knew. Not Braddock's implacable Judge. The God of the old hymns—— "He maketh us to lie down in green pastures——" "His loving kindness—loving kindness——" "Even as a father pitieth his children."

The boy (for he was nothing but a boy) said these scraps over and over, staring straight on. He understood now! Oh, he understood! How he had turned his back on Him. Had the punishment come? Or was there yet a chance? The loving kindness——

The hour which enters once into every man's life had come at last to the merry, social, weak fellow: friends and lovers were gone, and his soul was alone with God in judgment.

The snow had drifted here but lightly. He could not be mistaken: there were marks of heavy trampling. There had been a struggle.

Stooping to follow the tracks of horses' feet, he hurried on into the now unbroken silence. After a mile was passed, a low, shapeless figure came up the gorge, meeting them. It was Heltzer from Millheim, on his donkey. Jack remembered both well. But it was no time for greetings.

"Have you met any travellers before us in the gorge?"

"Yes," grunted Heltzer from out his mufflers.

Jack left the sleigh and came up close to the donkey, out of Isabel's hearing. It was a minute before his dry lips could ask the question.

"How many men did you meet?"

"Only one, riding alone."

Andross walked on, holding the horse, holding his pistol also more tightly. In a moment or two the soft thud of a horse's feet was heard, and Braddock rode up behind him. Jack did not look up. Clay stooped beside him.

"I met Heltzer," he said. "It is all over."

"Yes, it is all over."

"Where are you going?"

"Voss is alive—and I——"

"There shall be no bloodshed, Andross. I will go with you; we will arrest the man."

The silence was unbroken until Heltzer remembering

at last that he had not finished all he wished to say, jogged back after them.

"That man I met went to the cabin in the Black Wolf Hollow—if you want him."

"I want him," said Andross, and dropping the rein, ran on quickly out of Braddock's sight or reach of call.

The gleam of light from the cabin lay like a red bar across the darkness for a mile ahead. But as he neared it, Voss, on a powerful gray pony, rode boldly up out of a dark gap, and stopped with his horse's nostrils breathing hotly in Jack's face. Jack leaped at him with the strength of a wild beast.

"Where is Colonel Latimer?"

"Take care, Mr. Andross," coolly, "I'm armed."

"You have murdered him!"

"That was what you bargained with me to do, I believe. Look there!"

Jack turned to the cabin. In the open door, the firelight showing his big bony body from head to foot, stood Colonel Latimer.

When Andross turned again, he found that Voss was talking.

"Of course I'm sorry to miss any job. And Wilkins was liberal to me—very liberal. Wilkins knows a good man's worth a good price. If it had been himself or your friend Laird, or any of that kind of currency I had to give a lesson to, I'd not have backed out. But I rode from Harrisburgh to here with this old man. You didn't tell me what sort of stuff he was, Mr. Andross. I was taken at a disadvantage, as I might say."

"And—and what did you find him, Voss?" Jack laughed aloud with a fierce, convulsive clutching in the throat. It seemed to him for a minute as if the heat of summer weather was about him, and Voss was the best of good fellows.

"I don't know what you'd call him. But he treated *me* as if I was a man. After I'd knowed him for an hour, talkin' free-like, I couldn't have put a bullet through his head no more that if it had been my mother's. D'ye think Wilkins 'll allow nothing on the pay? I don't often go back on my word, and I can't well afford to lose the money, neither. It's been an infernally cold jaunt—"

But Andross, seeing the sleigh close at hand, had run to it, lifted Isabel out as if she were a baby, and carried her to her father—putting her right into his arms.

"There, there!" he shouted, and then groped blindly about for a seat. Somebody placed him in one, and presently, when he could see, he found that Braddock had loosened his cravat, and was quietly holding snow to his face; but Isabel was still sobbing over the astonished colonel, stroking his bony hands and gray hair as if not yet sure that she had him safe again.

CHAPTER XXXVI.

VAN METER, the owner of the cabin, bustled to and fro heaping up the fires, shutting the colonel and his daughter into an inner room, bringing out whiskey and urging it on everybody. What explanation Isabel made to her father no one knew; nor how much he received as fact. He came out presently, with a more bewildered look than before; but his old habit of military command always stood him in good stead in an emergency.

"Isabel has been telling me some wild story of forged letters and assassinations; women always do make a mess of business. One would suppose she had been reading Mrs. Radcliffe's romances."

Andross came up to him. He had not yet confessed his guilt to the old man, he remembered. "She has told you the truth," he began, "and I——"

"No, no, Mr. Andross! have done with it!" laughing nervously. "I want no more tales of horrors. I shall believe just as much as I please of the whole story. That man Voss appears to me to be a very decent, well-meaning sort of fellow, and I'm not often mistaken in human nature. One thing is certain, however, that my nephew, Hale Latimer, is not with our friend Van Meter here, as I expected to find him. We are only three miles from Nittany. We will go on at once to the old house. I left a man in it, so that it might be ready for us whenever we chose to go back home for a day or two. Home will be welcome to us all, just now."

He looked direct at Andross as he spoke, but Jack drew back. "I cau not go. You would not bring me under your roof, Colonel Latimer, if you knew——"

"But I would, sir!" laying his both hands on the young man's shoulders, his face kindling. "I know all about you, boy. Better than you do yourself: much better! There's no man living who is a more honoured and welcome guest at my hearth than you. Now," changing his tone hurriedly to prevent any answer, "look to the horses, will you, Jack? Van Meter will give them a meal, and in an hour we'll all be under the old roof again, thank God!"

He turned to Braddock, drawing himself up formally; his hospitable soul could not withhold an invitation, though in truth it cut sorely against the grain to give it. But the doctor, sterner and stiffer than usual in his wet clothes and frozen black whiskers about his lean face, stood by the great chimney-place looking down with a dull despair into Isabel's face, as she sat drying her feet by the fire. His coat and trousers and whiskers were thawing and steaming together, but he did not know it. He knew nothing but that he had wakened from a befogged, impure dream to the old daylight-world again, and that he stood alone in it.

Neither Clay nor Isabel were people used to dramatize their feelings. She looked steadily into Van Meter's roaring fire, because she was afraid to meet his eye. She knew he had come back to her; should she trust to him again? If she gave a look or sign of forgiveness, it must hold good forever. Isabel gave no half pledges.

The colonel, after a momentary scrutiny of the pair, wheeled around in his opinion, and silently took Braddock's part violently. "It's all been a cursed mistake, somehow. There's no lie in that boy's face," he thought. "Isabel ought to see that. But women are as unforgiving as the devil, and as unreasonable." Afraid that he might be led in his wrath to interfere, he went out to help Andross and Van Meter with the horses.

They were alone. It might be the last minute they would ever be alone. If he lost this chance——

But Braddock, trembling with fear and real, honest love, was yet eminently practical in his wooing.

"Your gloves are wet," he said, stooping nearer her. "Your wrists look frozen with cold."

She drew them off, and tried to answer him; but could not—broke down with the first word. She would have him now think she was crying because her hands were cold!

She held them up to the fire, resolutely, and then caught sight of his sad, thin face.

"You used to give me your hands to warm, to keep them from aching," he said, with a miserable smile. "You would not do that now, Isabel."

She had meant that he should humble himself so low, before she forgave him—and he had not humbled himself at all! He had asked nothing but to warm her hands. They were cold; God knows, she was all cold, body and soul, since he left her.

She turned her honest eyes full on his, and after a moment's searching, held out the blue, stiff hands.

The heat rushed to his face. She had not thought such fire and passion was in the man. He held them close to his breast. "Am I to keep them, Isabel?" he asked, under his breath.

"Yes, Clay." She rose, and they stood face to face.

"But you told me that you no longer loved me, Isabel?"

"That was a mistake of mine then," with a shy blush.

"You do love me as much as before?" eagerly. "There is no change in your love for me?"

"I did not say that." She looked gravely at him, deliberating. "No," said the honest, dull creature, shaking her head slowly. "I can never say that I love you as I did, Clay."

The colonel sat radiant at the foot of the breakfast table the next morning. The house was warmed and in order; they all slept late, and just before the meal was ready, who should appear in the kitchen door, like the genial black genius of the place, but Oth? The old man had gathered from Miss Morgan's terrors and from the boy Dick, the facts of his master's danger, and followed Isabel on the next train. He had cried and prayed out his thankfulness, in the colonel's room, and then rushed out to find vent for his remaining emotion in raids upon the neighborhood for venison and coffee for the breakfast table.

"This is home at last!" cried the colonel, turning from old Nittany, towering without, his feet in snow and head in the misty sky, to the faces of the guests beside him. No winter morning in town was ever so exhilarating in its cold; the creek babbled a subdued welcome under its icy cover, all about the house; the honeysuckles on the window glittered with hoar frost; the very cocks and hens, perched on the barn fence, clucked and crowed a good morning to him. A heap of fragrant pine logs crackled and roared on the hearth; the venison sent up a savory smell. Oth could not hide his delighted grin as he passed the cups.

"It is all just as it should be—just as it should be!" said the colonel rubbing his hands, looking at Bell, Braddock, and Andross in turn, his face in a glow. "If the bear skin was back, and my arm-chair, and pipes! What if we send for them, and settle down for a week's holiday?" He kept silence for a minute or two, and then brought down his fist on his knee.

"By George! What, if we bring up the bear skin and pipes, and settle down here altogether? The Works are in the market again. I can buy them—part cash down, and you two boys shall run them. What do you say? What do you say?"

"There would be no better investment for your money, Colonel. The works have yielded twenty per cent this fall," said Braddock guardedly, although his lean face had reddened with excitement.

"Confound the per cent! We four are not a money-making fraternity, Clay. We've had enough of the eternal digging for dollars in town; now we'll try for something better. Well, what do you say, Andross?" leaning over the table to take him by the hand. "You are to live in the house with us, remember. We'll all make a fresh start again in old Nittany, please God."

But Andross replied so gravely and rationally that the colonel grew silent. "The boy's hearty spirit is killed within him," he said to Bell, shaking his head sorrowfully when the two young men had gone out. "There's no use in trying to bring him to life again."

"We'll try, papa," said Isabel quietly.

Braddock and Jack walked over to the Works, to look about them. Braddock, who usually cared but little for men's moods, was startled at the change in Andross. He sat dully in his old office, scarcely noticing even the books which he had left upon the shelves; and when the men crowded about the door, hearing he was within, and cheering as he came out, his greeting was so lifeless and unsmiling that the cheer died away half uttered.

Braddock, observing him closely with a physician's eye, found more cause for alarm than did even the colonel. Andross, he saw, had reached one of those crises which occur in the lives of nervous men, when mental and physical vitality are exhausted by some work or disappointment which has produced a mortal overdrain. The chances are even in such a case, he told Isabel, whether, through strong new interests the ducts of the man's life fill again with healthy currents, or whether he sink into disease, inability, or death. With Andross's full, vehement temperament, the latter road would be but a short one.

But once, Andross was roused to a likeness of his old self. He was going over the books of the firm, with Braddock, preparatory to the final purchase. "I have a sum of about six thousand dollars saved," he said, "which I could have put into this to help the colonel with his first payment; but I owe it to Judge Maddox."

Braddock found it hard to bring himself to speak; but he could not let his hard earnings go to the Maddoxes, father or daughter.

"You owe it to me, Jack," he said gently, without pausing as he jotted down a line of figures. When he looked up, Andross was standing in front of him.

"I never knew you before, Clay," he whispered hoarsely. "Why did you keep this from me?"

"I don't like a fuss," dipping his pen again in the ink.

———◦◦◦———

CHAPTER XXXVII.

OLD Nittany never relapsed into its ancient depth of melancholy again. Braddock and Isabel were married in the homestead early in May. The Works were soon in full and successful operation. The colonel did propose to try wood instead of charcoal, but was contented at last to leave the business in the younger men's hands, and to carry on his divers experiments in an adjacent shed. · His next proposition was that Houston Laird should be invited to take part of the stock, but this idea was received so coldly by the rest of the family, that he wisely dropped it. He always retained his old faith in Laird's honour, however, in spite of the prejudices of the young people, and was delighted to find, when he ran down to New York once a year, that the failure of the Transit Company had not seriously injured that gentleman's credit in Wall street. "He certainly passed through bankruptcy," he told Isabel, after one visit four years later. "But he seems to have renewed his strength as speedily as that fabulous bird the phœnix, or Job. It always struck me that Job must have had remarkable financial ability with his other virtues. You remember the story of the recovery of his fortune, Isabel? I assure you, my dear, I consider Houston Laird one of the most remarkable men of this day. Just as unflagging as ever, too, in his efforts to do good—president of the Christian Brotherhood, and so on. He gave me a dinner at his club; very nice—very nice indeed. All the best men in New York were there."

"Do you ever hear anything of that unfortunate man, Ware, papa?"

"You pity him because he married little Anna? Now, she really makes a most admirable wife; she has grown stout, to be sure. But she is devoted to her husband, Laird tells me. Oh there's no doubt that Ware is a most devout person—lives wholly by faith : it is wonderful to read the anecdotes about him in the papers, how he relies on Providence. Still, if it wasn't for Anna's music teaching, and the help which Maddox gives them, she and the children, Laird says, would absolutely starve. I—I was thinking we might make up a little box of clothes, country produce, and so on—eh—my dear? They're quite used to that sort of thing. Living by faith, you see?"

"No, papa." Isabel shook her head quietly, but a portentous heat rose into her pale cheeks. "I shall send them no box, I am sure," she added with acrimony, "the sight of that wreck yonder," nodding to Andross outside, "ought to convince you what manner of woman she is!"

"Yes, that's true. Tut, tut! Andross will never be his old self. The jolliest, heartiest fellow! But he's very far from being a wreck, Bell. Braddock says his attention to business is wonderful, and I'm sure he is a slave to little Tom. Look there!" watching Jack romping with Isabel's child with sparkling eyes, and then taking up his hat to join them.

"*I* call him a wreck," persisted Isabel. In fact, she carried Andross in her heart and head very much as she did her father or her baby—regarding them all as unable, irresponsible beings. "He ought to have a wife and Toms of his own to slave for," she secretly thought.

As year after year passed, and Jack went and came on the business of the firm, and friends, both men and women, began to gather about him in the old eager, cordial fashion, the colonel declared the lad was his old self again. "He sings and whistles even over his accounts; he is like a gust of fresh wind coming into the house, with his jokes and romps with Tom: he is flinging his money away on old crockery again—what more do you want?"

But Isabel saw with shrewder eyes. "God only could see," she said, "how deep were the scars and hurts left in his soul after that pink, drabbled little creature had handled and flung it from her."

It was in accordance with a plan of Isabel's that the whole family went one August to a quiet little watering place on the coast, when she knew that Ware and his wife were there. Anna was undeniably stout and slovenly; she made a demi-god of the handsome, well-dressed Julius, and insisted that all other people should worship, or at least pay tithes to him. But shrill and shrewish and fat as she was, she served and drudged for her big, lazy Baal sincerely and unselfishly, and never had deserved as much respect and love from Andross as now, when he seemed disposed to give her the least.

He watched her every day, toiling after Julius, carrying a subscription book in her pocket, which she presented unblushingly to every new acquaintance with the old story of the life of faith, Jung Stilling, etc. "Ware has brought her down to his own level," he said, indifferently, to Isabel.

"He is cured," she thought, triumphantly.

One evening, when she was alone with him on the beach, as he lay in the sand at her feet, watching the tide come in, she spoke to him, for the first time in her life, of himself. She had meant to do it for years, but never had been able to find the courage; and now she did it half by accident, unconsciously. Andross had carelessly mentioned some one who passed as "a successful man."

"Wealth or high position hardly seems to me to deserve the name of success in life," Isabel said slowly, and then glancing down at him, her colour suddenly rose and she went on hastily. "A man who, through years and years, fights against his besetting folly or his weakness, and conquers it—that is the successful man, Jack."

He made no answer. She was not fluent at any time, and was, after all, a good deal daunted now by the large strong man's figure, even when his face was turned away from her.

"It seems to me," she said, swallowing a choking in her throat, "that the man who steadily does honest, thorough work in the world, with no hope of pleasure, nobody to applaud, is the one to whom *I* would say, 'Well done!'"

He knew what it cost the dumb, reserved woman, with her dread of intermeddling in the lives of others, to put out her hand thus to him, but he answered her only by a quick grateful smile. In her zeal her whole countenance was trembling, and the water stood in her eyes. Seeing this, he turned away from her.

"I—I have wished to say this to you for a long time. I want you to see yourself—what these years were—how well done the work has been. You have no mother, nobody to tell you. I want you to take comfort again in the world. It is a good, beautiful world, Jack."

He looked over the crimson sky, and the sea below, and turned to her, their light reflected in his eyes.

"You have hosts of friends, too: sincere, cultured men and women; you can find such friends everywhere; the world is full of them."

He nodded again slowly, a tender, fine smile on his face. She took fresh courage from it, and, after a moment's pause, went on desperately.

"There are lovely women in it, too; sweet, genuine girls, who would love you as few men can be loved. If you had a home now, Jack, and—and—— Indeed, you must forgive me. It has seemed so long as if you were my brother, and Clay and I being so happy—and Tom and all——" and there she began to cry, and Andross took her hand in his for a moment, and then walked away from her across the sands, blushing like a young girl.

The fancy of a fresh, real love which might be waiting for him somewhere, was rare and strangely sweet to him.

There was a sudden outburst of noise in the quiet evening, half laughter and half shrieks of terror. A little boat, in which were a woman and two or three men, had been carried out a few feet too far beyond the surf.

Isabel came up to Andross, and they both looked on amused, and glad of the trifle, too, on which to turn away from the gravity of their last words. "There is no danger," said Jack. "Ten strokes of the oar should bring them in. But they do not know how to give the strokes, apparently."

The woman's voice rose just then—a shrill little pipe.

"It is Anna!" cried Andross. "Isabel, it is Anna!"

He ran toward the beach, throwing off his coat and jacket as he went.

"She is perfectly safe," said Bell, coldly, trying to hold him.

But he had plunged into the surf, and was swimming toward her.

"The creature is the old, sweet, fair Anna to him, and always will be," said Isabel, despairingly, watching his headlong haste to reach the boat. She had no other cause for anxiety. Andross was an expert swimmer—the boat within easy reach; but owing to Anna's hysteric struggles or Ware's awkwardness in steering, the little vessel turned over, and in a minute they were all struggling in the water.

Ware and his companion reached the shore almost without effort. Anna was sucked under a current, and carried out beyond the surf.

"Jack!" she cried as she rose. "Oh Jack, save me!"

His strength had begun to give way before he reached her: if she had been the old Anna, fairy-like in size and proportion, he could have brought her in on the tide with ease; but she was a heavy dead weight; recovering strength from time to time, only to struggle and drag him farther down.

Ware ran wildly up and down the shore, shouting out directions and orders.

"I wish she had died in her cradle!" said Isabel, with white lips watching Jack's strokes grow more feeble.

Ware, with his friend, waded cautiously out at last to be ready to receive her. The heavy incoming wave lifted Andross at the moment, and dashed him against the upturned boat. His hold of the woman loosened, his arms relaxed, and were washed to and fro by the water. He was stunned and senseless; but the wave drove her within reach of her husband, who dragged her in; and after he had given a vigorous roll or two, she staggered to her feet. Ware and the other man would have remained to help Andross, if help were possible. But Anna cried and wailed so wildly, sinking helpless on the sand, that they were obliged to support her between them, and took her up the beach.

"Ugh—h!" she shivered, "I am sure I shall die before we reach the house! Let us hurry and get some dry clothes. I'm afraid you'll have a wretched cold, Julius, dear. I'm afraid that poor Andross is drowned. He always was the unluckiest creature!"——

The breakers rolled in again and again before they brought him within Isabel's reach. She drew him, with the help of the wave, up on the beach, and then tried to turn him on his side. But he was too heavy a weight for her, even in the force of her terror, to move. She stopped one breathless moment, and then, praying to God as she ran, darted up the beach for help.

He opened his eyes presently, and looked up the stretch of yellow sand. Anna was still in sight, wet and broad-backed, clinging to her husband, and leaving him unnoticed, to die or live.

"Poor little thing! She weighs two hundred pounds!" thought Jack, with an inward laugh, and, oddly enough, for the first time, he saw the woman as she was in soul as well as body, and in that moment her hold on him was gone forever.

There was a sharp pain in his chest, his breath came and went in spasms.

Was this death?

The tide flowed in with a dull, constant murmur, but there was no other answer. Jack, as always, needed a human voice—a human hand to touch.

The sea, the beautiful world he had loved differently from other men, were strangely quiet in the hush of evening — the heaven close overhead more quiet still. Must he go—now? There were other lives to live in the Hereafter, out of sight of this reddened sunset sky—— he did not forget that.

He had thought out many truths in these later, lonely years, unknown even to Isabel, and made them real to himself. He could go now willingly, like a child, holding his Master's hand. It would only be Jack Andross beginning his life again beyond, with the same God above him.

But, oh God, if he only could live!

He knew this world: he was used to it. He thought in that minute of all the people he loved: of his old books, of a queer bric-a-brac shop he meant to explore next week; of pleasant, shady places where he and Tom had gone fishing together.

He was so strong and alive; to die now—in the vigour of his youth? Somewhere, as Isabel had said, there might be a home of his own, and a woman who would love him, as no other had done——

There were Isabel and Braddock, and the old colonel, running toward him—and little Tom far behind. He raised his head and tried to shout "Tom!"

He knew that if he could only bear it until the boy should reach him, he would live.

Could he bear it?

Meanwhile the tide flowed steadily inward, but gave no answer.